"Box sets up an impressive dual perspective in the novel, shifting between Joe Pickett's life as a game warden in Saddlestring, Wyoming, and the wanderings of two hired killers . . . a tense chase." —*The Washington Post*

"Riveting . . . Box weaves in a history that gives the action a rich context . . . harrowing." —*USA Today*

"Brilliantly crafted . . . bears comparison to the best work of mystery giants such as Tony Hillerman and James Lee Burke . . . It won't spoil the plot to say that after the dust clears, it looks like this twenty-first-century range war is far from over, and that we'll be hearing more from Joe Pickett soon. Let's hope he brings the cavalry." —*Minneapolis Star Tribune*

PRAISE FOR
OPEN SEASON

A *New York Times* Notable Book

Los Angeles Times Book Prize Award Nominee,
Best Mystery/Thriller

"Buy two copies of *Open Season,* and save one in mint condition to sell to first-edition collectors. C. J. Box is a great storyteller." —Tony Hillerman

"Intriguing, with a forest setting so treacherous it makes Nevada Barr's locales look positively comfy, with a motive for murder that is as unique as any in modern fiction. Pickett is a refreshingly human and befuddled hero. . . . But it's Box's offbeat way of telling the story that puts it on the best of the year track." —*Los Angeles Times*

"A muscular first novel . . . Box writes as straight as his characters shoot, and he has a stand-up hero to shoulder his passionate concerns about endangered lives and liberties." —*The New York Times Book Review*

"A fascinating, well-scripted debut novel . . . In Gary Cooper style, Pickett is transformed into a man with a mission to save his family, then exact his vengeance. It's a classic tale of Wild West justice." —*USA Today*

Titles by C. J. Box

The Joe Pickett Novels

TROPHY HUNT

C. J. BOX

BERKLEY BOOKS, NEW YORK

THE BERKLEY PUBLISHING GROUP
Published by the Penguin Group
Penguin Group (USA) Inc.
375 Hudson Street, New York, New York 10014, USA

Penguin Group (Canada), 90 Eglinton Avenue East, Suite 700, Toronto, Ontario M4P 2Y3, Canada
(a division of Pearson Penguin Canada Inc.) • Penguin Books Ltd., 80 Strand, London WC2R 0RL,
England • Penguin Group Ireland, 25 St. Stephen's Green, Dublin 2, Ireland (a division of Penguin
Books Ltd.) • Penguin Group (Australia), 250 Camberwell Road, Camberwell, Victoria 3124, Australia
(a division of Pearson Australia Group Pty. Ltd.) • Penguin Books India Pvt. Ltd., 11 Community
Centre, Panchsheel Park, New Delhi—110 017, India • Penguin Group (NZ), 67 Apollo Drive,
Rosedale, Auckland 0632, New Zealand (a division of Pearson New Zealand Ltd.) • Penguin Books
(South Africa) (Pty.) Ltd., 24 Sturdee Avenue, Rosebank, Johannesburg 2196, South Africa

Penguin Books Ltd., Registered Offices: 80 Strand, London WC2R 0RL, England

This is a work of fiction. Names, characters, places, and incidents either are the product of the author's
imagination or are used fictitiously, and any resemblance to actual persons, living or dead, business
establishments, events, or locales is entirely coincidental. The publisher does not have any control over
and does not assume any responsibility for author or third-party websites or their content.

TROPHY HUNT

A Berkley Book / published by arrangement with the author

PUBLISHING HISTORY
G. P. Putnam's Sons hardcover edition / June 2004
Berkley Prime Crime mass-market edition / April 2005
Berkley mass-market edition / February 2012

ISBN: 978-0-425-20293-7

BERKLEY®
Berkley Books are published by The Berkley Publishing Group,
a division of Penguin Group (USA) Inc.,
375 Hudson Street, New York, New York 10014.
BERKLEY® is a registered trademark of Penguin Group (USA) Inc.
The "B" design is a trademark of Penguin Group (USA) Inc.

PRINTED IN THE UNITED STATES OF AMERICA

25   24   23   22   21   20   19   18   17   16   15   14

PART
ONE

PART
ONE

IN TWELVE-YEAR-OLD SHERIDAN Pickett's dream, she was in the Bighorn Mountains in the timber at the edge of a clearing. She was alone. Behind her, the forest was achingly silent. Before her, a quiet wind rippled through the long meadow grass in the clearing.

Then the clouds came, dark and imposing, roiling over the top of the mountains in a wall. Soon the sky was completely covered, a lid placed on a pot. In the center of the clouds was a lighter cloud that seemed to be lit from within. It grew bigger and closer, as if lowering itself to the earth. Black spoors of smoke snaked down in tendrils from the cloud, dropping into the trees. In moments, the smoke became ground-hugging mist that coursed through the tree trunks like soundless, rushing water. Then it seeped into the ground to rest, or to hide.

As quickly as the clouds had come, the sky cleared.

In her dream, she knew the mist stayed for a reason. The purpose, though, was beyond her understanding. When would it emerge, and why? Those were questions she couldn't answer.

———

Sheridan awoke with a start, and it took a few terrifying moments to realize that the darkness surrounding her was actually her bedroom, and that the breathy windlike stirring she heard was her little sister Lucy, asleep on the bunk beneath her bed.

Sheridan found her glasses where she had propped them on her headboard, and swung her bare feet out from beneath the covers. She dropped to the cold floor with her nightgown ballooning around her.

Parting the curtain, she looked at the night sky. Hard white stars, like blue pinpricks, stared back. There were no clouds, either dark or glowing.

1

IT HAD BEEN A GOOD DAY of fly-fishing until Joe Pickett and his daughters encountered a massive bull moose that appeared to be grinning at them.

Until then, Joe, Sheridan, and seven-year-old Lucy had spent the entire afternoon working their way upstream on Crazy Woman Creek on a brilliant, early-September day. Maxine, their yellow Labrador, was with them. The tall streamside grass hummed with insects, hoppers mainly, and a high breeze swayed the crowns of the musky lodgepole pine forest.

They fished methodically, overtaking each other in wide loops away from the water, passing silently while the person they were passing cast at a pool or promising riffle. The water was lower than usual—it was a drought year—but the stream was clear and still very cold. Joe was in his late thirties, lean and of average height. His face and the backs of his hands were sunburned from being outside at altitude.

Hopscotching over dry river rocks, Joe had crossed the stream so he could keep a better eye on his girls as they worked the other side with their fly rods. Maxine shadowed

Joe, as she always did, fighting her natural instinct to plunge into the water and retrieve fly casts.

Sheridan stood waist deep in brush upstream and was momentarily still, concentrating on tying a new hopper pattern to her tippet. Her glasses glinted in the afternoon sun, so Joe couldn't tell if she was watching him observe her. She wore her new fishing vest (a recent birthday present) over a T-shirt, baggy shorts, and water sandals for wading. A sweat-stained Wyoming Game and Fish Department cap—one of Joe's old ones—was pulled down tightly on her head. Her bare arms and legs were crosshatched with fresh scratches from thorns and branches she had crashed through to get closer to the water. She was a serious fly-fisher, and a serious girl overall.

But while Sheridan was the fisher, Lucy seemed to be catching most of the fish, much to Sheridan's consternation. Lucy did not share her older sister's passion for fishing. She came because Joe insisted, and because he had promised her a good lunch. She wore a sundress and white sandals, her shiny blond hair tied in a ponytail.

With each fish Lucy caught, Sheridan's glare toward her little sister intensified, and she moved farther upstream away from her. *It's not fair,* Joe knew she was thinking.

"Dad, come here and look at this," Sheridan called, breaking into his rumination. He pulled the slack tight on his rod and looped his line through his fingers before walking up the bank toward her. She was pointing down at something in the water beneath her feet.

It was a dead trout, white belly up, lodged between two exposed stones. The fish bobbed in a natural cul-de-sac dark with pine needles and sheaths of algae that had washed down with the current. He could tell from the wet, vinyl-like sheen on the fish's pale underside and the still-bright twin slashes of red beneath its gills that it hadn't been dead very long.

"That's a nice fish," Sheridan said to Joe. "A cutthroat. How big do you think it is?"

"Thirteen, fourteen inches," Joe replied. "It's a dandy." Instinctively, he reached down for Maxine's collar. He could feel her trembling under her skin through her coat, anxious to retrieve the dead fish.

"What do you think happened to it?" she asked. "Do you think somebody caught it and threw it back after it was dead?"

Joe shrugged, "Don't know." On a previous trip, Joe had instructed Sheridan how to properly release a fish back into the water after he caught it. He had shown her how to cradle it under its belly and lower it slowly into the water so that the natural current would revive it, and how to let the fish dart away under its own power once it was fit to do so.

She had asked him about the ethics of eating caught fish versus releasing them, and he told her that fish were for eating but that there was no reason to be greedy, and that keeping dead fish in a hot creel all day and throwing them away later because they were ruined was an ethical problem, if not a legal one. He knew this is what she was thinking about when she pointed out the dead fish.

I t wasn't long before Sheridan pointed out another dead fish. It hadn't been dead as long as the other one, Joe noted, because it floated on its side, flaunting the rainbow colors that gave the fish its name. It had not yet turned belly-up. This fish was not as large as the first, but still impressive.

Sheridan was righteously indignant.

"Something is killing these fish, and it makes me mad," she said, her eyes flashing. Joe didn't like it either but was impressed by her outrage, although he didn't know whether her anger came from her outdoor ethics or if she was angry because someone was killing fish she felt *she* deserved to catch.

"Can you tell what's killing them?" she asked.

This time, he let Maxine retrieve the rainbow. The Lab unnecessarily launched herself into the water with a splash that soaked both of them, and came back with the trout in her mouth. Joe pried it loose from Maxine's jaws and turned it over in his palm. He could see nothing unusual about the fish.

"This isn't like finding a dead deer or elk, where I can

check for bullets," he told Sheridan. "I can't see any wounds or disease on this fish. They may have been overstressed after being caught by someone."

Sheridan huffed with disappointment, and strode upstream. Joe tossed the fish into a stand of willows behind him.

While he waited for Lucy to mosey her way closer, he reached behind him and felt the heavy sag of his .40 Beretta semiautomatic, his service weapon, hidden away in the large back pocket creel of his fishing vest. He also affirmed that his wallet-badge was there, as well as several strands of Flexcuffs. Although he wasn't working, he was still the game warden, and still charged with enforcing regulations.

That morning, as he packed, he had taken the unusual step of adding another item to his fishing-vest arsenal: bear spray. He strummed his fingers over the large aerosol can through the fabric of his vest. The bear spray was wicked stuff, ten times more powerful than the pepper spray used for disabling humans. A whiff of the spray, even at a distance, brought men to their knees. Joe thought about the series of reports and cryptic e-mails he'd received regarding a rogue 400-pound male grizzly that was causing havoc in northwestern Wyoming. For the past month, the bear had damaged cars, campsites, and cabins, but as yet there had been no human-bear encounters. The bear had originally been located near the east entrance of Yellowstone Park through a weakening signal from its radio collar, but he had not yet been sighted. When the "bear guys"—a team of Wyoming Game and Fish Department and U.S. Fish and Wildlife Service bear specialists—tried to cut it off, the bear eluded them and they lost the signal. Joe couldn't recall a runaway bear incident quite like this before. It was like the wilderness version of an escaped convict. He blamed the drought, as the biologists did, and the need for the grizzly to cover new ground in search of something, anything, to eat. It had not been lost on him that the damage reports indicated that the grizzly was moving to the east, through the Shoshone National Forest. If the bear kept up his march, he would enter the Bighorn Mountains, where grizzlies had not roamed for eighty years.

Joe disliked bringing his weapon and badge with him on his day off. He felt oddly ashamed that his daughters were seeing his day-to-day equipment as they caught fish and he cooked them over an open fire for lunch. It was different when he was out in the field, in his red chamois Game and Fish shirt and driving his green pickup, checking hunters and fishers. Now, he just wanted to be Dad.

Working their way upstream, they stumbled upon another party. Sheridan saw them first and stopped, looking back for Joe. He could see flashes of color through the trees upstream, and he heard a cough.

Joe noticed a strange odor in the air when the wind shifted. The odor was sickly sweet and metallic, and he winced when a particularly strong waft of it blew through.

Making sure Lucy was well behind them, Joe winked at Sheridan as he overtook her, and she fell in behind him as he closed in on the two fishers. He debated whether or not to show his badge before saying hello, and decided against it. Joe noticed the unpleasant odor again. It seemed to get worse as he walked upstream.

As he approached them, he felt Sheridan tug on his sleeve, and he turned and saw her point toward the water. A small brook trout, not more than six inches long, was floating on the top of the water on its side. It wasn't dead yet, and he could see its gills working as it pathetically tried to right itself and swim away.

"The fish killers," Sheridan whispered ominously at the man and woman in front of them, and he nodded to her in agreement.

The man looked to be in his late fifties, and was dressed as if he were a cover model for *Fly-Fisherman* magazine. He wore ultralight Gore-Tex waders and leather wading boots, a pale blue Cool-Max shirt, and a fishing vest with dozens of bulging pockets filled with gear. A wooden net hung down his back from a ring on his collar. A leather-bound journal for documenting the species and size of the fish he caught was on a lanyard on his vest, as was a small digital camera for recording the catch. The man was large and ruddy, with a thick chest. He had a salt-and-pepper mustache and pale, watery eyes. He looked like a hungover CEO on vacation, Joe thought.

Behind and off to the side of the man was a much younger woman with blond hair; long sunburned legs; and a fishing vest so new that the tag from the Bighorn Angler Fly Shop was still attached to the front zipper. She held her rod away from her body with the unease of someone holding a dead snake.

It was obvious, Joe thought, that the man was teaching the woman how to fish. Or, more accurately, the man was showing the woman what a fine fisherman *he* was. Joe assumed that the couple had stopped at the fly store on their way up the mountain and that the man had outfitted her with the new vest.

The man had been concentrating on dropping a fly into a deep pool but now glared at Joe and Sheridan, clearly annoyed that he had been disturbed.

"Jeff . . ." the woman cautioned in a low voice, attempting to get Jeff's attention.

"Good afternoon," Joe said and smiled. "How's fishing?"

Jeff stepped back from the stream in an exaggerated way. His movement wasn't aggressive but clearly designed to show Joe and Sheridan that he wasn't pleased with the interruption and that he planned to resume his cast as soon as possible.

"Thirty-fish day," Jeff said gruffly.

"Twenty-eight," the woman corrected, and Jeff instantly flashed a look at her.

"It's an *expression*," he said as if scolding a child. "Twenty-fish day, thirty-fish day, they're fucking *expressions*. It's what fishermen tell each other if one of them is rude enough to ask."

The woman shrank back and nodded.

Joe didn't like this guy. He knew the type: a fly-fisherman who thought he knew everything and who could afford all of the equipment he read about in the magazines. Often, these men were fairly new to the sport. Too often, these men had never learned about outdoor etiquette, or common courtesy. To them it was all about thirty-fish days.

"Keeping any?" Joe asked, still smiling. He reached into

the back pocket of his vest, bringing out his wallet-badge and holding it up so Jeff could understand why Joe was asking the question.

"There's a limit of six on this stream," Joe said. "Mind if I look at what you've kept?"

Jeff snorted and his face hardened.

"So you're the game warden?"

"Yes," Joe said. "And this is my daughter Sheridan."

"And his daughter Lucy," Lucy said, having caught up with them. "What's that smell, Dad?"

"And Lucy," Joe added, looking back at her. She was pinching her nose with her fingers. "So I would appreciate it if you watched your language around them."

Jeff started to say something but caught himself. Then he rolled his eyes heavenward.

"Tell you what," Joe said, looking at the woman—who appeared to be fearing a fight—and Jeff. "How about you show me your licenses and conservation stamps and I'll show you how to properly release a fish so that there aren't any more dead ones?"

The woman immediately began digging in her tight shorts, and Jeff seemed to make up his mind that he didn't really want a fight, either. Still glaring at Joe, he reached behind his back for his wallet.

Joe checked the licenses. Both were perfectly legal. She was from Colorado and had a temporary fishing license. Jeff O'Bannon was local, although Joe couldn't remember ever seeing him before. Joe noted that O'Bannon's address was on Red Cloud Road, which meant he lived in one of the new $500,000 ranchettes south of town in the Elkhorn Ranches subdivision. That didn't surprise Joe.

"Do you know what that awful smell is?" Joe asked conversationally as he handed the licenses back.

"It's a dead moose," Jeff O'Bannon said sullenly. "In that meadow up there." He gestured through the trees to the west, vaguely pointing with the peaked extra-long bill of his Orvis fishing cap. "That's one reason why we're fucking leaving."

"Jeff . . ." The woman cautioned.

O'Bannon growled at her, "There's no law against the word *fucking*."

Joe felt a rise of anger. "I think, Jeff, that I'll see you again some time out here," Joe said, leaning in close to Jeff. "Given your bad attitude, you'll probably be doing something wrong. I'll arrest you when you do."

O'Bannon started to step toward Joe but the woman held his arm. Joe slipped his hand in the back pocket of his fishing vest and thumbed off the safety bar on the bear spray.

"Aw, to hell with it," O'Bannon said, leaning back. "Let's get out of here, Cindy. He's already ruined my good mood."

Joe watched as Cindy breathed a long sigh of relief and shook her head in bewilderment for Joe's benefit, keeping out of Jeff's line of vision. Joe stepped aside as the man stormed past him, followed by Cindy.

"Bye, girls," Cindy called to Sheridan and Lucy, who watched the two walk downstream. Jeff led the way, snapping branches and cursing. Cindy tried to keep up.

"Dad, can we leave, too?" Lucy asked. "It stinks here."

"Go ahead and go downstream a little ways and get out of the smell if you want to," Joe said. "I need to check this moose out."

"We're going with you," Lucy honked back, still holding her nose. Joe turned to argue when he noticed that O'Bannon and Cindy hadn't moved very far downstream after all. O'Bannon stood in a clearing, glaring through pine branches at Joe while Cindy tugged at him.

"Okay," Joe said, knowing it was best to keep his girls near him.

The moose wasn't hard to find, and the sight jarred Joe. A full-grown bull moose lay on its side in the ankle-high grass in the center of the meadow, which was walled on three sides by dark trees that continued in force up the mountain. The dead moose was horribly bloated to nearly twice its normal size, its mottled purple skin stretched nearly to breaking. Two black legs, knobby-kneed and surprisingly long, were suspended over the ground, like a chair that had been tipped over. Its face, half-hidden in the grass, seemed to leer at him with bared long teeth and a single, bulging, wide-open eye that looked like it was primed and ready to fire right out of the socket.

Joe turned on his heels and told his girls to stop so they wouldn't see it. Too late.

Lucy shrieked, and covered her mouth with her hands. Sheridan stared, her eyes wide, her mouth set grimly.

"It's alive!" Lucy cried.

"No it isn't," Sheridan countered. "But there's something wrong with it."

"Stay put," Joe said sternly. "I mean that."

Drawing a bandanna out of his Wranglers, he tied it over his nose and mouth like a highwayman, and approached the bloated carcass. Sheridan was right, Joe thought. There was something wrong with it. And there was something else; he had a fuzzy, slightly dizzy feeling. For a moment, he was light-headed, and thought that perhaps he had moved too quickly or something. He blinked, and when he looked around he saw faint, slow motion sparkling in the air for a moment.

Shaking his head to try and clear it, Joe circled the carcass, never getting closer than a few feet from it. The animal had been mutilated. Its genitals and musk glands had been cut out, and its rectum was cored. Half of its face had been removed, leaving a grinning skull and long, yellowed teeth. He could see where the skin and glands had been cut away, and noted that the incisions were smooth, almost surgical, in their precision. He could not imagine an animal, any animal, leaving wounds like that. Where the skin had been cut away the exposed flesh was dark purple and black, speckled with tiny commas of bright yellow. When he stopped and stared, he realized that the commas were writhing. Maggots. Besides the incisions, he could see no exterior wounds on the carcass.

Turning his head for a big gulp of air, he strode forward and squatted and grasped one of the bony, stiff forelegs. Grunting, he lifted, using the leg as a lever. He shinnied around the obscenely smiling face and massive, inverted palm-frond antlers and pulled, using his legs and back, trying to turn the stiff carcass. For a moment, the sheer weight of the animal stymied him, and he feared losing his footing and falling over it. Worse yet would be if the leg pulled loose from the putrefied shoulder, leaving a long, hairy club in his hands. But with a sickening kissing sound the body detached from the ground and began to roll toward him. He pulled hard on the leg and jumped back as the carcass flopped over in the grass. Gasses burbled inside the carcass, sounding like something subterranean. He searched the grass-matted hide for external injuries. Again, he found none.

He expected to see the flattened grass black with congealed blood, as was usually the case when he found animals that had been poached. The entry wound was often hard to see but the exit wound would bleed and drain into the turf, leaving a black-and-red pudding. But there was no blood underneath the moose at all, only more insects, madly scrambling, running from sunlight.

Joe stepped back and looked around. The grass was lush and thick in the meadow, and he noticed, for the first time, that there were no tracks of any kind in it. When he looked back on the slope he had walked up, his own footprints were glaringly obvious in the crushed, dry grass. It appeared that the moose had chosen the center of the meadow to suddenly drop dead. So what could possibly have removed the animal's genitals, glands, and face? And not left so much as a print?

He pulled the bandanna from his mouth and let it hang around his neck. His necropsy kit was in his pickup, which was a one-hour walk away. Dusk would be approaching soon, and he had promised Marybeth he would have the girls home in time for dinner and homework. Tomorrow, when he returned, he expected that with the kit and his metal detector he would find a bullet or two in the carcass. Usually, the lead caught up just beneath the hide on the opposite side of where the animal had been shot.

Joe walked back to where Sheridan and Lucy were standing. They had moved back down the hill from the meadow, close enough that they could watch him but far enough away that the smell of the carcass wouldn't make them sick to their stomachs. Jeff and Cindy were nowhere in sight.

As they worked their way down the slope to Crazy Woman Creek, his girls fired questions at him.

"Who killed the moose, Dad?" Lucy asked. "I like moose."

"Me too. And I don't know what killed it."

"Isn't that strange to find an animal just dead like that?" Lucy again.

"Very strange," Joe said. "Unless somebody shot it and left it."

"That's a crime, right? A big one?" Sheridan asked.

Joe nodded. "Wanton destruction of a game animal."

"I hope you find out who did it," Sheridan said, "and take away all of his stuff."

"Yup," Joe agreed, but his mind was racing. Besides the mutilation and the lack of tracks around the animal, something else bothered him that he couldn't put his finger on. But as the three of them walked downstream, he saw a raccoon ahead of them splash through a pool and vanish into a stand of trees. The raccoon had found one of the dead fish that Jeff had "released."

Suddenly, Joe stopped. That was it, he thought. The bull moose had been dead for at least several days, lying in the open, and *nothing* had fed on it. The mountains were filled with scavengers—eagles, coyotes, badgers, hawks, ravens, even mice—who were usually the first on the scene of a dead animal. Joe had discovered scores of game animals, which had been lost or left by hunters, by the squawking, feeding magpies that usually marked a kill. But the moose looked untouched, except for the incisions.

As a big fist of cumulous clouds punched across the sun and flattened the shadows and dropped the temperature by a quick ten degrees, Joe heard a snapping sound and turned slowly, looking back toward the meadow where they had found the moose. He could see nothing, but he felt a ripple through the hairs on the back of his neck.

"What is it, Dad?" Sheridan asked.

Joe shook his head, listening.

"I heard it," Lucy said. "It sounded like somebody stepped

on a branch or a twig. Or maybe they were eating potato chips."

"Potato chips," Sheridan scoffed. "That's stupid."

"I'm not stupid."

"Girls." Joe admonished them, still trying to listen. But he heard nothing beyond the liquid sound of the flowing breeze through the swaying crowns of the pine trees. He thought of how, in just a few moments, the mountain setting had changed from warm and welcoming to cold and oddly silent.

2

I T WAS A HALF HOUR BEFORE DUSK when they arrived at their small, two-story, state-owned home eight miles out of Saddlestring. Joe swung the pickup off Bighorn Road and parked it in front of the detached garage that needed painting. Sheridan and Lucy were out of the passenger door even before he set the brake, rushing across the grass in the front yard into the house to tell their mother what they had seen. Maxine bounded behind them but paused at the door to look back at Joe.

"Go ahead," Joe said, "I'm coming."

Assured, the Labrador bolted into the house.

After putting the rods, vests, and cooler into the garage, Joe walked around the house toward the corral. Toby, their eight-year-old paint gelding, nickered as soon as Joe was in sight, which meant he was hungry. Doc, their new sorrel yearling, nickered as well, following the older horse's lead. Joe shooed them aside as he entered the corral, then fed them two flake sections each of grass hay. He filled the trough and checked the gate on his way out. While he did so, he wondered why Marybeth hadn't fed them earlier, because she usually did.

As he opened the door at the back of the house, Sheridan stormed out of it in a dark mood.

"Did you tell your mom about the moose?" Joe asked her.

"She's busy," Sheridan snapped, "maybe I should have made an appointment."

"Sherry . . ." Joe admonished, but Sheridan was out the back gate toward the corral.

He turned and entered the kitchen. Marybeth sat at the kitchen table wearing a sweatshirt and jeans, surrounded by manila files, stacks of paper, facedown open books, a calculator, and a laptop computer. Boxes of files were stacked on either side of her chair, their lids on the floor. She was concentrating on her laptop screen, and barely acknowledged him as he entered the kitchen.

"Hey, babe," he greeted her and swept her blond hair away from the side of her face and kissed her on the cheek.

"Just a second," she said, tapping on her keyboard.

Joe felt a pang of annoyance. It was obvious that nothing was cooking on the stove, and the oven light was dark. The table was a shambles, and so was Marybeth. It wasn't as if he expected dinner on the table every night. But she had asked him to be home early with the girls, for dinner, and he had lived up to his part of the bargain.

"Okay," she announced and snapped the screen down on her laptop. "Got it."

"Got what?"

"The Logue Country Realty account is finally reconciled," she said. "What a mess that one was."

"Well, good," he said flatly, opening the refrigerator to see if a covered dish was ready to heat. Nope.

"I don't know how they stayed in business after they bought it, Joe," she explained, filing bank statements and canceled checks into folders and envelopes. "The previous owners left them an unbelievable mess. Their cash flow was an absolute mystery for the last twelve quarters."

"Mmm."

There weren't even frozen pizzas in the freezer, he saw. Just some rock-hard packages of deer burger and elk roasts from the previous year, and a box of Popsicles that had been in the freezer as long as Joe could remember.

"I thought we'd go out tonight," Marybeth said. "Or maybe one of us could run into town to get something and bring it back."

He was surprised. "We can afford to?"

Marybeth's smile disappeared. "No, we really can't," she sighed. "Not until the end of the month, anyway."

"We could thaw out that burger in the microwave," Joe suggested.

"Do you mind grilling out?" she asked.

"That's fine," he said evenly.

"Honey . . ."

Joe held up his hand. "Don't worry about it. You got caught up in your work. It's okay."

For a second, he thought she would tear up. That happened more and more lately. But she didn't. Instead, she bit her lower lip and looked at him.

"Really," he said.

As he scraped the grate of the barbecue grill in the backyard, Joe battled with himself over his disappointment that there was no dinner planned and his growing worry about Marybeth and their marriage. There was no doubt that the violent death of April, their foster daughter, last winter had severely affected Marybeth. Joe had hoped that the dawn of spring would help Marybeth heal but it hadn't. Spring had only brought the realization that their situation in general was no different than it had been before.

Sometimes, he caught her staring. She would fix on the window, or sometimes on something that seemed to be between the window and her eyes. Her face would look slightly wistful, and her eyes softened. A couple of times he asked her what she was thinking about. When he did, she shook her head as if shaking off a vision, and said, "nothing."

He knew their finances troubled her, as they troubled him. There was a statewide budget crunch, and salaries had been frozen. In Joe's case, this meant he would make $32,000 a year as far ahead as he could see. The long hours he worked also meant that any kind of extra income was out of the question. The department provided housing and equipment, but recently the house, which had at one time seemed wonderful, felt like a trap.

After April died, Joe and Marybeth had discussed their future. They needed normalcy, they agreed, they needed routine. Faith and hope would return naturally, because they were strong people and they loved each other and, given time, they'd all heal. Joe had promised to look at other job options, or request a change of districts within the state. A change of scenery might help, they agreed. But he had not really researched the job postings recently, because in his heart he loved his job and never wanted to leave it. That reality shrouded him, at times, with secret guilt.

Marybeth was no longer working at the library and the stables, the two part-time jobs she had held. Even combined, they were too low-paying, and involved too much public contact, she told him. She was uncomfortable with library patrons who assessed her and asked her questions about April, and the events that had lead to her death.

But they needed additional income, and in the summer Marybeth had started her own business, setting up accounting, office management, and inventory control for small businesses in Saddlestring. Joe thought it was a perfect choice, with her education, toughness, and organizational skills. So far, her clients included Barrett's Pharmacy, Sandvick Taxidermy, the Saddlestring Burg-O-Pardner, and Logue Country Realty. She was working hard to get established, and the business was close to being a success.

Which made him feel even more guilty that he had been angry with her about dinner.

"Tell me about that moose," she asked after dinner, while they washed and rinsed dishes in the sink. Joe was surprised by the question, because Sheridan and Lucy had described the incident in such graphic detail while they were eating that Joe had asked them to stop.

"What about it?"

She smiled slyly. "For the past fifteen minutes, you've been thinking about it."

He flushed. "How do you know that?"

"You mean besides the fact that you've been staring off into space the entire time that we've been doing the dishes? Or that you're drying that glass for the fourth time?" she said, grinning. "You're standing right here but your mind is elsewhere."

"It isn't fair that you do that," he said, "because I can never tell what you're thinking about."

"As it should be," she said, giving him a mischievous hip-check as they stood side-by-side at the sink.

"The girls described it pretty accurately," he said. "Not much I can add to that."

"So why does it bother you?"

He rinsed a plate and slid it into the drying rack, pausing until he could articulate what he had been thinking about. "I've seen a lot of dead animals," he said, looking over his shoulder at her. "And, unfortunately, some dead human beings."

She nodded him on.

"But everything about that scene was, well, different—extremely so."

"Do you mean that you couldn't figure out what made the wounds?"

"That too," he said. "But you just don't find a dead moose in the middle of a meadow like that. There were no tracks; no indication that whoever shot it went to check it out afterward. Even the really bad poachers, the ones who leave the bodies on the ground, usually go check out the target."

"Maybe it was just sick and it died," she said reasonably.

Joe had turned and was leaning back against the sink with the towel still over his forearm.

He said, "Of course animals die of natural causes all the time. But you just never *find* them. You may find some bones if the skeleton hasn't been too scattered by predators, but you just don't happen upon animals that have died of old age. Or if you do, it's damned rare. Dying animals tend to seek out cover where nothing can find them. They don't just keel over in the middle of a meadow like that."

"But you don't know that it wasn't shot, or hit by lightning or something," she said.

"It wasn't lightning. There were no scorch marks. It may have been shot; I'll find that out tomorrow. But my gut tells me I won't find any lead."

"Maybe it was poisoned somehow?" Marybeth asked.

Joe was silent for a moment before answering, reviewing the scene in his head. He was pleased that Marybeth was so wrapped up in what had happened to the moose. She'd been so distracted by her new business that it had been a long time since she'd been interested in anything he'd been doing.

"Again, I think the bull would have sought cover to die. Unless the poison killed him so quick he just dropped, which doesn't sound very likely to me. And those wounds . . ."

"You described them as incisions earlier," Marybeth said.

"Yes, they were more like surgery than butchery. No animal I know of makes perfect cuts like that. And the parts that were cut away were removed from the scene, taken away. As if they were trophies of some kind."

Marybeth grimaced. "I'd hate to see *that* trophy collection."

Joe laughed uncomfortably, agreeing with her.

"It's almost as if the moose was dropped from the sky," Marybeth said.

"Aw, jeez," he moaned. "I was hoping you wouldn't say that."

She prodded him hard in the ribs with her finger. "But that's what you were thinking, weren't you, Joe?"

At first he thought about denying it. But she was so damnably keyed into his thoughts that he didn't dare.

"Yup," he said.

"I can't wait to hear what you find out," she said, turning and reaching through the wash water for the plug. "Should I ask my mother what she thinks about it?"

Joe bristled, as Marybeth knew he would, and she laughed to assure him she was kidding. Her mother, the former Missy Vankueran, was soon to marry a local rancher named Bud Longbrake. In addition to getting remarried (she had four ex-husbands), and discussing exactly how Joe had stifled Marybeth's potential, Missy's top passion was reading books and watching television shows and movies about the paranormal. She loved to speculate about situations and events around Twelve Sleep County—and the world—and ascribe supernatural explanations to them.

"Don't tell her, please," Joe begged, exaggerating his please, but not really. "You know how I hate that woo-woo crap."

"Speaking of woo-woo crap," Sheridan said as she entered the kitchen from where she'd been eavesdropping, "did I tell you I had that dream again?"

3

THE NEXT MORNING, MONDAY, Joe hiked up the Crazy Woman Creek drainage with his necropsy kit to discover that the grinning moose was no longer there. The absence of the dead moose in the meadow stopped him outright, and he stood still for a moment, surveying the crushed grass. He was thinking about Sheridan's dream, which made him uncomfortable. Joe refused to believe in aliens or creeping mist or anything else he couldn't see or touch. Had there been a time when he believed in monsters and things that went bump in the night? *Nope,* he thought. He had always been a skeptic. He remembered when neighborhood kids gathered around a Ouija board, and urged him to join them. Instead, he went fishing. When his friends stayed up late at night to watch creature movies, Joe fell asleep. Sheridan was different, though, and always had been. He hoped she'd outgrow the dreams.

Something had dragged, or carried, the carcass away. The trail was obvious; a spoor of flattened grass led across the meadow in a stuttering S-curve toward the northern wall of pine trees. Puzzled, he followed it.

The mature bull moose weighed at least 600 pounds, he guessed. Whatever had moved it had tremendous strength. He wouldn't have been surprised to see a set of pickup or ATV tracks in the meadow, but they weren't there. He wondered if it could be the grizzly. As he walked silently across the meadow in the flattened grass track of the moose, he tried to peer ahead into the dark trees and see into them. He listened intently for sounds, and noted the absence of them. There were no chattering squirrels in the trees, or calling jays. Except for the low hum of insects in the grass near his feet and the high, airy flow of a cold fall breeze through the branches, it was deathly silent in the meadow. Again, he felt a chill run up his spine, which raised the hairs on his neck and forearms.

He couldn't explain the odd feeling he got again from the meadow. It felt as if something was physically pushing against him from all sides. Not hard, but steadily. The crisp fall mountain air tasted thicker than it should have, and when he breathed in, his lungs felt heavy and wet. He sensed a kind of shimmer in the air when he looked at the wall of trees and the granite mountains that pushed up behind them. He didn't like the feeling at all, and tried to shake it off.

Joe slipped the strap of the necropsy kit over his head so that his hands were free. He drew his semiautomatic weapon and worked the slide, seating a cartridge in the chamber. With his left hand, he unclipped the large can of bear spray from his belt and thumbed off the guard. He cautiously approached the wall of trees, his weapon in his right hand and the spray in his left. All of his senses were tuned to high, and he strained to see, hear, or smell anything that would give him a warning before it was too late.

That's when he saw the bear track in the center of the crushed grass. The huge paw was the size of a pie plate and had pushed down through the mat of grass into dark soil. He could see the heel imprint clearly; it was pressed into the dirt, as were the prints of all five toes. Nearly two inches from the end of the toe marks were sharp punctures in the ground, as if a curved garden rake had been swung overhead and embedded deeply into the earth. The creature that had made the tracks was the rogue grizzly bear, he was sure of it. None of the native black bears could leave a track that large. The odd thing, he thought, was that the track was pointed toward him, and not toward the wall of trees. Why wasn't the track heading away from the meadow?

Then he answered his own question. If the bear was dragging the moose out of the meadow, he would have clamped down on the moose's neck with his teeth and pulled it backward, like a puppy dragging a sock. The fact that the heel print was deeper than the claws indicated that the bear was struggling with the heavy carcass, backing up and digging deep into the earth for traction.

He glanced at the bear spray he carried and then at the .40 Beretta. *Too small,* he thought, *too puny.* Not only would he likely miss because he was such a poor shot with a handgun, but even if he hit his target it would probably do no more than make the bear angry.

He stood, thought, and shrugged, then plunged forward, toward the trees that lined the meadow. There was a hole in the brush where something—the bear?—had already blazed through. Branches had been bent and snapped back and broken. Entering the pool of shadow cast by the wall of pine trees, Joe squinted to see better. The forest was unnaturally dense and cluttered with wicked snarls of dry deadfall. The tree trunks were the thickness of the barrel of a baseball bat and extremely close together. Joe lowered his shoulder and pushed through.

The forest floor was dark, dry, and carpeted thickly with several inches of bronze pine needles. His boots sank with each step, and the earth was springy. The smell inside was a combination of dried pine, vegetative decay, and the sudden strong odor of the dead moose that for some reason Joe had not noticed until now.

As his eyes adjusted to the half-light filtering through the pine boughs, the carcass of the moose seemed to emerge on the forest floor right in front of him. The stench was suddenly overpowering, and Joe stepped back and thumped his shoulder blade against two tree trunks that prevented further flight. Holstering his gun, he held his breath while he dug a thick surgical face-mask from the kit, pulled the rubber band over the back of his head, and fitted the mask over his nose and mouth. He smeared Vicks VapoRub across the front of the mask from a small plastic jar in the kit to further block the smell. Then he approached the carcass and got to work.

The carcass had obviously decomposed even more. Blooms of entrails had burst through several places in the abdomen of the moose, where the hide had been stretched so tightly that it split. Again, he marveled at the surgical precision of the incisions that had been made. He could see no wounds that he had missed the day before, except for the gouged rips in the neck from the teeth of the bear that had dragged it from the meadow. Joe photographed the wounds from several angles using his digital camera. The photos, he thought, didn't convey the dread and fear he felt. They looked clinical, and somehow cleaner than the real thing.

He put on thick rubber gloves and squatted next to the carcass with his kit open. Using dental charts, he noted the size of the pre-molars as well as their stain and wear and guessed that the bull was at least seven years old, in its prime. Pushing a stainless steel probe through the hide along the spine of the moose between the shoulders, then in the middle of the back, and finally between the haunches, he noted that the body fat of the animal was normal, even a little excessive. Joe thought it was unusual in a drought year that the moose seemed so robust and healthy. Whatever had happened to the moose, it was clear that it hadn't died from either starvation or old age.

He ran a telescopic metal detector over the animal from its tail to the rounded end of its bulbous snout. No metal. If the animal had been shot, the bullet had passed through the body. But there was no exit wound. Conventional high-powered hunting bullets were designed to mushroom inside the body and do horrendous damage inside. But they were engineered to stay inside the body somewhere, not to exit. There was the possibility, Joe thought, that the shooter was using specialized armor-piercing type rounds that could pass straight through. But he doubted that scenario. In fact, the more he studied the body, the less he could convince himself that somebody had shot it.

Using a razor, Joe sliced tissue samples from the places on the moose's hindquarters, neck, and head where its hide had been cut away. He dropped the strips of meat into thick paper envelopes to send to the lab in Laramie. Plastic would spoil the samples, and he didn't want his effort to go to waste. He duplicated the procedure with another set of envelopes he would send to another lab.

After he completed his work, he stood above the carcass and stared at it. If anything, the face stripped of its flesh seemed more gruesome in the dark silence of the forest floor. The smell of the decaying body was working its way through the mask, overpowering even the Vicks. Joe looked around, suddenly realizing that he had been so intent on collecting the samples and completing the necropsy that he hadn't thought about the grizzly. Was he out there now, somewhere in the shadows? Would he be coming back?

Why would the bear go to all the effort of dragging the huge corpse into the trees and not feed on it? Moose was highly choice meat, for hunters and for bears. If the bear wasn't hungry, why would he have worked so hard? If the bear intended to eat the moose later, why hadn't he buried the carcass or covered it with brush as bears usually did?

Joe zipped up his kit and retraced his steps. Nothing about this dead moose made sense. His only hope to solve the puzzle, he thought, was if the lab boys could come up with something from the photos and the samples. But even if the moose died of some strange disease, how would they account for the incisions and the missing skin, glands, and organs?

As he neared the meadow, the light fused yellow, and when he emerged from the forest he had the same feeling a swimmer does as he breaks the surface from below. In the meadow, Joe turned. He listened closely for the sounds of a bear approaching or, for that matter, any sound at all. There was none. But there was still that shimmer in the air, and the closed-in feeling of density.

Maybe, Joe thought, *somebody or something is watching me.* Maybe that was why he felt so unnatural and out of sorts in the meadow. He swept the forest with his eyes, trying to find something out of the ordinary. A set of eyes, perhaps, or the glint of the lenses from binoculars. He turned slowly in the center of the meadow, not far from where the moose had originally lain. He scanned the three walls of trees, and the creek bed, even the high, slick faces of the mountains. He saw nothing unusual. But he was thoroughly and ashamedly spooked.

Still clutching his weapon and the bear spray, Joe walked across the meadow and dropped down into Crazy Woman Creek. As he walked downstream, he felt the pressure lessen. Eventually, he couldn't feel it at all. The sun seemed warmer and brighter overhead. A raven cawed rudely somewhere on the opposite bank.

In the afternoon, Joe sat in his truck on the crest of a sagebrush-covered hilltop in the breaklands east of Saddlestring. Behind him, the terrain arched and transformed into the foothills of the Bighorns, where he had come from. In front of him were miles of blue-gray sagebrush plains cut through with slashes of red ravines. From his vantage point, the breaklands looked like the ocean caught in freeze-frame; wavelike rolls of undulation stopped in time. This was pronghorn antelope country but there were few hunters out. He had identified only two vehicles over the past three hours, distant sparkles of glass and steel over two miles away. Watching through his window-mounted spotting scope, he observed the four-wheel drives move slowly on BLM roads. *Road hunters,* Joe thought. He had heard no shots. After the first weekend of antelope season, hunting activity was minimal in the breaklands. Pronghorns were so plentiful and easy to hunt that serious hunters had harvested their game within hours of the season opening. Those still out were either stubborn trophy hunters looking for the perfect rack, or local meat hunters who felt no sense of urgency.

Joe sat back from the spotting scope and rubbed his eyes. Maxine sighed and rolled over on the passenger seat, still sleeping.

He had stopped in town and mailed the tissue samples of the moose. The packages should arrive at the lab in Laramie and his other source in Montana the next morning. He had called both recipients on his cell phone and left messages asking that the examinations be expedited. He promised to forward the digital photos of the moose via e-mail that evening, when he got back to his house, so they could see the source of the samples.

From his vantage point, looking out at the plains, he could see forever. He loved this particular time in the fall for many reasons, but one of the major reasons was how the air and light seemed to sharpen, and everything was in perfect focus. In the summer, waves of rising heat rose from the plains and limited his field of vision. In the winter, moisture in the air or windborne snow did the same thing. This time in the fall the air was crisp and fresh and clear, and the colors from the trees that filled the valleys gave the landscape a festive, celebratory quality. Yet, today, the spectacular view failed to fill him with the same sense of awe that it usually did. He just couldn't stop thinking about the dead bull moose.

Even without the strange feeling he'd had in the meadow—which he now seriously doubted had come from anywhere other than his own imagination—the circumstances of the animal's death made even less sense than they had the day before.

Joe shook his head. He hoped some answers would come from the Wildlife Veterinary Research Services, where he'd sent the samples.

Then something caught his eye—a glint—and he leaned into the spotting scope again and tilted it upward, past the breaks into the private ranch lands miles beyond. Focusing the eyepiece, he simultaneously tightened the mount on the window to steady the telescope.

The glint, it turned out, was not from glass but from water forming around a freshly drilled well. The drilling rig that produced it was surrounded by three large pickup trucks, all the same make, model, and color. Men moved quickly between the pickups and the well, splashing through the growing pool of water. Joe couldn't see them clearly enough to make out their faces, or read the logos on the pickup doors, but he recognized what was going on. He had seen it dozens of times in the past year.

The trucks and rig were drilling for coal-bed methane in the basin. Judging by the rush of water to the surface and the urgency in the men's movements, they had obviously found it once again.

Underground coal seams covered the concentrated natural gas like a blanket, which in the past had made it difficult to retrieve. Joe had read, however, that since the technology had been perfected to extract the gas 5,000 CBM wells had been drilled in the Powder River Basin. An additional 5,000 to 8,000 wells were planned. Gas was being found everywhere they looked, and locating the underground pockets was now a fairly easy thing for geologists to do. Methane that had once been vented and released into the air during oil exploration as waste was now funneled into pipelines bound for the Midwest, the West Coast, and beyond. The coal-bed methane boom was being called the largest new energy discovery in North America.

In less than two years, Northern Wyoming was unexpectedly awash in the two things that, prior to that, were rare: money and water. Although Joe only understood the details of the boom from what he read and the snippets of conversation he heard from developers and locals in town, the price of methane gas ranged from seventy-five cents to three dollars per million British thermal unit, or mmbtus, depending on demand. And from what the energy developers were claiming, the underground coal in Twelve Sleep County could hold trillions of mmbtus of methane gas.

The CBM boom had invigorated the economy, and the county population, for the first time in a decade, was increasing. And it was only the beginning.

Although local businesses were certainly benefiting from the CBM boom, the developers, energy companies, and people who owned the mineral rights to the areas where the gas was being developed stood to gain the most. Stories abounded of instant millionaires, as well as of landowners who, after selling off what they thought were worthless mineral rights to their lands years before, could now only stand by while millions of dollars in gas were being pumped from wells on their ranches. Marybeth had told Joe the story of the Overstreet sisters, who owned the Timberline Ranch north of Saddlestring. The ranch was for sale through Logue Country Realty, her favorite client, but there were no buyers. Six hundred CBM wells were planned. Walter Overstreet, the patriarch of the ranch, had sold the mineral rights years ago, before he died. Despite the wells, the Overstreet sisters could be found in line for free lunch every day at the Saddlestring Senior Center.

But the controversial byproduct of CBM development was water. Far underground, water was trapped beneath the coal. Once a drill bit tapped the pocket, water rushed to the surface with great pressure. As the pressure eased, methane followed. Eventually, the water cleared out of the mix, and pure methane was produced. Although water had always been considered the single most precious commodity in the state, the effect of huge releases of underground water on the surface due to CBM wells was still unknown. Some tracts of land that had been parched for generations were now covered with standing water. Various landowners and many environmental groups claimed that CBM wells were depleting the aquifers, transforming the landscape and polluting the rivers with bitter water. The developers and other landowners countered that at last there was finally some water available for stock and wildlife. The battle raged on, although developers were now required to receive approval from state and federal environmental regulators before drilling.

Joe didn't know which side he was on. On the one hand, residents of Saddlestring were practically giddy with optimism for the first time since he had lived there. A new school was being built, the hospital was in the process of renovation, and the small airport was expanding. New restaurants and retail stores were filling the empty downtown buildings that had been boarded up the year before. The nation lusted for clean burning natural gas.

But there was no doubt that the thousands of wells were a blight to the landscape, even though the country they occupied was flat, barren, and stark to begin with. If the CBM wells sucked up so much underground water that water wells went dry or surface land collapsed, that wasn't good, either. And if the water being released to the surface was as mineral-heavy and tainted as some people claimed, it could poison the rivers and reservoirs, harming both people and wildlife.

Joe shook his head. Twelve Sleep County, Wyoming, was usually considered to be behind the rest of the world in all things modern or progressive. But when it came to this new kind of energy development, it was ahead of everyplace else.

The breaklands seemed empty of hunters, and before Joe moved to patrol a different area, he scanned the channels on his radio. While he usually listened to the channel reserved for the Game and Fish Departments in Wyoming, which was shared by brand inspectors and state park employees, he liked to check out what was going on in other areas of law enforcement. He listened to a highway patrol officer flirt with the dispatcher 200 miles away from his lonely location south of Jeffrey City, and a local Saddlestring police department request officers to check out a domestic disturbance. Joe had noted more domestic disturbance calls with the influx of CBM workers.

When he switched to the mutual aid channel, used by all agencies to communicate with each other in crises or emergencies, he found it crackling with traffic.

He recognized the first voice as that of Sheriff O. R. "Bud" Barnum, the longtime sheriff of Twelve Sleep County.

"Come again on that one?" Barnum said to someone. Even hearing his voice set Joe on edge. Over the years, Joe had come to despise Barnum. The feeling went both ways.

"You aren't going to believe this," someone answered, and Joe recognized the voice as that of Barnum's top deputy, Kyle McLanahan. "We've got a dozen dead cows on the Hawkins Ranch. It looks like they've been . . . well, *operated* on."

"What do you mean, operated on?" Barnum asked.

"Jeez, it's hard to describe," McLanahan said. "Half their faces are gone. And, uh, their peckers are missing, it looks like."

Joe felt a jolt of familiarity.

"Their *peckers*?" Barnum sounded angry.

"Well, if they had peckers," McLanahan reported. "If they was females, then their female parts have been cut out."

More trophies, Joe thought. He reached down and started his pickup. The Hawkins Ranch was an hour away on bad roads.

4

IN THE TOWN OF SADDLESTRING, behind a battered desk that came with the building, Marybeth Pickett shot her arm out and looked at her wristwatch. She had twenty minutes to finish up and print out the cash-flow spreadsheet she had been working on for Logue Country Realty, meet with the Logues, gather up her computer and files, and pick up her children from school. This is what it was like now, she thought. Her life was on the clock.

She had spent the morning meeting with the office manager of Barrett's Pharmacy going over accounts receivable, then at Sandvick Taxidermy working with the owner to establish a new billing system. Once they wrapped up, Marybeth asked the taxidermist, Matt Sandvick, if he had ever seen an animal brought in with the kind of wounds Joe had found on the dead moose the day before.

"Yup, I have," Sandvick had answered, his eyes widening behind thick lenses.

"Where?"

"On that show that used to be on. *The X-Files*." And Sandvick laughed.

After a quick lunch with her friend Marie Logue, co-owner of Logue Country Realty, Marybeth set up her portable office in a shabby back room at the real estate office and worked under a bare bulb. A small metal electric heater rattled to life whenever the temperature dropped below 60 degrees, and blew out dust-smelling heat through bent orange coils.

Of her three accounts, Marybeth preferred working with the Logues, although the account also presented the most challenges. While Marybeth did her best to straighten out the Byzantine finances of the business they had bought into, there was no doubt that the company and the Logues were in trouble. Despite this, she had come to like and admire them and wanted to do what she could to help them make the company survive, including undercharging for her time. She knew they couldn't afford her full rate just yet.

But if Sheridan and Lucy were to progress to college, as they should, it would take two full-time incomes. Joe's salary was barely enough to live on, considering Sheridan's basketball, volleyball, speech and debate interests, and Lucy's piano, dance, and Young Writers' Club. The real estate license would potentially create the cushion they needed for their family. When it came to college for the girls, they would be considered a low-income family, a designation that affected Marybeth deeply. She tried not to blame Joe, because he loved what he did and was good at it. But it didn't pay the bills.

Cam and Marie Logue bought what was then called Ranch Country Realty from its previous owner, a longtime local institution named Wild Bill Dubois. The purchase included the storefront on Main Street sandwiched between the Stockman's Bar and Big Suds Laundromat. With their seven-year-old daughter, Jessica, they had moved from Rapid City the previous winter and leased one of the oldest Victorian homes in town with the goal of restoring it while they lived there. They changed the name of the business to Logue Country Realty and sincerely did their best to establish themselves in the small community. They joined the Presbyterian church, the chamber of commerce, the realty association, the PTO, and gave to the high school activities groups and the United Way. In a sleepy town like Saddlestring, where the population trend until recently was a net loss, the arrival of the energetic, optimistic Logues was a welcome deviation from the norm. Or so Marybeth thought, despite knowing that there would be the usual bitter clucking from the old-timers and third-generation types. These were the longtime residents of Twelve Sleep County who referred to Mayor Ty Stockton—who had arrived with his parents from Massachusetts as a toddler—as "that guy from Boston."

Marybeth's younger daughter, Lucy, and Jessica Logue became fast friends on the first day of school and were joined by a third girl, named Hailey Bond, to round out the trio. Lucy was much more social than her older sister, Sheridan, and the three quickly formed a new ruling triumvirate of the first grade. Lucy and Jessica schemed to have their parents meet each other during school orientation, and Marybeth and Marie struck it off immediately. Marie told her later, over coffee, that she saw in the Picketts a young, growing, struggling family much like their own. Marybeth agreed, welcoming Marie's vitality and friendship and the fact that they were new to the area and had no preconceptions. They had discussed how similar they were; they had both gone to college the same year with goals of becoming professionals (Marybeth aimed for a law degree and Marie wanted an MBA in public administration). Marie had met Cam, and Marybeth had met Joe, and neither woman had applied for graduate school.

When Cam and Marie Logue approached Marybeth about looking into the accounts they had just bought, Marybeth agreed, even though Wild Bill Dubois had been known for comingling his funds and cooking his books. What she had found was even worse than she had anticipated. The Logues had bought a business that was a rat's nest of bad deals, expired contracts, and unfiled documents. When she told them what she found, they stared back at her in white-faced horror.

But instead of giving up or suing Wild Bill, who had quietly moved to Yuma, they decided to make the best of it. With their backs against the wall, they made the decision to work hard and turn their business around. Cam became even more prominent, calling on property owners throughout the county, reminding them that he was there if they needed to buy or sell, trying to win their trust.

His hard work had paid off recently in the listing of the Timberline Ranch by the squabbling Overstreet sisters. If Cam were able to sell it, even at the drastically reduced price it was likely to get, his commission would turn the company around.

So, when Cam Logue stuck his face in Marybeth's office, beaming a high-wattage smile she had never seen before, and asked if she could meet with him and Marie to hear some good news, Marybeth grinned and pushed back in her chair.

Ladies," Cam Logue announced once he had closed the door to his office, "we've got a secret client interested in the Timberline Ranch!"

Marie, who was petite, dark-haired, and attractive in an open-faced way, clapped her hands together. Her eyes shone. Marybeth was very happy for her.

"So who is it?" asked Marie.

Cam laughed. "I just said it was a *secret* client, Marie."

"I know, I know . . ."

Marybeth asked, "How serious is he?"

Cam turned to her. Cam was handsome, with light, wavy hair and sharp, blue eyes. He was ambitious in a way that seemed to encourage others to root for him. At least it worked for Marybeth. Her impression of him was that he was straightforward and entrepreneurial, if a little combative. He wanted to succeed not only for his business and his family, but also to prove something. Marie had told Marybeth that Cam had grown up as the youngest on a ranch outside of Saddlestring. She said that Cam's parents had doted on Cam's older brother, Eric, literally mortgaging the ranch in order to pay for Eric's medical school so he could become a surgeon. The Logue ranch was absorbed by the Overstreet sisters' Timberline Ranch, and his parents bought a small place in western South Dakota, near the Pine Ridge Reservation. When cattle prices bottomed out, there was no money left over for Cam, who went to Black Hills State (where he met Marie) and later into real estate. Cam's return to Saddlestring was a homecoming of sorts.

Yet if Cam recognized the irony of now selling the property he had grown up on, he didn't indicate it to Marybeth.

"He's serious," he said, "but he's doing due diligence. He's no dummy."

"Due diligence?" Marie asked.

Cam nodded. "He knows all about those CBM wells, and all of the water they discharge. Even though he knows he won't have the mineral rights, he wants to get that water tested to make sure it's okay when it flows down the river. He's afraid if something is wrong with the water the enviros or the downstream users might sue him as the landowner."

"That's smart," Marybeth said.

"He's a pretty smart guy."

Marie sat down in Cam's desk chair. "What if there's something wrong with the water?"

"There's nothing wrong with the water, Marie," Cam said, as if speaking to a child. "The water's fine. It's been tested before they sunk all of those wells, and it's fine. It's as sweet as honey."

"Then why . . . ?"

"Marie," Cam's reaction was sharp, "it's complicated. All of the testing that's been done has been piecemeal, before each new set of wells. By different companies at different times in the last couple of years. Our buyer wants water collected from all of those different well sites and tested again to make sure they're okay. To make sure, I don't know, that they haven't hit any bad water since they tested the first time, I guess. But you don't need to worry about it. The water's going to be just fine."

Marybeth thought Cam was a little more prickly than necessary. But she had never seen him this excited before.

"Our . . . difficulties may be over soon," Marie said as much to herself as to Cam or Marybeth. Cam beamed at her, then turned his full-force grin on Marybeth. As suddenly as a lightbulb going out, Cam's face fell into a mask of seriousness.

"But we need to keep this absolutely quiet," he said gravely. "It's got to be kept in the strictest professional confidence."

Marybeth nodded. The sale of property of this magnitude would electrify the valley, she knew. Other realtors would try to poach the secret buyer and try to get him to look at other ranches that might have more appeal or fewer wells. Property owners on the fence about selling may suddenly decide to try the market.

"It'll be hard to keep this a secret," Marie grinned. "But we can do it."

"Marybeth?" Cam asked.

"I'll tell my husband," she said, meeting their eyes. "We don't keep secrets from each other. But it will go no further than that."

When neither of the Logues spoke, Marybeth felt compelled to explain. "He tells me things that go on in his job that need to be kept confidential, and I do that. I've never breached Joe's confidence, and he wouldn't breach mine. Besides," she said, "he doesn't talk much as it is."

Marie snorted a laugh and turned in her chair to Cam. "You remember meeting Joe, don't you? At that back-to-school night? I think the only thing he said all evening when Marybeth introduced us was 'Pleasure.' That's it. One word in three hours."

"Okay then," Cam said, clapping his hands once as if to dispel the hint of suspicion that had entered the room.

Marybeth glanced at her watch.

"Oh my goodness, I've got to go. The girls are out of school."

Marie said, "Feel free to have Lucy come over to our house with Jessica. Hailey Bond is already coming. Those three have a great time together."

"But . . ."

"Don't worry. I'll bring Lucy home later. Around five or five-thirty, right?"

Marybeth nodded, and left them both in their giddy state.

As she left the office, pulling on her jacket, she noticed a man sitting in the reception area reading a magazine from the stack on the side table. He was lanky and in his sixties, with round, steel-framed glasses.

"I'm sorry," she said. "Do you need to see somebody?" Marie worked as the receptionist as well as the office manager, and she had obviously not been available.

The man looked up. He wore heavy boots, faded jeans, and a khaki work shirt. On his lap was a thick manila file. He had an experienced and kindly manner.

"I'm here to see Mr. Logue, but don't worry, I didn't have an appointment."

Marie overheard the conversation and entered the room.

"I'll let him know you're here," Marie said. She was bursting with cheerfulness, Marybeth thought, and for good reason.

Lucy Pickett and Jessica Logue were waiting at the pickup spot with Sheridan when Marybeth arrived. The playground was empty except for a few students on the swings. Marybeth felt guilty for being late.

Marybeth swung her minivan to the curb and the three girls piled in. Lucy and Jessica tossed their backpacks on the floor and immediately started telling Marybeth about their day in overlapping bursts, while Sheridan settled into the backseat alone and rolled her eyes. Lucy and Jessica were inseparable in a way that Sheridan never had been with another girl. Lucy and Jessica loved to dress up, do each other's hair, talk on the telephone, and play together. They even looked alike, as much like sisters as Lucy and Sheridan did.

"Jessica, your mom suggested you and Lucy play at your house this afternoon instead of ours," Marybeth said, pulling out into the road. "She'll bring Lucy home later."

"I hope dropping them off won't take too long," Sheridan interjected from the back. "I've got a falconry lesson in a little while."

Marybeth nodded, again feeling guilty that she was late. Sheridan had been learning falconry from Nate Romanowski, a loner and Joe's friend. He lived in a cabin on the bank of the Twelve Sleep River.

"It'll just take a minute," Marybeth said. "I'm sorry I'm running late."

"You seem to be running late a lot these days," Sheridan said under her breath but loud enough that Marybeth heard her. Both Lucy and Jessica immediately stopped talking and waited for what they hoped would be an argument.

"Please don't use that tone with me, Sheridan," Marybeth said evenly, locking eyes with Sheridan in the rearview mirror. "We can discuss this later."

Sheridan broke the gaze and shrugged. Marybeth noticed that Lucy and Jessica had huddled together and shrunk out of view, no doubt trying not to giggle.

The Logue home was one of Saddlestring's fading treasures; a classic Victorian, one of the original homes built at the edge of town near the river by an 1890s cattle baron. The faded house was hard to see behind the mature cottonwoods that towered around it. In addition to the old, magnificent house there was wooded acreage and a few outbuildings, including a carriage house. The house had sat vacant for fifteen years, in disrepair, until the Logues bought it last winter. Marie had walked Marybeth through the place recently, apologizing endlessly for its condition. Only two rooms had been modernized so far, the kitchen and a bathroom. The rest looked as it had in the mid-1980s, when the longtime county clerk of Twelve Sleep County died there in his seventy-eighth year. The rumor was that the county clerk used to store records in the house and the buildings and charge the county for rent.

Maybe now, Marybeth thought as she watched Lucy and Jessica skip away, *Cam and Marie would have the means to accelerate the remodeling on the great old house.*

"Mom?" Sheridan said from the backseat. "She's getting bigger. You don't have to wait until she gets in the house before we leave."

"I'm just not used to this yet Sheridan," Marybeth said.

"You two have so many things going on these days. I struggle with letting you go."

"Mom, my falconry lesson?"

As Marybeth pulled away and turned left on Centennial Street toward Bighorn Road, her phone chirped. It was Joe, telling her about the call he had overheard concerning mutilated cows. He told her he would likely be late for dinner.

Dinner, Marybeth thought, the guilt rushing back. She had forgotten to plan dinner.

5

THE HAWKINS RANCH was a checkerboard of private land and state and federal leases spread across the lee side of the foothills, and Joe had to cross through seven barbed-wire fence gates to get to it. Most of the ranch was blanketed with tall sagebrush and scrub oak, buffalo grass and biscuit root, except for several large fingers of heavy timber that reached down from the mountains through saddle-slope draws.

Joe pulled into the ranch yard, a packed-gravel courtyard surrounded by structures. The Hawkins place was an old-line working outfit, unlike many of the hobby ranches that were taking over the state. The largest buildings in the yard were vast metal Quonset huts that served as vehicle sheds, barns, and equipment storage. A maze of wooden-slat corrals bordered the small, white-framed ranch house. There were no adornments of any kind anywhere; nothing to suggest anything other than what the place was—the business center for a large-scale beef-and-hay operation.

Joe turned toward the small house and saw Mrs. Hawkins step out on an unpainted porch and gesture sternly to the mountains. There was no need to stop and visit, Joe thought, and he drove through the middle of the ranch yard until his wheels fell into the long-established ruts of a dirt road that pointed straight toward the timber five miles away. Ahead of him in the ruts were the fresh tread tracks of several vehicles.

Approaching the scene, Joe noted that two identical GMC Blazers belonging to the Twelve Sleep County Sheriff's Department, and a light-blue Ford pickup, were parked nose-to-tail on the two-track where the scrub thinned and the pine trees began. To the right of the vehicles were three figures in the middle of what appeared to be a glacial-boulder field.

As Joe closed in, the front of his pickup bucked suddenly and a cascade of maps fell from a clip on the sunshade. Maxine lost her footing on the dashboard and scrambled back to her place on the seat, looking at him for an explanation.

"Rock," he said. "Didn't see it."

The figures turned out to be Deputy Kyle McLanahan, Sheriff Barnum, and a visibly upset Don Hawkins. What Joe had thought were boulders strewn across the ground were actually carcasses of cattle, at least a dozen of them. The sour-sweet smell of death filtered into the cab of the pickup through the vents, and Maxine sat up ramrod straight, her brow wrinkled with concern.

Even from this distance, Joe could see that Barnum was glaring at him. The old man's eyes bored across the brush and through the windshield of the pickup. McLanahan stood to the side of Barnum with a 35-mm camera hanging from his hand, looking from Barnum to Joe's pickup and back to Barnum. Don Hawkins wore a bandanna over his face and paced among the dead cows.

"Stay, girl," Joe told Maxine as he parked to the side of the Sheriff's Department vehicles and swung out of his pickup. He fitted his gray Stetson on his head and skirted the Blazers. The smell of the cows was not as ripe as the smell of the moose had been, and he was grateful for that.

"Who called you out here?" Barnum asked. His deep-set eyes were cold, bordered by blue folds of loose skin. He lowered a cigarette from his lips and jetted twin streams of smoke from his nostrils.

"Heard it on the mutual-aid band."

"This look like a Game and Fish matter to you?"

"I'm not sure what it looks like yet, Sheriff," Joe said, walking among the carcasses, "but I found something similar done to a bull moose on Crazy Woman Creek."

It had been months since Joe had seen Barnum, and that had been fine with Joe. He despised Barnum, knowing the sheriff was as corrupt as he was legendary. There were rumors that Sheriff Barnum was in his last term of office, that he would retire within the next year. The electorate that had supported him for twenty-eight years seemed to be turning on him for the first time. The local weekly newspaper, the *Saddlestring Roundup,* had run a series of editorials in the spring saying outright that it was time for Barnum to go.

Deputy McLanahan said, "Your moose have his pecker cut off?"

Joe turned his head to McLanahan. This guy was just as bad, Joe thought, if not worse. Although the deputy wasn't as smart or calculating as Barnum, he made up for it with his cruelty. He was a loose cannon, and he liked to pull the trigger.

"Yup," Joe said, dropping to his haunches to examine a heifer. "Something took off most of his face, as well as his genitals and musk glands from the back legs."

"I ain't never seen nothing like this," Don Hawkins said, bending over one of the dead cows. "These cows are worth six, seven hundred bucks each. Something or somebody owes me nine thousand bucks, goddamit."

The reason the smell was not as bad, Joe realized, was that the cattle had been dead for at least two weeks. Although still somewhat bloated, the bodies had begun to deflate and collapse in on themselves in fleshy folds. The wounds looked similar to the bull moose's, with some differences. Skin had been removed from most of the heads in precise patches. One heifer's head had been completely denuded of hide, which made it look like a turkey buzzard with its thin neck and red head. In some cases, tongues and eyes had been removed, and oval patches were missing from shoulders. On the females, their bags had been removed. Half of the cows had missing rectums, showing large dark holes between their flanks.

Joe felt a distinct chill as he walked from body to body. This was like the moose, times twelve. It also meant that whatever had been doing this had been in action for at least two weeks.

"The blood's drained right out of 'em," Hawkins said, shaking his head. "This is crazy."

"Are you sure about that?" Joe asked, looking up at the rancher.

"Look at 'em," Hawkins cried, holding his hands palms-out. "You see any blood anywhere? How in the hell can you cut up a damned cow like that and not have any blood on the ground? Do you know how much blood there is in a cow?"

"Nope, I don't," Joe said.

"I don't know either," Hawkins said, flustered. "A shitload for sure."

McLanahan said, "No matter how much there is in a cow, there's none of it on the ground. It's like the blood got sucked right out of them."

"Oh, for Christ's sake . . ." Barnum growled, turning his back to McLanahan. "Don't start saying things like *that*."

"So what did it?"

"How in the hell should I know?"

"Maybe some kind of predator?" McLanahan asked. "A bear or a mountain lion or something?"

"There is a bear," Joe said. "A big grizzly. I saw his tracks this morning. But I can't believe a bear could do this."

"That's all I need," Barnum said, his voice rising, "a bunch of mutilated cattle and a goddamned grizzly bear on the loose."

"Not to mention space aliens sucking the blood out of domestic animals in the middle of ranch country," McLanahan said dramatically. "It's happened before, you know."

"Stop that!" Barnum spat. "*I mean it.*"

Joe battled a smile and addressed Don Hawkins.

"When did you find these cattle?"

Hawkins was slow to answer, and when he did, it was with hesitation. McLanahan's speculating had rattled him.

"My guy Juan found 'em a-horseback this morning. He called me at the ranch house on his radio."

"Have you been missing these cattle?"

Hawkins nodded. "We moved most of our herd up to Montana where they have some grass. The drought here forced us to move our cows this fall. We knew we had stragglers in the timber, and Juan's been looking for them and herding them down."

"Did you see anything unusual? Hear anything?"

Something washed across Hawkins's face. Joe waited. He could tell that Hawkins seemed a little embarrassed about something.

"This is stupid," Hawkins said. "Juan told me a few days ago he was getting dizzy when he rode up here. He thought it was the elevation or something. I thought it was laziness. It's easier to look for cows on flat ground than in the timber, so I figured he was angling for easier work."

Joe didn't say that he thought he knew the feeling.

"Dizzy?" McLanahan asked. "Like dizzy how?"

"I don't know," Hawkins said, rolling his eyes. "He's always complaining about something."

"Anything else?" Joe asked. "Maybe a couple of weeks ago?"

Hawkins shook his head. "We were delivering cattle north to Montana. We weren't even around."

"In all your years, have you ever seen cattle that looked like this?" Joe asked.

"Nope," Hawkins said, his eyes widening. "I once seen a badger make a den in the belly of a dead cow, but I never seen nothing like this."

Joe said, "Have you heard anything from your neighbors? Have they called about missing cattle?"

Hawkins rubbed his stubbled chin, then gestured north with his hat rim. "That's Bud Longbrake's place, and I haven't heard anything from Bud in a while. We both have a couple of cricks running through that we share in common, and our cows get mixed up in the bottoms sometimes. But like I said, he hasn't called me about anything."

Joe felt a twinge at the mention of Bud Longbrake. Marybeth's mother, Missy, had already moved to his ranch and their wedding was looming.

Hawkins turned his head to the south. "That's the Timberline Ranch that way," he said, and a grin broke across his face. "Do you know the Overstreet sisters?"

McLanahan snorted from ten feet away and shook his head. "I know of them."

"When they aren't scratching each other's eyes out or in court suing each other over something, they're accusing me or rustlers of making off with some of their cows," Hawkins said. "I bet the sheriff's been out here ten times over the years because one of those crazy Overstreet broads called and said they had cattle missing."

"At least ten," Barnum sighed. "Never found anything, and the sisters can't produce records of any missing stock."

The Timberline Ranch was the one for sale, Joe recalled. No wonder, he thought, if they couldn't keep track of their cattle.

"So whatever they say is less than . . . credible," Hawkins said.

"If anybody saw a flying saucer up here it would have been them," McLanahan said. "I'll guarantee you that."

"Shut up, *please,* Kyle," Barnum said.

As Joe listened to the exchange, another question came to him. "Were there any vehicle tracks up here before the sheriff arrived?"

"Not that I could see."

"What are you saying, that we messed up the crime scene?" Barnum asked.

"Not saying that at all."

Even McLanahan glanced over his shoulder at Barnum.

"Well, you better not be," Barnum said defensively. "This is my investigation and no one has requested you here."

"The wounds are similar to my moose," Joe said. "It's likely the same thing. No predation, either, even though all that beef has just been sitting out here in plain sight."

"That bothers me," Hawkins said, shaking his head. "There's just something real wrong with that. We should have knowed those cows were up here. There should have been big flocks of birds feeding on them. That's how we usually find dead cows. And not one of these cattle has been fed on, or scattered."

Joe had received calls from Don Hawkins the previous spring about mountain lions that had killed several calves. Joe had looked for the cats and not found them. When the calls stopped, he knew that Hawkins *had* found them. Nevertheless, the ranch was prime habitat for lions, coyotes, and black bears.

"Just like my moose," Joe said. "Nothing will eat the meat. It makes you wonder why."

"Tell you what," Barnum said as he lit a cigarette and exhaled a blue cloud of smoke, "you worry about your moose and I'll worry about Mr. Hawkins's cows."

"You've got jurisdiction," said Joe.

"You are correct."

"So I guess you're planning to talk with Juan then, as well as Bud Longbrake and the Overstreet sisters?"

"I know how to do my job, Pickett."

Not that you've always done it before, Joe thought but didn't say. But he knew Barnum was practically reading his thoughts.

"I sent tissue samples of the moose to the lab in Laramie," Joe said, not mentioning where else he had sent them. "I asked that they expedite the analysis. When there are some results I'll share them with you. You were going to get these cattle tested, weren't you?"

Barnum's eyes narrowed and he didn't answer.

"Who is *that*?" McLanahan said, pointing down the road at an approaching vehicle.

They waited, watching, as an older pickup bucked and heaved up the washed-out road. Joe recognized her first. He had met her the winter before but couldn't recall her name.

"Reporter," Joe said. "Works for the *Saddlestring Roundup*. She must have been listening in on the scanner."

"Damn it," Barnum said, his face darkening. "I do *not* want this in the newspaper."

"Too late," McLanahan said.

"How in the hell are we going to explain this?" Barnum asked the sky.

Joe wondered the same thing.

6

WE'RE SUPPOSED TO STAY in my room," Jessica Logue told Lucy Pickett and Hailey Bond. "My dad says we need to stay out of those old buildings out back. He says they're unsafe for us to play in."

Lucy and Hailey protested. One of the things the girls loved was exploring the old outbuildings in the thick trees behind the house. It was spooky back there, and dark.

"Can't we play hide-and-seek?" Lucy asked.

"That's what my dad said," Jessica shrugged. "He said he's afraid the buildings might collapse when we're playing in them and he says he doesn't have enough insurance if we get hurt."

"Oooh," Hailey said, widening her eyes. "Maybe the roofs will fall in and crush us. And there will be blood and guts all over, like those gophers that get squished on the highway . . ."

"Stop it, Hailey," Jessica said. Hailey, who was dark-haired with big brown eyes, liked to talk about gore. She also liked scaring people. Lucy and Jessica had made her promise to stop hiding in the worst places out back and refusing to answer their calls. Several times, Lucy and Jessica were on the verge of panic when Hailey would suddenly jump out from a pile of lumber or from behind the door of an ancient shed and shout, "Now you die!"

"There's stuff we can do in here," Jessica said, trying to make the best of it.

Yes there is, Lucy thought. Jessica had the best collection of cool old clothes she had ever seen. Both Lucy and Jessica loved to play dress-up in the old clothes, and loved applying makeup from an old makeup case Jessica's mom had given her. Hailey sighed, but went along. Hailey, like Lucy's older sister, Sheridan, seemed to think that the girl things Lucy and Jessica liked were boring. She would rather play hide-and-seek in the woods and scare the other girls. Just like something Sheridan would do.

The box of old clothes was wonderful, and the three girls plowed through it. There were formal ball gowns, high-heeled shoes, tiaras (Jessica's mom had once won the Miss Sunflower beauty contest as a girl in South Dakota), boas, bathrobes, and some men's clothes.

Hailey unfolded a dark green set of surgeon's scrubs with the name LOGUE stenciled over the breast pocket.

"Are these your dad's?" she asked.

"My uncle is a doctor," Jessica said. "They used to be his."

"Is he still a doctor?"

"I think so," Jessica said.

"Hey, this one's pretty!" Lucy squealed, pulling a long, maroon velvet gown from the box. She felt the material and liked the lushness of it. And she liked the white fur trim of the collar. "This would look good on me with those shoes," she said, pointing at a pair of spike heels.

"I want to go outside," Hailey said, pouting. "Do you think you could ask your dad?"

"He's not home yet," Jessica said, fishing a small black hat with a net out of the bundle and putting it on. "I'll ask him when he gets home, though."

The three girls stood shoulder-to-shoulder at the mirror over Jessica's dresser, their faces inches from the glass while they applied their makeup. They were dressed up; Hailey in the surgeon's scrubs, Jessica in a white satin dress with fake pearls, Lucy in the velvet dress and spike heels and the Miss Sunflower sash hung across her chest.

Despite their giggling, they could hear an argument coming from downstairs, from the living room at the foot of the stairs.

"What are they fighting about?" Hailey whispered, leaning into mirror to apply the blush to her cheeks.

Jessica shrugged, "I don't know."

"Are you going to ask your dad if we can go outside?"

"When we're done. Lucy, you look beautiful."

Lucy kissed at herself in the mirror, and the other girls laughed. Her lips were bright red with lipstick, and her eyelids were covered in blue shadow.

"Will your mom get mad if I wear her Miss Sunflower banner?"

"I don't think so. And it's called a sash."

Lucy was disconcerted by the loud voices from downstairs. It wasn't like her parents never had an argument—they certainly did. There were times at dinner when she knew there had been a disagreement, by the silence, the lack of small talk, or the extra helping of politeness when one of them asked for the salt. But she hardly even heard them raise their voices to each other, even behind closed doors. Their arguments, whenever they occurred, happened someplace else or when no one else was home. Hearing the voices from downstairs, she thought it was better to argue away from the children.

They stood at Jessica's upstairs window, looking, Lucy thought, like pretty hot young women. They had applied perfume—overdone it, actually—and the smell was overpowering. They were watching as two dark, late-model sedans pulled up the driveway and stopped near the front porch.

"Who are those people?" Hailey asked, as both cars stopped and the driver-side doors opened. Two older women emerged from their separate vehicles. Each woman was tall, angular, and wearing a print dress that was out-of-date as well as out of season, Lucy thought. The women looked similar but different. Like sisters, maybe.

"I think their name is Overcast," Jessica said. "Something like that."

"Are they sisters?" Lucy asked.

"Yes."

"So they're not married to anyone?"

"I don't know. I don't think so."

"Look how they pretend the other one isn't there," Hailey said. "Isn't that weird?"

Lucy had noticed. The two women had emerged from their cars, shut the doors, and proceeded to the front door without even acknowledging each other. They were now out of sight below, under the roof of the portico.

"Overstreet," Jessica said. "Now I remember their names. They own a ranch or something."

"Both of them?" Lucy asked. "Without husbands?"

"I think so," Jessica said. "I met them a couple of times but I don't like them."

"Why not?" Lucy asked.

Jessica shuddered. "They're just icky. And they smell bad."

Hailey laughed nervously. "Maybe now is a good time to ask about playing outside."

The three girls looked at each other, knowing Hailey was right. There was no better time to ask parents to do something than when guests distracted them.

Lucy was the second down the stairs, after Jessica. There was a discussion going on between the Overstreet sisters and Jessica's parents.

Jessica's dad said, "Yes, I heard about those cows today."

"And you know we've been losing stock that we can't account for," one of the sisters said.

"What will this do to the sale?" the other sister asked.

"I don't know," Jessica's dad said. "But we may want to consider lowering the price to keep it attractive."

"I knew you would say that."

"We're against that, you know."

"It's just that . . ."

"Cam, we have visitors," Jessica's mother said, interrupting him.

Lucy watched as Mr. Logue and the Overstreet sisters paused and looked up toward the stairs.

"My, my," one of the sisters said. "Look at *them*."

Despite their dresses, the women looked hard, Lucy thought. There was no warmth in their stares. One of the sisters had blue eyes and the other green. Their eyes looked like old jewelry.

"They look like little tarts," the other sister said, and received a glare from Jessica's mom.

"What do you girls want?" Jessica's dad asked.

"Can we play outside?" Jessica asked. "In the back?"

"Dressed like *that*?" the older Overstreet sister asked, smiling with her mouth only.

"We can change," Jessica said weakly.

Jessica's dad gestured toward Hailey. "Didn't we agree to throw out those old clothes?" He looked upset, Lucy thought.

"It's okay, girls," Jessica's mom said, standing up, not addressing Mr. Logue's question. "You can go out back."

Mr. Logue shot her a look, but didn't intervene. The three girls fluttered down the stairs and across the foyer and out the back door.

"That worked," Hailey said as soon as the door slammed behind them.

"Did you smell them?" Jessica asked.

"I smelled something," Lucy said. But even though they were outside and could play hide-and-seek, she wished she were home.

7

THE NEXT EVENING, after the dinner dishes were cleared, Joe entered his small office near the mudroom and shut the door. The office was cramped and poorly heated. It consisted of a metal government-surplus desk, two four-drawer filing cabinets, and bookshelves crammed with books of statutes, biology and range-management texts, the complete John McPhee collection, and spiral notebooks of department directives. A set of antlers from the first five-point buck he had ever shot hung from the wall behind him. Caps, hats, binoculars, and his gray, sweat-stained Stetson covered the tines. As he clicked on his desk lamp and booted up his computer, he glanced at the front page of the weekly *Saddlestring Roundup* that was delivered that morning.

THEY'RE BAAAACK . . .
MUTILATED CATTLE DISCOVERED IN COUNTY
A BULL MOOSE ANOTHER VICTIM?

The photo on the front page that accompanied the article showed the carcasses on the Hawkins Ranch, with Sheriff

Barnum standing in the middle of them. The story contained quotes from Don Hawkins, the sheriff, Deputy McLanahan, and Joe. Although the story was accurate, Joe winced while he read it. He could imagine Barnum doing the same. There was a disagreeable sense of unreality about it, he thought. It was the kind of subject matter he ignored with contempt when he saw something similar on the front of a supermarket tabloid.

At least a dozen cattle and a bull moose have been found recently in the county, bearing mutilations similar to those reported in the mid-1970s, according to Twelve Sleep County Sheriff O. R. "Bud" Barnum. . . .

The article summarized the scene at the ranch, describing the dead cattle as "gruesome and unearthly" and calling the mutilations "inexplicable" before jumping to inside pages. Joe read on:

. . . In the mid-1970s, a rash of cattle mutilations were reported throughout the Mountain West, primarily in Montana, Wyoming, and Utah.

Cattle, as well as sheep and some domestic livestock, were reported dead, with genitals and other organs missing. In most of the documented incidents, skin had been removed from the faces of the victims as well as eyes, tongues, ears, and glands. Blood was reportedly drained from the bodies . . .

. . . Speculation as to the cause of the deaths ranged from government experiments to cults, as well as extraterrestrial visitations. Despite local investigations, no definitive cause was ever determined, although an FBI report issued in 1978 seemed to conclude that the deaths were natural and that the "mutilations" were a result of predation and decomposition. A review of county records revealed that the cattle mutilations seemed to have ceased after the initial reports, and there is no record of additional incidents. . . .

The reporter had interviewed several area ranchers who had reported cattle mutilations thirty years earlier, as well as the long-retired county coroner who recalled the cases but couldn't locate his files on them. Joe noted the similarities with a rising feeling of unease. The mutilations indeed sounded similar. The removal of genitals and skin, the bloating, no evidence of predation, the lack of a logical conclusion. Several cattle, it had been reported, were found in what looked like craters of four or five inches in depth, making it appear as though they had been dropped from the sky. One blatant similarity was the precision of the cuts, which seemed to have been made by an extremely sharp and very precise instrument.

. . . "There is nothing to fear," Sheriff Barnum cautioned. "There could be an easy explanation for this."

When pressed, Barnum declined further comment.

"We don't want the good citizens of this county gathering up their pets and searching the skies for aliens," said Sheriff's Deputy Kyle McLanahan.

Joe smiled despite himself. He bet Barnum just loved that quote.

Launching his e-mail program, Joe scanned the incoming messages. Nothing yet from the laboratory in Laramie regarding the samples he had sent them.

One e-mail was from his district supervisor, Trey Crump, in Cody. The subject line said "???" He opened it.

"What in the hell is going on with these cows and a moose?" Crump asked. "And what is it with you and dead cows?"

Joe paused before responding. He ignored Crump's jibe about dead cows. Two years before, an environmental terrorist, his wife, and another man were killed by cows strapped with explosives. Joe had inadvertently been involved in the case. In regard to Crump's initial question, Joe didn't want to speculate.

"It's true," he typed. "Tissue samples have been sent to Laramie for analysis. I'm keeping an eye on any future incidents, especially with the game population."

Joe opened his browser, went to the Web site for the *Roundup,* and copied the link for the mutilation story to his e-mail, so Trey could read it for himself.

"There is probably an explanation," Joe wrote. "I haven't figured it out yet but I will try."

He wrote that he had found massive bear tracks near the moose. "Could this be our rogue grizzly?"

Then he reread his e-mail, deleted the last line, and sent it.

Just as Joe was about to exit his e-mail program, a large file appeared in his inbox, and he waited as it slowly loaded. He recognized the return address as Dave Avery's. Since the time years before, when samples he had sent for analysis had been "lost" at headquarters, Joe had never regained complete trust in the agency bureaucracy. So sometimes he chose to seek two opinions, one from the lab in Laramie and the other from Dave Avery, an old college roommate, who was now chief wildlife biologist for the Montana Fish and Game Department in Helena. Joe had been best man at Avery's first two weddings, but had begged off when asked the third time last summer, claiming he might be bad luck.

There was no subject line, and no text, only six JPEG photos attached to the e-mail. Joe leaned back and waited for them to open, annoyed as always at his low-speed connection.

He scrolled down through the photos and felt the hair rise on the back of his neck.

The photos were of mutilated cattle in a meadow. He recognized the wounds, the bloated bellies, the madly grinning skulls. Joe wondered how Dave could have gotten a hold of these photos so quickly, but then Joe noticed something.

The sky in the top right corner of the second photo was dark and leaden. In the fourth photo, a skiff of snow could be seen in the foreground. The grass was yellowed, almost gray.

These photos had been taken in winter. And they had been taken somewhere else.

Breaking the online connection so he could use the telephone, Joe found Dave Avery's contact details and punched the numbers. His friend answered on the third ring.

"Avery."

"Dave, this is Joe Pickett."

"Joe! How in the hell are you?"

"Fine."

"I thought you'd be calling."

"Yup," Joe said, scrolling again through the photos on the screen. "I'm looking at these shots of mutilated cattle and wondering where they were taken."

"Gee, Joe, ever heard of small talk? Like how am I doing these days, or how is the weather in Helena?"

Joe sighed. "So, Dave, how are you doing? What's the weather like in Helena?"

"They were all taken outside of Conrad, Montana," Avery answered, "last January. Do you know where Conrad is?"

"Nope."

"Conrad and Dupeyer. Pondera County. Northwestern part of the state. East of Great Falls."

"Okay . . ."

"Sixteen of 'em, from July through January of this year," Avery said. "Maybe eight more, but we couldn't be sure because the bodies were too old. So maybe two dozen cattle in all. They were found in groups of four to six, although there were a couple loners. No tracks, no reports of vehicles or lights in the area. Unfortunately, no one ever brought in a fresh one. All of the carcasses were bloated and old."

"Any predation?"

There was a long pause, then "No."

"Was the blood drained out of them?"

"No. It just looks like that. Natural coagulation makes it look like they're bloodless. Once you run some tests you'll find that out."

"Then you got the samples I sent you," Joe said.

"Got 'em at the lab."

Joe waited. He could hear a Chris LeDoux CD playing somewhere in the background, and somebody—he guessed Dave's new wife—singing along.

"And?" Joe finally asked.

"I haven't dug into them yet, Joe, but I know what I'll find."

"What's that?"

"A whole lot of nothing," Avery said. "Well, one thing, I guess, but I'm not sure it's significant. Believe me, we've been analyzing tissue samples up here for nine months. My freezer's full of cow heads and cored rectums in paper bags."

"I hadn't heard a single thing about cattle mutilations up there," Joe confessed.

"I'm not that surprised," Avery said. "Conrad's pretty remote, even in Montana. Besides, they're just *cows.*"

Joe smiled at that. He remembered a paper Avery had written in college, proposing that ninety percent of the cattle in the West be removed and replaced with bison. The paper had not been very well received at the University of Wyoming, home of the Wyoming Cowboys.

"Even so," Avery continued, his voice rising with annoyance, "I got calls from kooks all over the place. The newspaper stories ran in the *Great Falls Tribune,* so of course they showed up on the Internet, and crazies from all over who are into this kind of thing took an interest. They're like train buffs, Joe. You never know they're even out there living among us normal people until some rare train comes through town and they rush the tracks."

"What about wildlife?" Joe asked. "I found a bull moose mutilated in the same way."

"Hmmm, no shit?"

"The samples I sent were from the moose."

There was a pause. "I'll take a look tomorrow," Avery said in a serious tone.

"So there weren't any wildlife deaths reported?" Joe asked again. He sensed that Avery had something to say but was holding back.

"Actually, there were a couple of reports, but they weren't very credible."

"Who made them?" Joe asked.

Avery sighed. "Joe, there was a guy up here, a self-described expert in the paranormal. He just showed up out of the blue with a kind of laboratory-on-wheels. It's a retrofitted RV with all kinds of equipment and shit inside. He claimed to represent some foundation somewhere in Arizona or New Mexico that funds him to do research. His name is Cleve Garrett"—Avery spat the name out as if it were a curse word—"and he practically camped on top of me all last summer. He's got all kinds of theories about how these are alien abductions and how I'm engaged in a governmental conspiracy to keep it all quiet. The fucking dweeb. The moron."

"So you don't like him much?" Joe asked facetiously.

"Hah!"

"Is he the one who reported the wildlife deaths?"

Joe heard Avery take a swallow of something before answering. "He claimed there were hundreds of cases of wildlife mutilations. He said they were all over the place—on the sides of highways, in the timber, all over. He said the reason we didn't know about them was because we never thought to look. He said 25 percent of the deer killed on the highway were actually mutilated and dumped, but no one cared to notice. He loves talking to reporters and stirring this stuff up."

Joe thought about that, his mind racing. How many dead deer, elk, moose, fox, antelope bordered the highways? Hundreds, perhaps thousands. Who *would* think to examine them? They were roadkill.

"He brought in a mule deer carcass once," Avery said. "And yes, it did look like it had been cut on. But the body was too old to determine anything conclusive. Plus, I didn't trust the guy not to have done it himself."

"Is he still up there?" Joe asked.

"You know, I don't think so," Avery said. "I haven't seen him in quite a while. I heard he had a following of like-minded kooks and had taken up with some young girl. He probably took her back to wherever he came from so he could practice alien probes on her or something."

Joe didn't know what to ask next. Then he recalled something Avery had said earlier.

"Dave, you said there was something about the tissue samples you looked at?"

"Oh, yeah. But like I said, don't put too much significance in it."

"Yes?"

"One thing we found in the cattle that were the freshest—I think they had been dead a week or so—was an above-normal level of a compound called oxindole. Ever heard of it?"

"It sounds vaguely familiar," Joe said, searching his memory.

"Probably from biology class. Oxindole is a natural chemical that can have a sedative effect. Cattle release it within their own bodies under stress. We found excessive amounts in the tissue samples, especially in the brains and in the eyeballs that hadn't been removed already."

"So it probably came from the cow itself?" Joe asked, confused.

"Well, probably, yes," Avery said. Unconvincingly, Joe thought.

"The older cows, the ones that had been dead longer, did you find oxindole in them?"

"Some. But we think it dissipates with age."

"So why even mention it?"

"Because there was so damned much of it," Avery sighed. "Maybe enough to literally sedate the cow, to knock it out. Much more than we know that a cow is capable of producing."

Joe was silent.

"Look, you've got to keep it in perspective," Avery cautioned. "We don't know very much about the compound. We don't know, for example, if maybe it doesn't become concentrated, postmortem, in certain organs, and those were the organs we just happened to test. The compound may intensify due to a traumatic or stressful death, or it could be that the presence of it is triggered by a virus or something. We're still researching it, but quite frankly we aren't getting anywhere. We have real work to do up here, as you know. I've got a break-out of pinkeye in our mountain sheep population right now. So we can't be spending too much time or energy on dead cows, especially since the mutilations seem to have stopped."

"They stopped in Montana, anyway," Joe said.

"Now you've got 'em," Avery said, his voice heavy. "Maybe you'll get my friend Cleve Garrett as well."

Joe grunted. "I'm still a little surprised that this is the first I've heard of it. I'd think those ranchers would be demanding some kind of action."

Avery laughed, which Joe thought was an odd response.

"I don't get it," Joe said, annoyed.

"At first, they wanted to call in the National Guard," Avery said. "A couple of 'em were on the phone to the governor right away. Then they realized how it looked."

"What do you mean?"

"Cattle prices were at record lows at the time. Most of these ranchers barely scrape by as it is. They're one bank payment away from losing their ranches. So they're either trying to sell their spreads for big bucks to Hollywood celebrities, or selling their beef for a few pennies in profit. If word got out that the cattle are dying *unnatural* deaths, those landowners are shit out of luck. When they realized that, they pressured the governor *not* to do anything."

"So, Dave, can I ask you something?"

"Shoot."

"What do you think this is? Not a scientific explanation, or your professional opinion. What does your gut tell you?"

Joe heard Avery take another sip of his drink. He heard another Chris LeDoux rodeo song.

"Joe, I don't know what the fuck it is," Avery said, his voice dropping, "but for a while there I was scared as hell."

Joe asked Avery to contact him if he found anything unusual in the tissue samples. They talked for a few moments about game-management issues, and Avery reported what was happening in Montana with whirling disease in the rivers. Joe told Avery about confirmed findings of chronic wasting disease in mule deer in southern Wyoming. They agreed to keep in better touch.

Then Joe cradled the telephone and sat back.

He was still sitting there when Marybeth rapped on the door and opened it. She was in her nightgown; the short, black one he liked.

"Are you coming to bed?" she asked.

Joe looked at his wristwatch, surprised to see that it was 11:30.

"I didn't kiss the girls good night," he said, alarmed.

"What have you been doing in here?"

"Work. I talked to Dave Avery."

Marybeth smiled, rolling her eyes.

"I remember Dave being sober on his wedding day," she said. "I realized I didn't even know him. He was drunk almost all of college."

"He's a good biologist, though," Joe said, "and a good friend."

"What did he say about the moose?"

Joe looked away, then back. "We may have a problem."

"What do you mean?"

"Are the horses in the barn or in the corral tonight?" Joe asked.

Marybeth frowned. "They're in the corral, why?"

"I think we need to start putting them in the barn at night," Joe said, standing up and clamping on his hat.

8

SHERIDAN PICKETT STEPPED OUT of the shadowed gnarl of river-bottom cottonwoods. She looked up and searched the dull, gray sky in silence until she saw what she was looking for. She felt a small shiver of excitement, and dread. They were up there, all right.

As she had been instructed, she went no farther into the clearing. Behind her, on the other side of the thick old trees, was the Twelve Sleep River. The river was placid and low, the water in it clear and nearly still this late in the season. A rusted metal bridge spanned the river but was blocked off to vehicles, because it was old and unsafe. She had walked across it a half hour before, trying not to look down at the gaps between the wood planks where she could see the water. Her footfalls on the bridge seemed unnaturally loud as they crossed. Her breath came in puffs of condensation. It was a cold fall day, and the clouds that had pulled a blind over the wide-open sky looked like they could bring rain or even snow.

She was dressed warmly in jeans and her mother's old, canvas barn coat with the corduroy collar and too-long sleeves. Her dad had insisted that she wear a pullover blaze-orange vest, since it was hunting season, and she did so, even though she felt a little like a human highway cone. A black headband held back her blond hair and had a dual use if she needed to pull it over her ears to keep them warm.

She waited, as she had been told to do. Before her was a clearing bordered by skeletal dark trees. Tall, khaki-colored grass furred the clearing, broken up by solitary sagebrush and a few young river cottonwoods. A lone, deep green pine—a perfect-sized Christmas tree, she thought—added the only real color. The tree was as out of place as she was, she thought. The clearing was eerily still. She felt a little scared.

The night before, she had the dream again. It was the same as before, with the mist pouring across the forest like water released from a small dam. But the dream continued on. This time, the mist stopped at the forest edge and proceeded no farther. There was something out there that stopped it, made it cautious. A standoff was taking place, but in the dream she couldn't see what opposed the advance of the mist. Whatever it was had a solid presence, and it had traveled a long way to get there to mount a challenge. This time, she didn't tell her dad about the dream.

After nearly a year of apprenticeship in falconry, which consisted mainly of the care and feeding of Nate Romanowski's two peregrine falcons, and his almost whispered lectures concerning the philosophy of falconry, this was a special lesson. For the first time, Nate had brought her hunting. Hunting with falcons, Nate had told her, was a whole different thing than the kind of hunting she might be familiar with from her father, the game warden. In this instance the agents of the kill weren't rifles or shotguns, but the birds themselves. Humans were there to flush out the prey like bird dogs, so the falcons could rocket down from the sky and kill what had been scared out into the open. Nate had told her that many times she wouldn't even see the prey she had flushed until the falcon swept down and hit it.

"This is how mankind conceived of an air force," Nate had

said. "This is where it all started, the idea of striking targets from the air."

"What are you talking about?" Sheridan had asked.

"Fire from the sky. Hell from the heavens," Nate had said. "This is where it all began."

"Huh?"

The lessons took place after school, unless she had basketball or choir practice or Nate was out of town. Her mom or dad would drive her out to Nate Romanowski's cabin near the river, and Nate took her home afterward and often stayed for dinner. Her mom and dad seemed to have a special relationship with Nate, although they never really talked about it with her. They seemed to trust Nate, or they never would have okayed the lessons. After all, Nate was unmarried and solitary, and Sheridan was twelve. She knew there was something different about Nate, something *serious*. He was not like anybody she had ever met, certainly not like anyone her parents hung around with, like the Logues.

Nevertheless, her dad seemed oddly comfortable with Nate, like they shared some kind of old experience together, while at the same time she saw her father eyeing Nate coolly when he thought no one was looking. It was as if he were trying to decide something. Her mother, on the other hand, made special meals on Fridays, including salads and desserts. While this hadn't meant much at first, it did now, since her mom had become so busy with her new business that regular sit-down dinners had become more infrequent. Sheridan had noticed an expression on her mother's face at times when Nate was at their table. It was a look Sheridan had rarely seen before. It was a kind of a glow, the kind of look her mother sometimes had when she and Dad were going out somewhere—dinner or a movie—at night. The look reminded Sheridan just how attractive her mother was to some men. The expression didn't last long but it made Sheridan uncomfortable and made her want to act out. Sometimes, Sheridan knew, she acted like a brat at the table when this happened, like picking on Lucy or demanding a second helping of something that was no longer there. She didn't know why she did this, other than to divert attention. But there was something about the way her mom looked at Nate. Maybe that was why her dad acted so differently when Nate was around. There was something adult going on, Sheridan knew, but she wasn't sure what it was. But she didn't want to ask about it, or say anything. She didn't want to give them a reason to question the propriety of the falconry lessons.

Not that the lessons were anything special so far. The first few months it seemed like all she did with the falcons was clean the mews where they lived and help feed them. The feeding was kind of gross, with the way Nate pulled freshly killed rabbits and pigeons apart to give to the birds. She was fascinated by the way the falcons ate—they finished off not only the flesh but the fur, feathers, and bone—but wondered when they would ever actually do some *falconry*. Nate had shown her the tools of the sport, such as leather hoods, jesses (strips of leather attached to their talons so he could hold them upright in his hand without them flying away), and lures made of duck wings or leather, which could be swung in a circle by a string to draw the birds' interest. He had given her old books to read about the ancient sport, mostly written by dead Scotsmen. Some of the books had old black-and-white photos in them. What got Sheridan, though, was that in the old photos the only thing that looked authentic and real were the birds themselves. The falconers in the pictures were from another age. The men (she had yet to see a photo of a woman falconer) wore silly hats with short brims, and baggy knee-length pants, and they were smoking huge, drooping pipes that made her want to laugh out loud. They reminded her of Sherlock Holmes, except fatter. Luckily, Nate looked nothing like that.

She stood dutifully still, as Nate had instructed, and waited for him to break from the opposite tree line as he had said he would. He said he would come out once the birds had been successfully released to the sky and after they had climbed to the right altitude.

It had been six days since the mutilated cattle had been discovered on the Hawkins Ranch, and Sheridan noticed how something that had been a family thing—the dead moose in the meadow—had now become the subject of discussion not only in town but also in school. Her sixth-grade teacher, Mr. Morris, had even asked her to remain in her desk after school so he could ask her about it. Since she had thought his request was related to a history research paper she had practically copied off of the Internet, she had been relieved to find out he was only interested in the moose and the cows.

Sheridan had thought it was cool that her teachers asked her about things like this; things that her dad was in the middle of. She told Mr. Morris about finding the moose, and what the animal looked like. He asked about the cows, and she was coy, as if she knew more than she was telling, which she didn't. She wished she had paid more attention to her mom and dad when they had been discussing it at dinner, but she didn't say anything to Mr. Morris about that.

She heard the sharp snap of branches breaking, and looked around. Nate Romanowski emerged from the dense trees on the other side of the opening. Sheridan studied him. Nate's movements were liquid and rangy and had a cautious, feline quality about them, as if he were ready to pounce on something or somebody in an instant if he had to. He was tall, with wide shoulders, and had a long, blond ponytail. His sharp, green eyes engaged hers. She had never encountered a stare like Nate's. He was strange in that when he looked at her, his eyes never wavered. He was so direct. Sometimes, he unnerved her with his stare and she looked away. She had learned that he meant nothing by it. That was just the way he was.

For some reason, he was slowly shaking his head.

"Do you want me to go?" she asked, thinking that perhaps she had done something wrong.

"No."

She noticed that he had tilted his face skyward. She followed and looked up. As she watched, the once-distant black specks were becoming more pronounced. The two peregrines he had released were diving back down.

"Why are they coming down?" Sheridan asked, thinking—hoping—that the birds were diving toward unseen prey.

Nate shrugged. "I don't know."

"Did I do anything wrong?"

Nate looked across the clearing at Sheridan. His voice dropped apologetically. "You didn't do anything wrong. You were perfect."

"Then why are they coming down?"

Nate took another step into the clearing.

Nate said, "I've never seen this happen before."

"You haven't?"

"No," he said so softly that she barely heard him. "I've had them take off when they saw a rabbit or something in a different clearing, or I've had birds fly away forever. But I've never seen peregrines just take themselves out of the hunt altogether."

The falcons dropped as if they were about to strike targets—wings tucked, talons out and balled—but they suddenly flared at treetop level. She could hear the urgent whispering sound as their wings shot out and caught the air to slow them down. Seconds later, both birds flapped noisily and their feet outstretched before descending into the tall grass. She watched as Nate approached them. When he bent and lowered his thick, leather welder's glove, the birds refused to mount it, and stayed hunkered down in the grass.

Nate said, "This is not normal."

"Why don't they come to the fist?" Sheridan asked.

"I don't know," Nate said. "It's like they're afraid to show themselves."

Sheridan walked slowly across the opening, toward where the birds had landed.

"Feel it?" Nate asked, his eyes narrowed. "There's something in the air. Low pressure or something."

Sheridan stopped again. Her heart was beating fast, and she

did feel it, although she couldn't describe what it was. It was like pressure being applied from above, from the sky. In a fog, she watched Nate bend over and physically place one of the peregrines on his fist. Usually, they were eager to hop up on it. He straightened up with the falcon on his arm, only to have the bird release its grip and drop to the side. The leather jesses that were tied to its talons were grasped in his fist, and the bird flopped upside down, shrieking and flapping violently. Sheridan felt a puff of air from them as the falcon beat its wings.

"Shit," Nate cursed, lowering the bird to the ground. "He's going to hurt himself."

"Be careful with him."

"I will, and sorry about saying *shit*."

"It's okay."

Nate met her eyes, then slowly looked up at the sky.

Sheridan also looked up, but could see nothing in the clouds. She felt the pressure on her face, a kind of gravity pull on her skin as if she were on a fast ride at the county fair.

"I don't know what to tell you," Nate said, his voice thin. "It's like there is something up there the birds are afraid of. They *refuse* to fly."

9

_____

AN HOUR LATER and twenty miles away, a man named Tuff Montegue clucked his tongue to get his horse moving and pointed the gelding north, toward the timber. It was nearly dusk, and Tuff had the blues. He sang "Night Riders' Lament," his favorite cowboy song:

> *While I was out a-ridin'*
> *The graveyard shift midnight till dawn,*
> *The moon was as bright as a reading light*
> *For a letter from an old friend back home. . . .*

Despite his current profession, which was ranch hand for the Longbrake Ranch, Tuff despised riding horses. He had nothing against them personally, and enjoyed singing and listening to songs about them, but he preferred tooling around in a ranch pickup. Nevertheless, he was a cowboy. A real one. In his mid-fifties, he looked the part, because he *was* the real number. Droopy mustache that curled to jawline, sharp nose, weathered face, sweat-stained Gus McCrae hat, Wranglers that bunched on his boot-tops and stayed up as if by a trick of magic over his nonexistent butt.

He liked to tell people, especially tourists who bought him a whiskey in the Stockman's Bar, that he was the only bona-fide cowboy left in the Bighorns that spoke American. It was sort of true, since most of the ranchers couldn't find cowboys anymore except from Mexico, South America, or wannabes from former East Germany and the Czech Republic. Even when he left the profession, as he often did, he found himself coming back. Between stints at five different ranches in Park, Teton, and Twelve Sleep Counties, Tuff had been a satellite-dish salesman, a mechanic, a surveyor's assistant, a cellular-phone customer-service representative, and a mountain man in a chuck-wagon dinner theater in Jackson Hole, where his job, every night, was to ride a horse into the tent where the tourists were and select a "wife" and toss her over his shoulder. This had resulted in a back injury when he stupidly selected a young mother the size of a heifer (she was one of those women who looked slim sitting down but had beer-keg thighs hidden under the table) and he had crashed beneath her weight. The injury had been a stroke of luck, because up until recently he had collected disability payments and didn't have to ride horses or do much of anything except occupy a barstool at the Stockman's. But the damned chuck-wagon din-ner show, owned by a large family of Mormons, was disputing his injury. Apparently one of the owners had reported that he had seen him riding a mechanical bull in a saloon in Cody. Which was sort of true also, although Tuff wanted to know what a good Mormon had been doing in a bar in the first place. Until the matter was resolved, he had to once again seek em-ployment.

But that was only part of the reason why Tuff had the blues. Another big contributing factor was that it was Friday night and he was stuck on the ranch and couldn't go into town. Since his DUI arrest the previous week—his third in two years—his driving privileges had been revoked. The only other Longbrake employee, a Mexican national named Eduardo, was laid up in the bunkhouse with a broken leg from falling off a damned horse. Therefore, Tuff had no ride. That, and the fact that Bud Longbrake, the peckerhead, followed the letter of the law and refused to let Tuff use a ranch vehicle even within the ranch itself, where no law enforcement would ever see him. Tuff knew that if Bud Longbrake wanted to make a case about allowing him to drive only on his private roads, Sheriff Barnum and the highway patrol wouldn't object. But Bud Longbrake, who seemed to care a hell of a lot more about the needs and wants of his fiancée, Missy, than the operation of his own place, had not made meeting with the sheriff a priority.

Shit.

Despite his predicament, Tuff smiled to himself. The weekend before had been something. It had almost been worth the DUI on the way home. The barmaid at the Stockman's, Evelyn Wolters, had set up a threesome after the bar closed. Tuff, Evelyn, and Jim Beam in one bed. What a night that had been. He wished he could remember certain parts of it more clearly. It had been at her apartment, a studio over the VFW, within walking distance of the Stockman's. Evelyn had been doing something besides alcohol, but he wasn't sure what. Whatever it was, it was fine by him, because she had been a tigress. She was no looker—his age, skinny legs that were just skinny, not shapely, pendulous breasts that hung down and swung back and forth like oranges in tube socks—but she had been *wild.* It had been her idea to use the neck of the bottle that way once it was empty.

He had left Evelyn promising to be back in a week, and she had told him she was already looking forward to it. Tuff had said he was, too, but the truth was he was tired and drunk as hell. It would be several days before he had his energy, and his urges, back. He kept wondering if some of the things he recalled she had done—and let him do to her—were more a result of his delirium and fantasy than what had actually taken place. But the more he thought about it, and he thought about it often, the more he convinced himself that the acts had actually happened. It was the first time he had done some of those things since he'd been on shore leave in the navy. And then he had to pay for them. Evelyn, though, seemed to enjoy it. Which made him think: *woo-hoo!*

But now he was literally grounded. He had called and left messages for her at the bar, but she hadn't returned them. No doubt she had heard about the DUI. It had been in the *Saddlestring Roundup,* that one with the cattle mutilations in it. He had hoped that maybe with all of the hullabaloo about the dead cows she had missed the weekly police-blotter. Unfortunately, the police report was usually the only thing in the paper everybody read. And she was probably at the Stockman's now, damn it, targeting another lone drinker. Giving him a couple of whiskeys on the house, like she had done with him. Then, when the bar closed at two, she would grab his hand and a fifth of Jim Beam and take him up the street to her apartment. It should have been him, Tuff thought. He leaned forward in his saddle and hit his horse between its ears so hard that his hand stung. The gelding crow-hopped, but Tuff was prepared for it and had a good hold on the saddle horn. The horse recovered and resumed slow-walking to the dark timber, exhibiting no malice toward its abusive rider. Which was another reason Tuff disliked horses. They were stupid.

So, after a week of herding the cattle down from the mountains into the holding pens near the ranch, they had counted and come up with ten missing cows. Ever since the cattle mutilations had been reported on the Hawkins Place, Bud Longbrake had been acting paranoid. He ordered Tuff and Eduardo to ride the timber and see what they could find or spook out. Eduardo had found six strays the day before, prior to falling off of his horse. Tuff had found none. Bud had put the screws to Tuff, telling him that he wasn't holding up his end.

"I want those cows found, Tuff," Bud had said, leaning over the breakfast table with his palms flat on the surface. "Dead or alive."

Tuff had said, *Then go find 'em yourself, you pussy-whipped phony!*

No, he hadn't said that. But he had thought that. And someday, when he retold the story in the Stockman's Bar, that was how it would be recalled.

Tuff wished he had more light, but the sun was now behind the mountains. He blamed the horse for delaying him. The gelding had a smooth ride, but was the damned slowest walking horse he had ever ridden. He could have walked up the draw faster his own self, he thought. And if he could have taken one of the ATVs, he would have been goddamned back by now and watching television in the bunkhouse with Eduardo.

Shit.

Tuff reached back on the saddle and unbuckled a saddlebag that was stiff with age. His fingers closed around the smooth, cool neck of a fifth of Jim Beam. He had his memories of Evelyn Wolters, and this brought them back. He cracked the top and drank straight from the bottle. It was harsh, but tongues of familiar fire spread through his chest and belly. Sometimes, he thought, his memories—and what he could do with them—were almost better than the real thing. But he needed that original foundation before he could embellish them to his liking.

He rode up the mountain slowly. He stared in resentment at the back of the gelding's head, settling on the bony protrusion between the horse's ears. He fired mental curses at the spot, hoping some would soak through into the gelding's brain. Not for the first time, he wondered what a fencing tool would do to the skull of a horse.

He rode the fence line, just like the song. The reins were in his left hand and the bottle was in his right. It was turning into a cold night. There was a hint of moisture in the air— probably brought with the cloud cover—that accentuated the smell of dry, dust-covered sage leading up into sharp pine. He smelled his own breath. Not pretty.

The gelding was breathing hard as he climbed a rocky hill toward a stand of aspen trees. Not that the horse was moving any faster—he had only one speed, which was similar to four-wheel drive low—and Tuff was just about ready to call it a night. With no stars or moon, he would not be able to see whether there were strays on this saddle slope or not. And damned if he would use his flashlight. He wasn't *that* dedicated.

He wished he could find the missing cows, though, to get Bud Longbrake off of his back.

The aspens stood out from the dark timber that climbed up the mountain into the sky. The aspen leaves had turned already, and were in that stage between yellow-red and falling off. The aspens soaked up what little light there still was, making the stand look like a tan brushstroke on the huge, dark landscape.

"Whoa."

Tuff stopped the gelding and got his bearings. He slid one boot out of the stirrup so he could twist in the saddle and look around. It was easy to get lost up here, he had learned. But he wasn't. Far below were the crystal-clear blue lights of the ranch yard. Twenty-five miles farther, the lights of the town of Saddlestring shimmered in wavering rows.

He turned back, looking at the aspens. He saw movement in the trees. Or was it a drunken illusion? Tuff wiped his eyes with his sleeve and looked again. This had happened before, him seeing things while he was drinking. But this time there was something authentic about it, something that made his chest clutch. Movement again. Something, or somebody, moved from one tree to another. The form was thicker than the tree trunks, but once hidden it seemed to meld into the darkness. He heard a twig snap, and his horse, who suddenly pricked his ears, confirmed the sound.

He let his breath out slowly. Certainly, it was deer or elk. But game animals didn't hide, they *ran*. Under him, his horse started wuffing, emitting a deep, staccato, coughing sound. He feared that sound—all horsemen feared that sound—because it meant trouble was imminent. His horse, his slow-moving, docile horse, was about to throw off hundreds of years of domesticity and become a wild animal again.

Suddenly, the gelding crow-hopped, nearly unsaddling Tuff. His balance was goofy because of his position and the bourbon.

"What in the *hell* is wrong with you?" he growled, taking an empty swing at the gelding's ear with the flat of his hand.

Unlike before, the horse didn't shrug off his action. In fact, the horse began backpedaling down the slope in a panic.

"Damn you, what's the problem?" he shouted. The gelding was backtracking down the mountain much faster than he had walked up. Tuff tried to turn him, to face him away from whatever had spooked him in the aspens. Sloshing bourbon on his bare hand, Tuff tried to grasp the reins near the bit in the gelding's mouth to jerk him around hard. The bourbon splashed out of the bottle and into the gelding's eye, igniting the horse and making him explode into a wild, tight spin.

Tuff clamped down with his thighs and held on. His hat flew off. He let the bottle drop—not something he wanted to do—and found himself knocked forward in the saddle, hugging the gelding's neck. He had lost the reins, and several things flashed through his mind. With the reins down, the lunatic horse could inadvertently step on them as he spun and jerk both of them to the ground, breaking their necks. He thought of his broken bottle of Jim Beam. He imagined what he must look like, spiraling down a rocky slope in the dark, hugging the neck of a horse. He thought of how unbelievably strong and powerful a horse—a 1,000-pound animal—was when fully charged, like now.

Even as he spun, faster and harder than he had ever spun before, even when he used to rodeo, he wondered what had made the horse spook. Bears could do it, he knew. The smell of a bear in the wrong circumstances could make even a good ranch mount go crazy. *This horse is going to fall,* Tuff thought, *and I'm going to get hurt real bad.*

And then the horse tripped on something, recovered momentarily, then bucked. Tuff was thrown through the air—he could feel the actual moment of release when no part of his body was in contact with the saddle or the horse—and time seemed to literally slow down as he went airborne until it fast-forwarded as he flew face-first into a cold, sharp rock and heard a crunch in his ears like a door slamming shut.

10

J OE WAS UP AND SHOWERED when the telephone rang at
5:45 A.M. With a towel around his waist but still dripping, he
padded down the dark hallway toward their bedroom to find
Marybeth sitting bolt upright in bed, rubbing her eyes, with
the receiver pressed against her ear. From across the room, he
recognized the voice on the other end of the phone as that of
Missy Vankueran, Marybeth's mother. He noted the high-
pitched urgency in Missy's voice.

"Just a second," Marybeth said to her mother, then clamped
her palm over the speaker and looked up with wide eyes. "It's
my mother, Joe. They just found one of their hands dead on the
ranch."

"Oh, no."

"They called the sheriff, but she's wondering if you can go
out there."

"Why me?"

"I didn't ask her," Marybeth said, a hint of annoyance peek-
ing through. "She's very upset. She wants you there, I assume,
because you're *family*."

Joe had planned to get an early start. It was Saturday, and

archery season was in full swing, and an early deer rifle season was opening in one of the areas in his district. Hunters would be out in force. The death of a ranch hand was the sheriff's responsibility, or the county coroner's.

"She says he's been mutilated, like those cows."

"Tell her I'll be there in half an hour."

Normally, he would have savored the fall morning as he hurled down the old two-lane state highway toward the turnoff for the Longbrake Ranch, Joe thought. The sun had just broken over the mountains and fused the valley with color. Lowland cottonwoods were bursting with red and yellow, and the moisture sparkled on the grass. It was clear and crisp and cloudless. Mule deer still fed in the meadows and had not yet retreated to their daytime shelter of the trees and draws.

He slowed and turned off the blacktop onto a red dirt road made of crushed and packed gravel, where he passed under a massive log archway. Sun-bleached moose, deer, and elk antlers climbed up the logs and across the top beam. A weathered sign—LONGBRAKE RANCHES, SADDLESTRING, WYO.—hung from heavy chain attached to the beam. There were less than a dozen bullet holes in the sign, Joe noted, which meant that the sign had probably been hung just a year or two before. In Twelve Sleep County, older signs had many more holes in them.

The gravel road paralleled a narrow, meandering spring creek with thick, grassy banks. The fact that deer, coyotes, and ducks didn't flush from the creek as Joe drove told him that he wasn't the first to drive up the road that morning.

He thought: *Missy must be wrong.*

Although he had no doubt that a ranch hand had been found, Joe had trouble believing the man had been mutilated as well. Missy was inclined to let her imagination run away with her, and was prone to high drama. Joe hoped like hell that this would be the case. If a human was actually killed and mutilated like the moose and the cattle had been, it would be a whole new, and horrific, development.

The buildings that made up the headquarters of the Long-brake Ranch had an entirely different feel than the spartan and businesslike Hawkins Ranch. The main ranch house was a massive log structure with gabled upper-floor windows and a wide porch railed with knotty pine. It was a monument to the gentleman rancher Bud Longbrake aspired to be, as it had been the monument to his father and his grandfather before him. Guest cabins were tucked into the trees behind the home, and the bunkhouse which at one time housed a dozen cowboys.

Joe felt a clutch in his stomach as he saw Missy Vankueran push a screened door open and emerge from the house. She waved him over.

Despite the events of the morning, Joe noticed, Missy had managed to do her hair and apply the exquisite makeup that made her look thirty-five instead of her real sixty-one years. Her eyes shone from a porcelain mask featuring sharp, high cheekbones and a full, red mouth. She was slim and neat, and wore a flannel shirt covered with bucking horses, and a suede vest with Shoshone wild roses in beadwork on the lapels. She looked every bit the chic ranchwoman, Joe thought with grudging admiration.

Maxine bounded up in her seat next to Joe and whined to be let out. That Maxine, Joe thought. She liked *everybody*.

Joe told his dog to stay and got out. Missy met him near the front of his pickup. She was obviously distressed.

"The horse Tuff was riding showed up around three in the morning," she began, dispensing with greetings. "Bud looked outside and saw the horse near the corrals, with its saddle hanging upside down. He thought Tuff must have fallen off in the mountains, so he got in his truck and went to look for him. Bud came back down a couple of hours later and said he found Tuff's body up there."

Missy gestured vaguely toward the mountains. The sun had risen enough that a yellow strip banded the snow-dusted tops of the peaks.

"Did Bud say the body had been mutilated?"

Missy paused and her eyes widened almost grotesquely. "*Yes!* He said it was awful."

"Is Bud up there now?"

"Yes, he took the sheriff up there to the scene."

Joe nodded.

"What does this all mean?" Missy asked.

Joe was thinking the same thing. First moose, then cattle, now possibly a man.

"I'm not sure," he said. "If what Bud says is true then we really have a problem on our hands."

"No, not that," Missy shook her head. "I meant in terms of Bud. We're working on plans for the wedding, and I don't want him to be distracted."

Joe looked at her and fought an urge to ask, *Are you really Marybeth's mother?*

Instead, he stepped back from her as if she were radioactive.

"How far is the body?" he asked.

With one exception, the scene was eerily similiar to the scene on the Hawkins Ranch. Just below an aspen grove and before the slope darkened with heavy pine, the two Sheriff's Department vehicles were there again, as well as a ranch pickup, no doubt driven by Bud Longbrake. The addition to the group was the lone four-wheel-drive ambulance from the Twelve Sleep County Hospital.

As he approached in his pickup, he could see a small crowd of men bending over something in knee-high sagebrush. Bud Longbrake, in a gray, wide-brimmed Stetson, looked up and waved to Joe. Barnum straightened up and glowered. Deputy McLanahan and two EMTs made up the rest of the group. One of the EMTs, a squat bruiser with a whisp of tawny facial hair, looked pale and distressed. While Joe pulled up next to the Longbrake truck and swung out, he saw the EMT turn quickly and retch into the brush behind him. The other EMT walked over to his colleague and led him away by the arm, apparently for some air.

"Joe," Longbrake said.

"Bud."

"Missy call you?"

"Yup."

"She all right?"

Joe paused for a beat. "Fine," he said.

Barnum snorted and exchanged glances with McLanahan.

"What do we have?" Joe asked, stepping through the sage-brush. The ground was spongy and soft, except for the football-sized fists of granite that punched through it on the slope.

When he saw what the men were standing over, Joe stopped abruptly. Although he had seen hundreds of harvested game animals as well as the moose and cattle, he was not prepared for what was left of Tuff Montegue. The body lay on its back, legs askew. One arm was thrown out away from the body, as if caught making a sweeping gesture. For a moment, Joe thought that the other arm was missing, but then he realized it was ac-tually broken and pinned beneath the trunk. Tuff was disem-boweled; his blue-gray entrails blooming out of a foot-long hole in his abdomen like some kind of sea plant in the corral. His Wranglers had been pulled down to mid-thigh—Tuff had bone-white skin—and his genitals had been cut out, leaving a maroon-and-black oval. Huge chunks of clothing and flesh had been ripped from Tuff's thighs.

Tuff's face was gone. It had been removed from his jaw-bone to his high forehead. All that was left were obscenely grinning teeth, wide-open eyes the size of Ping-Pong balls, a shiny, white wishbone protrusion where his nose had been, and a mass of drying blood and muscle. There was also the smell; a light but potent stew of sweet-smelling sage, spilled blood, exposed entrails, and the half-digested breakfast of the squat EMT. Joe gagged and tried to swallow.

He turned away, closing his eyes tightly and trying to breathe steadily. He heard Barnum snort behind him.

"Something the matter, Joe?" Barnum asked.

Then, *damn it,* Joe could no longer fight the wave of nau-sea and he threw up his morning coffee onto the soft ground.

Joe was there for most of the morning, keeping his distance as the hillside was photographed, measured, and tied off with yellow crime-scene tape wrapped around hastily driven T-posts. Additional deputies had arrived from Saddlestring, as well as a Wyoming highway patrolman who had heard the chatter on his radio.

Sheriff Barnum seemed more distressed than Joe had ever seen him, barking orders at his underlings and marching up and down the hillside with no apparent intent. Several times, he climbed into his Blazer and slammed the door to work the radio channels.

Bud Longbrake stood near Joe, leaning against the grille of his pickup. Longbrake was a large man, with wide shoulders, silver hair, and thick ears that stuck out almost at right angles from his temples. His face was weathered, his eyes sharp blue, his expression inscrutable. He wore a starched, white cowboy shirt and a silver belt buckle the size of a softball that celebrated an ancient rodeo win. Longbrake watched the procedures carefully but dispassionately, as if trying to guess the conclusions of the investigators before they announced them.

"I ain't never seen a body in that shape before," Longbrake told Joe after nearly an hour of silence.

"Nope."

"I've seen calves hamstrung and gutted by coyotes while they were still alive, and I've seen a damn wolf eat the private parts out of a calf elk while the elk bawled for his mama, but I never seen a man like that."

Joe nodded, agreeing. The EMTs were trying to slide Tuff's body into a body bag without any of his parts detaching. Joe looked away.

"I never knew a bear could do that to a man," Longbrake said.

It took Joe a moment, then he turned toward the rancher.

"*What* did you just say?"

Longbrake shrugged. "I said I never heard of no grizzly making cuts like that."

"Grizzly?"

"Didn't Barnum tell you?"

Joe kept his voice low so he wouldn't be overheard. "The sheriff has told me exactly nothing."

"Oh. Well, when I drove up here this morning in the dark I saw a big-ass grizzly bear feeding on something. Caught him in the headlights from a long way away. He looked up with a big piece of meat in his mouth. When I drove up here I found Tuff."

Joe was perplexed. This explained the horrible chunks of flesh missing from Tuff's legs, and maybe even his disembowelment. But . . .

"But how could a grizzly bear do that to his face?" Joe asked.

Longbrake shrugged again. "That's what I was talking about. I've never heard of such a thing. Maybe that bear just peeled it off. You know, like when you're skinning an animal."

Joe shivered thinking about it. For a second he imagined the two-and-a-half-inch teeth of a grizzly bear tearing back human skin, like peeling a banana. He quickly shook off the vision.

Longbrake shook his head, then squinted. "And Jesus, to get your balls bit right off by a bear like that. Poor dumb Tuff. He was probably glad that bear finished him off after he did *that*."

Joe didn't respond. What he had seen of the body, as quick as it had been before he got sick, didn't seem to fit the scenario Longbrake was suggesting. Tuff's face hadn't been chewed off by a bear. It had been *removed*. Joe thought of how clean and straight the cut was. Same with his genitals, Joe thought. They weren't ripped out. They were *cut* out. He felt a second wave of nausea and breathed deeply again, looking away. At least there was no more in his stomach to throw up.

There was a shout a hundred yards up the hillside, and Joe looked up. A deputy waved at Barnum from a spot nearly in the aspen trees. Barnum sighed, tossed his cigarette aside, and started climbing. Joe fell in behind him.

"Excuse me, Bud."

"Sure."

Halfway up the hill, away from the others, Joe noticed that Barnum had stolen a look back at him to see if he was still there. Barnum was slowing down as he climbed, and Joe slowed as well. Not because he was wheezing, like Barnum, but because he didn't want to walk beside the man. It was that bad between them, Joe thought.

"Why are you following me?" Barnum didn't turn around.

"I want to see what your deputy found. Same as you."

Barnum climbed several more steps. When he spoke, his voice was strained with exertion. "I want you to stay the hell away. For once."

Joe had been waiting for that.

"Sorry, Sheriff, I'm involved whether you want me to be or not. That first moose is my responsibility and if Tuff's death is connected then I need all the facts."

"Save your breath," Barnum growled.

"And Bud back there was telling me he saw a grizzly bear this morning."

Barnum stopped suddenly and Joe nearly ran into him. Barnum turned slowly. His face was red. Joe didn't know if it was from the hike, or anger, or both.

"That's right, we've got a grizzly bear up here," Barnum hissed. "*Your* fucking bear. I don't need or want any goddamn bears in my county. I don't want any goddamn wolves, either. But you people keep chasing them here. Now we've got what looks like an outlaw bear killing my citizens. So what are you going to do about that bear, Pickett?"

Joe shook his head, incredulous at Barnum's twisted reasoning. "You don't really think a bear did that, do you?"

"What else? Fucking aliens? That's what my idiot deputy keeps saying."

Joe and Barnum stared at each other, neither speaking. Joe looked into the eyes of the old man, and it reminded him of half a dozen reasons why Barnum couldn't be trusted.

"Just stay the hell away, unless you want to bring me the head of that bear," Barnum said.

Joe paused, not breaking the stare. "I won't be staying away, and I won't be bringing you the head of a bear," he said.

Joe watched the veins on Barnum's temples pulse.

"Then fuck you, Pickett. You're useless." Barnum turned. Joe followed.

The deputy was straddling a sharp rock that poked out from the ground. The rock was granite, and green in color because of the lichen on it. It was green except for the spatter of dark blood on its surface.

"Don't touch it," Barnum told his deputy, a man named Reed. Joe liked Reed.

"I haven't," Reed said, clearly miffed that Barnum had felt the need to tell him something so obvious. "As soon as I found it I waved down to you. It sure took you a while to get up here."

"The sheriff and I were visiting," Joe said.

Barnum glared at him.

Deputy Reed said, "The way I figure it—based on the hoofprints up here—is that this is as far as Tuff got last night. As you can see, the prints stop right here. I figure the horse bolted and Tuff got thrown off, right on this rock."

Tuff's hat was crown-down in sagebrush to the left of the rock.

"Then how did he get all the way down there?" Barnum asked.

"Either he walked a ways or something dragged him down there," the deputy said.

"Like a bear," Barnum said.

"Maybe."

"But unlikely," Joe interrupted. "A bear would probably feed on him where he found him, or drag him into the cover up there on the mountain." Joe pointed at the aspens, and both Barnum and the deputy followed his arm. "It wouldn't be likely a bear would drag a body into the open and *then* start feeding on it."

Barnum didn't even try to hide his contempt. "So what do you think happened?"

Joe looked back. "I think the deputy's right. Tuff got thrown right here. My guess is that he somehow got up and started walking toward the lights of the ranch down there. Then something stopped him."

"The bear?" the deputy asked.

"Something," Joe said. "I don't think the bear came along

until much later. Maybe just a few minutes before Bud Long-brake showed up this morning."

The deputy nodded, mulling it over. He looked to the sheriff for confirmation.

"That's a goddamned horseshit theory," Barnum scoffed, shaking his head. "The bear did it."

Barnum turned and started to trudge down the hill.

Joe called after him, "Did a bear kill my moose and mutilate it? Did a bear kill and mutilate a dozen cows?"

Barnum waved his hand over his head, dismissing Joe with the gesture.

This time, Joe didn't follow.

"The sheriff wants it to be a bear real bad," the deputy whispered.

Joe grunted.

"Because if it isn't a bear, we've got a very, very bad situation here."

When Joe returned to his truck, the ambulance was pulling away with the body. The deputies remained, scouring the scene. During breaks they drank coffee and speculated on what had happened. Joe overheard the word "aliens" from Deputy McLanahan. Another deputy suggested a satanic cult. A third advanced a theory involving the government.

Joe looked around for Barnum and finally saw the sheriff sitting in his Blazer with the door closed and the windows up. Barnum looked like he was yelling at someone on his radio.

"Did you hear?" Bud Longbrake asked, as Joe passed by him.

"Hear what?"

Longbrake nodded his hat brim toward Barnum's Blazer.

"They found another body. In Park County, about fifty miles away."

Joe froze. "Who was it?"

Longbrake raised his palms. "Didn't get a name. Some older guy. They found him by his cabin."

"Mutilated?" Joe asked.

"That's what I hear."

PART
TWO

11

"GENTLEMEN," County Attorney Robey Hersig said, "let's convene the first-ever strategy meeting of the newly formed Northern Wyoming Murder and Mutilations Task Force."

Sheriff Barnum said, "Jesus, I hate that name."

It was 10:00 A.M. on Wednesday, four days after Tuff's body and the body of Stuart Tanner had been found. There were seven people seated around an oval table in the Twelve Sleep County courthouse, in a room usually used for jury deliberations. The door was shut and the shades were pulled.

Joe sat at the far end of the table from Robey Hersig, and for an instant they exchanged glances. Hersig, Joe thought, already looked slightly frustrated and the meeting had barely begun. Hersig and Joe were friends and fly-fishing partners. When the governor said he wanted a representative from the Wyoming Game and Fish Department on the task force, Hersig had fought for Joe's inclusion, much to Joe's, Barnum's, and even the governor's objections. The governor wanted a biologist on the task force, for forensic and scientific expertise, and Barnum wanted anybody but Joe—just because. Joe had told Hersig he preferred to work on his own, but a call to Joe from his district supervisor Trey Crump made it clear he *would* be the G&F's representative on the task force.

The task force itself was Governor Budd's response to calls to his office in Cheyenne from both the statewide news media and business interests in Twelve Sleep and Park Counties, where the murders had taken place. Brian Scott, who did a statewide radio broadcast out of KTWO in Casper, had begun a tongue-in-cheek "Mutilation Moment" update on his morning show, where he breathlessly read the body count of wildlife, cattle, and humans and contrasted it with the lack of response from the governor's office. With his reelection campaign looming in less than a year, the governor reacted to the pressure quickly, announcing the creation of the task force. He did so after his chief of staff called Robey Hersig and Hersig confessed that the Sheriff's Department was stymied in their investigation. Knowing Barnum, Joe assumed that the sheriff viewed the formation of the task force as a personal slap in the face.

As Hersig circulated agendas and manila folders, Joe surveyed the room. In addition to Joe, Hersig, Barnum, McLanahan, and the Park County Sheriff Dan Harvey, there were two men from the outside whom Joe had met before: Wyoming Department of Criminal Investigation (DCI) agent Bob Brazille and FBI Special Agent Tony Portenson. Seeing Portenson again made Joe's mouth go dry.

While Brazille was affable behind a jowly, alcoholic face, Portenson was dark, pinched, and had close-set eyes and a scar that hitched up his upper lip so that it looked like he was sneering. Portenson had already been seated when Joe entered the room, and had offered no greeting. Instead, he'd stared at Joe as if they shared a conspiracy.

"As you all know, Governor Budd has promised a swift resolution and justice in regard to these crimes," Hersig said by way of introduction. "It's our job to make that happen. I've given you each a file of what we've got so far, and I hope you'll take a moment to review it with me."

Joe had already begun. In the file were copies of the incident reports written by the Sheriff's Department on the Hawkins

cattle as well as on Tuff Montegue's body. His own preliminary necropsy report on the moose was in the file as well, and
Joe was a little surprised that Hersig had obtained it from
headquarters without mentioning this to him. There were
dozens of pages of crime-scene photos that had been printed
out in color and black-and-white, as well as maps of Twelve
Sleep and Park Counties with circles drawn where the crimes
had occured. A preliminary autopsy report was included from
Park County on the body found there, as well as the autopsy
report on Tuff Montegue. Both bodies had been shipped to the
FBI laboratories in Virginia for further examination. Clip-
pings from both local and national papers on the murders and
cattle mutilations were also in the file.

It came as no surprise that the autopsy and necropsy de-
scriptions were very similar, whether of the moose, cattle, or
men. Skin had been removed from faces. Tongues, eyes, and all
or part of ears had been removed. Udders were removed from
female cattle. Genitals were gone, and anuses had been cored
out. Cuts were described as "clean and made with surgical precision."

The exception, Joe noted with a start, was in the autopsy report for Tuff Montegue. In his case, the cut on Tuff's face was
described as a "notched or serrated mutilation cut similar to
serrated cuts near the genitals and anus."

To make sure, Joe thumbed back through the reports. The
notes of "serrated cuts" were unique to the Tuff Montegue autopsy. It could just be an aberration, Joe thought, or a mistake.
The county coroner did not do many autopsies. He spent more
time in his fly shop than the one-room morgue. Joe planned to
ask about the discrepancy once the discussion got started.

There was something else. Or, rather, the lack of something
else. There was no mention of oxindole, Joe noticed.

"Let's start at the beginning," Hersig said, sliding Joe's report on the moose from the file.

Under Robey Hersig's direction, the task force methodically
reviewed the reports in the file. It was decided early on that

the aspects of the investigation would be divided up among the principals; Sheriffs Barnum and Harvey would concentrate on the murders that took place within their counties, Agent Portenson would facilitate communication access between the local authorities and the FBI, Brazille would coordinate with the governor's office, and Joe would follow up on the wildlife mutilations and "anything out of the ordinary." When Joe heard Hersig say that, he winced. Hersig smiled back.

"Reports will be shared with my office, and we will serve as the communications center," Hersig said, looking hard at each person at the table. "Nothing will be withheld from this office. Territory doesn't matter, jurisdiction doesn't matter. We're all on the same team here."

FBI Special Agent Tony Portenson seemed to have an agenda of his own, and Joe couldn't yet determine what it was. Portenson paid cursory attention to Hersig, reviewing the documents in the order Hersig referred to them, but periodically rolling his eyes and staring at the ceiling. Joe wished Portenson wasn't there, because Portenson brought back dark memories of the death of his foster daughter the winter before, as well as the death of a federal-land manager. When Joe looked at Portenson, he imagined that the agent was there to observe *him,* to possibly catch him at something. Joe vowed to be careful. Trouble was, Joe actually liked Portenson.

Sheriff Dan Harvey of Park County didn't seem to agree that the attacks that had happened in Twelve Sleep County had any bearing on *his* interest, which was investigating the death and mutilation of the older man found near his cabin on the same night Tuff Montegue was killed.

Because Joe knew only a few sketchy details about this aspect of the case, he paid special attention to the Park County report. The sixty-four-year-old victim was named Stuart Tanner. He was a married father of three grown children and CEO of a Texas-based water-engineering firm that had contracts in Wyoming doing purity assessments for the state Department of Environmental Quality and the CBM developers. Tanner's family had owned the cabin and mountain property for over thirty years, according to people in Cody who knew him, and

Tanner preferred staying at his cabin rather than at a hotel while doing work in the area. He was physically fit and enjoyed long hikes on his property in all kinds of weather. It was presumed that he was on one of his walks when he died, or was killed. His mutilated body was found in a meadow in full view of a remote county road. Someone had seen the body and reported it by calling the Park County 911 emergency number. The preliminary autopsy listed the cause of death as "unknown."

As Hersig moved to the case of Tuff Montegue, Joe interrupted. It was the first time he had spoken.

"Yes, Joe?"

He turned to Sheriff Harvey. "The report doesn't indicate predation of any kind. Did you see any?"

"You mean like coyotes or something eating the body?"

Joe nodded.

Harvey thought, stroked his chin. "I don't recall any," he said. "I wasn't the first on the scene, but my guys didn't mention any animals and the coroner didn't say anything about that, either."

Joe nodded, sat back, and turned his attention back to Hersig.

Tony Portenson cleared his throat. "Before we go off in too many directions, I've got something here that might give you all a great big headache."

From a briefcase near his chair, Portenson withdrew a thick sheaf of bound documents. Like a card dealer, he slid them across the table to all of the task force members.

Portenson said, "This stuff isn't new, cowboys."

Joe picked up the one-inch-thick binder and read the title: SUMMARY INVESTIGATIVE ANALYSIS OF "CATTLE MUTILATIONS" IN WYOMING, MONTANA, AND NEW MEXICO.

The report was dated 1974.

"I found this when the bureau was asked to assist on this investigation," Portenson said, a little wearily. "Somebody in our office remembered seeing it back in the archives."

Joe flipped through the binder. The report had been typed

on a typewriter. There were dark photographs of cattle, much like the newer ones he had just looked at in the file Hersig had assembled. There were pages of necropsy reports, and transcripts of interviews with law enforcement personnel and ranchers.

"Shit," McLanahan said, "this has all happened before."

"Not exactly," Hersig said quickly. Joe guessed that Hersig didn't like the way Portenson had taken over the meeting and surprised him with the reports. "There's no mention of what I've found about wildlife or human mutilations here."

Portenson conceded the point with a shrug, but did it in a way that indicated that it didn't matter.

"So what was the conclusion of the FBI?" Barnum asked. "Or do I have to read this whole goddamned thing?"

Portenson smiled. "A forensic investigative team at Quantico devoted three years to that report. Three years they could have been working on real crimes. But your senators and congressmen out here in the sticks *insisted* that the bureau devote precious time and man-hours to a bunch of dead cows instead."

"And?" Sheriff Harvey prompted.

Portenson sighed theatrically. "Their conclusion was that this cattle-mutilation stuff is a pile of horseshit. Let me read . . ." He flipped open the report to a page near the back he had marked with a Post-it. "I quote: 'It was concluded that the mutilations were caused by scavenging birds, pecking away at exposed soft tissues like eye, tongue, rectum, etc. The smoothness of the "incisions"—note the quote marks around that word, fellows—is produced as a result of postmortem gas production in the cattle's bodies that stretched the tissues . . .' "

Portenson looked up from the report and his upper lip hitched into a sneer. "So how did the cattle die?" Joe asked.

To answer, Portenson found another marker in his report and turned the page.

" 'The cows examined died of mundane causes, such as eating poisonous plants.' "

Joe sat back and rubbed his face with his hands. Birds? That was what the FBI concluded? *Birds?* The report made him angry, as well as Portenson's delivery of it. There was a long, uncomfortable silence.

Hersig broke it. "I guess I don't see how a thirty-year-old report and our crimes here—including the deaths of two men—have anything to do with each other."

Portenson shrugged. "Maybe nothing, I grant you that. But maybe you all need to step back a little and take a deep breath and look at the whole situation from another angle. That's all I'm saying."

"What other angle?" Brazille asked.

Portenson slowly looked at each person seated at the table. Joe noticed the brief hardness in Portenson's eyes when they fell on him.

"Let's say that the cattle died naturally. Maybe they got a virus, or ate some bad plants. Hell, I don't know shit about cows. But let's say that happened. So the cows died. Birds found them and started pecking at the soft stuff, like the report says. It could have happened that way here, gentlemen. After all, the carcasses weren't really fresh when they were found.

"But in this atmosphere of near hysteria, a cowboy falls off of his horse in one county and an old man dies of a heart attack in another county. That's a strange coincidence, but that's maybe all it is: a coincidence. People die. Two men dying in the same night wouldn't be a very big deal in any American city. No one would even make a connection. Only out here, where the deer and the antelope play and hardly any people live, would it be a big deal.

"So the cowboy gets pecked on a little while he's on the ground and then he gets mauled by Joe Pickett's grizzly bear. And the other guy gets found by birds and other critters that start eating on him. So what?"

Portenson stood up and slammed his report shut. "What you may have here, boys, is a whole lot of nothing."

During a break, Joe stood in the hallway with Hersig as the others used the restroom, refilled their coffee cups, or checked their messages. Hersig sagged against the wall near the doorway to the deliberation room. He winced and shook his head slowly.

"Portenson's report sucked all the air out of the room," Hersig said morosely.

Joe said evenly, "It's *not* birds."

"I don't know what to think," Hersig sighed. "Are we jumping to wild conclusions here, like he said?"

Joe shook his head.

"It's going to be you and me, Joe."

"I came to the same conclusion," Joe said.

"Shit." Hersig said, rolling his eyes. He had made no secrets about his own political ambitions. He wanted to be thought of when Governor Budd replaced the soon-to-be-retiring state attorney general. If the investigation floundered, so would his chances of moving to the capital, Cheyenne.

"I do admire you, Joe," he said. "You don't have much of a dog in this fight, but you seem to be the only guy in that room who wants to figure out what happened. The others are concerned with protecting their turf."

"I wanted to work on my own, anyway," Joe said. "Looks like I'll be doing that."

Hersig smiled. "That wasn't exactly the idea, you know."

"Yup," Joe said. "What does Portenson want?"

Hersig folded his arms across his chest and frowned. "That I can't figure out."

"Me," Joe said. "I think he wants *me*."

"Think he's got a hard-on for you and Nate Romanowski because of that bad business last winter?"

"Maybe so."

Robey Hersig was the only man who knew enough about the circumstances surrounding the death of Melinda Strickland, a federal land manager, to legitimately suspect that Joe knew more about it than he let on. But Hersig had never asked Joe anything about the incident, and Hersig's silence in the matter told Joe everything he needed to know about his friend's suspicions. Justice had been done, and Robey asked no questions.

————

When they got back to work, Hersig asked the members of the task force for additional theories on the crimes.

He addressed the group. "We know what the FBI concluded thirty years ago, and we can't discount that. But I think we'd be doing a disservice if we didn't consider other possibilities. So fire away, gentlemen. The ideas can be off the wall," Hersig urged. "Nothing is too crazy. Remember, it's just us in this room. Who or what is killing and mutilating wildlife, cattle, and people in our county?"

"*Your* county," Sheriff Harvey corrected, "the wildlife and cattle in my county are just fine, thanks."

Robey stood up, approached a whiteboard, and uncapped a red felt-tip marker. He wrote BIRDS.

"Gentlemen?"

No one spoke. *Great,* Joe thought.

"Maybe it's some kind of cult," McLanahan said finally. "Some kind of satanic cult that gets their jollies by collecting animal and human organs."

Under BIRDS, Hersig wrote CULTS on the board.

"Or just one or two sickos," Sheriff Harvey said. "A couple of lowlifes who like headlines and attention. They started with the moose, then moved on to cows. Then they took a giant step to humans."

Hersig wrote DISTURBED INDIVIDUALS.

"Not that I agree with any of this," McLanahan said, sitting back in his chair and stretching out with his fingers laced behind his head, "but I've heard some things around town. Hell, I've heard 'em in the department."

McLanahan didn't see Barnum shoot a glare at him for that, but Joe did.

"One theory is that it's the government. CIA or somebody like that. The thought is that they're testing new weapons. Maybe practicing some counterterrorism tactics."

"Maybe it's the FBI?" Barnum said, smiling at Portenson.

"Fuck that," Portenson replied sharply. "We've got enough on our plate."

"Another theory I've heard is that it's Arabs," McLanahan said. Joe snorted, and the deputy turned slightly in his chair to scowl at Joe. His voice rose in volume as he spoke. "There was a report of a white van filled with Middle Eastern–looking men in town during the past week, Mr. Pickett. No one knows why they were in town."

Since there was little color in Saddlestring other than Mexican ranch hands, Indians from the reservation who occasionally shopped in town, and only two black citizens, Joe wasn't surprised that a van containing dark-skinned people would result in calls to the sheriff. But still . . . *Arabs?* Terrorizing Wyoming? Regardless, Hersig wrote ARABS on the board.

"What about that bear?" Barnum asked, turning to Joe. "Longbrake saw a grizzly and Montegue was chewed up. Maybe we've got a crazy-ass bear on our hands that likes to eat faces and dicks? Maybe years of animal lovers coddling bears has turned one of them into a murderer."

"I think the killer Arab theory makes more sense than that," Joe said.

Barnum angrily slapped the table. "I would like to know why Joe Pickett is on this task force. He's a pain in my ass."

There, Joe thought. It was out.

"Because Governor Budd wanted a Game and Fish representative," Hersig answered coolly. "And if I recall, Joe has been involved in some real big cases in this county."

"Bring it on, Sheriff," Joe said, feeling his neck get hot. "Let's get this on the table right now."

Barnum swiveled in his chair and acted as if he were about to argue but he apparently thought better of it. Instead, he glared at his coffee cup.

To divert this unexpected turn in the discussion back to the subject at hand, Hersig wrote GOVERNMENT AGENTS and GRIZZLY BEAR on the board.

"Maybe a virus of some kind?" Brazille offered. It was the first time he had spoken during the meeting.

"There's one more, and all of you know it," McLanahan said, slowly sitting upright. "But since no one wants to say it, I will."

Hersig was writing even before McLanahan said the word. ALIENS.

We've even got some guy calling the department offering his expertise in extraterrestrials mutilating cattle," McLanahan smiled. "He says he's got experience in the 'field of the paranormal.'"

"Who is it?" Hersig asked.

"Some guy named . . ." McLanahan searched his spiral notebook for a moment, "Cleve Garrett."

Joe sat up. That was the name Dave Avery had mentioned. The "expert" who had shown up in Helena.

"Apparently, he's in town because he heard about the mutilations. He came down from Montana and set up shop at the Riverside RV Park."

"Have you talked with him?" Hersig asked.

"Are you kidding?"

"I'll talk to him," Joe volunteered.

"He's yours!" McLanahan laughed.

"You get the nut cases," Hersig said, assigning the job to Joe.

Joe briefed the room on what he had learned from Dave Avery. He noticed that even Barnum's eyes got wide when he heard that other mutilations had taken place in Montana the winter before. And he saw Brazille and Barnum write the word "oxindole" in their files as he told them about it.

"We'll need that in a report, Joe," Hersig said.

"I'll write it up."

Hersig said, "Agent Portenson, can you request that chemical analysis of the blood and tissue be done on the two human victims in Virginia to determine if there is oxindole or anything else unusual in their systems?"

"I'm sure they'll cover that," Portenson said. "But yes, I'll make the request."

After the meeting had finally drawn to a close Joe walked across the parking lot from the county building. He was confused. He needed time to sort out all he had heard today. The puzzle had, in his mind, suddenly mushroomed into something bigger and murkier than it had been before. Portenson's explanation—if that's what it was—had unsettled him.

As he approached his pickup, he looked back at the county building. Portenson stood in the doorway with Sheriff Barnum. They were having a heated discussion, but Joe was too far away to hear what it was about. Joe watched as Portenson and Barnum stepped closer to each other, still talking. Suddenly, Portenson turned and pointed at Joe. Barnum's face turned to Joe as well.

What were they saying? Joe wondered.

Portenson left Barnum in the doorway and made his way across the parking lot.

Joe stepped around the front of his pickup to meet him. He felt a flutter in his stomach as he did. Portenson obviously had something to say.

"The sheriff and I were just agreeing that it would be best if you took a backseat in this investigation," Portenson said.

Joe didn't hide his annoyance. "I don't know what your problem is," Joe said. "The FBI was exonerated last year. You guys did an investigation of yourselves and determined that you were a bunch of heroes."

Portenson grimaced. "Officially, yeah. Unofficially, it's different on the inside with my fellow agents. I'm a fucking leper. Because I helped you and didn't support my brethren."

"You did the right thing."

"As if *that* had anything to do with anything. Tell that to my office, okay? I'm going nowhere fast. I don't want to be stuck here for the rest of my career. I really don't."

"Unless you redeem yourself to get promoted out of here," Joe said. "Unless you do something big."

"Like if I figure out how you and your pal Nate Romanowski were involved in the suicide of a federal-land manager." Portenson said the word "suicide" with dripping contempt.

Joe said nothing. He knew this would always hang over him, always weigh him down. And it should, he thought, it should. He tried to think of something to say.

"Birds?" Joe asked.

"What?"

"Do you really think *birds* are the answer to the mutilations?"

Portenson got close to Joe, his face inches away. Joe could smell coffee and tobacco on his breath.

"It's as good as any other theory in that room and better than most of them."

"It wasn't birds," Joe said.

12

On the other side of town, Marybeth Pickett glanced into her rearview mirror to check on her passengers. Lucy and Jessica Logue were huddled together on the middle bench seat, and Sheridan occupied the rear seat of the van. Sheridan sported an expression that shouted: I AM EXTREMELY BORED!

Lucy and Jessica had once again made plans to play at the Logues' home after school.

"Why does she have to be so *social*?" Sheridan asked Marybeth.

"I can hear you, you know," Lucy said over her shoulder to Sheridan. "Maybe it's because I have good friends."

"She'll probably be a *cheerleader*, for goodness sake."

"That's because I'll have something to cheer about and won't be crabby all the time, like some people."

Which caused Jessica to giggle.

"Put a gag in it, Lucy."

"Girls . . ." Marybeth cautioned.

Driving down Second Street, Marybeth smiled to herself. Although Sheridan participated in plenty of activities at school and church, she had never felt the need to fill her social calendar beyond that. She didn't get many calls at home, and rarely made any to classmates. Sheridan's best friend, Marybeth thought with a gulp, was probably Nate Romanowski.

Marybeth turned into the winding, tree-shrouded driveway out of habit and nearly rear-ended a stopped vehicle. She slammed on her brakes, the van did a quick shimmy, and they avoided hitting the pickup with a camper in the back of it by less than a foot.

"Cool," Sheridan said. "Nice maneuver."

Marybeth blew out a breath and sat back. That had been too close. It was her fault. She had assumed the driveway would be empty the way it always was.

"Everybody okay?"

They all said they were, and then Lucy and Jessica were scrambling for the door handles.

Because the van was designed to automatically lock all the doors when it was in gear, Marybeth had to hit a toggle switch to open them. She hesitated as she reached for the switch to let the girls out.

The camper pickup she had almost slammed into was old, red, dented, and splashed with mud. It listed a bit to the side, as if one of the shocks was bad. The old truck had dirty South Dakota plates.

"Do you have visitors, Jessica?" Marybeth asked, turning in her seat.

Jessica gave up on the door and looked up nodding. "My grandma and my grandpa are here."

"Well, I'm sure that's nice for you," Marybeth said, trying to think if either Cam or Marie had mentioned their company at the office. If they had, she couldn't remember it. The atmosphere in the office had been tense all week, with lots of closed doors.

"Yeah," Jessica said without enthusiasm.

"They're from South Dakota?"

"Um-hmmm."

"Will they be staying with you very long?"

Marybeth saw Sheridan look up at her with an exasperated

expression. She wanted to go home, not listen to her mother pry for information.

"I don't know."

"How long have they been here?"

"A week, maybe more."

Maybe that's why Cam has been so irritable at work, Marybeth thought. It was bad enough with the mutilations in the news, the stubborn Overstreet sisters causing problems, the poor financial conditions in general for the Logues—and now his parents were visiting. Cam's dark moods seemed to make a little more sense.

"Lucy, maybe it would be best to skip it tonight if the Logues have company," Marybeth said.

Both Lucy and Jessica howled in protest.

"You're sure it's okay?"

"Yes!" Jessica insisted.

"And you're sure your mom said she'll bring Lucy home tonight?"

"YES!"

"Okay, then," Marybeth said, pushing the toggle to unlock the doors.

Lucy bolted forward and gave Marybeth a quick kiss on the cheek. "See you, Mom."

Marybeth watched both girls skip around the pickup and toward the house. Sheridan sighed from the back. Marybeth started to put the transmission into reverse, then halted. Something didn't seem right to her. Nothing logical, nothing she could articulate. But when it came to her children, she always let her feelings hold sway, and she did that now.

"Mom? Are we leaving?"

Maybe it was simply because Marie had not said anything to her, Marybeth thought. They shared everything, Marie and Marybeth, things she knew Joe would blanch at if he overheard. They discussed wants, needs, ambitions, sometimes like schoolgirls. Marybeth knew, for instance, that Cam had not been interested in sex since he got the Timberline Ranch listing. This troubled Marie, especially since they had agreed to try to get pregnant again. Marybeth was more guarded with her secrets, although she had poured out her frustration on the disheartening state of the Pickett family finances.

The arrival of a father- and mother-in-law was a big event, Marybeth knew. How could Marie have failed to mention it? Or had Marie said something and Marybeth, in the nonstop rush her life had recently become, simply not heard?

"Okay," Marybeth said, as she began to back out of the driveway. She saw Sheridan slump back into her seat in over-obvious relief. "I just . . ."

". . . *have trouble letting go,*" Sheridan finished for her.

Marybeth backed out of the driveway and onto the road and started back through town toward the Bighorn Road.

13

THERE'S SOMETHING OUTSIDE I've got to show you that will scare the pants off Hailey Bond," Jessica Logue told Lucy Pickett as they entered the house.

"Are you sure it's okay?"

"Of *course* it's not okay, Lucy."

They smiled at each other.

Because Jessica's parents weren't yet home from work, Jessica and Lucy dropped their backpacks in the living room and went straight through the house toward the back door. Lucy heard the sound of a television from the darkened family room, and as they passed by she saw the blue glow from the screen.

"Jessica, honey," someone called.

"Hi, Grandma," Jessica said but didn't slow her stride.

"Come in here so we can see you. Who is your friend?"

Jessica stopped abruptly, then turned to Lucy and rolled her eyes. She led Lucy into the dark room.

It took a moment for Lucy's eyes to adjust to the darkness. When she could see, she could make out two people in the gloom. They were lit softly by the light of the television, which reflected in two pairs of old-fashioned, metal-framed eyeglasses.

"Lucy, this is Grandma and Grandpa Logue."

"Hi," Lucy said. Jessica's grandparents were small, thin people. Her grandmother wore an oversized sweatshirt with a heart embroidered across the front of it. Her hair was dull gray and cropped close. Jessica's grandfather looked like something out of an old movie about farmers: flannel shirt buttoned to his chin, wide suspenders, baggy, stained trousers, and heavy work shoes. They were watching a talk show about bad families.

Lucy saw that Jessica's grandmother had a pile of knitting on her lap, and could see the glint from the metal knitting needles. How could she even see what she was doing?

"Why don't you have the lights on?" Lucy asked.

"Why waste electricity?" Jessica's grandmother asked back.

"We don't waste electricity in our family," Jessica's grandfather said with a high twang. "Don't waste water, either."

Lucy didn't know what to say to that.

"We're going to play," Jessica said, and Lucy was grateful to her changing the subject.

"You be careful," Jessica's grandmother cautioned. "Stay close to the house. Nice to meet you, little girl."

"Nice to meet you too," Lucy said.

Outside, Jessica widened her eyes and gestured "follow me." They were in the heavy trees behind the house. It was cool and still, and the curled cottonwood leaves crunched beneath their feet. Lucy was glad to be outside, away from Jessica's grandparents.

Lucy thought how old Jessica's grandparents seemed to be, especially compared to Grandmother Missy, who was now out on that ranch. Grandmother Missy seemed years younger. Lucy sometimes wished she was more like a real grandmother, but Jessica's grandparents took being old a little too far, she thought.

They were a long way from the house.

"Jessica . . ."

"I know. We'll take a look at it and get right back to the house before my mom and dad get home."

Lucy nodded. What, she wondered, was "it"? She was frightened, but a little thrilled. She reached between the buttons of her jacket with the palm of her hand, to see if she could feel her heart beating. She could.

"Now, whatever you do, don't look up . . ." Jessica whispered. Both girls laughed, and it broke the tension for a moment. *"Don't look up"* had become a comic mantra at school ever since the news of the mutilations had come out. Sixth-graders, some from Sheridan's class, said it to scare the little kids on the playground. When the kids *did* look up, usually with a fleeting, half-terrified glance, the sixth-graders would lunge forward and either tickle the youngsters or push them backward over a coconspirator who was on their hands and knees behind them.

The funniest thing to have happened so far though was when two boys in their class had started selling foil-covered baseball caps for seven dollars apiece. One of the boys had stolen the caps from his father's collection, and the other had borrowed a large roll of aluminum foil from his own mother.

"Why get mutilated?" They cried out like carnival barkers. "Protect yourself with these babies . . . only seven dollars each or two for twelve dollars. . . ."

How much farther?" Lucy asked. They must be near the edge of the property, she thought. They had never been this far from the house before.

"It's right up here," Jessica said. "Man, wait until the next time Hailey comes over. We'll ditch her right here. It'll serve her right for always trying to scare us."

Nervous, but giggling, they ducked under a low-hanging branch and pushed through tall, dried brush. Lucy froze when she saw the dark building in front of her. She looked it over. It wasn't as large as she initially thought it was. In fact, it was more of a shack. It was old, unpainted, with one window that still had glass in it. The other front windows were boarded up. There was a sagging porch with missing slats where yellowed grass had grown through and died. The roof was uneven, and an old, tin chimney was black with age.

"Wow," Lucy said. "When did you find this?"

"Yesterday," Jessica said.

Lucy looked over at her friend. Jessica smiled and raised her eyebrows expectantly. Lucy wasn't sure she liked this, even a bit.

"You want to look inside?" Jessica asked.

"Maybe we should go back now."

"Don't you want to know what's inside?"

Lucy folded her arms across her coat. "I'm not going inside of that place."

Jessica looked disappointed, but not as disappointed as she could have looked. This made Lucy feel a little better, knowing that Jessica was scared too.

"How about if we just look in the window?" Jessica said.

Lucy weighed the idea. Her first impulse was to go back to the house. But she didn't want to show she was afraid and give Jessica something to tease her about later.

Lucy quickly nodded yes. She chose not to speak, because she was worried her voice would betray her fright.

The two girls walked tentatively to the shack. Lucy could see that the window would be too high to look in without standing on her tiptoes. Jessica was an inch or two taller, maybe tall enough that she could see into the window without extra effort. Lucy wished it wasn't overcast, and thought that everything might feel different if the sun was out.

They approached the window silently. The bottom sill was gray and warped, and Lucy reached up and closed her fingers around it to help her stretch higher. Lucy strained, balanced on the toes of her shoes, and pulled herself up so her nose touched the top of the sill.

There was just enough light inside the building that they could see.

They both suddenly gasped.

What terrified them wasn't the pile of dirty bedding, or the opened food cans and cartons, or the pile of books on the floor. It was the sound of rustling from somewhere in the shadows out of view, and the thump of a footfall as if something was trying to get away.

They ran back to the house, screaming all the way.

14

AFTER THE TASK-FORCE MEETING, Joe Pickett drove his pickup through the breaklands into the foothills of the mountains. He pulled off the road, on a steep overlook to eat his lunch—a salami sandwich, and an apple—while surveying the vast valley below. The day was cloudless and cool, the eastern horizon limitless. Below him, several miles away, was a small camp of three vehicles and a pop-up camper near the brushy crux of small streams. He glassed the camp through his spotting scope recognizing a group of antelope hunters he had checked a few days before. They had asked him if he thought they were in danger from the sky. He didn't know how to answer the question then, and he still didn't.

Despite the new task force, Joe still had a job to do. Pronghorn antelope season was open, as was archery season for elk in the high country. Deer season would open in two weeks, and for a short, furiously busy time, all of the big game seasons would be open simultaneously. Joe hoped that the task force would have reached some conclusions by then, or his absence in the field would be noted. Most hunters were dutiful, but the criminal element—the lowlifes who would try to take too many animals or leave the wounded in search of a bigger trophy—would keep close track of his comings and goings.

Portenson's presence and threat that he was going to look deeper into Joe and Nate's roles in the federal-land manager's death last winter wormed through his thoughts. When he saw his reflection in the rearview mirror, he saw a man with a tense, worried scowl.

Joe got out of his pickup and sat down on the tailgate, flipping open his notebook to his notes from the meeting.

- CULTS
- DISTURBED INDIVIDUALS
- GOVERNMENT AGENTS
- GRIZZLY BEAR
- ~~ARABS~~ (stupid)
- UNKNOWN VIRUS
- ALIENS
- BIRDS (FBI theory)

1. Tuff Montegue / Twelve Sleep County / Contusions mutilation / Grizzly breakfast / Oxindole?
2. Stuart Tanner / Park County (50 miles away) / No predation / 911 call / Oxindole?
3. Cleve Garrett / Paranormal guy / Riverside RV Park
4. Portenson / Happened before in the 1970s / *BIRDS???*

He reviewed the theories and shook his head. If there were cults of any kind in the area, they operated in complete and total anonymity, because he hadn't heard anything about them. Obviously, from the lack of reaction at the table, no one else had either.

In his mind, he classified "Government Agents," "Unknown Virus," "Aliens," and "Birds" into the "most improbable" category. It was conceivable that the government might conduct secret experiments on animals with new weapons, but only in a weird *X-Files* kind of way. How did the deaths of Tuff Montegue and Stuart Tanner fit in? He didn't believe the government was murdering and skinning old cowboys to test new weapons.

He conceded that it was remotely possible that a virus of some kind killed the animals and humans, although it made no sense to him that the virus could operate externally as well and cause the kinds of mutilation he had seen.

"Aliens" were a possibility he refused to seriously acknowledge. The word itself produced an instinctive inner scoff. Was he being closed-minded, he wondered, or was he scared to examine the possibilities? He didn't know the answer to that question, but thought that it was likely a combination of both. And, he reasoned, if the cause of the murders and mutilations were alien beings, then there wasn't going to be much the task force, or anybody else, could do about it.

Birds?

"Birds?" he said aloud. "How idiotic is *that*?"

Joe wanted to toss aside the "Grizzly Bear" theory as well but couldn't. The fact was that a bear had been present at both the bull moose and Tuff Montegue locations. Joe had seen the tracks in the meadow, and determined that the bear dragged the moose into the trees. The savage wounds on Montegue's torso, aside from the mutilations, were undoubtedly caused by a bear. But it had appeared the bear had shown up only after they were dead. The grizzly had happened by and checked out two bodies already on the ground, Joe thought, choosing not to sample the moose but having no objections to feeding on the old cowboy.

Joe also couldn't discount the bear theory because bears were his responsibility. Because once the grizzly had left its federally protected enclave in Yellowstone, it was now the responsibility of the Game and Fish Department. With responsibility came liability, and if it turned out that the bear was the cause of the crimes, Joe's agency would be blamed. If so, blame would cascade downhill, pooling around Joe Pickett's boots.

If the radio collar on the bear hadn't malfunctioned, the bear biologists tracking it could either clear—or implicate—the bear. As it was, they had no better idea of the bear's location than Joe did.

"Disturbed Individuals" merited more consideration, he thought. He drew a star next to it. The likelihood of a nut—or nuts—with cutting tools was the most likely prospect of all, he thought. Perhaps the bad guy had been practicing on animals for months or years without suspicion. He had started, maybe, with small animals or pets, and perfected his technique. Then he moved up the food chain; an antelope or deer for starters, then a single cow or horse. Without the atmosphere of suspicion that now existed, the lone deaths of single animals would not have aroused any notice. A mutilated carcass that wasn't found immediately—predation or not—wouldn't appear all that different from a natural death if the discovery was a month or so afterward. Maybe, Joe thought, this had been going on for *years* in the area. How many animal bodies had he seen himself over the years on the sides of highways, in ditches, in the landfill? Hundreds, he thought.

But then, for some reason, the animals weren't enough, so the killer moved on to human beings. Not just one, either. He went after two people in one night in a bloody explosion of . . . *something.*

Both men were killed in isolated locations accessible by either private dirt roads, in Montegue's case, or remote county roads, in Stuart Tanner's case. Joe wondered how long it would take to drive from one crime location to the other, and guessed an hour and a half without stopping. Which meant, if this theory played out, that the killer was local and knew his way around.

What kind of person is capable of this? Joe wondered, trying to picture a face or eyes. Neither came.

Joe's mind spun with questions.

Was this the same person who had mutilated cattle in the 1970s? If so, why had the killer stopped for over thirty years before beginning again? Had the killer, in the meanwhile, contented himself with the death and mutilation of wildlife, like the bull moose Joe found, or perhaps the cattle mutilations in Montana?

And whoever it was, why had the killer chosen to escalate the horrors to a new level? Since Joe and the task force had virtually no leads of any kind—despite what Barnum might tell the public—what was to stop this person?

Joe looked up and stared out at the breaklands. The dull headache that had started behind his left ear an hour ago had become a full-fledged skull-pounder. The more he thought about the killings, the worse it got.

This is a job for somebody a hell of a lot smarter than I am, he thought.

The sun was still two hours from dropping behind the mountains, but the sagebrush flats and red arroyos were beginning to light up. Pockets of cottonwoods and aspen pulsed with fall color. He loved this time of the evening on the high plains, when it seemed like the dying sun infused the landscape with every last pulse of color and drama before withdrawing the favor.

He shoved his notebook into his pocket, climbed into the cab of his truck, and drove farther up the mountain into the trees, peering out from behind his headache.

Joe cruised slowly, with his windows open. As it darkened, he had switched on the sneak lights under his front bumper, illuminating only the road surface directly in front of him. With his headlights off, he was almost invisible to a hunter or another vehicle until he was practically on top of them.

A half mile from the turnoff to Hazelton Road, in the low light of timber dusk, two camouflaged hunters stepped out of the trees onto the road.

When the hunters saw him, he could tell from their body language that he had surprised them. They consulted with each other, heads bent together, as he approached them. He waved, eased the pickup to a stop, clamped his Stetson on, and swung out of the truck. Before he closed his door, he reached in and turned his headlights on full, bathing the hunters in white light. It was a tactic he had learned over countless similar stops; approaching armed men on foot with his headlights behind him.

Joe quickly sized up the men as elk hunters out for the archery season. Their faces were painted in green and black, as were the backs of their hands. Each carried high-tech compound bows with extra arrows attached by side quivers. Their eyes, in the headlights, blinked out from their face paint.

"Are you doing any good?" Joe asked pleasantly, although he'd noted that neither was spotted with blood from a kill.

"It's too damned warm up here," the taller hunter said. "It's too dry for any stealthy movement."

His voice sounded familiar to Joe, although Joe couldn't place it.

"See anything?"

"Cow and a calf this morning," the shorter hunter said. "I missed her, damn it."

The shorter hunter's quiver was missing an arrow, Joe noticed.

"Couldn't find your arrow, I see."

The shorter hunter shook his head. "Nope."

"I hope you didn't wound her," Joe said. Although archery hunting was certainly more sporting to the prey than rifle season, too many inexperienced or overexcited hunters often wounded game animals and then lost track of them. He had seen too many crippled elk, deer, and antelope in the field with errant arrows stuck in them.

The shorter hunter started to speak.

"I don't think—"

"He missed her clean," the taller one interrupted, annoyance in his voice. "He just fucking missed her, all right?"

Joe was now close enough to see their faces and to recognize the taller hunter through his face paint.

"You again," Joe said to Jeff O'Bannon, the belligerent fisherman he had met before on Crazy Woman Creek with his daughters. "I hope you've learned how to release a fish since then."

O'Bannon's eyes flashed. Joe thought they looked bigger behind the face paint.

"What's this about?" the shorter hunter asked O'Bannon.

"Never mind, Pete," O'Bannon said through clenched teeth.

"Can I please see your licenses and conservation stamps?" Joe asked, still polite.

"You've already seen my stamp," O'Bannon said.

"Yup, but not the elk tag."

O'Bannon rolled his eyes and sighed, clearly annoyed.

While the hunters set their bows aside and dug for their wallets, Joe waited with his thumbs hooked into the front pockets of his Wranglers.

"Have you heard anything lately about those murders?" the short hunter asked, giving Joe his license.

"Like what?" Joe asked, checking it over. Pete was a state resident from Gillette. His license and stamp were okay, so Joe handed it back.

"Have there been any more sightings around here? Any more, you know, *incidents*?"

O'Bannon chuckled when he heard the question.

"Not since last week," Joe said. "I'm sure you heard about that."

"No little green men?" O'Bannon asked, smiling so that his teeth glinted in the headlights.

"Nope, just hunters." Joe said, looking over the license. "You need to sign this," he told O'Bannon, pointing toward the signature line.

"Jesus," O'Bannon sighed, shaking his head "I knew you'd find something to hassle me over."

I told you I would, Joe thought.

"I'm glad things are quiet," Pete said. "I almost didn't come over here to go hunting when I read about them murders. Jeff had to work hard to convince me to come hunting with him."

Joe nodded, wondering how many hunters were thinking twice about traveling to his district.

"Jeff said he'd take care of those little green bastards if they showed up."

Joe had started to turn toward his pickup when he stopped.

"Really, how?"

He could see the blood drain from O'Bannon's face, even through the face paint.

"Pete . . ." O'Bannon whispered.

"Show him, Jeff," Pete said enthusiastically.

"Show me, Jeff," Joe said, raising his eyebrows.

O'Bannon didn't move. Pete looked at Jeff, and slowly realized what he had done.

"Show me, Jeff," Joe repeated.

"Shit, it's for self-protection only. Self-protection!" O'Bannon said, raising his voice. "When people are getting cut up in the woods by something, it only makes sense!"

"Show me, Jeff."

Sighing, O'Bannon pulled back his camouflage coat to reveal a heavy, stainless-steel revolver in a holster on his hip.

"What's that, a .357 Magnum?" Joe asked.

O'Bannon nodded.

"I used to carry one of those myself," Joe said. "I couldn't hit anything with it. Well, once . . ." he let his voice trail off.

"Jeff's won some trophies in open-range pistol shoots," Pete volunteered, trying to ease the situation.

"That's good," Joe said, reaching for the ticket book that he kept in his back pocket, "but it's *archery* season, fellows. *Archery.* Bows and arrows. When you carry a handgun, you're violating regulations as well as the whole spirit of the season."

"I told you it was for self-protection only," O'Bannon said. "I didn't even shoot it!"

"I understand," Joe said, flipping the ticket book open. "And in other circumstances—like if you were somebody else—I would likely issue you a strong verbal warning. But, Jeff, you're special."

Thumbing through his well-worn booklet of regulations, Joe found the page he was looking for and read out loud from the light of the headlights: "Statute 23-2-104(d). No person holding an archery license shall take big game or trophy game animals during a special hunting season while in possession of any type of firearm."

Joe wrote the ticket while O'Bannon glared at his former friend.

"You're also in violation of the concealed-weapons statutes unless you have a valid permit signed by Sheriff Barnum," Joe said. "If I remember correctly, you could be looking at six months or so in jail. Do you have a permit?"

"I'm contesting this," O'Bannon said, snatching the violation sheet from Joe and wadding it into his front pocket. "I'll see you in fucking court!"

"Yes, you will," Joe said. "In the meantime, I'd advise you to stay home for a while. It'll play better with Judge Pennock if you show some remorse, even if you're just faking it."

O'Bannon looked like he was about to have a stroke. His eyes bulged and his jaw was thrust forward. His hands had clenched into meaty fists.

Joe tensed and laid a hand on his gun as a warning. He felt slightly ashamed for taking the frustration of the day out on Jeff O'Bannon. But only slightly.

Pete looked from O'Bannon to Joe, and back to O'Bannon.

"Can I get a ride to town with you?" he asked Joe.

Joe smiled. "Jump in."

After dinner—takeout again that Marybeth grabbed from the Burg-O-Pardner on her way home from work—Joe checked his messages. Nothing from the lab on the samples he had sent, nothing from Trey Crump on the bear, nothing from Hersig on any progress in the investigation.

Marybeth came into the office and shut the door behind her.

"Did you notice anything odd at dinner tonight?" she asked.

Joe grimaced. He studied her quickly. No new haircut, her clothes looked familiar. Something else, then.

"When Cam brought Lucy home earlier, she was pretty upset. Cam had asked the girls not to explore the outbuildings at their place, so guess where they went after school?"

"Is she all right?"

Marybeth nodded. "She's fine. She's upset that she got in trouble, though. She said Cam was pretty angry with them and told Jessica she couldn't play with Lucy for a while."

"Nobody hurt, though?"

"No. I told Lucy it was her job to listen to Cam and Marie when she was at their house, and to follow their rules."

Joe nodded.

"You didn't notice that Lucy never said a word during dinner?"

"Sorry, my mind was elsewhere."

"So how *did* your task-force meeting go?"

Joe leaned against his desk and filled her in. She made faces as he described the meeting, and laughed when he told her about McLanahan's theory about Arabs.

"I bet you wish they would have forgotten about you when it came to naming the members of that group," Marybeth said.

"I've got Trey and Hersig to thank for that."

She stood in silence, studying Joe. "Do you think Portenson will be trouble for us?"

Joe nodded. "I'm sure he'll be watching me closely. He also mentioned Nate."

"I'm sorry, Joe."

He shrugged, as if to say *we knew this was possible.*

Anxious to change the subject, he asked about her day.

"Cam's listing more homes and ranches every day. Ranchers are talking to each other and singing his praises. But those mutilations are big news. . . . No one wants to buy right now. Cam's trying to get them to lower their prices. It's a little tense around the office right now. But if things go well, he asked me if I'd be interested in going full-time, Joe. As a realtor." She beamed.

Inwardly, Joe moaned and guilt washed over him.

"That's great, honey."

"That's not really what you think, is it?" she asked, smiling slightly.

"Of course it is. We need the money."

"Joe, I like the Logues. I admire them. And you know I'd be a hell of a good realtor."

"Yes, you would. You are good at everything you do."

"Damn straight," she said.

He smiled and reached out for her. If only he could provide

enough for the family. He silently vowed that as soon as the task force investigation wrapped up, he would start exploring his options in earnest.

"Don't forget that we're having dinner with Mom and Bud Longbrake tomorrow night," Marybeth said, dashing his mood further.

An overnight envelope lay in the in-box on his desk. When he saw that it was from the forensics laboratory in Laramie, he anxiously ripped it open and pulled out the documents. It was the toxicology report on his moose. He fanned through the pages listing the details of the analysis and found the conclusion in a memo at the end.

The lab had found no unusual substances, and no abnormal levels of natural substances. He scanned the pages for the word "oxindole," but it simply wasn't there.

"Damn," he said, and threw the report on his desk.

Sheridan was snoring, but Lucy was still awake when Joe came into their bedroom to kiss them good night. The room was small and there wasn't much space between the two single beds. He sidled between them and sat down on Lucy's bed, smoothing her blond hair.

"I heard what happened," Joe said softly.

Lucy nodded, "Did Mom tell you about that shack we found?"

"No," Joe said, "she didn't."

"Somebody was living out there. We saw where he slept and we thought we heard something. We were so scared, Dad."

Joe wondered why Marybeth hadn't told him about this, but figured that probably it wasn't the issue. He assumed that a transient was using the shack, which alarmed him. Who knew how long ago somebody had been there? The house had been unoccupied for years before the Logues bought it and began restoration. Had Cam called the sheriff? He would need to ask Marybeth.

"You need to stay out of those buildings, Lucy," he said firmly. "There are strange people in town because of what's going on. You need to listen to Mr. Logue and to us."

Lucy nodded, her eyes wide.

As he climbed the stairs, he thought: My wife the *realtor,* imagining a photo of her face at the bottom of an advertisement in the *Roundup* real estate section.

15

THE NEXT MORNING, Joe headed out to the Riverside RV Park to pay a visit to Cleve Garrett, self-proclaimed expert in the paranormal. Joe prayed that his mother-in-law would never find out about this. He cringed just thinking about the multitude of woo-woo questions she'd have for him. The RV park was located on the west bank of the river and was surrounded by three acres of heavily wooded and seriously overgrown river cottonwoods.

As Joe nosed his pickup onto the ancient steel bridge, he thought that the RV park looked like the aftermath of a giant garbage can tipped over in the wind. Bits of glass, metal, weathered plywood, and old tires looked like they were caught in the spidery silver trees that had just lost the last of their leaves. On closer inspection, however, he saw that the trash was actually a number of aging mobile homes tucked into alcoves among the trees. The old tires had been placed on the tops of the mobile homes to keep the roofs from blowing off in the wind.

Under the bridge, he noticed a single fisherman in the water below, and smiled. It was the man known as Not Ike, who since his arrival in Saddlestring, had become the single most dedicated fly-fisherman Joe had ever seen. Not Ike was the "slow" cousin of Ike Easter, the county clerk. Because Ike Easter had been the only black face in Saddlestring for ten years, when his cousin the fly-fisherman moved to town he found himself being called Ike everywhere he went, so he had a sweatshirt printed up that said I'M NOT IKE. But instead of being called by his actual name, which was George, he became known as Not Ike.

Along with a couple of retired local men named Hans and Jack, Not Ike worked the pocket waters near the two bridges that crossed the Twelve Sleep River for trout, and Joe had seen him out there in every kind of weather. Because Not Ike couldn't yet afford an annual nonresident license, he bought cheaper, three- and five-day temporary licenses, one after the other, as they expired, so he could keep fishing. At least Joe hoped Not Ike was still buying the licenses, and made a mental note to check him out later.

As he reached the other side of the bridge, Joe turned left and passed under a faded hanging sign announcing his entrance to the Riverside Resort and RV Park.

Although once conceived as a "resort," the Riverside RV Park had declined and amalgamated into a sort of idiosyncratic hybrid. Most of the spaces were occupied by permanent residents; retirees from the lumber mill, service workers for the Eagle Mountain Club, transients, and now CBM crews. A few new model mobile homes with strips of neat landscaped lawn sat next to sagging, dented trailers mounted on cinder blocks, with out-of-plumb wooden storage sheds occupying every foot of the property. From the entrance, the road branched into three lanes, with mobile homes lining both sides of the lanes.

Joe had been to the Riverside two years before, following up on an anonymous poaching tip, so he was somewhat familiar with the layout. He had caught two employees of a highway construction crew skinning pronghorn antelopes hung from trees behind a rented trailer, and he had arrested them both for taking the animals out of season. The RV park had changed very little since then, although due to the influx of CBM workers, it now looked as if most of the spaces were occupied.

He stopped at the first trailer, the one with RESORT MANAGER in sculpted wrought-iron above the gate. The trailer had been there long enough that the silver skin of the unit had oxidized into pewter. A basket of frosted plastic flowers hung from a sun porch near the door.

Leaving his truck idling with Maxine curled and sleeping under the dashboard heater vent, he swung out and clamped on his gray Stetson. It was a cold, still morning, and the park was silent. He zipped his coat up a few inches, and thrust his hands into his coat pockets.

He could smell coffee brewing and bacon frying from inside the manager's office as he approached the door. The doorbell rang, and he stepped back on the porch and waited, wishing the bright morning sun could find him through the trees and warm his back.

The interior door clicked and opened inward, then the manager pushed the screen door open.

"Good morning, Jimbo," Joe said.

Jimbo Francis had been the manager of the Riverside since Joe had moved to the Saddlestring District. He was a big man with a massive belly. His face was as round as a hubcap, with protruding ears and a band of wispy, white cotton under a bald dome that expanded into a full mustache and beard stained with streaks of yellow. Jimbo had once been a government trapper, in charge of eradicating predators in the Bighorns and valleys by shooting, trapping, or poisoning them. When federal funding was withdrawn, he had taken the job of managing the "resort" temporarily, until funding for the program was restored. That was twenty-five years before, and he was still waiting. Jimbo was also a self-proclaimed patron of the arts, and was the chairman of the Saddlestring Library Foundation. He had once told Joe and Marybeth that his passions in life were "reading books and eradicating vermin." Now that he was in his late seventies and his eyes were failing—he had been instrumental in creating the books-on-tape section in the library—both of his passions were waning. As was his sanity, Joe suspected.

"And a good morning to you, Vern Dunnegan!" Jimbo boomed.

"Joe Pickett," Joe corrected. "Vern's been gone for six years. I replaced him." *Vern's in prison where he belongs,* Joe thought but didn't say. No reason to confuse Jimbo further.

"I knew that, I guess," Jimbo said, rubbing his hand through his hair. "Of course I knew that. I don't know what I was thinking. Vern was here so damned long, I guess, that I still think of him. That just goes to show you that a man shouldn't open his door in the morning until he's had his first three cups of coffee. I *knew* Vern was gone."

"Sure you did," Joe said, patting Jimbo on the shoulder.

"Is Marybeth still working at the library?" he asked, as if trying to further prove he was lucid.

"Not anymore, I'm afraid."

"That's too goddamn bad," Jimbo said. "She was a looker." Joe sighed.

"You need some coffee? You're here pretty early, Joe. I've got breakfast started. Do you want some eggs and bacon?"

"No thanks, Jimbo. I need to check with you on a new renter."

"We call them *guests.*"

"Okay. On a new guest. The name is Cleve Garrett."

Jimbo rolled his eyes into his head, as if trying to find his mental rental list. Joe waited for Jimbo's eyes to reappear. When they did, Jimbo said, "It's a cold morning. Do you want to come in?"

"That's okay," Joe said patiently. He remembered the interior of Jimbo's trailer from before. The place was claustrophobic, books crammed among Jimbo's collection of coyote, badger, beaver, and mountain lion skulls, empty eye sockets of dozens of predators looking out over everything. "If you could just tell me what space Cleve Garrett is renting, I'll be off."

"He's got a girl with him," Jimbo said. "Skinny little number."

Joe nodded. He could have simply cruised the lanes, looking for the new RV. But he'd wanted to clear it with Jimbo first. Now he was regretting his choice.

"He's here, then."

"He's here, all right," Jimbo said. "Been a parade of folks through here lately, all asking about 'Cleve Garrett, Cleve Garrett.' They're all starstruck. He's some kind of big expert in the paranormal, I guess. He's giving lectures on it. I plan to attend a couple. Maybe we can get him to speak at the library while he's here."

"Maybe," Joe said, his patience just about gone. "Which space is he in?"

"Lot C-17," Jimbo said finally. "You know, I've seen him before, but I can't figure out where. Maybe on television or something. These mutilations in our community are weighing heavily on my mind. You want a strip of bacon to go?"

C hewing on the bacon, Joe drove down lane C. He tossed the second half of the strip to Maxine.

Cleve Garrett's trailer was obvious before Joe even looked at the lot numbers. It couldn't have been more out of place. Joe fought an urge to laugh out loud, but at the same time he felt an icy electric tingle shoot up his spine. The huge trailer stood out as if it were a spacecraft that had docked in a cemetery. A bulging, extremely expensive, gleaming silver Airstream—the Lexus of trailers—bristled with antennae and small satellite dishes. A device shaped like a tuning fork rotated in the air near the front of the trailer. The Airstream was unhitched, and the modified, dual-wheeled diesel Suburban that had pulled it was parked to the side. Joe stopped his truck briefly behind the Suburban, jotting down the Nevada license plate numbers in his notebook before pulling to the other side of the trailer.

A Formica plate was bolted to the front door. It read:

DR. CLEVE GARRETT
ICONOCLAST SOCIETY
RENO, NEVADA

Joe turned off his motor and shut his door when the Airstream door opened and a smiling, owlish man stepped out.

"Cleve Garrett?"

"*Dr.* Cleve Garrett," the man corrected, pulling an oversized sweater around him. Garrett was in his late forties, thin, with a limp helmet of hair that gave him a disagreeably youthful appearance. His mouth was wide, with almost nonexistent lips, and it turned down sharply at each corner. His nose was long and aquiline, and his big eyes dominated his face, appearing even larger through thick, round lenses.

"Joe Pickett. I'm the game warden and a member of the task force investigating the mutilations."

Garrett tilted his head back, as if looking at Joe through his thin nostrils.

"I was wondering when someone was going to show up. I'm a little surprised they sent a game warden."

"Sorry to disappoint you," Joe said, although he wasn't.

Garrett waved it away. "Never mind. Come on in, I've been waiting. Everything is ready."

Joe hesitated. *Everything is ready?* He pondered revealing to Garrett that he had some background on him, and his "work" in Montana, courtesy of Dave Avery. Joe chose not to say anything yet, to let Garrett do the talking.

"Iconoclast Society?" Joe asked. "What's that?"

Garrett's large eyes widened even further, filling the lenses, unnerving Joe.

"Iconoclast," Garrett said. "Breaker of images. Burster of bubbles. Denouncer. Decrier. Without passion. I'm a scientist, Mr. Pickett."

Joe said, "Oh," wondering why he had volunteered to Hersig to take this part of the investigation.

"Let me show you what you people are up against," Garrett said.

Stepping into the Airstream was like stepping inside a computer, Joe thought. On three of the four walls were shelf brackets that held stacks of electronic equipment and gauges, monitors, and keyboards. There was the low hum of high-tech equipment and the hushing sound of tiny interior fans. Wires and cables bound by duct tape snaked through the equipment and across the ceiling.

On the back wall of the room was a closed door that obviously led to the rest of the trailer. On either side of the door were stainless steel counters and sinks, littered beakers, and glass tubing. The pegboard walls near the door displayed medical and mechanical tools.

Joe folded himself onto a stool on one side of a small metal table stacked high with files, folders, and printouts. Garrett took the other stool and started arranging the folders in front of him.

"Quite a place," Joe said, removing his hat and looking around.

"The trailer was modified to be a mobile lab and command center," Garrett said brusquely, as if he'd explained it a thousand times to others and wanted to get it out of the way quickly so they could move on with things.

"A million and a half dollars worth of the latest hardware, software, and monitoring devices. The lab takes up the front half of the trailer, living quarters take up the back. We've got an interior generator, although I prefer to pull into a place like this," he gestured vaguely toward the outside, referring to the Riverside Park, "so I can plug in. All of our data and findings are synched via satellite to our center in Nevada, where half a dozen other scientists analyze it as well. I can be totally mobile and on the road within two hours to get to a site. I was here in Saddlestring, for example, within forty-eight hours of the first discovery of the mutilated cattle."

Joe nodded. "Who pays for all of this?"

"We're totally, completely private," Garrett said. "We accept no corporate or government funds at all. Therefore, we're not compromised. We're a completely independent center devoted to impartial scientific research into paranormal activities."

"So," Joe asked again, "who pays for all of this?"

Garrett showed a hint of annoyance. "Ninety-eight percent of our funding comes from a single source. He's a highly successful entrepreneur named Marco Weakland. You've probably heard of him."

"I haven't," Joe said.

"Among his many ventures, he has a particular interest in paranormal psychology and science. It fascinates him. He uses a very small part of his fortune to fund this project and to employ some of the best alternative scientists in the world. Our job is to get to the scene of unexplained activity and analyze it in pure scientific terms. Mr. Weakland doesn't trust government conclusions, and frankly we've disproved and debunked more phenomena as hoaxes than found actual evidence of paranormal or supernatural activity. And we've found completely natural explanations for most of the phenomena we've investigated in the three short years we've been in operation. Don't get me wrong, Mr. Weakland sincerely believes in the possibility of alien beings, civilizations, and incursions, as do I. But he wants them proven, scientifically, before he brings them to light. What I don't quite understand, Mr. Pickett, is why I'm explaining all of this to you when I already went into it in some detail with the Sheriff's Department."

Joe had a mental image of Deputy McLanahan listening to Garrett over the telephone while doing the crossword puzzle in the back of the *TV Guide*.

"The deputy communicated very little of your conversation," Joe said, not liking to make excuses for McLanahan.

"Well," Garrett said, looking annoyed, "then that explains why I wasn't asked to participate in your task-force meeting."

Joe looked at Garrett blankly.

"In fact, if you people were really interested in getting to the bottom of these mutilations and murders, you would appoint me cochair of the task force."

"You'd need to talk to the county DA about that," Joe said. "His name is Robey Hersig." Joe made a mental note to call Hersig as soon as he could and warn him that Dr. Cleve Garrett would be contacting him.

For thirty minutes, Garrett spoke nonstop and Joe listened. Cleve Garrett showed Joe photographs of mutilated cattle, sheep, horses, and goats that had been taken over the last four decades in the United States and Canada, and throughout South and Central America. Mutilated dairy cattle had been reported in the United Kingdom and Europe in the 1960s, often at the same time alleged crop circles were discovered. Official explanations for the mutilations were as varied as their geography, but most involved birds, insects, or cults.

The photos and case files—many of them ancient carbon copies and several written in Spanish and Portuguese—piled up on the table in front of them. The last few case files held photos and names of places Joe recognized. Conrad, Montana. Helena, Montana.

"Last winter, mutilated cattle were discovered in Montana," Garrett said. "Someone up there was familiar with our group and called us. Unfortunately, they called us three weeks too late. By the time I got there, the local yokels had completely tromped all over the crime scenes, and they refused our assistance."

Joe listened silently, not letting on that he had heard Dave Avery's side of this story.

"We were able to obtain the heads of several of the cattle, but they were nearly two months old at that point. We shipped them to our facility in Reno for technical analysis."

Garrett dropped a thick file of necropsy photos on the table. Joe opened the folder to see the skinless head of a cow with the top of its skull cut off. Someone probed a flat metal tool into the cow's withered brain in a gesture that looked uncomfortably like the act of scooping peanut butter from a jar with a butter knife. Gently closing the folder, Joe felt his morning coffee burble in his stomach.

"What we found were levels of a chemical in the brains and organs in excess of what should be there naturally."

Joe thought *oxindole,* but said: "What was it?"

Garrett started to answer, pulled back, and said coyly, "I'll save the results for the task-force meeting."

"So we're playing games here?"

"I don't play games. I just don't want to show all of my cards until we're in an official setting and I've been given some standing in the task force."

Joe nodded. "Go on."

Garrett continued, "Some of the trace chemicals discovered were absolutely unknown to our scientists. You understand? *Unknown!* Poisons or sedatives not of this world were found in the brain tissue of Montana cattle. Not only that, but the incisions had been performed by ultrahigh-temperature laser instruments—instruments available only in leading surgical hospitals, not in the field. Certainly, this type of procedure could not have been done in the elements outside of Conrad, Montana."

Joe was intrigued. He looked up, needing a break from the photos, which, in their quantity alone, were numbing.

"So what did you determine?" Joe asked.

Garrett sighed. "What we determined was that we were too late to do proper on-site analysis. We kept waiting for fresh incidents in Montana, but they never came. We were very disappointed. Our scientists were begging for fresher tissue to study before natural decomposition occurred. But whatever had mutilated the cattle had moved on."

"Here to Twelve Sleep County," Joe said.

"YES!" Garrett shouted, nearly upsetting the table. His sudden exclamation sounded like a gunshot in the silent room. "Now we're right in the middle of it, right where it's happening. Not only cattle and wildlife, but perhaps, for the first time, *human beings*! This is why I need to be on the task force. Why I need to be involved, and to be kept informed. You people have a resource here," he thumped his chest, indicating himself, "that you can't ignore, that you shouldn't ignore. Look at the equipment in this laboratory. Can you even imagine a more fortuitous circumstance?"

Joe looked up. "I can't speak for the task force."

"From what we can determine," Garrett said, plowing ahead as if Joe hadn't spoken, "wildlife and livestock mutilations aren't random at all. What we're beginning to believe is that the mutilations are ongoing, and perpetual, and have been for at least forty years."

"You lost me," Joe said.

"You lost yourself," Garrett snapped. He had been getting

more and more animated as he spoke, and was now highly agitated. His hands flew about as he spoke and his eyes, if possible, had become even wider.

"What we're saying is that the mutilations are like the worldwide circulation of the flu bug. They never really stop, they just keep moving around the earth. There are blank spots in time—years, in fact—where there are no reported incidents, but that's because we don't have information from places like Africa or the Asian continent or Russia. And we certainly don't have data about the hundreds—or *thousands*—of incidents that are never even discovered or recognized for what they were. Do you know what this means?"

"What's that?" Joe asked, knowing he sounded doltish.

Garrett rose and leaned forward on the small table. His damp palms stuck to papers and files, puckering them. "It could well be that beings are conducting full-time research on our planet. Whether they're doing it for genetic or physiological reasons, we don't know. But they're digging rather aggressively in our own Petri dish, trying to discover, or confirm, or create something."

Garrett let his words hang in the air, obviously hoping that Joe would understand their significance

"If they're here now, we have the best opportunity we've ever had of contacting them directly. We can let them know we're on to their little game, and maybe offer to assist them. Perhaps we can start to build trust, exchange ideas. What is happening out there right now may be one of the most important opportunities to happen in our lifetime!"

Or not, Joe thought.

"What about the human victims? Where do they fit into your theory?" Joe asked.

Garrett stifled a smile. Actually, a mad grin, Joe thought.

"This is where things get interesting," Garrett said, his voice nearly a whisper. "They've obviously stepped up their research in one bold stroke."

"Why now?" Joe asked. "And why two men, for that matter?"

Garrett shook his head. "That I can't quite figure out,

although I have some ideas on it. One of my ideas you're not going to want to hear."

He said it in a way that led Joe to believe that Garrett couldn't wait to continue. Joe responded by raising his eyebrows.

"At least one of the two men was killed by other means," Garrett said quickly for maximum impact.

Joe felt his stomach churn. He would have to get out of the trailer soon, he thought.

"What makes you say that?"

Garrett raised his hands, palms up. "From what I understand, the two men were killed at least fifty miles apart on the same night. Both were mutilated in similar fashion to the cattle and wildlife. But one of the men was dragged from the murder scene and fed on by a bear and the other was found in pristine condition."

Joe nodded.

"Obviously, something is wrong here. One of the primary characteristics of cattle and wildlife mutilations has been the lack of predation. I've got hundreds of photos to prove it. But a predator fed on the corpse of one of the murdered men only hours after he was killed. Doesn't this strike you as odd?"

"Yes," Joe admitted.

"There's more, much more." Garrett said, his hands flying around like doves released from a cage.

"Yes?"

"I'll save the rest for the task-force meeting."

Joe noticed something different in the room, smelled something, and turned his head.

The door at the end of the room near the sinks was ajar. He hadn't heard it open, but the odor he smelled was cigarette smoke.

As he watched, the door pushed open and a woman stepped through it. She was young, pale, and thin, with straight, shoulder-length blond hair parted in the middle. She wore all black—black jeans, Doc Martens boots, long-sleeved turtleneck. Her lips were painted black and her dark blue eyes were bordered by heavy mascara. *She is not beautiful,* Joe thought. *Without the statement in black, she would be unremarkable.*

Garrett turned as well, angry. "Deena, what have I told you about letting smoke in here with my expensive equipment?"

Deena fixed her eyes on Joe, and when she answered she didn't shift them.

"I'm sorry, Cleve. I heard loud voices, so I . . ."

"Please shut the door," Garrett said sternly. As if talking to a child, Joe thought.

Joe looked back. Her eyes and expression were remarkable in their lack of content. But it seemed as if she were trying to connect with him in some way, for some reason.

"Deena . . ." Garrett cautioned.

"Bye," Deena said in a little-girl voice, and stepped back through the door, closing it.

Joe looked to Garrett for an explanation. Garrett, again, looked agitated. His dramatic monologue had been interrupted.

"Deena's been with me since Montana," Garrett said, his eyes icy. But Joe noticed a flush in his cheeks, as if he were embarrassed to have to explain anything. "She's a hanger-on, I guess you'd call her. My line of work attracts people who are a bit on the edge of the rest of society. I'm doing what I can to help her out with her journey."

"Is she even seventeen?" Joe said coldly.

"She's nineteen!" Garrett hissed. "More than legal age. She knows what she's doing."

Joe simply nodded, then pushed his stool back.

"What, you're leaving?"

"I've heard enough from you for today, I think."

Joe stood, picked up his hat, and turned for the door. Garrett followed.

"I think I know what's happening out there, Mr. Pickett. I'm so close to it I can almost shout it out! But you've got to give me access to the task force and your findings. I need to see the case files, and the investigative notes. And you must make sure I'm notified immediately in the instance of another discovery."

"I gave you Robey's name, right? You'll have to call him for all of that," Joe said over his shoulder as he stepped out of the trailer.

"I need you to vouch for me," Garrett pleaded. "I beg of you, sir!"

Joe opened the door of his pickup, hesitating for a moment. Garrett stood near the front of his Airstream, palms out, pleading.

"I'll talk to them," Joe said. "I need to settle on exactly what I'm going to say."

"That's all I ask," Garrett said, his face lighting up. "That's all I ask."

He saw her in the heavy trees before he made the turn to leave the Riverside Resort and RV Park. It was a glimpse through the passenger window; amidst the tree trunks were her eyes, framed by dark makeup.

Joe checked his rearview mirror. Cleve Garrett had returned to his trailer, and the front window of the Airstream was obscured by overgrown branches that reached down from the side of the lane. Garrett would not be able to see him.

He stopped and got out. "Deena?"

"Yes."

He walked across the gravel lane into the soft mulch on the floor of the tree stand. She leaned against a massive old-growth river cottonwood trunk. She had no coat, and her face was even paler than he recalled from a few moments before. She hugged herself, her long, white fingers with black painted nails gripping opposite shoulders.

He asked, "Were you trying to tell me something back there?"

She searched his face with her eyes, trying to read him.

"I guess so." Her voice trembled. "Maybe . . ." Was she cold or scared? he wondered.

Joe stripped his jacket off and fitted it over her shoulders.

"What year were you born, Deena?" he asked. As he suspected, he saw a twitch of confusion as she tried to do the math. Did she know that Garrett had said she was nineteen?

Deena gave up, not even trying to lie. "Please don't send me back to Montana. There's nothing I want to go back to. There's nobody up there who wants me back."

"What did you want to tell me, Deena?"

Joe searched her face, looked her over. Beneath the cover of foundation was a road map of acne scars on both cheeks. A smear of shiny, black lip gloss dropped from the corner of her mouth like a comma.

"I didn't hear very much of what you two were talking about," she said in a voice so weak he strained to hear it, "but I know there's more to Cleve than meets the eye. And there's less, too, I guess." She looked up and smiled hauntingly, as if sharing a secret.

Unfortunately, Joe didn't know what she meant.

"You don't understand, do you?"

"Nope."

She looked furtively over her shoulder in the direction of the Airstream, as if calculating how much time she had.

"Do you have an e-mail address?" she asked Joe.

He nodded.

"I'll e-mail you, then. I don't think we have the time to get into all of it here. I have an e-mail account Cleve doesn't know about."

"Deena, are you being held against your will?" he asked. "Do you need a place to stay?"

She grinned icily and shook her head. "There's no place in the world, in the cosmos, that I'd rather be than right here, right now. I'm no prisoner. Cleve will help make things *happen,* and I want to be here to see it. To experience it. The other stuff doesn't much matter."

"What other stuff? And what will Cleve make happen?"

She shifted away from the trunk she was leaning on, stepping back from Joe.

"I can handle Cleve, don't worry," she said, smiling provocatively. "I can handle most men. It's really not that tough."

Joe started to speak, but she held up her hand. "I've got to go. I'll e-mail you."

He wrote his address on the back of a Wyoming Game and Fish business card and handed it to her.

"Thank you for the coat," she said, before shrugging it off and turning back to the Airstream.

As he pulled it back on, he could smell her inside of his coat. Makeup, cigarette smoke, and something else. Something medical, he thought. Ointment, or lotion, he thought.

When he looked up she was gone.

As he crossed the bridge, Joe glanced over the railing. Jack, the retired guy, was fishing upstream near a sand spit. Not Ike was still down there, completing a long, looping fly cast into ripples that flowed into a deep pool. There were some big fish in the pool, Joe knew. Twenty-two- to twenty-four-inch browns, three to four pounds, big enough to be called "hogs" by serious fishermen. Not Ike looked up, saw Joe, and waved. Joe waved back and made another mental note to check out his license. Later, though, after he sorted out what had just happened in the Riverside Resort and RV Park. Later, when he could get back to being a game warden.

16

"I BET CAM ten dollars I could get you to say three words tonight," Marie Logue told Joe between courses that evening at the Longbrake Ranch.

"You lose," Joe said, deadpan.

Marie at first looked disappointed, even a little shocked, then she shared a glance with Marybeth and both women whooped. Joe smiled.

"He's been waiting for *years* to use that line," Marybeth laughed. "You offered the perfect setup. Calvin Coolidge said it first."

"Good one," Cam said gruffly from across the table. "I'll have to remember that one."

"It's not like you've ever had a problem talking," Marie said through a false smile. "Except to me. Lately, especially."

Cam rolled his eyes and looked away, dismissing her.

Uh-oh, Joe thought. *They're not kidding.* He noticed that Marybeth caught it, too. She had mentioned the increasing tension at Logue Country Realty to him recently, saying that despite Cam's success in listing ranches, homes, and commercial property, nothing was selling.

Dinner at the Longbrake Ranch had become a twice-monthly event since Missy had moved in with Bud. In addition to Joe and Marybeth and the grandchildren, Missy often invited a number of other people, all of them influential: ranchers, business owners, the editor of the *Roundup,* and state senators and representatives. Tonight, however, it was just the Picketts and the Logues. Missy was, Joe grudgingly admitted, an excellent hostess. It was something she was born to do and she thrived at it. The events typically began with drinks beneath the canopy of old cottonwoods out back or in the huge living room when it was cool or windy, then moved to the dining room for dinner and wine, and ended up with the men in Bud's cavernous study and the women in the living room. Missy moved graciously from guest to guest, asking innocuous questions, showing them the renovations she was supervising in the old ranch house, laughing at their jokes, discussing her wedding plans, urging them to top off their drinks. Her face assumed a luminescence that made her truly beautiful, if one didn't know any better, Joe thought.

Joe had made halfhearted attempts to get out of the dinners before but hadn't succeeded. Marybeth felt obligated to attend, she said, and made the case that it was important for their girls to have a good relationship with their grandmother. Joe suspected that Marybeth enjoyed the socialization and discussion, although she claimed it didn't matter that much to her. Sheridan and Lucy, Joe guessed, leaned more toward his point of view than their mother's. Rarely were there other children at the dinners.

May we be excused?" Lucy asked. She sat with Jessica Logue and Sheridan. She was asking on behalf of all three girls.

Marybeth looked to Marie, and both mothers nodded. Lucy and Jessica had not played with each other since they got in trouble and both were transparently pleased that the dinner had brought them together again.

"Should they go outside?" Marybeth asked Joe.

"They'll be within sight," Missy broke in, dismissing her daughter's concern. Then whispered: "Nothing has ever happened out in the *open,* honey."

"Stay close to the house," Marybeth called after them as the three girls thanked Missy for dinner before scrambling away from the table and out the front door.

"We're just going to see the horses," Sheridan called out as the screen door slammed.

After dinner, talk turned to the mutilations and the death of Tuff Montegue. Bud Longbrake questioned Cam Logue about the economic effects the crimes had had on the valley, particularly in regard to land values.

"We can only pray it's temporary," Cam said. "But it's reduced land values and home values at least twenty percent, by my guess. Twelve Sleep County is radioactive."

He shook his head. "In one case, I've got a willing seller and a willing buyer, but the buyer has decided now to hold out a little longer for a price reduction. The sellers are battling among themselves whether to reduce the price a little or not. Meanwhile, nothing is happening."

Bud smiled knowingly. "I think I know the ranch you're talking about. Those crazy sisters. They'd be rich if their daddy hadn't sold the mineral rights to the place. Nobody ever used to think that much about it. Everyone figured if there wasn't oil on their land—and there never was—that selling the mineral rights was just free money from suckers. I hear the plan is to put two thousand CBM wells on the land."

Cam nodded vaguely. He obviously felt uncomfortable talking about the specifics of the ranch or the terms. But Bud liked to needle and pry, and was good-natured about it.

"It's been crazy," Marie said, shaking her head.

"Marybeth mentioned that on top of everything else you have company right now," Missy said to Cam and Marie.

Cam laughed and ran his hand through his thick, blond hair.

"Yes, it's not exactly the best time in the world to have my whole family here for a visit."

"It never is," Missy cooed sympathetically. This from the woman who camped out in his house for a month and a half before moving in with Bud Longbrake, Joe thought sourly.

As the talk turned back to more mundane topics, Joe's thoughts drifted away from the table. He kept replaying the morning at the Riverside Park and his conversation with Cleve Garrett. He still could not shake his discomfort. The point Garrett had made about the differences in the deaths of Tuff Montegue and Stuart Tanner had eaten at him all afternoon. Yet again, nothing seemed to make sense or connect as it should.

Joe?" Marybeth said, her voice breaking into his thoughts. "Bud is talking to you. Are you going to answer his question?"

Joe looked around and realized that Missy had paused in midserve of dessert and was looking at him expectantly. Cam and Marie were silent, waiting for the answer to the question that Joe hadn't heard. The conversation, which a few moments before had been lively and flowing around him, had died. He could hear the clock tick in the next room. Marybeth looked exasperated, as she often did when he lapsed into what she called "Joe Zone." It particularly annoyed her when he did it in front of Missy because Marybeth thought it made him look ignorant.

Joe cleared his throat. "I'm sorry," he said. "What was the question?"

The three girls lined up outside of the corral looking at Bud Longbrake's horses in the last moments of dusk. They leaned forward and rested their arms on the rails, peering inside at a dozen stout ranch horses. Roberto, the remaining ranch hand, broke open bales and tossed hay to them over the fence. Sheridan cocked a foot on the bottom rail. She found the *grumm-grumm* sound of horses eating extremely soothing.

Sheridan said, "I heard Grandmother Missy say that Mister

Bud brought all of his horses in from the mountains and put them in the corral because of the aliens."

Lucy looked up at her with wide eyes. "Did she really say 'aliens'?"

"Yes, she did. I heard her tell Mrs. Logue that."

"Man, oh, man."

Behind them, in the ranch yard, the sensor on the light pole hummed and the light clicked on as the sky darkened. Although it really didn't make sense that it could get colder from one moment to the next simply because the sun dropped behind the mountains, Sheridan gathered her coat closer around her. It had to do with the altitude and the thin air, her dad had told her.

Jessica said, "If we're going to be out here, maybe we should have bought those aluminum-foil hats those boys were selling in the cafeteria."

"What are you talking about?" Sheridan said, and Lucy laughed. They told Sheridan about the caps. Then they said they thought it was unfair that their parents had not allowed them to play together after school for the last week because of their visit to the "haunted shack." Sheridan needed to see it, Lucy said. The shack would scare her, as it did them. Maybe they would see who lived there.

"It's probably a poor homeless guy," Sheridan said.

"Or . . ." Jessica said, pausing dramatically, "it's the Mutilator!"

"Jessica!" Lucy exclaimed. "Stop that. You're acting like Hailey, trying to scare everyone."

Jessica giggled, and after a short pause, Lucy joined in. Once their giggles had stopped, the two girls changed the subject to a mutual friend's upcoming birthday party. While they chattered, Sheridan watched the horses in the corral. Something seemed wrong. She knew from their own horses that once the hay was tossed out the horses were single-minded about eating for the next few hours until it was gone. It was odd, she thought, that the horses hadn't settled into their eating routine, but continued to mill about in the corral. They ate for a few minutes, then shuffled restlessly.

"Don't the horses seem nervous?" she asked.

Lucy and Jessica had been in deep conversation about things that had happened in school that day, and how Hailey Bond had gone home sick.

"What about them?" Lucy asked.

"I don't know anything about horses," Jessica said. "Ask me about something I know about, like piano lessons."

Sheridan dropped it. "Girlie girls," she said, dismissing them.

But she was sure that something was wrong in the corral. One of the horses, a dun, broke from the herd and rushed toward the girls, stopping short just in front of them and causing all three to step back momentarily. The dun faced them, his nostrils flared and his eyes showing wild flashes of white. His ears were pinned back. Then just as suddenly, the horse relaxed and bent his head down for a mouthful of hay.

"What did *she* want?" Jessica asked Sheridan.

"He's a he," Sheridan said. "He's a gelding, do you know what *that* means?"

"No."

"Then I won't tell you. But I don't know what he wanted. Horses shouldn't do that when they have dinner to worry about. Something's wrong."

Tuff could be a pain in the ass," Bud Longbrake said over a snifter of after-dinner brandy in his study, "but no one deserves to die like that."

Cam murmured his agreement and sipped his own drink. Joe had passed on the brandy and poured bourbon into his glass.

All three men were now in the book-lined study.

"Most employees can never be counted on," Bud said. "Loyalty lasts as long as the next paycheck. They all feel like they're owed a damned living, like they're entitled to it. That's why I like hiring guys like Roberto, who know they're getting a hell of a fair shake. But Tuff worked here at least five times over the years. Twice I fired his ass, but the other three times he quit to do something else. He was a surveyor's assistant for a while, then a cell phone customer cervice rep. Imagine that—a cowboy service rep.

"Then after being a fake mountain man in Jackson Hole for a while, old Tuff was back in this very office with his hat in his hand, begging for his old job back. Now he's gone."

Joe had looked up sharply as Bud talked; something had tripped a switch.

"Bud, did you say Tuff worked with a surveyor?"

"Yup. Why?"

"I'm not sure," Joe shrugged. "It's just interesting."

Joe noticed that Cam Logue was looking him over closely, apparently trying to figure something out. He met Cam's eyes, and Cam looked away.

"Tuff did lots of things," Bud said, laughing. "Did I tell you the story he told me about trying to lift some woman at a chuck-wagon dinner theater for tourists? When he was playing a mountain man?"

While Joe listened, he refreshed the ice in his glass from a bucket on Bud's desk. The curtains on the window were open, and it was dark outside. It was getting late. He could use this as a reason to move Marybeth on, he thought. There was school tomorrow, after all.

Outside, he could see his daughters and Jessica Logue in the dim cast of the yard light.

"Something's definitely weird with the horses," Sheridan said to Lucy and Jessica, interrupting their debate over who was the cutest boy in the sixth grade.

It was getting too dark to see individual horses in the corral but the herd was a dark, writhing mass. Occasionally, a horse would break loose like the dun had earlier, charge and stop abruptly, and she could see its shape against the opposite rails. But, like the dun that had bluff-charged them, the stray would inevitably return to the herd. The footfalls of the horses were distinct, and muffled in the dirt, as was the sound of them eating.

"Maybe it's the Mutilator," Jessica said.

"Stop it," Lucy said sharply. "I'm not kidding."

"I agree," Sheridan said. "Knock it off."

"I'm sorry," Jessica said in a near whisper.

Then, from the corner of the corral, within the dark herd, a horse screamed.

Inside the house, Marybeth jumped. "What was *that*?"

"Just the horses," Missy said, wearing her hostess smile and filling coffee cups on a silver tray. "Bud brought them down to the corral."

"Mom," Marybeth asked, "why did he bring them down?" The tone in her voice caused Missy to frown.

"You know," she said, "since Tuff was killed, Bud's been a little nervous about the stock."

Marybeth cursed. *"The girls are out there."*

Marie covered her mouth with her hand.

Marybeth was halfway to the front door when Joe suddenly strode out of the study and over to her. Cam appeared at the study door with a drink in his hand, watching Joe with concern.

"Did you hear that?" Marybeth asked him.

"I did," he said.

The deep bass drumming sound of horses' hooves filled the night and reverberated through the ground itself as Joe ran from the porch toward the ranch yard and called aloud. "Sheridan! Lucy! Jessica!"

Grabbing a flashlight from the glove compartment of their van as he passed, Joe thumbed the switch. No light. The batteries were dead, damn it. He thumped the flashlight against his thigh and a weak light beamed. He hoped the dying batteries held.

Looking up toward the corral, he could see a kind of fluttering across the ground that made his heart jump. The fluttering, though, turned out to be his daughters and Jessica Logue who were running across the ranch yard toward him from the corral with coats, hair, and dresses flying.

Thank you, God, he whispered to himself as they neared. "Dad! Dad!"

They met him at the same instant that the outside porch lights came on and the front door opened. He could hear a rush of footsteps behind him as Sheridan and Lucy flew into him, hugging him tight. Jessica veered toward the house and buried her face in her mother's waist.

"Something happened with the horses while we were out there," Sheridan said, her words rushing out. "They just went crazy and started screaming."

"It's okay," Joe said, rubbing their backs. "You two seem all right."

"Dad, I'm scared," Lucy said.

Marybeth came down from the porch and both girls released Joe and went to her. Joe looked up to see Bud Longbrake filling the door, a .30-.30 Winchester rifle in his hands. He was looking toward the corral.

"Do you have a flashlight, Joe?" Bud asked, walking heavily from the porch.

"Yes, a bad one," Joe said.

"Bring it," Bud said, passing the van and walking across the ranch yard toward the corral.

Joe nodded, even though he knew Bud couldn't see him in the dark. He wished he had brought his pickup, with his good flashlight as well as a spotlight, instead of the van. His shotgun—the only weapon he could hit anything with—was nestled behind the coiled springs of his pickup bench seat.

As they approached the corral, which was still exploding with the fury of pounding hooves and the whinnies and guttural grunts of spooked horses, Joe felt rather than heard someone close in next to him. Cam.

"Okay, calm down, goddamit!" Bud shouted to his horses in the corral. Joe lifted his weak beam through the railing. Horses shot through the dim pool of light as they ran and thundered through the corral. He caught flashing glimpses of wild eyes, exposed yellow teeth, heavy, blood-engorged muscles flexing under thin hide, billowing nostrils, flying manes and tails.

Joe, Cam, and Bud climbed the rails and dropped into the soft turf of the corral.

"Take it easy, take it easy," Bud sang, trying to calm them. They walked shoulder-to-shoulder through the corral. Horses swirled around them. Joe could feel the weight of the animals shaking the ground through his boot soles. A horse ran too close, clipping Cam and spinning him around.

"Shit, he hit me!"

"Are you all right?" Joe asked.

"Fine," Cam said, turning back around and joining Joe and Bud.

Then with a mutual, collective sigh, the horses in the corral stopped running. It was suddenly quiet, except for the labored breathing of the animals who looked at them from shadows in each corner of the corral.

"Finally," Bud said.

Joe could see a few of the horses, who moments before had been in a frenzy, drop their heads to eat hay.

"How strange," Cam said. "Remind me never to get any horses."

Joe smiled at that.

Bud lowered his rifle and whistled. "Whatever got them going is gone now."

"Could have been anything," Joe said, knowing that something as innocuous as a windblown plastic sack could sometimes create a stampede within a herd.

"Probably one horse establishing dominance over another one," Bud said. "Administering a little discipline within the herd. Or maybe a coyote or mountain lion came down from the mountains. Or Joe's damned grizzly bear."

Why is it always my *bear,* Joe wondered, annoyed.

He moved his light beam across the horses. Most were now eating calmly.

"Okay, fun's over," Bud declared. "Thanks for the help, boys."

Cam chuckled. "I think this is enough action for one evening."

No one said what Joe knew they were all thinking: that

somebody, or something, had attacked the herd. *And the girls were right there,* he thought as a shudder rippled though him.

As they turned to go back to the house, Joe shone his light into a tight grouping of four horses drinking from the water trough. He could hear them sipping and sucking in water by the quart. The light bounced from the rippling surface of the water on the velvety snouts of the animals, and it reflected in their eyes as they drank. As he raised the flash, he saw something.

He felt a blade of ice slice into him.

"Bud."

Joe held the faltering light steady on the second horse from the left, a blue roan. Bud and Cam were starting to climb the railing to get out of the corral.

"BUD."

Bud stopped as he straddled the top rail, and turned back to Joe.

"What is it?"

"Look."

"Oh, Jesus," Bud Longbrake whispered.

Cam said, "My God," his voice cracking.

The horse Joe shined the flashlight on raised its head from the trough. Excess water shone on its thick lips with growing beads of bright red. A thin stream of blood ran from the chin of the animal into the trough, changing the color of the water to pink. The eyes, much larger than they should be, bulged obscenely from the sides of its head. They were lidless.

Most of the roan's face had been cut away, and it hung in a strip from its jawbone, looking like a bloody bib.

On their way home, Joe listened in as Sheridan and Lucy described what they had seen, felt, and heard at the corral. He knew it was important for them to talk it out, even though they had told him everything after the mutilated horse was first discovered.

Bud had been kind enough to put the rifle back in the house until the Picketts were down the road, Joe had observed. When they were gone, the rancher would destroy the injured animal before it bled to death, out of the sight of Missy's grandchildren. Joe appreciated the gesture.

Bud hadn't said whether he planned to call Sheriff Barnum or Hersig before the morning.

"Dad, I just thought of something," Sheridan said from the back.

"What's that?"

"Remember that feeling we had when we found the moose in the meadow?"

"Yes," Joe said cautiously.

"I felt the same thing during my falconry lesson with Nate, when the falcons wouldn't fly."

"Okay."

"Well, this time I didn't feel anything at all. What do you suppose that means?"

Joe drove for a few miles but couldn't come up with an answer.

In the driveway, he waited outside until Marybeth and his daughters were inside. Then he leaned against the hood of the van and crossed his arms, looking up. The sky was clear and milky with stars. It didn't *look* threatening, but it did appear endless and immensely complicated. There was a sliver of a moon. Over the mountains to the west was the fine chalk-line of a jet trail. He saw nothing else up there that shouldn't be there. He didn't know what exactly he was looking for, or what he would do if he saw anything unusual.

This thing was beyond him, he thought.

Unless . . .

Marybeth opened the front door and looked out.

"Joe, are you coming in?"

"Yup."

Later that night, at 3:30 A.M., Joe was jolted awake when Marybeth suddenly sat up in bed.

"Are you all right?" he asked her.

She was breathing deeply, trying to calm down.

"I had a bad dream," she said. "I heard that horse screaming again and again."

"Are you sure it was a dream?" he asked.

"Yes," she said. "Positive."

"Do you want me to check our horses?"

She eased back down into bed. "That's not necessary. I know it was a dream."

He pulled her close and cupped her breast beneath her nightgown. He could feel her heart thumping. He held her until the beating slowed and her breathing flattened out. When she was asleep, he untangled himself from her and slid out of the bed.

Pulling his boots over his bare feet, clamping on his hat, and cinching the belt on his robe, Joe went outside to check the horses. He took his shotgun with him. The horses were fine, and he sighed in relief.

He was wide awake when he came back into the house. He entered his small office and closed the door, leaning the shotgun against the wall. It was so quiet in the house that he flinched at the noise his computer made as he booted it up.

Opening his e-mail program, he sat back and waited while mail flooded his inbox. Directives and press releases from the Cheyenne headquarters, spam, a message from Trey Crump with the subject line "How's it going?," nothing from Hersig or Dave Avery, nothing from the lab, and a very large file that took a few moments to download.

There was no subject line in the large e-mail. But the return address was "deenadoomed666@aol.com."

He clicked on it.

As the e-mail opened, Joe felt his breath stop. "Oh, no," he whispered.

17

Ready and waiting for Joe Pickett . . . it said in a stylized color font.

Beneath the header was a digital photo. As he scrolled down, Joe noticed how cold he suddenly felt, and cinched his robe tighter.

The photo was of Deena. She was posed on top of the metal table in the Airstream he had sat at with Garrett that morning. She was nude except for thick-soled Doc Martens boots. She sat on the table with her legs spread open, smiling coyly. She had a light blond wisp of pubic hair, and her vagina was pink and slightly parted. Her breasts were small and her nipples were pierced with silver rings and erect. Her skin was so white it hurt to look at it, except for the tattoos on her inner thighs and upper arms, and the bruises that mottled her ribs and neck. There was a compress bandage the size of a hand on her left shoulder. The bandage looked moist, the skin around it glistening. The ointment he had smelled in his coat, he thought. Across her abdomen was a tattoo that said ABDUCTEE.

"Oh, no," he said again.

She looked so young, so unbearably thin and unhealthy. He was not aroused. He was sickened.

Beneath the photo was another stylized caption.

Strong, tall, and silent, he tries to save her. But she doesn't want saving. She wants him inside of her like an animal. She wants him to know he can do anything to her. . . .

I'm not that strong, not that tall, not that silent, Joe thought, feeling his face flush.

A second photo. On her hands and knees on the table, her buttocks aimed at the camera, her face peering back at him with a grin.

Whatever he wants, however he wants it, she is agree-able. There is nothing he can do to her that hasn't been done. She likes his hat and wants to wear it. . . .

Another photo. This time, she is clothed. Standing outside of the Airstream wearing all black except for blood-red lip-stick. She's mugging for the camera, head tilted forward, mouth parted, trying for a seductive come-hither look.

He knows where she lives, and he can't stay away. She won't be there forever, he knows. She will be gone soon, permanently out of here. She knows things, and she does things. . . .

Then, of all things, a graphic of a garish, yellow, smiley face.

Will he write back soon?

Joe slumped in his chair. The air in his office seemed oddly thin. He could hear the clock ticking in the living room, and Maxine snuffling outside the door to be let in.

What, he wondered, could create a girl like this? What had happened to her that resulted in this? Deena wasn't that much older than Sheridan, but she was so different.

What had caused the horrible bruises, or the wound? Had Cleve Garrett hurt her? Or were the injuries self-inflicted? Joe shook his head. He didn't understand why she had approached him this way. Is this what she thought all men wanted?

He rubbed his face hard with both hands, inadvertently knocking his hat off. His hat. She liked his hat.

"Joe?"

He nearly pitched out of his chair.

"Joe, what are you doing in here?" Marybeth asked, squinting from the light but looking at his computer screen.

He turned in his chair toward her.

"It's not what you think," he said.

"And what is it I think, Joe?" Her voice had a sharp edge.

"That I'm looking at pornography."

"Well?" She jutted her chin toward the screen, her arms crossed in front of her chest.

"Come here, Marybeth," he said. "Remember that girl with Cleve Garrett I told you about?"

"Sheena something?"

"Deena. Sheena would be the jungle girl."

"Yes, what about her?"

"This is from her. I guess it *is* pornography though. In the very worst kind of way."

Marybeth stood beside Joe and he showed her the message. He watched her face as he scrolled through the e-mail.

"That's disgusting," she said.

"Yup, it is. I don't know what she's thinking."

"She's thinking this will get you hot and bothered, Joe. It's like she's trying to lure you back there in the worst kind of way. Like she's desperate."

Joe nodded, sighed. "It just makes me, I don't know . . ."

"It's pathetic, isn't it?" Marybeth agreed. She leaned into Joe and he held her, pressing her hip into his chest.

"You need to stay away from her," Marybeth said. "She's trouble. It looks like she's been severely abused." She paused for a moment, before continuing. "Do you think she took the pictures herself?"

That jolted him. "I assumed she did."

"But what if she didn't, Joe?"

His mind spun. What if Cleve had taken the photos and the whole thing was his idea to lure Joe back out there? To get something on him, to get some leverage Cleve could use to get into the task force? If so, Joe thought, it was despicable to use Deena in this way. Unless, of course, she was in on it as well.

"This is too much right now," Marybeth said, giving his shoulder a good-bye squeeze. "Tonight was bad enough without adding this on top of it. I'll meet you in bed. We need to try and get some sleep."

Joe sat there for a few minutes. He wasn't sure what to do with the e-mail. Should he show Hersig? Call someone? He couldn't help thinking Deena was in trouble, that Garrett was abusing her in terrible ways. Even if she let him—and Joe found that very likely, given her age and situation—that didn't mean she didn't need saving. But what could he do? Rush out to Riverside Park with his shotgun, create the Wyoming version of the seminal scene in *Taxi Driver*?

Finally, he closed down the e-mail program and shut his computer off.

Back in bed, Joe stared at the ceiling and waited for the alarm to ring. It took two hours, and he shut it off immediately when it sounded.

Marybeth sighed and turned over toward him, her warm hand finding his chest. He moved to her, but his thoughts were elsewhere.

Nate Romanowski. He needed to find Nate and talk to him, get Nate's take on everything.

Joe slipped from the bed. Marybeth stirred.

"You're up early," she murmured.

"I'll make coffee," he said.

"While you were gone last night, did you check the horses?" she asked.

"Yup."

"Are they okay?"

"They're fine."

She opened her eyes. "Joe, are you okay?"

He hesitated. "Dandy," he lied.

The phone rang, jarring them both. Joe grabbed it from the bedstand.

"Joe Pickett."

"You the guy that's on that task force?" It was a man, and he spoke in a rushed, no-nonsense way.

"Yes, I'm on the task force."

"I asked because I called the sheriff, and the dispatcher said the sheriff is out at some ranch investigating a mutilation. A horse this time, she said. Anyway, she suggested I call you. She said you were on the team."

"What can I help you with?"

"Well, it's not as bad as a murder or a mutilation," the man said.

"I'm glad to hear that."

There was a pause. "You ever heard of a crop circle?"

It took Joe by surprise. He said, "I think so."

"Well, I think I've got one out in my pasture. I found it this morning."

18

DAVID THOMPSON, THE RANCHER who called, had a 200-acre place adjacent to the exclusive Elkhorn Ranches subdivision in the foothills of the Bighorns. Like the Elkhorn tract, Thompson's "ranch" had been carved from the much larger V Bar U Ranch once owned by a deceased lawyer Jim Finotta. By Wyoming standards, Thompson's place was not really a ranch, Joe thought as he drove there. It was a nice house with a really big lawn.

Nevertheless, Thompson had clearly paid a good deal of money for the knotty-pine sign that announced BIGHORN VIEW RANCH that Joe passed by. The road curved up and over a sagebrush hill and descended into a green, landscaped pocket where the newly built home had been nestled among pines and young cottonwoods.

On the drive out to Thompson's ranch, Joe tried to recall what he knew of crop circles, and concluded that it wasn't much. He remembered that when he was young, he'd read some kind of "Believe It or Not" book with blurry black-and-white reproductions of aerial photographs in England or Scotland of sites where the grass had been blown flat into perfect

O's. There had also been photos of fields where intricately cut designs had supposedly appeared overnight, usually amid reports of cigar-shaped flying objects.

Jeez.

This made him grumpy, and anxious to discount whatever he found as quickly as he could.

Joe pulled into the ranch yard to find David Thompson was waiting. Thompson was a dark, trim man in his early sixties who had supposedly cashed out of a dot-com in Austin months before the company had crashed. With his new fortune, he had purchased a home in Galveston, Texas, for the winter and the Bighorn View Ranch for the summer. He raised and showed miniature horses. Joe didn't like miniature horses. He thought they were silly, in the same way that hairless cats were silly.

Thompson was wearing a crisp canvas barn coat and a cap that said BIGHORN VIEW MINIATURES. He opened the passenger-side door of Joe's truck and Maxine scrambled toward the middle to make room.

"Want me to show you where it is?" Thompson said, swinging into the seat.

"Might as well," Joe said, "since you're already in my truck."

Joe's sarcasm didn't register with Thompson, who appeared flushed with excitement over his discovery.

"Don't you want to ask me when I found it?" Thompson said.

"You told me it was this morning."

"I did?"

"Yup."

"Take that road," Thompson gestured, indicating an old two-track that ascended out of the pocket and over a hill. "I don't use this road very much. My corrals and miniatures are the other way. But when I got up this morning to feed the horses I just had this strange feeling urging me to go down the other road. Like a premonition, you know? Like somebody or something was willing me to take the other road."

Joe nodded.

"It's a lucky thing I found it," said Thompson. "Usually by

this late in the fall I've already moved down to Texas. And especially this year, with all of the supernatural crap that's been happening around here, I had plenty of reason to leave early. But I wouldn't leave without my horses, and my goddamned unreliable horse hauler got waylaid up in Alberta somewhere. He should be here any day, and when he comes, brother, I'm out of here. I'll leave the aliens to the locals, baby."

"We thank you for that," Joe said, deadpan.

"I was thinking of selling the place anyway, you know? Moving back and forth to Texas with my minis is getting to be a drag. I might look for somewhere in New Mexico or Arizona, where it doesn't get so damned cold, you know? And where it isn't *spooked.* Problem is I'm not sure I could sell the place for what I've got into it, you know? I hear land prices are in the toilet, thanks to what's going on. I went to list the place at Logue Country Realty and the realtor there said appraisals are coming in at 20 percent lower than what they should be. Fire-sale prices, damn it."

Joe kept quiet. Thompson didn't seem to need a response in order to keep talking.

"When I saw that crop circle I thought to myself, why me? Why now? Why my ranch? But now when I hear that there was another mutilation last night, it all seems to make sense," Thompson said, talking fast. "Do you think it's all related?"

"I don't know," Joe said.

Thompson shot Joe a perturbed look. "Aren't you on the task force?"

"Yes."

"Aren't you intrigued by my discovery, then?"

Joe shrugged. "I don't know yet whether I'm intrigued. I haven't seen it."

"Well, it's just over this hill."

They cleared the hill and Joe stopped his truck.

"*Voilà!*" Thompson said, sweeping his hand as if presenting what was behind door number three.

Joe looked. Below them, on a sagebrush flat, was a perfect

circle cut into the buffalo grass. Joe estimated that it was eighty feet in diameter. Joe rubbed his jaw, ignoring the look of triumph on David Thompson's face.

"Just like I told you, eh?" Thompson said.

"It's a circle, all right," Joe agreed.

"A *crop* circle."

Joe continued to size up the scene. "Don't you need crops for a crop circle?"

"Oh, for Christ's sake."

"I was just kidding."

"I," Thompson said slowly, "am less than impressed with your investigative technique, Mr. Pickett. Maybe I should have waited for the sheriff."

Joe arched his eyebrows. "Maybe. But let's go down there for a closer look."

He eased the pickup down the hill and parked it on the left side of the circle. Joe and Thompson climbed out. While Thompson leaned against Joe's pickup, Joe paralleled the ring on the outside, studying it. The ring cut through the buffalo grass turf to bare ground. It did not look singed on the edges, or ripped out. There were no pieces of broken-up turf along the edges. He was reminded of the ring of moisture a sweating, cold drink made on a countertop. He walked a full rotation around it until he was back at the truck.

Thompson looked expectant, his eyebrows raised as if to say, "See? What did I tell you?"

Joe turned, looked again at the circle, squinting.

"When was the last time you used that road we just took?" Joe asked.

"Oh, a few months, I suppose."

"Are you sure? Can you remember the last time you came down here?"

Thompson's eyebrows fell a little. "Why are you asking me this?"

Joe stuffed his hands into his Wranglers and rocked back a bit on his bootheels. "I'm trying to establish how long this thing has been here."

"I told you about that premonition I had . . ."

Joe nodded. "But that doesn't mean that because you just found this thing it was made last night. You see, if you look close at the dirt in the ring you can see that it's been weathered. There's old pockmarks from rain in it. This circle has been here quite a while—at least a month, and probably longer than that."

Thompson looked puzzled for a moment, obviously doubting himself, then rebounding, as Joe knew he would.

"What difference does it make if the crop circle was made last night or a month ago? It's still a damned crop circle."

Joe shook his head. "Don't you have caretakers who live here in the winter when you're in Texas?"

"A woman stays here," Thompson said impatiently, trying to figure out where Joe was going. "Heidi Moos. She stays in the guest house and watches over the place."

"I know Heidi," Joe said. She was an attractive, dark-haired woman who had moved to Wyoming from Alabama. "She moved here with her horse a few years ago. She's a horse trainer, right? I mean *real* horses."

Thompson puffed up. "I resent that, mister. Miniatures are real horses."

Joe raised his hand, palm up. "Calm down, that's not what I meant. I should have said 'full-sized' horses. My point is that she's a horse trainer. This is the only flat ground on this side of the hill. It's the best place to set up a portable round pen. You know what a round pen is, right?"

"Of course I do," Thompson said. "I've got one by my corral."

"My guess is that Heidi set up her round pen right here last winter and spring," Joe said, soldiering on. "I've seen how horses running in a controlled circle eventually cut right through the turf like this. I've got a couple of these 'crop circles' next to my own corral, where my wife, Marybeth, works our horses."

Thompson's face was red. "That's how you want to explain it away?"

"Yup."

"You think I'm overreacting? That what we're looking at is where Heidi set up her round pen?"

"Yup."

"Well for Christ's sake," Thompson said, shaking his head. "No wonder you people haven't figured out these mutilations yet, if this is how you work. . . ."

"Why don't we call Heidi?" Joe said. "And ask her where she set up her round pen?"

Thompson stared, his eyes boring into Joe. He clearly was not a man who was used to being questioned.

Joe thought about David Thompson's so-called crop circle—round pen—as he drove down the highway toward the turnoff to Nate Romanowski's house. David Thompson was not stupid, and, despite his faults and his miniature horses, he was a serious man. Yet the atmosphere in Twelve Sleep County was now such that when Thompson saw a ring on the ground he didn't think "round pen," he thought "crop circle."

This thing was warping the mindset of the valley, Joe thought. Football practice was being held indoors. Out-of-state hunters had cancelled $3,000 trips with local outfitters. A public meeting that was supposed to be held at the Holiday Inn by the Wyoming Business Council had been switched to Cody. Livestock was being housed in barns and loafing sheds. Schoolchildren were wearing aluminum foil over their caps as they walked to school.

Despite the CBM activity, Saddlestring was being squeezed economically. Residents had assumed a siege mentality, of sorts, and tempers flared more quickly. Marybeth had told him of a fistfight in line at the grocery store.

The task force was getting nowhere. There had not even been another meeting, because no one had anything to report.

But for a reason he couldn't quite articulate, Joe thought that there was an answer to what was happening. Whatever the answer was, it was just sitting there, obvious, waiting for Joe or someone to find it. He just hoped it could be discovered before any more animals, or people, died.

19

As JOE RUMBLED DOWN the rough dirt road that led to Nate Romanowski's stone cabin on the bank of the Twelve Sleep River, he searched the sky for falcons. The sky was empty.

Nate's battered Jeep was parked beside his home, and Joe swung in next to it and turned off his engine. "Stay," he told Maxine, and shut the door. If let out, she would have been drawn straight to the falcon mews, where Nate kept two or three birds, and she would upset them by sniffing around.

Joe knocked on the rough-hewn door, then opened it slightly. It was dark inside, but it smelled of coffee and recently cooked breakfast. Joe called for Nate but got no response. This wasn't unusual, because Nate often went on long treks on foot or horseback in the rough breaklands country surrounding his house. Joe checked the mews, then the corral. No Nate.

Nate Romanowski had a habit of vanishing for weeks at a time. He took clandestine trips to surrounding states—Idaho, mostly—although he sometimes went overseas. Joe and Sheridan fed his birds while he was gone. Nate told Joe little about the purpose of his journeys, and Joe didn't ask. He was involved in things Joe didn't want to know about, and their short history together already had too many skeletons in the closet as it was. Their relationship was unusual, but oddly comfortable, Joe thought. Nate had pledged his loyalty to Joe in exchange for proving his innocence in a murder, and that was that. Joe hadn't asked for the pledge, and was a little surprised and awed that Nate had remained steadfast, even extending his protection to Joe's family. Joe and Marybeth never discussed what they knew about Nate Romanowski—his years with no record when he worked for a mysterious federal agency, the murder of two men sent to find him in Montana, the death of a corrupt FBI agent, and his involvement in Melinda Strickland's suicide the winter before. Sheridan worshipped the man, and was learning falconry from him. Sheriff Barnum, his deputies, Agent Portenson—even Robey Hersig—feared Nate, and were suspicious of Joe's friendship with him. That was okay with Joe.

With the strange things that had been happening in the valley, Joe looked for Nate with a niggling feeling of dread forming in the back of his mind. The image of the defaced horse at the Longbrake Ranch had not yet left him. It bothered him more than anything he had seen, including the remains of Tuff Montegue.

"Nate!" His shout echoed from the deep red wall on the other side of the river. It was still, and the echo returned twice before it faded away.

He thought he heard a faint response, and he stood and listened. The sound had come from the direction of the river.

"Nate, are you down here?" Joe called as he walked. He scanned the near banks and followed the river downstream until it S-curved out of sight, but saw no one. He cocked his head and looked up—something he had never felt the need to do before—and saw nothing unusual in the clear blue sky.

When he looked down he saw it. A thin plastic tube broke the surface of the river in a calm back eddy ten feet from the bank. As he approached the water he could make out a dark form below the water, and long blond hair swirling gently in the current like kelp. Nate was underwater, breathing through the tube.

Joe shook his head and sat down on a large curl of driftwood. He removed his hat and ran his fingers through his hair. He noticed that in the hollow of the log was Nate's massive .454 Casull handgun in its holster, within quick reach if Nate needed it.

"Nate," Joe said, "do you have a minute?"

Nate tried to talk through the tube. It came out in a nasal gibberish. This was the sound Joe had heard earlier when he called.

"Should I come back?"

After a beat, the water puckered and Nate sat up, breaking the surface. He looked at Joe through strands of wet hair that stuck to his face. Nate was wearing a full-body wet suit that gleamed in the morning sun. He removed the tube with two fingers as if taking a cigarette from his mouth.

"Should I even ask?" Joe said.

Brushing his hair from his face, Nate grinned, fixing Joe with his hard-eyed stare. Nate had an angular face with a bladelike nose separating two sharp, lime green eyes.

"It's amazing what you can hear under the surface," he said. "I've been doing this since the river warmed up. I thought it would be relaxing, but there's a lot going on under the surface. The river looks calm but things are happening in it all the time."

Joe just nodded.

"It's like being one with the earth, as stupid as that probably sounds," Nate said. "When you're below the surface, you're out of the air and wind and everything is solid, connected to some degree. That's why you can hear and sense so much."

His eyes widened. "I've heard river rocks dislodging and rolling down the bed of the river in the current. They sound a little like bowling balls going down a lane. I hear fish whooshing by, going after nymphs. I heard you drive up, get out, and walk around. If I concentrated, I could even hear your footsteps from underneath walking toward the river."

Joe thought about it. It wasn't something he would want to do, but this was Nate.

"Pretty cool," Nate said.

———

Nate brewed more coffee in his house while Joe told him everything that had happened with the murders and mutilations. Nate listened in silence, but was obviously paying attention. He served two large mugs and sat down across from Joe.

They were on their third cup when Joe finished.

Nate leaned back and laced his fingers together behind his head. He stared at the ceiling, his mouth set. Joe waited.

"I think you're thinking too much like a damned cop," Nate finally said. "You're letting the events steer you. You need to get out of your cop mode and look at everything with a fresh eye, from a completely different angle."

"What angle would that be?" Joe had expected something like this from Nate, although he had hoped for more. Like an answer. Or at least a theory.

"I think you're assuming that everything is connected. That's a logical, coplike approach. But maybe everything isn't connected. Maybe there are a bunch of different things going on, and they just happen to be culminating around us."

"You sound a little like Cleve Garrett," Joe sighed.

Nate's eyebrows shot up. "Just because he's a weirdo doesn't mean he might not be on to something. But from what you told me, I disagree. Cleve Garrett is trying to attribute it all to one thing, aliens or whatever. What I'm saying is that maybe the connections really aren't there. That there are different threads running."

Joe sat up, tingling with recognition. This was what he had been speculating. "From what you've heard, can you pick out any of the threads?"

"Maybe. When was the last time there were credible reports in this area about cattle mutilations?"

"Thirty years ago," Joe said. "In the early and mid-seventies."

"What was going on then?"

"I don't know. Gas lines, recession, Jimmy Carter."

Nate smiled coldly. "But what was going on here, on the land around us?"

Joe thought, and he felt another glimmer of recognition. "Oil and gas development gone wild," he said. "It was the last big energy boom."

"Right," Nate said. "At least until today. It was a little like what we're seeing now, wouldn't you say?"

"I hadn't thought of that," Joe confessed.

"Of course not. You've been thinking like a cop. You need to think bigger, look at everything fresh."

"There are a lot of roughnecks here," Joe said. "They come in from all over the country to work the CBM wells and lay the pipe. The last time there were this many people around was the last time this area had a boom."

Nate said, "Right. I bet that makes you wonder if any of them were here before, doesn't it? Or maybe—and I already know what you'll think of this angle—somebody or something gets mad whenever we start drilling into the ground."

Joe moaned. "That's too screwy, Nate."

"It's fresh thinking, is what it is," Nate countered.

Joe was silent for a moment. "Anything else?"

Nate solemnly shook his head. "I'm worried about the bear. I had a dream about a bear the other night."

"What?"

"In my dream, the bear was sent here for a reason. He has a mission," Nate said, narrowing his eyes and whispering conspiratorially.

Wincing, Joe looked away. What was *this*? First Sheridan had ominous dreams, and now Nate. Was it something in the air? Had the two of them discussed this?

"So what are you saying, Nate?"

He shrugged. "I'm not sure. It's just that I have a feeling that the bear plays a central role somehow. Like I said, I dream about this bear."

Joe said nothing. Nate simply thought differently than anyone Joe had ever met. To Nate, anything was possible.

"One other thing," Nate said. "Have you considered the possibility that the two human murders have nothing to do with the cattle and animal mutilations?"

"Actually, yes I have," Joe said.

"Have you pursued it?" Nate asked.

"Barnum and Portenson are in charge of the murders."

"And you trust *them*?"

Joe drained his mug and stood up. His head was spinning.

As he walked out to his pickup, Nate followed. "I've got a special connection with that bear because of the dreams. I would like to meet the bear, get into his head," Nate said. "Will you call me if there are any more sightings?"

Joe said that he would. He didn't even pretend to understand what Nate was talking about.

"Start fresh, is my advice," Nate said as Joe climbed into his truck. "Fuck Barnum and Portenson. They're cops. They either want an easy explanation or they want the whole thing to just go away."

Joe started the engine and Nate leaned into the pickup, filling the open driver's-side window. "Call me if you need some help. Backup, or whatever."

"The last time I did that you cut off a guy's ear and handed it to me," Joe said.

N ate was right about one thing, Joe decided. Although a couple of the things he threw out seemed unlikely—a bear on a mission, for example—what Nate had said about thinking differently made some sense.

Joe plucked his cell phone off of the dashboard and speed-dialed Robey Hersig's office. Hersig was in.

"Robey, Joe."

"Hey, Joe." Hersig sounded tired.

"Anything of note from the task force?"

There was a long sigh. "Your notes from your interview with that Garrett guy have been quite a source of amusement, as you might have guessed."

Joe thought about telling Hersig about the e-mail from Deena, and decided against it for the moment. He hadn't decided how he should reply and he needed to reply, to keep her talking to him. Although he hoped she'd cool it with the digital photos of herself.

"Anything in regard to Tuff or the other guy?" Joe asked.

"Nothing of significance," Hersig said. "I know Barnum and Portenson have been interviewing people who knew them, that sort of thing. Standard procedure. But if either of them have anything, they haven't told me yet. The investigation is stone cold, and although I hate to say it, we're just sitting around waiting for another corpse, or a lucky break. But there's nothing so far. That's why I haven't called a new meeting."

"Robey," Joe said, "given the situation I want to widen my part of the investigation."

"You mean investigate the murders?" Hersig sounded hesitant.

"Yup."

"That'll piss off Barnum, for sure."

"I can live with that."

Hersig chuckled uncomfortably. "I'm not sure I can authorize that, Joe."

"You don't have to. I'm independent. I'm a game warden; they have no authority over what I do or don't do."

"Aw, Joe . . ." Then: "What's your angle?"

"I'm not sure I have one. But I can't see how it could hurt to look at the murders from another perspective. Maybe we can compare notes at a task-force meeting and find some discrepancies in our information. That might lead us somewhere."

Hersig didn't reply. In his mind, Joe could see Hersig sitting forward in his chair, elbows on his desk, concern on his face as he thought it through. "All right, all right," he said. "But out of courtesy I'll need to advise Barnum and Portenson."

"Fine."

"And that sound you'll hear will be the explosion when Barnum gets the news," Hersig said.

"Hey, those guys are welcome to go talk to Garrett or zoom around with their sirens on looking at crop circles that aren't crop circles," Joe said. "Maybe they'll figure out something I missed."

"As if they'd do that."

"Well . . ."

"Good luck, Joe."

"Thank you," he said, rolling toward town. *Here's where we start to make people angry.*

PART
THREE

20

His STARTING PLACE would be the site of Tuff Montegue's murder, Joe decided. For reasons he had trouble articulating even to himself, he felt that Tuff's death was the key to cracking things open.

After grabbing a quick lunch at the Burg-O-Pardner on the edge of town, Joe passed through the small downtown toward the bridge over the river. Not Ike was fishing again, looping a fly-line through the air. Joe pulled off the road on the other side of the bridge and got out. Maxine joined him, and he cautioned her to stay close. He had just about broken her habit of wanting to retrieve artificial flies that landed on the water.

Not Ike was a huge man with large, yellowed eyes, a quick smile, and a barrel chest so stout that his fishing vest strained to stay buttoned over the tattered I'M NOT IKE sweatshirt. When he saw Joe, the smile flashed, and he waved. Joe waited at the edge of the river, watching Not Ike's graceful cast play out. Not Ike placed a dry fly perfectly inside the muscle of a current, and mended his line back so the line wouldn't overtake the fly in the current. The dry fly drifted over the top of a dark, still pool. Joe saw a flash beneath the surface of the water, heard the *ploop* sound of the trout taking the fly, and watched the fly-line tighten and rise out of the water to the tip of Not Ike's rod, which bent in the shape of a boomerang.

"I got one!" Not Ike laughed. He had a booming laugh that made Joe smile.

Not Ike retrieved the trout patiently, not horsing it in, and eventually netted it. He held it up for Joe to see, and the sun flashed on the bright rainbow sides of the cut-bow trout—a hybrid of a native cutthroat and rainbow trout—and the beads of water that glistened on the net.

"Three for me!" Not Ike proclaimed.

Not Ike always claimed he had caught three fish, whether the actual number was one or twenty.

"Nice fish," Joe said when Not Ike reached the edge of the riverbank.

"Nice fish, nice fish," Ike repeated, then looked up, his brow furrowing. "What you need? You need to check my license again?"

"You know it," Joe said.

"All right, all right, gimme a minute." Joe watched as Not Ike walked back out a few feet, eased the net into the water, removed the fly, and released the fish. Joe could see the trout hover for a moment below the surface, then with a powerful twist it shot out of sight. *The man knows how to release a fish, God bless him,* Joe thought.

Not Ike waded noisily toward the shore, still grinning. "Three for me!"

Ike Easter had told Joe that his cousin had once been lucid, if a little mean, and that he had become mixed up with the wrong crowd in Denver. He'd gotten involved in gangs and drugs, and was in the middle of it during the Summer of Violence when he had taken three .22 bullets in the back of his head, was dumped in the Five Points district, and left for dead. When he finally recovered three years later, he was a different man. Easter said Not Ike now had the day-to-day intelligence of a five- or six-year-old boy, and so Easter had agreed to become his legal guardian. Soon after he arrived in Saddlestring, Robey Hersig had taught Not Ike how to fish. Fishing gave Not

Ike a purpose, and as far as Joe knew, fishing was what Not Ike *did*. Which was another reason for not coming down too hard on the man for having an improper license.

While Joe checked the license Not Ike handed him, the big man loomed over him with the blank but brilliant smile. The license had expired the week before. "Jeez, what would it take for me to drive you over to Barrett's right now and stand there with you while we bought you an annual fishing license?" Joe asked.

"Ain't got the money for the big one," Not Ike said.

"You say 'big one' like it costs a fortune. It's only fifteen dollars."

"Ain't got fifteen dollars, Joseph." Not Ike was the only person who had ever called Joe "Joseph." Joe didn't know why.

"Look, I'll buy you one," he said. "You don't even need to spend your own money."

Not Ike took this as a personal affront, and scowled. "Don't want your charity, Joseph. Never have, never will."

Joe sighed. He had offered to buy Not Ike a license before, and Not Ike had refused him then also.

"Maybe I should talk to Ike about it."

"Won't do no good," he said, shaking his head as if sharing Joe's frustration. "He knows I won't take charity."

Joe handed the license back. "Well, at least go get a valid temporary one when you can, okay?"

Not Ike nodded. He concentrated on refolding the permit and sliding it into his vest pocket. His big face furrowed as he did it. Not Ike had poor motor-skill coordination, and although his casting was graceful, it took him ten minutes to button up his fly-fishing vest, and longer than that to tie on a new fly. He had all the patience in the world, Joe thought, all the patience that didn't manifest itself in greedy, impatient fishermen like Jeff O'Bannon.

"Yeah, okay," Not Ike said. "You gonna give me a ticket?"

Joe shook his head. "Just get the new permit, okay?"

Not Ike looked up, his face dark with sudden concern. "You found the Ripper yet?"

"No."

Not Ike stepped close to Joe. "I think I seen them in the alley downtown the night before those two men got killed."

"Really."

"I was fishin' a ways upstream, around the corner. I told the sheriff and that deputy. Even the FBI guy."

Joe wasn't sure what to ask. "What did they look like?"

"Wiry. Hairy and wiry. Creepylike. They were up in the alley, in the shadows," Not Ike said and gestured toward downtown Saddlestring, toward the alley behind the buildings on Main Street.

"And there's something else."

"What's that?"

Not Ike leaned in even closer, until his lips were nearly touching Joe's ear, and his voice dropped dramatically. *"I caught three fish that night."*

Tuff's death was likely caused by massive head injury," the county coroner told Joe when he finally returned Joe's cell phone call. "It was obvious even before we sent the body to the FBI that there was severe head trauma. The wound looked like what a hammer or baseball bat would make, but most likely it was caused by a rock he hit when he was thrown from the horse. We found blood and tissue on a rock up there."

"What about the autopsy?" Joe asked, as he drove. "Anything unusual?"

"Nope. His blood alcohol level was .15, so he was legally drunk. But I don't think there are any laws against that if you're riding a horse."

"But nothing else you found that was odd? Toxicology?"

Joe could hear tinny country music playing in the background in the coroner's office.

"Nothing other than the obvious mutilations and the teeth marks of your grizzly bear."

Joe rolled his eyes. *His* bear again.

"Have you spoken to the coroner in Park County about the other guy?" Joe asked. "Or should I call him?"

"I talked to Frank yesterday," the coroner said. "He's a

friend of mine. Basically, he determined the same thing on Mr. Tanner: blunt trauma head injury likely caused the death, although Frank thought it was possible that the blow to the head didn't kill the victim outright. Frank said it was possible the man had a severe concussion, and that they started skinning him before he actually expired."

"Yikes," Joe said, feeling a chill.

"I agree."

"Anything else?"

"Well, Frank's guy didn't have any of the other wounds we saw with Tuff Montegue. The body seemed to be found in the same place it fell, and there was no predation of any kind on it. Your bear didn't make it over to Park County, I guess."

"Right," Joe said absently, but it made him think of something. "Thanks, Jim."

"You bet," the coroner said. "I've been over all of this with Sheriff Barnum and Agent Portenson."

"I know," Joe said, his mind elsewhere.

On the other side of town, outside the town limits, Joe pulled off of the highway into the rutted, unpaved parking lot of an after-hours club called the Bear Trap. The Bear Trap was a one-level cinder-block building with bars on the few small windows and a fading MEMBERS ONLY sign on the front door. The place looked like a bunker. There were five vehicles, battered pickups parked at odd angles near the front of the club. The Bear Trap skirted liquor laws by proclaiming itself a private club, and it catered to drinkers who were still thirsty after the bars in Saddlestring closed at 2 A.M. It made the Stockman's Bar in town seem like an upscale establishment. Joe had been to the Bear Trap once before, following up on an anonymous poaching hotline tip that a "member" had been seen taking a pronghorn antelope out of season and that the poacher had retired to the club after field-dressing the animal.

The poacher had been easy to find and arrest, because the still-warm carcass of the antelope was in the back of his pickup under a tarp, blood running in thick strings from beneath the tailgate into the mud, and the man himself was at the bar wearing a shirt matted with blood and clumps of bristly pronghorn hair. The poacher surrendered without a fight, and seemed to look forward to a calm night in jail. The Bear Trap was the kind of a place where a blood-stained shirt didn't really stand out, the bartender had told him later. The bartender's name was Terry Montegue, Tuff's brother.

Joe checked his gun and the pepper spray on his belt before entering. Once he was inside, it took a moment for his eyes to adjust to the darkness. The barred windows were shuttered closed, and the only light came from Coors, Bud, and Fat Tire beer signs, a fluorescent backlight over the bar, and an ancient jukebox playing Johnny Horton songs. Joe liked Johnny Horton, but wasn't sure he could ever justify the fact if somebody challenged him to say why.

Four drinkers were crowded together on stools in the middle of the bar, and Terry Montegue hovered over them behind the bar. Joe heard the sound of dice being scooped into a cup, and saw a clumsy flurry as the drinkers stuffed the cash they had been gambling into their coat pockets.

"Nothing to worry about," Terry told the drinkers, looking over them at Joe. "It's just the game warden."

Joe smiled to himself, gave the drinkers a wide berth, and sat on a stool at the end of the bar.

Montegue was tall and bald with a beer belly that hid the buckle on his belt. He had a fleshy, cruel drinker's face, made worse by the scar that cut a white, wormlike path up his cheek, through his eyelid, and into his brow. He wore a too-small short-sleeved shirt that showed off his arm muscles, as well as the rattlesnake-head tattoos on both forearms.

"Can I get you something?" Montegue asked.

Joe looked up at the drinkers, who were trying to look at him without being obvious. They looked like out-of-work ranch hands or CBM roughnecks between crew shifts. Joe guessed the latter, since their pockets were stuffed with cash. He wondered what he would turn up if he called their plates in.

"I thought you had to be a member to drink here?"

Montegue's upper lip arced, and Joe assumed it was a

smile. Montegue reached under the bar and tossed a thick pad of perforated cards on the counter. They were blank membership cards, Joe saw.

"Membership costs fifteen bucks a year, or ten with your first drink. You wanna join?"

"Nope," Joe said.

"What, then?"

"Your brother, Tuff. I'm a member of the task force . . ."

One of the drinkers snorted down the bar, and turned away. The others stared ahead, not looking at each other or, Joe surmised, they would be forced to laugh.

Joe started again. "I'm investigating the death of your brother, Tuff. I want to ask you a few questions."

Montegue sighed, leaned forward, and placed both of his palms on the bar. He rotated his arms to give Joe the full effect of his triceps. "The sheriff's been here, and some FBI dork. Are you guys just following each other around?"

"Sort of," Joe admitted.

"I bet whoever sucked the blood out of Tuff was bombed for a week," Montegue said. "Look for a drunk alien, is my suggestion."

This produced a big laugh from the drinkers.

"I'm interested in what Tuff had been doing for the last couple of years," Joe said. "I know he was working for Bud Longbrake at the time of his death, but what else was he into?"

Montegue went down the list: ranch hand, school bus driver, roofer, customer service rep, surveyor, and professional mountain man at a Wild West show, until he hurt his back.

"When was he a surveyor?"

"Well, he wasn't actually a surveyor. He was more like a surveyor's peon."

"He was a rodman," one of the eavesdropping drinkers said. "You know, the guy who walks out and holds the rod so the surveyor can shoot it."

"Who did he work for?"

Montegue leaned back and rubbed his chin. "I know he worked a little for the county on the roads, but he also worked for some big outfit based out of Texas that was doing work up here." He turned to the drinkers. "Anybody remember the name of that company Tuff worked for a while? I remember him bragging about it, but I can't remember the name."

"Something Engineering," one of the drinkers said. "Turner Engineering?"

Montegue frowned. "No, that ain't it. Something like that, though. Why does it matter?" he asked Joe.

Joe shrugged. "I'm not sure it does. I was just curious. I'll check around."

"Check away," Montegue said.

"Did Tuff have enemies? Someone who might want to kill him?"

Montegue snorted, "Me, at times. He owed me 850 bucks. He still does, I guess, and I aim to sell a couple of his rifles so we're even."

Joe nodded.

"He had his share of fights, I guess. But he's like all of these assholes. They fight, then they buy each other a drink, then they're butt-buddies for life. I can't think of any serious enemies Tuff had. Anything else you want to ask me?"

"Nothing I can think of," Joe said. "But I might come back."

"Feel free," Montegue said, then thought of something that brought a smile to his face. "In fact, bring your wife. I'll waive the first year of membership if you bring *her*."

"I'll *pay* for your membership if you bring her," one of the drinkers said, and the others laughed.

"Leave my wife out of it," Joe said with enough steel in his voice that Montegue raised his hands in an "I'm just kidding" gesture.

As he climbed into the Bighorn Mountains and neared Bud Longbrake's Ranch, Joe mulled over a theory that had been floating in the back of his mind. Something about Tuff's death was just a little bit wrong. It almost but not quite fit the pattern.

The wounds on the cattle and wildlife had been reported in gruesome detail in the *Saddlestring Roundup*, Joe thought.

What hadn't been reported was the exact kind of cut made in the hides of the cows. A person following the story would have known just enough to make Tuff's murder appear to be like the others, he thought. But the wrong knife or cutting instrument was used. And how could a killer possibly prevent predators from finding the body? While there was something extraordinary in the bodies of the cattle, moose, and Stuart Tanner that apparently prevented predation, Tuff's killer obviously hadn't been able to duplicate whatever it was.

Maybe, Joe thought, Tuff's murder was a copycat and entirely unrelated to the others. Maybe Tuff was killed for reasons wholly different from the other deaths, by someone who saw his opportunity to take advantage of the bizarre happenings to solve a personal problem with Tuff Montegue.

Again, Joe felt that if he could figure out what had happened to Tuff, and who murdered the man, the answers to the other and bigger parts of the puzzle might become more apparent.

"Or maybe not," Joe said aloud to Maxine, his voice rising with frustration. "Maybe all of this crap has been the work of two wiry, hairy, creepylike guys who hang out in an alley in Saddlestring, like Not Ike said."

21

MARYBETH DROVE LUCY, Jessica, Hailey Bond, and Sheridan to the Logues' home after school, but something felt wrong about it. The three younger girls shared the middle seat in the van, and she could see through the rearview mirror that they were conspiring; they were animated, sneaky, whispering directly into each other's ears, barely containing excitement. Something was going on, Marybeth thought. She could tell by their body language and sparkling eyes, and the way they shot glances at her while they whispered.

She said, "Jessica, are you sure it's okay with your parents that they drive Lucy home?"

Marybeth tried to read Jessica in the mirror. The little girl was good, Marybeth thought. She could lie well.

"Yes, Mrs. Pickett, it's okay," Jessica said, while Lucy and Hailey stopped talking and looked innocently—too innocently—at Marybeth.

"And Sheridan's coming too," Lucy said.

"What?"

Sheridan chimed in, bored, from the backseat, "It's okay, Mom. Really. I'll make sure we're home for dinner."

Now Marybeth knew that something was up. Why would Sheridan want to join Lucy at the Logues? A conspiracy was afoot, no doubt. Sheridan was in on it, which was unusual in itself. Marybeth tried to read Sheridan's face in the mirror while she drove. Sheridan, anticipating the scrutiny, looked casually out the side windows of the van, feigning a sudden interest in the homes along the street.

Marybeth felt a pang; her girls were growing up. They no longer wanted to share all of their secrets with her. It hurt to think that. Maybe if she didn't work so much, Marybeth thought, it would be different. Maybe if she was home when school was out, like she used to be, her girls would confide in her again. Sheridan, especially. Sheridan used to tell Marybeth everything, lay bare her feelings and concerns, bounce things off of her while Marybeth prepared dinner. She didn't do that anymore, because of Marybeth's schedule, her work, her burgeoning new enterprise. Dinner was rushed, something she thawed in the microwave and gave Joe to grill, or takeout. While Marybeth still insisted on a family dinner together, it wasn't the same anymore. Everything was rushed. Dinner was for eating, not catching up and visiting, talking about everyone's day. Dinner now was a fuel stop that preceded homework, showers, and bed. God, she felt guilty.

But when Cam Logue had come into her office earlier in the day, looking surprisingly interesting—she chose that word, rather than others—in a black turtleneck and blazer and blue jeans and cowboy boots, and perched on the corner of her desk with his hair askew in his eyes and an open, hangdog expression on his face, and asked her if she would consider becoming a full partner in the real estate firm, she had had a brief, giddy vision of what it would be like if she succeeded as she knew she was capable of succeeding. She pictured them moving to a home in Saddlestring with bedrooms for everyone and a stove where all four burners actually worked.

"I've been thinking about this," Cam had said, "and I believe it could be profitable for all of us." He looked at her in a way he had never looked at her before, she thought, as if he were sizing her up for the first time.

"I think it could work, too," she had said. "I could make you a lot of money."

"I don't doubt that for a second," he said, leaning toward her, inches away so she could smell his subtle scent—Joe never used aftershave lotion or cologne—"I think you would be a great asset to the company," he said.

"I know one thing," she told him, as he leaned closer. "I would bust my butt for you."

He had smiled, almost painfully. "Don't bust it, because it's perfect as it is."

Then she knew.

A line had been crossed. Cam was hitting on her, and she felt momentarily flattered. Then it passed. She wanted to be taken seriously as a professional, but now she wondered. Was this whole "get-your-real-estate-license" thing a ruse by Cam to get her into bed?

"Cam," she said, "you are way too close to me, physically, right now. Lean back. And if the reason why you want me to get my license is so something will happen with us, you're so wrong about that it makes my head hurt. Marie is my friend, and don't get me wrong—I think you're an admirable businessman—but if the reason you want me to become involved is what you're hinting at right now, well . . ."

Cam had shrunk back while she was talking, and was literally about to fall off of the desk.

". . . Joe is my guy. That's it. That's all there is. He may screw up on occasion, and he doesn't make much money, but he's my guy."

She was angry at herself at that moment, because she felt tears well in her eyes, which was the last thing she wanted to have happen. But she continued, narrowing her eyes, "And if you ever, and I mean EVER, even suggest again that there is anything more than a business relationship at all, I'll tell Joe. And then I'll tell Nate Romanowski . . ."

When she said the name "Nate Romanowski," Cam visibly flinched.

". . . And that will be that," Marybeth concluded.

All of this was coursing through Marybeth's thoughts as she wheeled into the Logue home, stopped fast, once again, by the pickup with South Dakota plates in the driveway. It had been moved to the opposite side of the driveway, but the rear of it still jutted out into the path.

"So Jessica, your grandparents are still here?" Marybeth asked, looking into the mirror.

"Yes, ma'am."

"Is your mom feeling better? She hasn't been in the office in a couple of days."

"I think so," Jessica said. But it was obvious she was bristling to get out of the car. So was Lucy. And Sheridan was glaring at her.

"Well," Marybeth said, "tell your mom hello from me and tell her I wish her to get well."

"Okay, Mrs. Pickett."

Marybeth turned in her seat, stern. "You girls be home in time for dinner. Stay away from those buildings in the back. And if Marie isn't feeling well enough to bring you home, you call me and I'll come get you, okay?"

Lucy nodded. Sheridan mumbled something, averting her eyes.

"What was that, Sherry?"

"Nothing."

But Marybeth had heard what Sheridan said. *Like you're going to cook dinner,* was what she mumbled.

Stung and hurt, Marybeth watched her girls skip toward the old house. They were leaning into each other, conspiring again. For the second time that day, she felt tears well in her eyes.

22

So HOW MUCH FARTHER IS IT?" Hailey Bond asked boldly, but there was a tremor of false courage in her voice.

"Right up here," Jessica said. "And don't talk so loud. Maybe we'll catch him in the shack."

Sheridan reluctantly followed the three younger girls. She couldn't believe she had let Lucy talk her into this. But Lucy had begged her older sister to accompany them, and Sheridan felt an obligation, and also responsibility for Lucy's well-being. If there was something to this crazy story, Sheridan thought, she wanted to be there for Lucy. It made her uncomfortable to be with the younger girls, with their chattering, and she wondered if she had ever been like that. Probably not.

"It's right up here," Jessica said, stopping and turning, holding her finger to her lips to shush everyone. "From now on, just *whisper*."

"You're trying to scare me," Hailey said aloud.

"Whisper!" Jessica admonished.

Hailey shrugged, trying to act brave.

This is silly, Sheridan thought. Lucy would get it for this later.

But Sheridan noticed Lucy looking at her with a false, frightened smile. Even if it was silly, Lucy was taking it seriously. Sheridan nodded to her, *go on.*

The shack seemed to morph out of the thick timber, as if it were a part of it. The shape of it seemed partly blurred, because it fit in so well with the trees. It was older, smaller, and more decrepit than Sheridan had imagined.

Jessica took a step ahead of the girls and turned, wide-eyed. She gestured toward the open window near the front door of the shack. This was as far as she and Lucy had been before. There was something in the air, maybe just the silence, but it got to Hailey Bond. Hailey shook her head, *no.*

"I'm not going closer," Hailey said in an urgent whisper. "You guys are just trying to scare me."

Sheridan noticed the smirk of satisfaction on Jessica's face. Sheridan hoped that the whole thing wasn't a setup, and that she had been asked along to legitimize it. If that turned out to be the case, Lucy would *really* get it later. But it didn't seem like something she would do. In fact, she had stepped back and was standing next to Sheridan, clutching at her hand.

"Let me look," Sheridan said, shaking off Lucy's hand.

The three younger girls stared at her, their eyes wide.

"Step aside," Sheridan whispered.

The girls parted, and Sheridan strode past them. She tried to walk with confidence, with courage. But she felt her knees weaken as she approached the window. She remembered Lucy saying that she and Jessica had trouble seeing in. For Sheridan, that should be no problem. Her chin was about the same height as the bottom of the windowsill.

She slowed as she neared the window. It was dark inside. She never even considered opening the door and walking in.

She approached the windowsill, stopping a few inches from it. She leaned forward, holding her breath.

There was a sleeping bag on the floor, all right. With nobody in it. There were magazines, papers, empty cans. A small gas stove. Books—hardbacks, thick ones. And, on a square of dark material, what looked like silverware. A lot of silverware.

She didn't exactly lose her nerve, but when she turned

around toward the younger girls she saw them running. Hailey was gone, Jessica was disappearing into the timber. Lucy held back, fear on her face, waiting for her older sister.

Sheridan was about to tell her sister there was nothing to worry about when she noticed that Lucy's eyes had shifted from her to the side of the shack. Sheridan followed Lucy's eyes, and felt her own heart whump against her chest.

He was a tall man, thick and dirty. Sheridan saw him in profile as he came from around the shack. He was looking at Lucy. He had long, greasy hair and a wispy beard. His nose was hooked, his mouth pursed, his eyes black and narrow. He wore a heavy, dirty coat. His trousers were baggy.

"Get the HELL out of here!" he snarled at Lucy. "Go away!"

Lucy turned on her heels and ran a few feet, then stopped again. Sheridan knew why. Lucy wouldn't run without her sister.

The man hadn't yet seen Sheridan, who was now hugging the side of the building.

Sheridan hoped he wouldn't turn his head and see her.

But he did.

For a second, she looked into his eyes, which were dark and enraged. Maybe a little frightened, she thought later.

"G-g-get OUT OF HERE, YOU l-l-little b-b-bitch!" he screamed. Her eyes slid down the front of him, at his coat. The name "Bob" was stenciled above a breast pocket.

He took a step toward her, and Sheridan ran. She had never run faster, and she overtook Lucy in seconds. She reached back, found the hand of her younger sister, and didn't let go as they weaved in and out of trees, around untrimmed brush, until they collapsed within sight of the Logue home.

23

AN HOUR AND A HALF AWAY, after calling Marybeth to
tell her that he'd be getting home later than usual, Joe drove up
the two-track on the Longbrake Ranch toward the treeline
where Tuff Montegue was killed. He wanted to retrace the
route of Tuff Montegue, to be there in the same place and at
the same time of night that the coroner suggested Tuff was
killed.

There was a crisp fall chill in the air. The beginning of
dusk had dropped the temperature a quick twenty degrees. The
chill, along with the last of the fall colors in the aspen pockets
that veined through the dark timber, seemed to heighten his
senses. Sounds seemed sharper; his vision extended; even the
dry, sharp smell of the sage seemed to have more of a bite.
Maybe it was because just prior to darkness the wind usually
stopped, and it was the stillness that brought everything out.

He was placing himself right square in the middle of it, using himself as bait. Marybeth wouldn't approve.

The grass around the murder scene was still flattened by all
of the vehicles that had been up there, so it was easy to find.

He stopped and killed the engine. Maxine eyed him desperately, her excitement barely contained.

"Yup, we're going to get out," he told her, "but you're sticking close to me."

With that, she began to tremble. Dogs were so easy to please, Joe thought.

Pulling on his jacket, he swung out of his pickup and drew his twelve-gauge Wingmaster pump shotgun from its scabbard behind the seat, loaded it with double-ought buckshot, and filled a jacket pocket with more shells. He pulled on a pair of thin buckskin gloves, clamped his Stetson on tight, and walked the perimeter of the crime scene. It had been cleaned up, he was glad to note. No cigarette butts or Coke cans in the grass. Maxine worked the area as well, nose to the ground, drinking in the literal cornucopia of smells—wildlife scat, blood, maybe the bear, a dozen Sheriff's Department people, the ME, the coroner, anything else that clung to the grass.

He turned and faced east, studying the shadowed tree-line above him, wondering what it was that Tuff and his horse had seen that caused the problem. Walking very slowly and stopping often, as if he were hunting elk, he moved up the slope. He had learned that moving too quickly dulled too many senses in the wilderness. If his breathing became labored, all he could hear was himself. By walking a hundred yards and then stopping, he could see more, hear more. As the light filtered out, his eyes adjusted to the darkness. The sky was brilliant and close with swirls of stars. A quarter moon turned the grass and sagebrush dark blue. Maxine stayed on his heels.

For an hour, he moved slowly up the mountain until the first few of the trees were behind him and the forest loomed in front.

It wasn't so much that Joe could see something in the trees as sense it. It was a hint, a barely perceptible hint, of the pressure he had felt at much greater volume when he found the moose.

Maxine moved up in front of him and set up on point. The hair on her back was raised, and she was sniffing the air.

He reached down and ran his fingers down her neck to calm her, but she was rigid. Her eyes were wild, her ears up and alert. "Stay," he whispered to her. "Stay, girl." She was staring into the dark trees the way she would if they were bird hunting and she had found pheasants in the cover. But he could see nothing.

Suddenly, the dog exploded with purpose. She launched herself into the trees ahead—Joe missed when he grabbed for her collar—and she barked with a manic, deep-throated, hound-like howl that sounded so loud in the stillness that it even scared him. He had never seen his mild-mannered Labrador act so crazy.

"Maxine!" he yelled. No point in proceeding quietly now. "MAXINE! Get back here! MAXINE!"

He glimpsed her in the shadows, her tail and hind legs illuminated by a dull shaft of moonlight. And then she was gone.

He chased her through the trees listening for her barking. It sounded like she had veered left, then right. She sounded so *mean,* he thought. And he thought he heard something else. Footfalls? Somebody running? He couldn't be sure.

He whistled for her, and kept shouting as her barking grew more and more distant. He unholstered his Mag-Lite and bathed the area in front of him with its beam, then sharpened it into focus and shot it up into the trees in the general direction of where she had run. He couldn't pick up her track.

"Oh, no," he moaned aloud. In the seven years he had had his dog, she had never run away from him.

He wondered whether she was stupid enough to have taken off after the grizzly bear.

Her barking was now so faint, he could barely hear it. It came from farther to the right in the forest, much deeper into the timber.

While she was still in earshot, he hoped, he fired two blasts from the shotgun into the sky. The flame from the muzzle strobed orange on the tree trunks near him.

Then he waited. Yelled. Whistled. Fired two more blasts and reloaded the shotgun with shells from his pocket. Nothing. It was now completely silent again.

"Shit, Maxine."

There was no way he could track her in the dark and find her.

He couldn't even be sure she was to the right, the way sounds bounced around in the mountains. Very reluctantly, he began to work his way back the way he had come, stopping periodically hoping to hear her bark. Joe knew that if she managed to emerge from whatever forces had turned her into the hell-hound she had become, she would know to return to the pickup. In normal circumstances, he would have given her a day or so before getting worried. But these weren't normal circumstances. He pictured her mutilated body and it made him shudder.

Joe sat in his pickup with his windows rolled down and his headlights on. Every few minutes, he honked the horn. Maxine would know the sound, recognize it as him. He scanned the slope and timber, hoping desperately to see her.

It pained him to think that Maxine had possibly charged at something in an effort to save him. Why else would she have become so ferocious, so single-minded? It wasn't for her own sake, he thought. She wasn't the kind of dog to embrace a confrontation or want to fight.

"Damn it all," he said and fought the urge to pound the steering wheel.

He kept looking over at the passenger seat, thinking that's where she should be. He thought that he'd probably spent more hours with Maxine than with Marybeth or the girls. Maxine was a part of him.

He tried not to get maudlin. Leaning on the horn, he let the sound of it express what he felt.

He sat up with a start when something light colored and low to the ground moved just beyond his headlights. Grabbing for the spotlight, he thumbed the switch, the beam bathing the acreage in front of him with white light, seeing something doglike . . . only to discover that it was a damned coyote. The coyote stopped for a moment, eyes reflecting red, then moved down the mountain.

Again, Joe cursed. And the curse released something that

started in the back of his throat like a hard, hot lump and burst forward, and he sat there in the dark and he cried.

The cell phone on the dashboard burred at 10 P.M., and Joe could see from the display that it was Marybeth. He had avoided calling her.

"So, are you coming home tonight?" she asked, an edge of irritation in her voice.

"Yes, I'm just about to leave. I'll be home in forty-five minutes."

She obviously picked up on the tone of his voice, the solemnity: "Joe, are you all right? Is something wrong?"

"Maxine ran away," he said, telling her in as few words as possible what happened.

For several moments, neither spoke.

"I don't want to tell the girls," Marybeth said.

"We'll have to."

"Okay, but in the morning. Otherwise, they'll cry all night long."

Joe nodded, knowing she couldn't see the gesture.

"Oh, *Joe,*" she said, in a way that made him feel guilty for once again bringing pain into their family.

"I'm sorry, honey," he said.

As Joe drove down the mountain, he kept honking. He wondered if Bud Longbrake could hear him down at the ranch, and figured that he probably could. He called Bud from his cell phone, told him why he was making so much noise, asked Bud to keep an eye out for his dog.

"Your dog?" Bud said, genuine sympathy in his voice. "Damn, I'm sorry, Joe."

"Yeah, me too."

"When my first wife left me I didn't feel nearly as bad as when my dog died."

Joe didn't dare respond to that one.

A quarter of a mile from where he would turn onto the highway, Joe looked into his rearview mirror and saw something in his taillights.

"YES!" he shouted, and slammed on his brakes.

Maxine was exhausted, her head hung low, her tongue lolled out of the side of her mouth like a fat, red necktie. She literally collapsed in the road.

Joe walked back and picked her up, seventy-five pounds of dog, and buried his face in her coat as he took her to his truck. He saw no obvious wounds on her, although she was shaking. He lay her on her seat, and she looked at him with her deep, brown eyes. Filling a bowl with water from his water bottle he tried to get her to drink, but she was too tired.

As he wheeled on to the highway with giddy relief, he called Marybeth, and she burst into tears at the news. He called Bud, and said not to worry about the dog. After punching off, Joe told Maxine, "Don't ever, ever do that again, or I'll shoot you like the dog you are." He meant the first part but not the second. She didn't hear him because she was sleeping, her head where it always was when he drove, on his lap.

As he pulled into his driveway, he glanced up to see Marybeth at the window pulling the shade aside. The porch light lit up the cab of the truck, and he looked down to see if Maxine was awake. He didn't really want to have to carry her again.

That was when he noticed something wrong. Her coat seemed lighter than it should.

He snapped on the dome light and simply stared. Whatever she had seen or experienced had scared her so badly that her coat was turning *white*.

"Okay," Joe said aloud. "Enough is enough. Now I'm starting to get mad."

Sheridan and Lucy were still up, even though it was past their bedtime, because Marybeth wanted them to tell Joe what had happened earlier on the Logue property. As Joe entered the house and hung his jacket on the rack in the mud-room, he saw two guilty-looking girls in their pajamas standing near the stair landing. Marybeth was behind them in the kitchen, wiping her hands on a towel.

"Tell him, girls," Marybeth said to them.

Sheridan sighed and took the lead. "Dad, we screwed up this afternoon and we're sorry for it. We went out to that shack on the Logue place . . ."

He leaned against the doorframe of his office and listened to Sheridan tell him how they had deceived their mother and how they snuck up to the old shack. She described the contents inside the shack; the bedroll, books, stove, the long line of gleaming silverware on a dark cloth, then the appearance of "Bob" who called her a bitch. Lucy twisted the bottom of her pajama top in her fingers while her sister spoke, betraying her guilt.

"He called Sherry a *bitch*!" she repeated unnecessarily.

"But he didn't follow you," Joe said, wary.

Both girls shook their heads.

"You're sure?"

Sheridan nodded. "We checked behind us when we were running. I saw him go back into the shack."

Joe asked Marybeth, "Did you call the sheriff?"

"No, I wasn't sure if you would want him involved. We still can, though."

"Cam Logue needs to call Barnum," Joe said. "I don't know why he didn't the first time the girls saw this guy."

"I think he was just some homeless guy," Sheridan said. "I feel bad about bothering him, now. I feel sorry for a grown man who has to live like that."

Marybeth shot Joe a look. She was admonishing him to hold the line, to reinforce the talking to she had given the girls earlier in the evening. She knew Joe well enough that she feared he would soften. She was right, he thought. He tried to keep his expression stern and fixed.

"Girls, it's past your bedtime now," Marybeth said. "Kiss your dad goodnight and get into bed. We'll discuss your punishment later."

Relieved to be done with it, both girls approached Joe. It

was then that Sheridan froze, looking around Joe toward the figure in the mudroom. "What's wrong with Maxine?"

"She's exhausted, girls," Joe said. "I thought for a while tonight I lost her."

Sheridan stepped around Joe and turned on the light switch in the mudroom.

"She's white!" she howled.

"What happened to her? Did she fall into some paint?" Lucy asked.

Joe said, "No. I think she got really scared. I've heard of it happening sometimes to animals. They get so scared that their hair turns white."

"Is she okay?" Sheridan asked, bending over the dog and patting her white fur.

"I think so," Joe said. "She's probably just tired from running to catch me."

He watched as both girls nuzzled the sleeping dog, telling Maxine that everything would be okay. Marybeth gave it a few moments before scooting the girls along.

When the girls were in bed, Marybeth turned to Joe. "I can't believe how white she is."

"I've never seen anything like it before," Joe said, slumping into his office chair. "I've never seen a lot of things before that have happened around here."

"What are you doing now?" she asked.

He sighed. "I need to check my messages, see if anything is happening. Then I'll be up."

"Don't be long."

"I won't. I promise."

He called to her before she went upstairs. "Try not to go to sleep right away, I've got some things I want to talk with you about."

"Oh, sure," she said, smiling at him. Her smile took him off guard, and he welcomed it. With her schedule, it had been a while since they had gone to bed together with both of them not too tired.

"Really," he said, grinning back. "It was quite a day. I investigated a crop circle that wasn't a crop circle, met with Nate, then lost our dog."

"Hmmmm," she purred, obviously thinking of what to say next. "I had an interesting day as well. Don't be long."

Nothing from Robey, nothing from Trey Crump, nothing from anyone. Except another email from deenadoomed666@ aol.com.

"Oh, no," he whispered aloud.

There were no photos this time, only text.

Dear Joe:
I hope you got my last e-mail—didn't hear from you so I wasn't sure :) I hope you liked the pictures ☺. things are getting a little crazy here now so this has to be short. i've got some very important things to tell you that you will want to know. don't know how much longer i'll be able to tell you these things. please come by as soon as you can or at least reply to me. i know a lot more now. i've got to go. He'll be back any minute. Just when you think that things can't get any weirder they get weirder.
    Love ☺,
    Deena

Joe replied:

Deena:
I'll be by in the morning. I hope you're okay. If you need to talk to me away from him let me know and we can go somewhere. It's important that you stay safe. If you need help now, call 911 or my direct line.
    Joe Pickett

As he prepared to go to bed, his head swimming once again with the unwanted images she had previously sent him, he saw a glow of light from beneath the closed bathroom door. He stopped and knocked.

"Come in." It was Lucy.

He opened the door wide enough to stick his head in. Lucy was standing at the sink, looking carefully at herself in the bathroom mirror.

"What are you doing, darling?"

Lucy's cheeks flushed red. "I was really scared today, Dad, when that man came out. Sherry said I looked funny. So I was just checking myself."

Joe smiled. "You were checking to see if your hair was turning white?"

"I guess so. That's what Sherry said."

"Don't worry, sweetie. It's still blond."

To Sheridan, as he passed their dark bedroom: "Quit scaring your sister, Sheridan."

"Sorry, Dad," Sheridan said from beneath her covers, where she had no doubt been hiding to muffle her giggles. "She deserved it, is all."

"Good *night*."

Marybeth was in bed and she looked as beautiful as he could ever remember. Her blond hair was loose and brushed to the side, fanning across a pillow. Her knees tented the covers, but the quilt was turned down enough that he could see she was wearing the dark-blue silk chemise that drove him crazy. One of the thin straps had fallen over a shoulder.

"Get in here now," she said. "We can talk later."

24

JOE WAS IN A FOUL MOOD at breakfast when he heard the sound of an engine and the crunching of gravel outside. He'd been stewing about what Marybeth had just told him about Cam Logue. Although she had handled it well—Marybeth always handled these things well, he thought—the very idea of it infuriated him. She had made Joe promise that he wouldn't do anything; wouldn't go to the office and confront Cam, or urge her to find another job. Chances of finding another job with this kind of promise in Saddlestring, as they both knew, were remote.

"I knew I never really liked him," he told her, buttering his toast.

"*Joe,*" she cautioned him, imploring him with her eyes to let it go. As she did, Sheridan came to the table. She was always first, before Lucy. Lucy took much more time to color-coordinate her outfit and determine what her hair would look like for the day.

"I had that dream again," Sheridan announced. "I'm starting to think I know where it's headed. It's a showdown of some kind."

Joe dropped his knife on the tabletop, looking at her. "A showdown between whom?"

"Good and evil," she said, matter-of-fact.

"Who wins?" he asked.

She shrugged. "The dream hasn't gotten that far along yet."

"Well, let me know," he said cautiously.

"I will," she said, reaching for the jam. "Oh, somebody's outside. They parked next to your truck."

"Did you see who it was?" Joe asked.

"A four-wheel drive with a light-bar on top," she said, filling a bowl with cereal. "Probably Sheriff Barnum."

"Great," he said, pushing away.

"*Joe,*" Marybeth cautioned again.

Joe strode outside feeling as if he were about to enter a boxing ring. He clamped his hat on his head while he walked, and pushed through the front gate harder than he had intended to, making it slam open.

It was Barnum, all right, as well as Agent Portenson. They both sat in a cloud of smoke inside the vehicle. They squinted at him as he approached. Simultaneously, the driver and passenger doors opened, and both men swung out. What a good morning for them to show up, Joe thought sardonically. If only they had Cam Logue with them, he could deal with two problems at once.

"Sorry to disturb your breakfast," Barnum said, his voice more gravelly than usual and his face more gray.

"No, you aren't," Joe said, taking a position on the other side of his truck and leaning his forearms on the hood. He did not trust Barnum, and the early-morning surprise meeting had a confrontational feel about it. If something was going to happen, he wanted his truck between him and Barnum and Portenson. At least until *he* bridged the gap.

"What do you want?" Joe asked. "Why don't you get right to it? I've got a busy day ahead of me."

"You could at least invite us in for a cup of coffee," Barnum said, pretending he was offended.

Portenson snorted, and lit another cigarette.

Joe said to Barnum, "You are not welcome in my house, Sheriff. This is where my family lives. If you need to talk with me all you have to do is call, and I'll meet you anywhere."

"It's also your office, right?" Barnum said, squinting. "Working among all of those girls, it must be tough to get anything done."

"Right," Joe said, looking squarely at Barnum. "Unlike the Sheriff's Department, where things get done but they're usually wrong."

Barnum stood still, but Joe saw the sheriff's jaw muscles twitch. Barnum's flat, blue eyes didn't look away.

"Boys," Portenson said, waving his cigarette in the air. "We are getting nowhere."

"What do you want?" Joe asked again. Barnum finally broke the stare-down. "I mean, that can't be discussed at a task-force meeting?"

"Sheriff," Portenson said, "you want to start?"

"Keep the fuck away from our investigation," Barnum growled. "Just stay the fuck away. You're wasting everyone's time."

Joe smiled bitterly. "I suspected that was what this was about."

"Just worry about your furry animals, and the alien hunter you were assigned by Robey," Barnum said. "Don't second-guess us and don't reinterview all of our leads. There's nothing you can find that we haven't already."

Joe looked to Portenson. The FBI agent seemed to be concentrating on his cigarette, and watching the morning sun hit Battle Mountain. He looked so out of place here, Joe thought. Portenson's coat was too heavy for the fall, and too outdoor-gear trendy. His slacks and black slip-on shoes belonged beneath a desk in a temperature-controlled office.

"I talked with Robey," Joe said to both of them. "I told him what I wanted to do. I'm not second-guessing anyone, but I thought that maybe I could find an angle on this whole mess that had been overlooked. You're welcome to go talk to Cleve Garrett, if you want to. Go ahead and check up on *me*. I don't care. Maybe you'll turn up something I missed. We've got nothing so far. Not a damned thing. If I can look at the murders with a fresh eye . . ."

"You're a goddamned *game warden*!" Barnum thundered, stepping around the nose of Joe's truck toward him. "You're no investigator. You're only on the task force because the governor needed somebody from your agency."

Joe watched as Barnum's face reddened. He had stopped just before he fully came around the truck.

"You should be out finding that bear, or counting fish, or whatever the hell it is you do. Leave the professional work to the professionals!"

"And who would that be?" Joe asked calmly.

"You son of a bitch!" Barnum spat, and Joe squared himself, ready.

This had been brewing for years. He noted that Barnum wore his gun. Joe was unarmed. Fine, Joe thought. He couldn't imagine Barnum actually shooting him, not in front of an FBI agent, anyway. And it would be against Barnum's nature to hurt him directly. Barnum was more of a corrupt, behind-the-scenes man.

Nevertheless . . .

Because of the rush in Joe's ears, he didn't hear the school bus on Bighorn Road until the brakes squealed to a stop and the accordion doors wheezed opened.

"Hello, Sheriff!" the bus driver called out cheerfully. "Hey, Joe!"

Out of the corner of his eye, Joe saw Portenson roll his eyes heavenward.

The front door of the house opened and Sheridan and Lucy came out. Both girls were pulling on jackets and fumbling with their backpacks and lunch boxes. Marybeth stood in the doorway, watching them skip up the walk. But she was really watching Joe, Barnum, and Agent Portenson, Joe knew.

Sheridan made a point of walking between Joe and Barnum, and stopped long enough in front of Joe to tilt her chin up for a good-bye kiss. Lucy was right behind her.

The men watched as the girls boarded the bus and the doors closed. Both girls took seats near the window and waved as the bus pulled away. Joe waved back. A thin roll of dust bloomed from the tires of the school bus as it labored away.

It was uncomfortably silent. Barnum still stood near Joe's fender, but his hand had dropped away from the butt of his weapon. Marybeth still stood in the open doorway, watching the bus. Portenson leaned back against the sheriff's Blazer, and laughed silently.

"This is over," Portenson said.

"No, it isn't," Barnum said, his voice low. "It's just postponed."

"Anytime, Sheriff," Joe said.

Barnum turned his back on Joe, nodded his head to Marybeth, and walked back to his GMC. He threw himself into the driver's seat with more dexterity than Joe would have guessed, given Barnum's age and health, and slammed his door shut.

"Agent Portenson," Joe said. "How come you're mixed up with *him*?"

Portenson stared at Joe, smiling coldly. "I've got to go."

"It isn't birds, Portenson."

Portenson waved his hand in front of his face, as if shooing away a fly. "Then what is it?"

"It's two things, I think," Joe said, keeping his voice low enough that Barnum wouldn't hear. "I think we've got one set of killers responsible for most of the animals and Stuart Tanner. I think we've got another entirely separate killer who did Tuff Montegue."

Portenson looked pained.

"Whether they're connected or not I don't know," Joe said. "But if nothing else, we've got to figure out one or the other. We can't look at the mutilations as one thing any longer, or we'll never get anywhere."

"We aren't anywhere now," Portenson said.

"No, we aren't. But if we change the focus of the investigation, we might find something out."

Portenson shook his head as if dispelling a bad thought.

"Look, Portenson, I know you're not a bad guy," Joe said. "I know what you did last winter, how you tried to stop the massacre. You blame me for putting you in that position, but you did the right thing. You can do it again."

"Oh, just shut up," Portenson said.

Joe grinned. "I can count on you, can't I?"

"Why do you even care?"

Joe shrugged. "I don't want this kind of thing happening in my mountains, or my district. Not around my family. They've gone through enough in the last few years without worrying about something like this."

Portenson looked genuinely sympathetic. Then something changed in his face.

"I still think you and that Nate Romanowski maniac are guilty of something. I'll find that out one of these days, and I'll bust you both. Then I'll get out of this hellhole I'm in."

Joe nodded. "That's fine. But right now, we've got killers out here who are just about as scary as anything I can think of. You know that."

Portenson lit another cigarette, then tossed it away angrily after one drag. "I'm hoping the whole thing just goes the fuck away," he said. "There haven't been any incidents in a few days, not since that stupid horse got his face ripped off. I just hope the whole thing goes away."

"Maybe it will," Joe said, thinking again of Cleve Garrett's theory. "Or maybe just part of it will. If that happens, we've still got the other part to figure out."

Barnum leaned on the horn, even though Portenson was just feet away from his vehicle.

"What an asshole," Portenson said.

"That's just the half of it," Joe said back.

25

LOT C-17 AT THE RIVERSIDE RESORT and RV Park was empty.

"Damn it," Joe said, thumping the steering wheel of his pickup with the heel of his hand. He looked over to Maxine, remembered that he had left her home to sleep today, then looked back at the vacated lot.

He wondered when they'd left. How long had the Airstream been gone?

A sick feeling welled up in Joe's stomach. He hoped that Deena was all right. He felt responsible for her, since she had reached out to him even in her pathetic way. If he had acted sooner, had come over to see Deena the morning after the first message, could he have averted something? Had Cleve Garrett discovered their correspondence and hurt her? Or had he simply moved his operation to some other place?

He found Jimbo behind his trailer, raking leaves in his postage-stamp backyard.

"Jimbo, when did Cleve Garrett pull out?" Joe asked the resort manager.

Jimbo froze, then slowly looked up. "What do you mean?"

Joe was confused for a moment. "Don't you know that he's gone? I just came from there. The lot is empty."

Jimbo let the rake fall into the pile of leaves he had made. "Well, what do you know," he said. "He musta' left during the night. He was all paid up, so he doesn't owe me anything. But he at least could have said good-bye so I'd have known I have another space to rent."

"Didn't you hear him go?" Joe asked, incredulous.

Jimbo pointed at his own head. "I don't hear nothing without my hearing aids anymore. I take 'em out to sleep, so I guess he left after I went to bed."

"When was that?"

Jimbo pondered the question. "Let's see, I watched the news, read a little. You ever read *Harry Potter*?"

Joe had, but he didn't want to discuss it.

"I'm hooked," Jimbo said. "I'm on the third one now. I never thought I'd care a good goddamn about a little Brit orphan, but . . ."

"Jimbo, what time?"

Jimbo's face lost enthusiasm, and he thought for a moment. "Must have been after 11:30 or so. I think that's when I packed it in."

Deena's last e-mail to Joe had been sent at 11:15, Joe remembered. In it, she hadn't said they were leaving. Maybe she hadn't known yet, he thought, the sick feeling coming back. Maybe Cleve read Joe's response over Deena's shoulder, and decided then that they needed to go immediately.

But what difference did it make what time they left? Joe thought. What was significant was the fact that they were gone, and that they felt a need to leave in the middle of the night.

Why?

As he crossed the Twelve Sleep County line into Park County, Joe called Hersig and told him that Cleve Garrett was gone and mentioned Deena's e-mail.

"I think we should put out an APB," Joe said. "Locating their truck and that big Airstream shouldn't be too difficult."

Hersig hesitated.

"What?" Joe asked.

"We don't have any grounds to stop him," Hersig said. "A man has a right to move his trailer from place to place, Joe."

"What about Deena?"

"What about her? Can you honestly make a case that you think she's in danger? Or threatened? From what you told me she hasn't ever indicated that she's in trouble. It doesn't sound like we have anything to go on at all here, Joe."

Joe held the phone away from his ear and looked at it, scowling at Hersig. Then he pulled it back. "They left right after she sent me an e-mail, like I said. She was going to tell me something this morning that she thought was important. I'm telling you, Cleve Garrett is dirty in some way. Why else would he hightail it out of town so quickly when just the other day he was begging me to get him on the task force? I think he's going to hurt her, if he hasn't already."

"Aw, Joe . . ."

"Damn it, Robey, if we find her body somewhere I hope you remember this conversation."

Hersig sighed, "Okay, I'll call the highway patrol. But if he's located, we need more than what you've given me to search the trailer or arrest the guy. If she's with him and looks okay we'll have to cut him loose with our apologies."

Joe hoped that if Garrett was stopped the man would give something away that would invite inquiry. At least Joe would know if Deena was with him, and if she was unharmed.

Maybe Barnum had a point, Joe thought, as he slowed his pickup to enter Cody. Maybe Joe didn't know what he was doing.

P ark County Sheriff Dan Harvey had agreed to meet with Joe in his office to go over the case file of Stuart Tanner's death. Harvey seemed younger and more at ease than he had been during the task-force meeting, Joe thought. Maybe he was just more comfortable on his own turf.

The sheriff offered coffee, and Joe accepted. They sat in the sheriff's office, which was larger and much neater than Barnum's rathole, Joe observed. There were even books on the bookshelves.

"I asked Deputy Cook to sit in with us, Joe. He received the callout and was the first officer on the scene."

Joe nodded to Cook, who nodded back. Joe thought the deputy seemed capable and serious.

"Anything happening in Twelve Sleep County?" Harvey asked, as a receptionist delivered three Styrofoam cups of see-through coffee.

"Need anything in it?" she asked Joe.

Maybe some coffee beans, Joe thought, but declined her offer.

"Has Robey been in contact with you?" Joe asked.

"Every afternoon."

"Then you know that we haven't made any progress. That paranormal guy Cleve Garrett has disappeared, though. We're looking for him. But nothing of significance has happened yet."

Harvey shrugged. "This is a bad case. I just wish it would go away somehow. There's just no real *evidence* anywhere."

Cook nodded in agreement. "The only good thing about it is that there haven't been any more murders or mutilations in Park County."

"We found a horse," Joe said, grimacing a little.

"I heard. You were there, right?"

Joe nodded.

"You heard that the FBI said there was no toxicology on Mr. Tanner, right?" Harvey said. "Nothing unusual, I mean. He died from a blow to the head, and he would have died from severe exposure anyway. His mutilation occurred post-mortem."

Cook said, "Basically, there's nothing we've found that we haven't already given to Robey Hersig," an edge of jurisdictional integrity creeping into his voice. "So frankly, I'm not sure why you're here."

"I'm just going over things again," Joe said. "Maybe I'm spinning my wheels. I'm not accusing you guys of withholding anything."

"That's good," the sheriff said, sipping his coffee and exchanging a glance with Cook. "Because we're not. Besides, practically everything happened in Twelve Sleep County. Our guy is dead just because the aliens or whatever couldn't see the county line."

Cook laughed at the sheriff's joke, and Joe smiled.

"So who called it in?" Joe asked.

Cook opened his file with a copy of the 911 log. "The call came in at 4:32 A.M. from an unknown male. The caller didn't identify himself, but he reported a body within sight of county road 212. Dispatch took down the information and called me at home because I'd just gotten off of my shift. Katherine, the night dispatcher, said it was hard to understand the caller, and she had to ask him to repeat himself a couple of times. Bad connection, I guess."

Joe was silent for a moment, considering the situation, turning the details over in his head. "Deputy Cook, you said the body was found within sight of the road, but was it parallel to the road, or somewhere on a turn?"

Cook sat back, not sure where this was headed. "It was parallel to the road, in the trees. We found the body in a clearing."

"You found it pretty easily, then?"

"Yup. The directions from the call-in were good. He told us it was 6.8 miles on the country road from the highway. It was exactly 6.8 miles, all right."

"So you drove 6.8 miles and then what? Shone your spotlight out to the side?" Joe asked.

Cook bobbed his head. "I picked up the body right where it was supposed to be."

"So," Joe asked, rubbing his jaw, "if you hadn't known the exact location of the body, could you have seen it from the road?"

Cook snorted, "In the daylight, hell yes. It was plainly visible from the road."

"But it wasn't daylight," Joe said, perking up. "It was night.

Would your headlights have picked up the body if you were driving down that road?"

Cook hesitated, then: "No. There's no way I could have seen it off to the side like that in the dark."

Sheriff Harvey slowly sat up, and leaned forward on his desk. "Shit," he said. "So how did the guy who called it in see the body? How did he know it was there?"

Joe said, "Yup."

"I never thought of that," Cook confessed. "Damn it all. The coroner said Tanner was killed between 10 P.M. and 2 A.M. which means the guy either saw it happen, or he fucking did it."

"Do you keep a tape of the calls?" Joe asked. His question betrayed his growing excitement.

Harvey's cheeks flushed. "We do, but the machine wasn't working that day. I'm sorry about that."

"The call came in at 4:30 A.M., right? Don't you think it's kind of odd that someone was driving around out there at that time of night?" Joe asked.

Harvey shook his head. "Not really. We know that there's been some drug activity on that road, some meth buys. It's also a road pretty popular with the high school crowd. They go out there to drink and jump each other's bones. My guess is that somebody like that called it in."

"So it was from a cell phone?"

"We assume so."

"Does your dispatcher have Caller ID?"

Harvey's eyebrows shot up. "You know, we honestly didn't think of that. We've got it but we never really pursued it because we didn't put much emphasis on the caller himself. Didn't seem important. The dispatcher said the guy was really hard to understand, and she kept having to ask him to repeat himself. It was like he was drunk or drugged, she said."

"I'll check the record," Cook said, standing up. "Be right back."

"Seems like a good guy," Joe said after Cook had left.

"He is," Harvey said, sipping his coffee. "I think he's a little miffed that he didn't have an answer for you."

"I'll tell him not to worry."

While they waited, Joe told Harvey about his encounter with Cleve Garrett and Deena, as well as the crop circles that weren't crop circles. Joe explained that he was currently operating under the theory that the murders and mutilations in Twelve Sleep and Park County were connected, with the exception of Tuff Montegue's death, which didn't fit the pattern. Harvey maintained a steady smile, and nodded from time to time. He was noncommittal overall and Joe suspected that Harvey would rather have the murder that was part of the pattern instead of the exception to it. That way, there would be no special expectations placed on him or his department. When Joe told Harvey about Maxine turning white, Harvey seemed genuinely shocked.

"Cows are one thing," Harvey said. "But you don't fuck with a man's dog."

"Damned right," Joe said.

Deputy Cook returned in a few minutes holding a printout. He closed the door behind him and sat down heavily in his chair.

"I don't know if this is helpful or not," he said. "It doesn't make a lot of sense to me anyway."

"You've got a number?" Harvey asked impatiently.

"Yup. But it's not a local number like I thought it would be. The area code is 910." He looked to Joe and Harvey to see if they recognized it. Both men shook their heads.

"Nine-one-oh," Cook repeated. "I looked it up. The cell phone is from Fayetteville, North Carolina."

"What?" Harvey said, his voice high-pitched. "We've got a guy from North Carolina driving around in the mountains at 4:30 A.M.?"

Joe tried to make sense of it, but couldn't. He wrote the number down in his notebook.

"Maybe he's one of those CBM guys," Cook said. "They're from all over. Is there natural gas in North Carolina? Or a company headquarters there?"

Harvey shrugged. "Arden, you need to follow up on this."

"I'll get on it right now," Cook said. He asked Harvey if he could use two of the other deputies so they could work faster. Harvey agreed.

After Cook left, Harvey turned to Joe and raised his eyebrows. "Maybe we've actually got something here."

"It's a start anyway. Will you call me when you've got a name?" Joe said, handing Harvey his card. "I'll fill Robey in on what we've got so far."

"Which really, when you think of it, isn't very damned much," Harvey said. "But at least I've got my guys running around all excited, instead of sitting there reading the *Pro Rodeo News*."

Joe stood, shook hands, and opened the door. Before he left, he remembered one of the questions he meant to ask when he arrived.

"You said Stuart Tanner owned an outfit called Tanner Engineering?"

Harvey nodded. "Right, based out of Texas, but his family's had a cabin up here for years, and he liked to stay there when his company was working in the area."

"Do you know what Tanner Engineering was working on? Specifically?"

While Harvey shuffled through the file, Joe recalled something from the day before. Tuff Montegue's brother had said Tuff worked for "Turner Engineering." Could it have been Tanner Engineering? Joe felt a twinge.

Harvey looked up after going through the file. "We don't have anything on what he was doing here," he said. "You know, I feel kind of stupid that we haven't really pursued this angle. To be honest, we've been sort of waiting for something to break in Twelve Sleep County."

That sounds about right, Joe thought.

"I've got to think about this," Harvey said, as much to himself as to Joe. "If some bad guy killed and mutilated Stuart Tanner, did he also do all of the livestock? And the moose? And the cowboy? It doesn't seem possible to me."

Joe didn't know what to say. But his mind was spinning.

B ack in his pickup heading for Saddlestring, Joe called Marybeth at Logue Country Realty.

"Are things okay today?" he asked.

"Fine," she said, sounding more cheerful than he would have anticipated. "Except Marie is sick again. I haven't seen her in three days. I'm starting to get a little worried about her, Joe. I asked Cam how she was doing, and he said he thought she'd be back in later this week."

"So you talked with Cam, huh?" he asked, feeling a surge of anger.

"Of course I talked with him," Marybeth said, admonishing Joe. "He's my boss. Nothing was said about our conversation yesterday, and I think he's a little ashamed of the whole thing. I'm not worried, Joe."

"You'll call me if something happens again, right?"

"Of course. But I can handle myself. I'm a big girl, and I'm smarter than hell."

"That you are," Joe said although he still felt like smashing his fist into Cam's face.

"But that's not the only reason why you're calling, is it?" she teased.

Man, she knew him well, he thought. "I was wondering if you would have any time to do some research. It can probably be done on the Internet and with a couple of calls."

"Is something happening, Joe?" She sounded intrigued.

"Maybe. But I'm not sure yet."

"I can grab some time over lunch," she said. "What do you need?"

"Do you have a pencil?"

I t was late afternoon when the town of Saddlestring came into view. From the distance on the highway, it looked insignificant beneath the slumping shoulders of the Bighorn Mountains. Joe could see a few buildings poking out of young trees, the Twelve Sleep River as it serpentined through the valley and through the middle of town, and four shining ribbons of highway that intersected within the tree-choked community.

He had tried to let his mind work during the drive back, to process what he had learned in Cody. He tried to think of what they might be overlooking that was sitting there right in front of them.

This was giving him a headache. But maybe this new information would sort itself out, start to fit into proper places.

Then something occurred to him. It was obvious, if risky. It could move the new track of the investigation forward, or screw it all up forever.

He could simply call the number with the 910 area code, and see who answered. Fayetteville, he said to himself. What is in Fayetteville?

Joe pulled his cell phone from its mount on the dash and was reaching for his notebook to look up the number, when the phone trilled.

"Joe, it's Trey Crump."

Joe hadn't talked to his district supervisor since before the task force was formed, although he had kept him up to date on the progress, or lack of it, via e-mailed reports.

"What's up?"

"You're not going to believe this, but I just got a call from the bear guys up in Yellowstone. Apparently, they just picked up a signal on our missing grizzly."

Joe had a feeling what was coming.

"They tracked him to a location that's literally in your backyard, so to speak. Just east of the mountains, in the breaklands. He appears to have stopped, because they said the signal is strong and not moving."

Joe grabbed his notebook from the seat, and flipped to a fresh page.

"Do you have the GPS coordinates?" Joe asked.

"Got 'em. You ready?"

"Sure," Joe said, scribbling.

—————

As he shot through Saddlestring and out the other side toward the breaklands, Joe called Nate Romanowski. As usual, he got Nate's unreliable answering machine.

"We located the bear," Joe said. "If you get this, you'll want to get right out to the BLM tract off Dreadnought Road. The bear is supposedly right in the middle of it, about six miles off-road to the north. Look for my truck."

26

THE BREAKLANDS COUNTRY beyond Dreadnought Road served as a kind of geological shelf before gradually rising into the foothills and then swelling into a sharp climb into the mountains. At first glance it looked flat and wide open, but in actuality it was deceptive terrain coursed through with deep draws of crumbly, yellow-white earth that created massive islands of grass-covered flats that were attractive to pronghorn antelope, mule deer, and ranchers. Before lamb and wool prices collapsed in the 1980s, the breaklands had been filled with sheep. Joe had seen photos from the forties and fifties on the wall at the Stockman's Bar of sheep herds clipping the grass in the Dreadnought breaklands as far as the photographer could see. There were still a few bands of sheep in the area, tended by Mexican or Basque herders, but nowhere near the amount there had been.

Joe slowed his pickup on Dreadnought Road while watching the GPS unit on his console, and scanned the surrounding area for Nate Romanowski. He was wary of striking off-road as it approached dusk because of the network of arroyos and draws that could cut him off, isolate him, or get him stuck.

Joe didn't find a road, and realized he had gone beyond where he should have turned right. He stopped and studied a well-worn topo map of the area, trying to find if there was another approach—one with roads—to where the bear had been located. There was an old road of some kind that entered the area from the exact opposite direction but he estimated it would take close to an hour to get to it. His only choice, he concluded, was to go off-road.

On the floor of the pickup was a tranquilizer gun in its plastic case. The gun had a pistol grip and shot a single fat dart loaded with a debilitating sedative. The warnings on the box of darts said that the sedative was extremely concentrated, and designed for animals weighing over 400 pounds. The dosage was lethal to humans. Reversing down the empty county road for nearly quarter of a mile, he slowed, cranked the wheel so that the nose of the pickup pointed straight out into the breaklands, punched the four-wheel-drive high switch, and started crawling across the sagebrush in the dusk. His tires crushed sagebrush, and the sharp, juniper-like smell perfumed the chilling air. As usual, he kept both windows open so he could see and hear better. As the front tires bucked down and up through a hidden, foot-deep channel, he instinctively reached over with his arm to prevent Maxine from toppling from the seat to the floorboards before remembering Maxine wasn't there.

Twenty minutes after he had left the road, Joe glanced up and saw a pair of bobbing headlights in his rearview mirror. The vehicle was at least ten minutes behind him, and seemed to be using the same set of tracks that he had cut across the grass and brush.

Who could possibly be following him, or even know where he was? Maybe Nate got his message after all.

While he was watching the mirror instead of where he was going, his left front tire dropped into a huge badger hole and jerked the truck to a stop. The steering wheel spun sharply left as the tire fell and twisted in the hole, and maps, memos, and other paperwork rained on him from where they had been wedged under rubber bands on his visor for safekeeping. The motor died. He picked up all the paper that had fallen on him and shoved it out of the way between the seats. He looked up and saw lazy dust swirling in his headlights, lit up with the last brilliant half hour of the ballooning sun.

Feeling his chest constrict, he checked his mirror. Because he had stalled out in a small dip in the terrain, he couldn't see the headlights behind him. He turned in his seat, looked through the glass, but couldn't see the vehicle.

Was it Nate? If Joe could see the headlights again, he could be sure. Nate's Jeep had a recognizable grille and set of lights. It looked like an owl's face.

He had a wild thought: what if it wasn't Nate? What if someone had used the same frequency as the bear collar to alert the biologists and lure Joe out here? The frequency itself, though assigned to the U.S. Fish and Wildlife Service, was available on the handheld radios favored by most hunters and fishers, even though use of it was discouraged.

Uh-oh, Joe thought. Did he have time to unsheath his shotgun before the vehicle behind him caught up?

Then headlights cleared the wash and Joe instantly recognized the grille of Nate's Jeep. Nate thrust his head out the window.

"Hey, Joe," Nate Romanowski, the driver, said in greeting. "I got your message about the bear and came straight out."

Joe sighed, relaxing. "Have you ever considered calling ahead, Nate? Have you ever thought about calling me on my cell phone or through my dispatcher and telling me that you're planning to find me?" Joe said, his voice rising. "Have you ever thought about that, Nate? Instead of scaring the hell out of me by chasing me across the prairie?"

Nate didn't respond right away, which was his way. Joe noticed that Nate was wearing his side-draw shoulder holster.

"So," Nate said, a smile tugging on his mouth, "where's your bear?"

They left Nate's Jeep in the ditch and, after working Joe's pickup out of the badger hole, Nate and Joe sat side by side on the bench seat in Joe's truck and churned forward through the prairie in the half-light of the last ten minutes of dusk.

"The bear might be out here," Joe said, "but I don't think the bear is the key to the mutilations."

Nate shrugged. "This is one of those instances where reasonable people can disagree."

"Okay," Joe said. "Explain."

Nate chuckled again, which sounded somewhat false.

"Things are happening with the investigation," Nate said. "I can tell by your mood. You're . . . *jaunty,* all of a sudden. A little excitable also, I'd say. If you give me the background I'll be able to let you know if I'm still in the ballpark or not. But I've had a few thoughts lately and a few more dreams. I've talked to some Indian friends."

Joe shot Nate a look. He knew Nate had contacts on the reservation. The mutual interest was falconry, which the Shoshone and Arapaho admired.

"So you need to tell me what's going on," Nate said.

Joe checked the GPS unit. They were close. So far, he was pleasantly surprised that they'd paralleled the worst draws in the breaklands, and hadn't been confronted with any ditches that stopped their progress.

"Things are getting interesting," Joe said, and told Nate about his confrontation with Barnum and Portenson, his interview with Montegue, and the meeting with Sheriff Dan Harvey.

"Okay," Nate said, after listening carefully. "There is something here."

"So what is it?" Joe asked.

Nate shrugged. "Hell, I don't know. But something ought to fit with something else. Tanner Engineering may be the place to start. But, Joe . . ."

"What?"

"Don't dismiss what I said earlier. About the energy booms and the fact that the murders and mutilations seem to come when the ground is being tapped. Or that the bear may be more than a bear. That bear is here for a reason."

Joe waved Nate away, as if swatting at a fly. "Nate, let's not even go down that road. It's crazy."

Nate clammed up, stung by Joe's attitude. Silence hung heavily in the cab.

"Okay, Nate, I haven't dismissed it completely," Joe said, sorry he'd snapped. "But I still can't see where it connects."

They hit another badger hole, which pitched the pickup like a sailboat in a choppy swell.

Nate said, "It probably doesn't. That's my point. I feel like there are things happening on different levels of reality but all at the same time. We happen to be in the right place at the right time where different levels of conflicts are overlapping."

"What?"

"You should open your mind a little."

"Perhaps."

Both Nate and Joe watched the GPS unit. They knew they were moments away from contact.

"What did you say that area code and telephone number was?" Nate asked, changing the subject. The pickup nose was pointed toward the sky, into a swirl of early-evening stars. When they broke over the rise Joe expected to see the bear. They were that close.

"Nine-one-oh something," Joe said. "Fayetteville, North Carolina. Wherever that is."

Nate laughed. "Here's a guy in the middle of Nowhere, Wyoming, asking where North Carolina is."

"We're just about over the top," Joe said. "Get ready for I don't know what."

"Nine-one-oh," Nate said suddenly. "That's the area code for Fort Bragg. The army base. I spent some time there. Forget Fayetteville, Joe. Think Fort Bragg."

With that, Joe felt another door open. As it did, they topped the hill and looked down on an immense flat basin that was lit up in the moonlight. He saw no bear. But in the center of the basin was a sheep wagon. There was no pickup next to the wagon, only a few white sheep, their backs absorbing the light blue moonlight. The sheep wagon was prototypical of the models that used to be found all over the Rockies: a compact living space mounted on wheels that could be pulled by a long tongue hitch and stationed amid the herds. It was the nineteenth-century precursor to the RV. There was a single door at the rear of the wagon, and a single window over the bunk-shelf near the front. A wood-stove chimney pipe poked out of the rounded top.

Joe stopped and checked the coordinates.

"This doesn't make any sense," Joe said.

"What?" Nate asked.

"We're here. This is where the bear boys said they caught the grizzly's signal. Right here. But I don't see anything besides the wagon and the sheep."

Nate leaned forward, looking back and forth from the GPS display into the basin. "Unless I'm wrong," he said, "our bear is inside that sheep wagon."

Joe turned his head toward Nate. "This is really strange."

Nate nodded.

"Do you have a lot of bullets for that gun?" Joe asked.

Nate arched his eyebrows. "I do. I just hope I don't have to use them."

Joe stopped the truck twenty yards from the sheep wagon. His headlights bathed the door, which appeared to be slightly ajar. There was no light from inside, and no curl of smoke from the chimney.

Nate spoke softly as Joe armed the tranquilizer gun under the glow of the dome light, twisting off the plastic cap from the needle, checking that the dart was filled with 4 cc's of Telazol, inserting the dart into the chamber, and snapping the barrel down on the assembly.

Nate said, "I've read where the methods of working with bears is similar in concept to working with raptors. On a much bigger scale, of course, but it's basically the same program of give-and-take, and mutual respect."

Joe checked over the tranquilizer pistol and found the button which engaged the CO_2 cartridge. He pushed the button and heard a short, angry hiss.

"Nate, are you saying you want to *train* the grizzly?" This was incomprehensible to Joe, not to mention illegal.

"Not at all," Nate said emphatically, "I want to get inside his head, see what makes him tick. Find out what he's thinking and why he came here. And who sent him."

Joe looked at Nate, hoping to see a hint of a smile but Nate was dead serious.

Joe's heart raced as he approached the sheep wagon. Their plan was for Joe to go to the left side of the wagon, the side the door would open up to, and for Nate to take the right. Joe had the tranquilizer gun in one fist and his Mag-Lite flashlight in the other. Once in position, Nate was to slip a cord over the handle of the door and ease it open. Joe would shine his light inside. If the bear was in there, he would shoot it point-blank, aiming for a haunch or shoulder. *Don't hit him in the head,* he told himself. If he missed, the dart could bounce right off.

So here he was, he thought, with his little dart gun and no place to run if things went bad. The sheep in the plain hadn't even looked up to note their presence.

Nate was his insurance policy in this situation. Despite his earlier statements, Nate had agreed that if the bear turned on either one of them Nate would fire. From the other side of the sheep wagon, Joe heard the faint *click-click* of Nate's revolver being cocked.

Joe heard no sound from inside the wagon as he stood next to it. No breathing, no rustling. He could smell a dank, musky odor—a bear.

He peered cautiously around the edge of the wagon and saw Nate slip the cord over the door handle. Slowly, the cord tightened and the door began to open. When a rusty hinge creaked, Joe nearly jumped out of his boots.

Then the door was fully open, and Joe pivoted around the side of the wagon and aimed his flashlight inside. The tranquilizer gun was held parallel to the flashlight.

The sheep wagon was empty.

"All clear," Joe croaked, his voice giving away his fear.

Nate wheeled around the door and looked down the sight of his handgun into the wagon.

"The place has been trashed," Nate said, easing the hammer down and holstering the gun.

Inside, in the naked white light of the flashlight, Joe could see that the table was splintered and the old mattress on the bunk was shredded, with rolls of foam blooming from the tears. The insides of the walls were battered.

Joe stepped up on the trailer hitch and shined his flashlight on the old cooking stove. It showed deep scratches from huge claws, as did the cupboards and shelves.

"He's been here, all right," Joe said. "But where is he now?"

Nate shouldered Joe aside and reached down into the gloom. Joe shined his light down to see what he was after. A battered, sun-faded nylon collar hung from the bent-back steel handle of an ancient icebox. Nate pried it loose and held it up.

Joe said, "He must have snagged his collar on that handle, and ripped it off when he pulled out. But what was he even doing here, going inside a sheep wagon? There are plenty of sheep out there to dine on."

He looked closely at the radio collar, surprised how old it looked. The collars Joe had seen had much smaller radio transmitters. This collar looked like an old model. Perhaps the underfunded bear researchers had had to dig into their storage containers to keep up with demand. No wonder it hadn't worked properly, he thought.

Joe dropped Nate off at the Jeep.

"Thanks for the adventure," Nate said.

"Are you going to follow me out?" Joe asked, before driving away.

Nate slowly shook his head. "I'm going in the other direction, back to the wagon."

"What?"

Nate shrugged. "That bear is close."

"He doesn't even have his collar anymore, Nate," Joe said. "How are you going to find him?"

Nate was silent for a moment. He seemed utterly calm. "I'm going to stay here and let him come to me. I think he'll come when he realizes I mean no harm."

Joe thought about it for a moment. There was no point in arguing, because it wouldn't do any good. Nate hunted for deer and antelope by staking out a spot and "letting the animals come to him." Joe had scoffed when he heard it the first time. He didn't scoff anymore.

"Don't disturb the crime scene, okay? And don't get hurt."

Nate was quiet for a few seconds. "Remember when you asked why the bear trashed the sheep wagon?"

"Yes."

"Maybe he was looking for somebody," Nate said and smiled wickedly.

As Joe made it back onto the highway, he listened to his radio after he called Trey Crump to let him know about the bear collar. His report had caused a firestorm of recrimination and controversy among the elite bear team. They openly doubted his claim that the collar was an old model. Trey promised to send it to them after he received it from Joe. One of the researchers accused another of using old equipment, and the man accused denied it. An argument started. Joe turned down the volume of the radio to a low roar.

He thought about the sheep wagon, the collar, what Nate had said. He thought about Nate out there in the dark, letting the grizzly come to him. And what had Nate meant about different levels of reality? Joe shook the thought off.

Then he remembered the telephone number.

Why not, he thought. He pulled over to the side of the road and found the number in his notebook. Grabbing his cell phone from the dashboard, he keyed the number, then held it to his ear.

It rang four times, then someone picked up.

"Nuss-bomb," a deep voice answered.

"Hello?" Joe said, not understanding.

"Nuss-bomb."

"What? Who is this?"

"NUSS-BOMB!"

"I can't understand you," Joe said, his voice betraying a hint of panic as well as the knowledge that he might have just done something really stupid.

"Nuss. Bomb," the man said patiently.

"Where are you?"

The phone clicked off.

"Damn it!" Joe shouted. What had he done?

He weighed calling again, but decided against it. This might be a matter for the task force. He pulled back on to the road, mentally kicking himself. Stupid, stupid, stupid.

Driving down Bighorn Road to his house, he reconsidered slightly. Why would the man who answered assume he was involved in any kind of investigation? As far as the man on the other end knew, it was a wrong number. Joe hadn't identified himself, or given any indication why he called.

Joe was pleased to see that Maxine was up and excited to see him when he came in the house. She was still white, though.

Sheridan worked on homework on the kitchen table, while Lucy watched television.

"Where's your mom?" he asked.

Sheridan gestured toward his office. The door was closed, which was unusual, and he opened it.

Marybeth sat behind his desk, the glow of the computer monitor making her features look harsh. But when she raised her face, Joe could see she was troubled.

"You've got some messages on the answering machine," she said. "Why don't you take care of those and then come back in here. We need to talk."

27

THE FIRST TELEPHONE MESSAGE was from Sheriff Harvey in Park County.

"We tracked the cell phone number down, Joe. It is leased from Cingular Wireless to a guy named L. Robert Eckhardt, RN, whose last known address is Fort Bragg in North Carolina."

Nate was right about that, Joe thought. He wrote the name down on a legal pad.

Harvey continued, "I'm assuming RN stands for registered nurse. We've got calls down there but we couldn't get much cooperation. One guy we talked to was friendly at first, then he put us on hold and came back and wouldn't say jack-shit. I got the impression he'd been told to stonewall us. We asked the FBI through Portenson to put some heat on them down there, and we should know more tomorrow. I'll give you a call."

The second message was from Robey Hersig: "The APB is out, Joe, but as of six this evening, there are no reports of Cleve Garrett and his traveling road show."

The third was from Sheriff Barnum. His voice was tight with anger. "Pickett, I got a call from Sheriff Harvey in Park

County. He says they may have an angle on somebody, but didn't give much detail." There was a long pause, and Joe pictured Barnum fuming at his desk, trying to keep calm, trying to find the right words to say. Finally, "You need to keep me in the goddamned *loop* here, Mr. Pickett." The telephone was slammed down violently on the other end. Joe saved the messages for later, in case he needed them.

"Done?" Marybeth asked, trying to contain her impatience.

Joe nodded. "Can I grab something to eat first?"

"Sure. There's some cold Wally's Pizza in the refrigerator."

"I haven't eaten since . . ."

"*Go,* Joe."

He returned with the box and a bottle of beer and sat down across from his desk. Except for some condiments, milk, and something old and green wrapped in plastic, the refrigerator was now officially empty. He tried not to let it get to him.

The look on her face shifted his line of thinking immediately. She looked agitated, yet sad. Maybe a little angry. He hoped it wasn't aimed at him.

"You wanted me to find out what I could about Tanner Engineering, and how long ago Tuff Montegue worked for them," Marybeth said, standing up and walking past Joe so she could close the door of his office. "There is a lot of information on them on the Internet. I started with a simple Google search."

Joe listened, eating cold pizza.

"It was really easy to find," she said, her eyes widening. She gestured at a stack of paper she had printed out and placed facedown on the edge of the desk. "Tanner Engineering is an environmental research firm that is contracted by the federal government and a lot of energy companies to assist with environmental impact statements. Their specialty is water-testing—and their most recent clients included all of the big firms drilling for coal-bed methane in Colorado, Montana, and Wyoming—but mainly Wyoming. Especially in the Powder River Basin and here in Twelve Sleep County.

"Once the company does its testing and produces a certified report signed by the primary engineer, who was Mr. Tanner, then the energy company bundles it with all of their paperwork and submits it to all of the state and federal agencies that approve drilling. Without that seal of approval, there's no drilling. If the company finds too many minerals—or salt—in the water, it's a lot harder for the company to get approval to drill. So that certificate is pretty important."

Joe twisted the cap off the bottle of beer, and drank a quarter of it. It was cold and good.

"I called the company down in Austin and talked to their personnel department," she said, and her cheeks flushed. "I sort of told them I was related to Tuff Montegue, which I know I shouldn't have. But I didn't know if they would help me or not."

"Don't worry about it," Joe said, saluting her with the beer bottle. "Good work."

Marybeth beamed a quick smile. "And yes, Tuff was employed by them as a contractor in the spring. He was with a survey crew that resurveyed a property and put the stakes in the ground so that the water-testers could follow up. Tuff worked for them for six weeks."

She was leading to something, Joe could see.

"And . . ." he said.

"When I asked what the property was, the lady in personnel got kind of suspicious. I guess I would, too, but I told her another lie. I told her that Tuff had passed away but that he'd said in the past that the place he was working in meant a lot to him, that he talked about how beautiful it was all the time, so we wanted to spread his ashes there. But we needed to know where exactly he worked."

"That's . . . inventive," Joe said, equally impressed and alarmed by her deceit.

Marybeth shot him an uneasy grin. "The whole time I was talking to her, I was afraid Cam or someone would come into my office and ask what I was doing. Luckily, nobody did.

"Anyway, the woman decided to help me out. I guess she believed me, or else she didn't see how helping me could hurt."

"Yes . . ."

"Joe, it was the Timberline Ranch."

Joe sat up.

"You're probably wondering who hired Tanner Engineering to do the water survey."

"Yes I am, darling," he said, feeling his interior motor start to run.

She took a deep breath, and her eyes closed briefly. Then she opened them: "Logue Country Realty, on behalf of an unnamed client."

Joe whistled, and sat back heavily in the chair. "So what does this mean?"

"I'm not sure, Joe, but it gives me a really bad feeling. And Joe, that's not all."

"What?"

She turned over the sheaf of papers on the desk, and thumbed through it. "On the Tanner Engineering Web site I went to the section on executives, and did a search. They had photos of their top management. There he is."

She slipped a page to Joe. He looked at the photo of Stuart Tanner, CEO and founder. In the photo, Tanner looked to be in his mid-sixties, but was lean and fit. His face looked weathered behind rimless glasses. He looked like a serious man. Joe wondered if Marybeth thought Joe would recognize Tanner from somewhere.

"I saw him, Joe. I talked to him," she said. "He was in the office that Monday when the first mutilated cows were discovered. He had a big file with him that he said he needed to deliver to Cam."

"You're sure it was Stuart Tanner?"

Marybeth nodded her head, somewhat reluctantly. "Yes, it was him. Which means Cam knew him, and maybe Marie did, too. That's fine, of course, but what troubles me is that neither of them ever mentioned it to me. Remember when we were talking about the murders at my mother's dinner? The Logues said nothing about knowing Stuart Tanner. Nothing."

"Of course, we weren't talking about Tanner, we were talking about Tuff," Joe said.

Marybeth leaned forward, now so still and tense that she looked like a snapshot. "Joe, you don't think Cam and Marie . . ."

Joe was silent, thinking.

"We can't rule anything out," Joe said finally. "But I think it's very, very unlikely they had anything to do with the crimes."

Marybeth let out a long breath of relief, but her eyes still had him fixed in their sights.

"That doesn't mean, though, that he didn't see some opportunity in the situation," Joe said. "That he didn't use the circumstances to advance an agenda of his own."

"I can't see it, Joe. I can't see Marie getting involved in something so awful."

Joe drained his beer and wished he had another in front of him. "Didn't you tell me she hasn't been in the office? That she's been sick? Maybe she can't face you anymore, or can't face the situation she's got herself in."

"I should go to her house," she said. "I should talk with her."

Joe held up his hand. "Maybe so. But I'd like to do some checking around before you do. I'll do it first thing in the morning. This thing still doesn't make much sense."

As he looked at her, tears welled in her eyes, and when she blinked the tears coursed down her cheeks.

"Marybeth . . ."

"Damn it," she said. "I liked and trusted them. How could I be so taken in? So blind?"

They both knew the answer to her question.

Joe stood up and went around the desk, and pulled her up and hugged her. She buried her face in his shirt, and he kissed her hair.

Although they were in bed and it was late, Joe could tell that Marybeth wasn't sleeping, and neither was he. He lay with his hands clasped behind his head on the pillow, and he stared at the ceiling. The half-moon outside striped the bed in pale blue coming in through the blinds.

He tried to set all of the other tracks of the case aside and work through what Marybeth had learned.

He wondered if he had been assuming the wrong thing all along by concentrating on Tuff's death instead of Stuart Tanner's. Even though Tuff's death seemed an aberration, maybe it was *intended* to look that way. To steer anyone looking into the crimes toward Tuff, away from Tanner. Maybe Tanner was the key to both murders, not Tuff. Maybe Tuff was killed to draw attention away from Tanner's death.

But who could be so calculated?

In Joe's experience, conspiracies like this simply didn't work out. People talked too much, made too many mistakes, had too many individual motives to keep a secret for long. The coordination of two deaths fifty miles apart in the same night suggested a level of planning and professionalism that just didn't seem likely, he thought. That was why no one even assumed it. The two murders, in the midst of the animal mutilations, were assumed by everyone—including him—to be part of the overall horror. But if someone used the cattle and wildlife mutilations as cover to murder Tanner in the same method, that suggested an icy, devious calculation. And if the killer was capable of that kind of subterfuge, maybe he took it to another level and went after Tuff for no reason other than to mask his true target.

Could it be Cam Logue?

He couldn't see it, although there had always been something about Cam that hadn't felt right to Joe. Cam seemed overeager, a bit too driven. Although both traits were the qualities of successful people, it seemed to Joe that just under the surface Cam seemed a little . . . *desperate*. Whatever drove him was powerful. But could it possibly drive him to murder? Joe didn't think so.

If the report that Tanner had delivered to Cam indicated that the water was bad beneath the surface of the Timberline Ranch, who would be hurt? Cam would, but only to the degree that the ranch likely wouldn't sell and he'd be out of a commission. But Cam had plenty of ranch listings, many larger than the Timberline Ranch.

Cam's secret buyer might be hurt, Joe thought. If the buyer knew that he could never drill, the ranch would be all but worthless. But the buyer wouldn't have had the mineral rights in the first place, since they had been sold off years ago. So why would he care?

Suddenly, Joe felt a spasm in his belly. Realtors didn't work for buyers, Joe thought. *Realtors worked for sellers.* The person—people—who would be hurt by the discovery would be the Overstreet sisters. But could two old, cranky women who hated each other be capable of this? Again, it didn't work, he thought. If the mineral rights didn't go with the property, a bad-water report wouldn't impact the sale to a buyer who wanted a ranch and not a CBM field.

So who was the secret buyer?

Then, as if a dam was breached, more questions poured forward.

Where were Cleve Garrett and Deena?

Who was L. Robert Eckhardt, the owner of the cell phone number, and what was he doing driving forest backroads in Wyoming at 4:30 in the morning?

What in the hell did "*Nuss-Bomb*" mean?

Joe moaned out loud.

"Are you okay, honey?" Marybeth asked sleepily.

"I'm sorry, I was thinking," he said. "I'm giving myself a headache."

"You're giving me one, too," she said.

It was an hour later, and although Joe hadn't come up with any answers, he had thought through a list of places where he might find them. Carefully, he swung out of the bed, trying not to disturb Marybeth.

"I'm not sleeping," she said. "Don't worry about it."

He looked at the clock next to his pillow. It was 3:48 A.M.

She turned over and snapped on the lamp.

"Joe, if the information I got was so easy to find, why didn't the task force do it earlier?"

"We weren't looking into the backgrounds of the victims," Joe said. "We were searching for aliens and birds, or not doing much at all. We were hoping the whole thing would go away, I think."

"That's . . ." she hesitated, then her eyes flashed, "that's *in-excusable*."

Joe nodded, "Yup."

"Aren't you cold standing there in your underwear?"

"I can't sleep. I was going to get up and make a list of things to do in the morning."

She looked at the clock. "It's practically morning now. Why don't you come to bed?"

"Can't," he said. "I'm too edgy. Every time I close my eyes, a million things charge at me and I can't stop any of 'em."

"What if I make it worth your while?" she said and smiled.

He hesitated, but not for long.

When they were through, Joe rolled over onto his back.

"Sorry," he said. "I couldn't concentrate."

"You did fine," she purred.

28

THE COUNTY CLERK'S OFFICE was located in the same building as the courtroom, jail, sheriff's office, and attorney. A man named Stovepipe manned the reception desk and metal detector, and he nodded at Joe and waived him through at 7:45 A.M.

"You're up early this morning," Stovepipe said, lowering the morning edition of the *Saddlestring Roundup*. Joe noted the headline: HERSIG SAYS NO PROGRESS IN MUTILATION DEATHS.

"Still broken?" Joe asked about the metal detector.

Stovepipe nodded. "Don't tell nobody, though."

"I never do. Is Ike in yet?"

"They don't open until eight, but I think I seen him come in earlier."

Ike Easter's glass-walled office was behind the counter where Twelve Sleep County citizens lined up daily to do business with the three matronly clerks who sat on tall stools and called out "NEXT!" Most of the business transactions involved titles on automobiles and property. This was also the place to get marriage licenses, so the clerks who worked for Ike Easter were among the better informed gossips in the county, and much sought after when they got their hair done.

When Joe opened the door to the main office, all three of the matronly clerks wheeled on their stools and glared at him. It was easily one of the most unwelcome receptions he had ever received, he thought. One of the clerks quickly raised an open palm to him as he entered. "Sir, we're not open for fifteen minutes," she said. "Please take a seat in the hall and . . ."

"I'm here to see Ike," Joe said flatly, ignoring her, and went through the batwing doors on the side of the counter.

"Sir . . ." The clerk was irritated.

"It's okay, Millie," Ike called out from his office when he saw Joe coming.

"I forgot about your elite Republican Guard," Joe smiled, stopping outside Ike's office and tipping his hat toward Millie. Millie huffed melodramatically. To Ike: "Do you have a few minutes? It's important."

Ike motioned Joe in, and Joe shut the door behind him.

"I'll ignore the Republican Guard comment," Ike said, not unpleasantly, "but they won't. Next time you need a new title for your car, expect delays."

Joe sat in a hardback chair across from Ike. "Unfortunately, it'll be a while before we get a new car."

"All my clerks are county employees," Ike said. "They work eight hours a day and not one minute longer. They take an hour for lunch and get two fifteen-minute breaks. If you woke one of them up in the middle of the night, she could tell you to the hour how long she has until retirement, how many days of sick leave she's got left this fiscal year, and to the penny what her pension will be. Those women keep me in a constant state of absolute fear."

Ike had a smooth, milk-chocolate face and wore large-framed glasses. He had a silver mustache and his receding hair was also going gray. Like his cousin, Not Ike, Ike was quick to smile and had dark, expressive eyes. He had been reading the newspaper as well, and it lay flat on his desk, opened to the page where the NO PROGRESS IN MUTILATION DEATHS front-page story was continued inside.

"Before you ask me whatever it is you're going to ask me, can I say one thing?" Ike said.

"Sure."

"Thank you for being so kind to my cousin, George. I know he gives you fits with all of those temporary licenses and all."

Joe grunted, and looked down.

"I've tried and tried to get him to get a yearly license," Ike said, "but I just can't break through to him. It's very generous of you to ease up on him a bit, Joe. I know you don't have to do that. His life is fly-fishing, and I figure as long as he's fishing he's not getting himself into any other kind of trouble."

"Okay, Ike, gotcha."

"But I do appreciate it, Joe. Both Dorothy and I are grateful."

"*Okay,* Ike. Enough," Joe said.

"So, what do you want from me so early in the morning?"

Joe looked up. "How do mineral rights work?"

Ike's eyes narrowed, and he paused. "Let me get another cup of coffee. This will take a few minutes."

Ike Easter used a legal pad to explain. He started out by writing "OG&M" on the top of the pad.

"When I say 'OG&M,' I'm referring to oil, gas, and mineral rights. They're usually sold for a term on a specific piece of land, or they can be retained by the landowner. If the OG&M are sold, it usually means that the developer pays the landowner a fee for the rights or, in some cases, a percentage of the gross that is derived if the OG&M is exploited."

Joe asked, "Are they like water rights?"

Ike shook his head. "No. Water rights go with the land. That means if you sell your land to somebody, the buyer gets your water rights. You don't keep them and lease them back, and you can't sell them separately to somebody else downstream or upstream.

"OG&M rights, however, can be bought and sold among companies or developers, or eventually returned to the land-owner if the terms of the sale run out."

Ike explained how the market for mineral rights in Wyoming peaked in the mid-twentieth century, during the boom years for oil, trona, coal, and uranium. Some landowners made much more from their mineral rights than they ever made from their cattle or sheep.

"Up until recently, we had almost forgotten about all of the intrigue and wheeling and dealing that gets done for mineral rights," Ike said. "I had a clerk here who didn't know what in the hell to do when some land man with a Texas accent walked into the office and wanted to file. But we all got back into the rhythm of it soon enough."

"Because of CBM?" Joe asked.

"Yes, because of CBM. See, no one realized after the last oil bust that natural gas was down there in the kind of quantity it is. Suddenly, all of those fields that everyone thought were played out or useless were valuable again. Quite a few of the ranches had changed hands since their first leases or sales, and some of the new landowners didn't even know that other people owned their OG&M rights. A lot of the squawking we all heard from ranchers bitching about the CBM companies on their land was because those ranchers discovered that the mineral rights had been sold years before."

Joe tried to work it through. "So even if a ranch sells, the mineral rights stay with whoever had them?"

"Right."

"The Timberline Ranch, for example, has six hundred wells planned for it. Those rights are owned by a mineral company, I assume, even though when they bought the rights they had never heard of coal-bed methane?"

"Right."

Joe rubbed his face. He was missing something. The incentive to sell, or buy, or manipulate the land value, wasn't there.

"Why would a company buy mineral rights to a ranch when they didn't know what was in the ground?" Joe asked.

Ike shrugged, "It happened—and happens—all the time, Joe. Companies speculate. They lock up land, betting that somewhere down the road their investment will pay off."

"Can I see the OG&M deed for the Timberline Ranch in the county record books?" Joe asked. "It would be interesting to know who has the mineral rights to the place. My understanding is that old man Overstreet sold the rights a long time ago."

"Of course you can," Ike said. "It's a public record. But it might be a bitch to find right away."

"Isn't it all on computer?"

Ike laughed. "Not hardly, Joe. The most recent stuff is, of course. But anything older than ten years was indexed in deed books. Anything beyond twenty-five years is in the archives, but completely disorganized. There was a flood in the vault back then, and the deed books all got soaked. Because all of those old deeds and patents were typed on parchment paper, somebody emptied the books and put them into files after they dried out. They never were put back into new books in sequential order."

"I'd still like to see it," Joe said.

"May I ask why?" Ike said, lowering his voice.

Joe sighed. "It may be relevant to a sale of the place. Or a murder."

"Really?"

"This is purely speculation on my part, Ike," Joe said. "Please keep this confidential."

Ike got up and opened his door. "Millie, can you please find and pull the OG&M file for the Timberline Ranch? Owned by the Overstreet sisters?"

Millie reluctantly got down from her stool, and gave Joe a look as she walked by.

"Why'd you ask *her*?" Joe said in a whisper.

Ike smiled sympathetically. "She's been assigned to the archives, Joe. She's the only one who can find any of that old stuff. We're in the process of going through all of the old county files—which were kept off-site in file boxes for over fifty years—and bringing them in-house to recreate the old deed index books."

"I heard something about that," Joe said. "How the old county clerk charged the county rent for storage in his own house."

"Um-hmmm," Ike said, raising his eyebrows. The scandal was one of the reasons Ike Easter was elected county clerk.

"We think we've recovered all of the old records," he said, "but every few months we find another box or two. The old county clerk had them in his basement, in bedrooms, and even in a couple of old locked garages in town."

While they waited, Ike asked Joe questions about the Murder and Mutilations Task Force, and the story in the newspaper. Joe confirmed that there was very little progress, but said that some things appeared to be emerging, although he couldn't get into them.

"Hold it," Joe said suddenly, looking at Ike.

"What?"

"The old county clerk's residence, where the old records were kept—that's where Cam and Marie Logue live now, isn't it?"

"Yes."

"Would Cam and Marie have had access to the boxes?"

Ike thought about it for a moment. "I suppose they would have. The boxes were sealed up with tape, but they weren't locked up or anything. Why do you ask?"

"It's just interesting," Joe said.

Finally, Millie returned to Ike's office, wiping her hands with a wet towel.

"Those old boxes are filthy," she said, glaring at Joe.

"Did you find the file?" Ike asked, even though she wasn't carrying anything.

She shook her head. "It must be in one of those boxes we've still got in storage. It hasn't been brought up to the filing room yet."

Ike groaned, thanked her, and waited for the door to close.

He told Joe, "We've got twenty or more boxes downstairs in the boiler room that still need to be brought up and gone through."

"How quickly can you do it?"

Ike said, "Are you serious?"

"Yup."

"Joe, I want to help you out and all, but can you at least give me a better reason so I can justify the overtime hours and feel good about it when the elite Republican Guard turns on me?"

Joe leaned forward on Ike's desk. "As I mentioned, I think that the murders have something to do with either the potential sale of the Timberline Ranch or the mineral rights. I think if we know who holds the rights, we might know who ordered—or did—the killings."

Ike swallowed. "Even the cows?" he asked.

"Maybe not the cows, but Tuff Montegue and Stuart Tanner."

"And you feel pretty confident about this?"

Joe sat back and rubbed his face. "Kind of," he confessed.

Joe found Robey Hersig in his office reading the *Roundup* and looking very sour.

"Tell me something good, Joe."

Joe sat down and recapped what he knew and suspected. Hersig grew increasingly interested, and began to take notes. When Joe was through, Hersig steepled his fingers and pressed them against the bridge of his nose.

"We don't have enough to arrest anyone yet, or even bring them in for questioning," Hersig said.

"I know."

"So what's your next step?"

"I'm going to go see Cam Logue."

Hersig winced. "It might be too soon."

"Maybe so. But it might break something loose. Or," Joe said, "Cam may blow my whole theory out of the water."

Robey sat for several moments, thinking things through. "What can I do to help?"

"A few things," Joe said. "Intensify the search for Cleve Garrett. We've got to find him and make sure the girl's okay. I can't see him just blowing out of town like he did, after wanting to get so involved with the task force. Then follow up with Sheriff Harvey and Deputy Cook. They've already involved Portenson, so maybe we can find out more about this Eckhardt guy. I don't know how or if Fort Bragg figures in, but Cook said he thought the army was stonewalling him when he called. Maybe if they heard from you, or the governor, we'd get some answers. Oh, and check up with Ike to see if they've located that Timberline Ranch file."

"I can do all of that," Hersig said, writing it down on the pad. "But you're forgetting somebody. What about Barnum?"

"Keep him the hell out of it," Joe said.

"Joe . . ."

"It's not just about this thing between Barnum and me," Joe said. "Barnum seems more hostile than usual. He called me at my house and all but warned me off of this thing. I think he's involved in some way, Robey."

Hersig slapped his desktop angrily. "Joe, do you realize what you're saying?"

Joe nodded. "Don't get me wrong. I don't think Barnum had anything to do with the mutilations or the murders. I think he's playing another angle, but I don't know what it is yet. Somehow, I think he's taking advantage of the situation."

Hersig stared at Joe, still upset. "I can't lie to him, Joe. He's the sheriff."

"But you can just sort of withhold information, can't you? Not return his calls? Just for the rest of the day and maybe to-morrow?"

Hersig shook his head. "Do you think we're that close?"

"I think we're close to something," Joe said, standing and clamping on his hat. "I just don't know what it is yet."

Hersig gave a low moan.

As Joe opened the door, Hersig called out to him.

"Give Cam my regards," Hersig said. "And call me the minute you know something."

29

I T FELT ODD, Joe thought, entering the front office of Logue Country Realty. In a few hours, Marybeth would be there.

Marie wasn't at the front desk, as she usually was. In her place was a thin, blond woman who pursed her lips, whom Joe caught reading a supermarket tabloid. She was the only person in Saddlestring, he thought with some relief, who wasn't aware that there was NO PROGRESS IN MUTILATION DEATHS.

"Is Marie still sick?" Joe asked.

"I guess so," the woman said. "All I know is that the temp agency called and asked me to come in again."

"Is Cam here?"

"May I ask your name?"

"Joe Pickett."

The temp hesitated and looked puzzled for a moment, as if she had heard the name but couldn't place it.

"My wife, Marybeth, works here," Joe said.

"Ah," the temp said. "She seems nice."

"She *is* nice," Joe said, impatience creeping in. "But I'm here to see Cam."

The temp looked at her wristwatch. "He usually comes in around nine, I think."

Joe glanced at his own watch. Ten to nine. "I'll wait in his office."

The temp wasn't sure if this was appropriate, but Joe strode by her as if he waited for Cam every day, and she said nothing.

J oe sat in a chair across from Cam's desk, and put his hat on the chair next to him. This would be interesting, he thought. He planned to watch Cam carefully as he asked him questions, and listen even more carefully. Joe dug his microrecorder out of his front shirt pocket, checked the cassette, and pushed the record button, then buttoned his pocket. By Wyoming law, the tape would be admissible in court, even if Cam wasn't aware he was being recorded.

Joe surveyed the office. Neat stacks of paper lined the credenza in columns. A large-scale map of Twelve Sleep County covered an entire wall in the room. Cam's realtor and insurance licenses were framed behind his desk, as were large portraits of Marie and Jessica, and several family photos of them all. There was a Twelve Sleep County Chamber of Commerce "Businessperson of the Year" plaque, as well as a photo of a boys' soccer team Cam obviously coached, signed by all of the players. On Cam's desk was a coffee cup that read "World's Greatest Dad." There was a "Volunteer of the Year" award from the United Way. *Jeez,* Joe thought. *What am I doing here?*

Cam entered his office a few moments later, without a hint of trepidation. He asked how Joe was with concerned sincerity, and if he wanted a cup of coffee.

Joe passed on the coffee, but stood and shook Cam's extended hand and returned a half-smile. Joe thought he detected a flash of discomfort in Cam's eyes as he shook Joe's hand, but wouldn't swear to it. Then Joe thought, *If I made a pass at a man's wife and the husband showed up in my office unannounced, I might be more than a little jittery too.*

Cam asked, "What can I do you for, Joe?" in a forced,

too-cheerful way, and sat in his big, leather chair across the desk from Joe. "I do have a meeting in twenty minutes, so I hope . . ."

"Shouldn't take that long," Joe said. "How's Marie?"

Again, the flash of discomfort, or maybe fear. Then it was gone. "Marie?" Cam said almost absently. Then: "I'm sorry, I guess Marybeth must have told you. Marie's had some kind of a bug for over a week that just won't go away. She has *not* been a happy camper."

"Is there anything we can do?" Joe asked.

Cam seemed to be thinking about it, then he shook his head. "That's a really nice offer, Joe. But she seems to be just about back to normal, now. I wouldn't be surprised if she came back to work this afternoon. Tomorrow for sure, I'll bet."

"Well, good," Joe said. "But don't hesitate to ask. Marybeth thinks the world of Marie."

"Yes, Marie and Marybeth have a great relationship, which is wonderful. Really wonderful," Cam said, agreeing enthusiastically. *Too enthusiastically,* Joe thought. But was Cam's nervousness because of what he had said to Marybeth, or something else?

"Cam, you know about the task force I'm on," Joe said, watching Cam's face carefully. "The investigation isn't going quite as badly as what you might have read in the paper this morning. We're pursuing some new leads."

Cam's eyebrows arced. He was interested.

"One of them involves you."

Cam seemed to freeze in place. Even his breathing stopped. His tanned face drained of color.

"Say again?" Cam asked, his voice a whisper.

"We're pursuing everything, even if it turns out to be a dead end," Joe said. "I'm here to ask you a couple of questions, if you don't mind."

Cam was clearly shaken. Joe tried to interpret it, but couldn't decide if Cam was displaying guilt, or shock.

"I guess I don't mind," Cam said. "Jesus. I can't believe you're even *here.* I can't believe you could even think . . ."

"Why did you think I was here?" Joe asked innocently, but the implication was clear. *Now you've done it,* Joe said to himself. *Whatever the Logues and the Picketts had together is now over. Marybeth and Marie. Lucy and Jessica. Maybe even Marybeth's future career. You've done it now, Joe, and there's no going back.*

"Gee, I guess I thought maybe it was because Marybeth and I had a misunderstanding a while back," Cam said, looking at his hands and not at Joe. "But I think she thought I meant something I didn't. That was bad enough. But to have you here saying I'm being investigated . . ." he trailed off.

Joe sat in silence, letting Cam talk.

"Should I call a lawyer?" Cam asked. "Is it that bad?"

"Only you can answer that," Joe said. Man, he felt cruel.

Cam still didn't meet Joe's eye, but reached for his telephone. Joe noticed that the man's hand was shaking.

"Please cancel my 9:30," Cam told the temp, then listened for a moment. "No, I don't want to reschedule it right now." When he replaced the receiver, it rattled in the cradle.

"What do you want to ask me, Joe?"

Joe thought that Cam looked just about as pathetic—or guilty—as anyone he had ever seen. He was either about to nail a killer, or make a horrible, unforgivable mistake.

"Cam, we have a theory that the murders of Tuff Montegue and Stuart Tanner were connected. We think there is a possibility that they were killed because of something they—or one of them—knew about the sale of the Timberline Ranch."

"You're kidding me," Cam said. The flash in his eyes this time was of anger.

Joe plowed on: "I think Stuart Tanner was going to nix the drilling of all of the CBM wells because there was too much salinity in the water. Or maybe he found something else, like silica or something. His report would cost some people a hell of a lot of money. The company that holds the mineral rights would be out millions, and the realtor who didn't get his commission would be out thousands. I think somebody wanted him dead, and saw the opportunity to kill him in the same method as the cattle and the moose."

Joe tried to make his face and eyes go dead. "So who is the secret buyer, Cam?"

Slowly, the color returned to Cam Logue's face, and kept going. Now his face was turning red.

"Joe, I can't believe you just said that to me. You're so goddamned off base." Cam said it with enough passion that Joe nearly flinched.

"You knew Stuart Tanner," Joe said. "You hired him. He delivered the water report to you personally, right in this office. But when the news came out that he died, you said nothing. You didn't report it to the sheriff, or even mention it to me."

"You're right about that," Cam said, his voice back to normal. "You're absolutely right. I got the report, and I knew the guy. I paid Tanner Engineering for his work. And damn it, I didn't say anything because given the current market, the less said about any of this shit the better. Hell, Joe, I can't even sell a ranch with a willing buyer and a willing seller. Everybody's waiting for your stupid task force to make a conclusion, or arrest somebody. But I can see why you're getting nowhere, if this is the best you can do. If all you can come up with is to target a guy who's made a huge commitment to this community."

Cam looked up and shook his head. He was upset, and visibly tried to calm himself. "Joe, there's a couple of things really wrong with your theory, and it pisses me off that you would be going in this direction."

"What's that?" Joe asked.

"First, Tanner Engineering cleared the way for the CBM drilling. The water is fine."

Cam turned quickly in his chair and dug through one of the neat stacks of paper on his credenza. He produced an inch-thick report bound in plastic, and tossed it across the desk. Joe picked it up and thumbed through it until he found the summary page.

"Tanner concluded that there was no excess salinity, or anything else in that water," Cam said. "The water's good, Joe. It's perfect. It's the best damned water in the Twelve Sleep Valley."

Joe read enough to see that Cam was right.

"Second," Cam said, his voice rising, "the secret client is me. And Sheriff Barnum."

Joe was stunned. *"What?"* So this is where Barnum figured in, he thought.

Cam stood quickly, sending his chair to roll back until it thumped against the credenza. He glared down at Joe.

"Barnum's a year away from retirement, and he's got one *hell* of a pension after twenty-five-plus years as sheriff," Cam said. "He planned to borrow against it for a down payment on 360 acres of the ranch we'd buy together. He wants to retire on it. But with all of this bullshit going on, the bank's been holding back. It's only temporary, but they're dragging it out. I've always wanted the family ranch back. I grew up there, Joe. It's my dream, Marie's and my dream. We couldn't say anything, even to Marybeth."

"You want it even with all of those CBM wells all over it?" Joe asked.

Cam shrugged. "They won't be there forever. And they're bound by law to clean up when they're gone."

"But that could be thirty years."

Cam smiled, but not warmly. "I'm willing to wait. Land is always a good investment. Especially the land I grew up on and still love."

Joe felt as though he had had the rug, the floor, and the joists pulled out from under him.

"How in the hell are you going to buy it?" Joe asked.

Cam's eyes lit up. "Okay, since you're asking, since you've spent a good deal of the morning trying to fuck up my life, I'll tell you."

Joe winced at that.

"Real estate sales is sizzle, Joe. It's flash and sizzle. If the market is hot, the realtor is hot. Everybody wants to work with a winner, and that's me. Once I listed the Timberline Ranch, the landowners around here figured that if I could get a couple of old crones like the Overstreet sisters to sign, then I must be hot shit indeed. As you know, we now have exclusive listings on just about every available ranch in this part of Northern

Wyoming. I did it by hard work, Joe, and by creating the sizzle of a winner."

Joe still felt pole-axed. "You figured a couple of the other ranches would sell first. That you could use the commission money from those other ranches for the down payment on the Timberline Ranch."

Cam opened his eyes in an exaggerated way, as if he were addressing a simpleton. "*Right,* Joe. There's not a single thing wrong with that. Not a single thing."

"But no property is selling, because of the mutilations," Joe said.

"Right again, Joe. Exactly what I've been telling you for a month. Nothing's selling because buyers think this county is spooked."

"Man," Joe said.

But Cam was on a roll. "Do you know who I'm not going to invite to the ranch when I finally own it?"

Joe didn't guess.

"My parents, Joe. Mom and Dad. The people who sold my birthright out from under me so they could devote more time and attention to sending my big brother, Eric, to medical school. You thought I was going to say you and Marybeth, didn't you?"

Joe looked up.

"Well, I probably won't invite you out, either. Not now." Cam's eyes had a fiendish intensity.

Despite feeling bad, feeling stupid, Joe caught a whiff of something in the air from Cam. It was the desperation he had recalled earlier, the over-the-top intensity that seemed a notch or two higher than it needed to be.

"Some day, all of you people are going to regret the way you treated Cam Logue," Cam said, his voice dropping but his face screwed up with rage. "You sit around and come up with some lunatic idea that it must be the new guy in town, it must be the guy who just moved here who's upsetting the sleepy little village by working his ass off and being aggressive."

"It wasn't like that," Joe said lamely.

Cam leaned across his desk, thrusting his face forward. "I

know what it's like, Joe. I remember what you people are like, and I don't forget. I remember you all looking down at the ground when we left this place. You wouldn't even say good-bye when I stood there with my stupid parents as they drove around this town and canceled their utilities, and their post office box, and got the transcripts from my school."

We didn't even live here then, Joe said to himself but not to Cam. Joe simply watched and listened.

"You people never even thought about me at all, trying to go to a school in South Dakota that was half-Indian and half-white and all fucked up. If anything, you wondered about my brother, the genius, the future doctor who would make my parents so proud. You wanted to be able to tell people you remembered when he was a student here, going to sixth grade when he should have been in third grade, winning all of those science contests. If only you knew . . ."

Suddenly, Cam stopped.

"Talking too much," Cam said, more to himself than to Joe.

He lumped back into his chair, staring at something over Joe's head, looking drained.

"I'm truly sorry, Cam."

No response.

"I screwed up," Joe said. "I came up with a conclusion and tried to find facts that would fit it, instead of the other way around." Putting his hat on his head, Joe stood up.

Cam still sat there, eerily drained, his concentration elsewhere.

"Cam?"

Joe thought that Cam was somewhere deep inside of himself now. What had he done?

"CAM!"

Thankfully, Cam Logue seemed to snap back to the present. He blinked rapidly, then his eyes settled on Joe.

"I'll be going," Joe said.

Cam nodded. "Okay."

Joe started to turn, then stopped himself. "Do you have any ideas on what's happening, Cam? With the mutilations and the murders? We obviously don't even have a clue."

Cam shook his head wearily.

"We've got bears, aliens, all sorts of bad ideas," Joe said. "Hell, somebody even claims he saw a couple of figures out in the alley behind your office a while back."

Joe was surprised that Cam's face blanched again, as it had when he first saw Joe.

"Who said that?" Cam asked.

Joe shrugged. "That's not important. My point was about all of the crazy theories."

"Tell me who said it."

"Cam, I'm sorry, I've got to go now. I'm sorry I took up so much of your time."

Cam stared at Joe and set his mouth.

"I really am sorry about all of this, Cam."

In his pickup, Joe thumped the steering wheel with the heel of his hand. He had been so wrong, he thought.

He called Hersig, who answered anxiously.

"You should take me off the task force," Joe said morosely. "I don't know what the hell I'm doing."

"Dry hole?" Hersig asked.

"Wrong county, even. Not even close."

Hersig sighed. "We're going to have to mend some fences with the business community after this."

"Worse than that, Robey, I've got to tell Marybeth."

Joe found her in her tiny back office at Barrett's Pharmacy. She looked up expectantly as he came in.

"I was wrong about Cam."

"Tell me."

He did, her face hardening as he spoke.

"Why did you come down on him so tough, Joe?"

He shrugged. "I thought it was the best way. I thought I could shock him into saying something."

"Well, I guess you did that all right."

He shook his head and stared at the tops of his boots. "I feel terrible."

"Don't."

He looked up, puzzled.

"It sounds like a hell of a performance," she said.

"I know, I just thought if I laid it right out . . ."

"No," she said, shushing him. "Not by you. By Cam. There's something there, Joe. I just know it. There's no good reason why Cam and Marie wouldn't have told me about getting back the ranch. They know I'd keep it confidential, and what difference would it make anyway? Marie and I shared everything, Joe. We talked about both you and Cam, and we talked about our children and our aspirations. Believe me, if Marie knew about Cam's plan to buy back that ranch, she would have told me about it. When Cam told us together about the 'secret buyer,' he was misleading Marie as well. Why would he go out of his way to do that?

"So, he's lying to you. Besides, there's nothing wrong with a realtor wanting to buy property. Realtors do it all the time."

Joe felt a wave of relief for a moment.

"But I sabotaged your career."

She smiled. "If I wanted a career, Joe, I'd have it. And I'd be damned good at it. Even now, without the Logues, my small business is chugging along. I just need to keep it small, I know now. More flexible. I've got to think about Sheridan, and Lucy, and you."

"Marybeth, I . . ."

"It's just another setback. No one said this would be easy."

Joe felt awful. "I wish I were as tough as you are," he said.

She smiled again, and pinched his cheek. "You're better than tough, Joe. You're good. I'll stick with good."

30

HIS MIND AND EMOTIONS ON EDGE, Joe spent the rest of the morning patrolling the breaklands and foothills close to town, checking hunters for licenses. He did his job mechanically, his thoughts elsewhere. The few hunters in the field were clean, and in every camp someone asked him about the mutilations. He found himself getting irritated with the entire subject.

Throughout the morning, he checked messages on his cell phone and home telephone, hoping to hear from Hersig, Ike, or Sheriff Harvey.

He decided to push things along, if for no other reason than to see if anyone pushed back, or panicked. He'd start at the county clerk's.

Ike Easter, Millie, and the two other clerks were assembled around a conference table covered with dozens of old file boxes and stacks of files that smelled of age and dampness when Joe entered the county clerk's office.

If his reception that morning was cold, this time it was something out of the Ice Age. The three clerks and Ike had hard scowls and dirt-smudged clothing.

"There he is," Millie said as Joe let the door wheeze shut behind him.

"Here I am," Joe said, looking at Ike. "Find it?"

Ike looked harried. Joe suspected that Ike had been abused for most of the day by his clerks as they searched the archives.

"Good timing," Ike said to Joe, raising a file into the air. "I've got something for you, but it's kind of a puzzlement."

Joe followed Ike into his office.

"Thanks for your hard work," Joe told the clerks as he passed them. "We really appreciate this."

Millie held his gaze for a moment, then rolled her eyes heavenward.

Ike fell into his chair and pushed the file across the desk to Joe. Joe noted that the tab on the file said "Overstreet" and was followed by the physical coordinates of the tract.

"Take a look," Ike said.

Joe opened the file. Inside was a clean copy of a deed and title originally made out to Mr. Walter Overstreet in 1921. An amendment was added in 1970, when additional acreage—the Logue property—was added to the document. Joe thumbed through the paperwork, then looked up at Ike for some kind of interpretation.

"Everything's there and in perfect order," Ike said. "Except for two things. One, there's no record of the OG&M. It should have been attached to the document. Second, it's a duplicate of the original deed."

Joe shook his head. "What's that mean?"

Ike shrugged. "As far as the OG&M lease goes, that could just be an error. We find plenty of those in these old files. It's not that big of a problem, because I can request a copy from the state easy enough . . ."

"How soon?"

Ike looked at his watch, mumbled "they'll kill me," before calling Millie on the intercom and asking her to contact

Cheyenne ASAP and have them fax a copy of the lease to the office. Joe didn't even turn around to see what kind of furor Ike's request had set in motion.

"What else?" Joe asked.

"Look at the deed in your hands, Joe."

Joe did. He saw nothing unusual about it. It had been typed, probably with a manual typewriter, on a deed form decades before. He looked at the dates and description and could see no alterations.

"It's a clean copy of the original," Ike said. "It's all pretty and nice. It's not a carbon copy, which is what they used in those days. It's a modern machine copy."

Joe felt a twitch in his scalp. "So somebody made the copy recently."

"That's what it looks like to me. The copy was made while it was still in the archives, for some reason, and the file was put back in the old box. We probably wouldn't have ever even noticed it if we weren't looking for this particular file on this particular day."

Joe looked up. "How many people had access to the archives, then?"

Ike raised his eyebrows. "All of us. The sheriff's deputies who transferred them. The old county clerk, of course. And the new owners of the old county clerk's home, where the files were kept."

"Cam Logue," Joe said. "And the sheriff."

"Maybe," Ike said, "but there's no crime here. There's nothing wrong with making a copy of a deed."

"What about taking the mineral rights lease terms?" Joe asked.

"Also not a crime," Ike said. "Why do you ask?"

A s Joe got up to leave, he asked Ike to call him on his cell phone as soon as the fax from Cheyenne showed up. Ike followed him to the door.

Joe thanked the clerks again, and one of them actually smiled back.

"Joe, can I ask you a favor?" Ike said.

"Of course."

"It's going to take me a while to get the office cleaned up after all of this." He gestured to the table and the boxes. "I was going to give George a ride home from where he's fishing on the river. Would you mind taking him to the house?"

"Not a problem, Ike. I'm headed that way now."

Ike smiled, and looked over at his shoulder at the clerks, as if assessing the threat before returning to battle.

31

MARYBETH DIDN'T GO TO WORK at Logue Realty that afternoon, assuming she was no longer employed, and she felt guilty about it. She hated to leave a job unfinished, even if it were for someone like Cam.

When she was through for the day at Barrett's Pharmacy, she used the telephone on the desk to call Logue Country Realty, and she asked for Cam. The temporary receptionist said Cam was out for the rest of the day.

"Is he on his cell phone?" Marybeth asked.

"He didn't say anything about that," the temp said. "He seemed a little mad about something, so I didn't even bring it up."

"Can you please put me through to his voice mail, then?"

After fumbling with the telephone system, the temp figured it out.

Marybeth listened to Cam's recorded greeting, then spoke softly. "Cam, I talked with Joe about what happened and I'm sure we'll both agree that it's best if you find another book-keeper. I just hope this won't affect the friendship between Lucy and Jessica. I hope we can both be better parents than that."

Marybeth paused. "And I hope Marie and I can still be friends. But you don't need to give this message to her. I'll go see her myself."

She hung up. After all, Marybeth thought, she now had the afternoon off.

Marybeth bought a quart of chicken noodle soup from the Burg-O-Pardner and chocolates from Barrett's Pharmacy and drove through downtown to the Logues'. This time, she anticipated the pickup and camper with the South Dakota plates, and swerved around it and parked near the front door. The house, she thought, looked lifeless, even though she knew there were people inside.

Carrying the bag with the soup and the chocolates, she rang the doorbell. She didn't hear it chime hollowly inside the house.

After a minute with no response, she rang it again. It was strange, she thought. She didn't hear rustling inside, or footfalls in response to the bell.

She knocked and waited, then knocked again hard.

Nothing.

Putting the bag down on the front step, she walked around the front of the house to the side. The garage door was closed, so she couldn't see if Marie's car was there. Maybe, Marybeth thought, Marie had taken her father- and mother-in-law somewhere for lunch. But Marie was supposed to be sick.

Maybe Marie was at the doctor's office, Marybeth reasoned, and for a moment her mood lightened. But if Marie went to the doctor, would she have taken her in-laws with her?

Puzzled, Marybeth found an envelope in the glove compartment of her van and scribbled a note to Marie, saying she was sorry she missed her and hoped she was feeling better. She wrote, "Please call me when you can." Marybeth left the note with the soup and chocolates on the front porch.

As she returned to the van, Marybeth took a last look at the house. Upstairs, in the second window to the right, she thought she saw a curtain move.

Marybeth stood stock-still, not breathing, and stared at the window. She felt a chill, despite the warm fall afternoon. But the curtain didn't move again, and she wondered if she had imagined it in the first place.

Then she had another thought: maybe Cam had already talked to Marie, told her what Joe had accused him of. Maybe, she thought with unexpected shame, Marie didn't want any part of Marybeth Pickett anymore.

32

THE WYOMING GAME AND FISH DEPARTMENT had a successful program where the department leased land from ranchers in exchange for allowing public access for hunters. Joe had negotiated most of the deals in his district the spring before, and it was his responsibility to keep the "walk-in areas" clearly marked. Unfortunately, the brutal winter before had damaged and knocked down a number of the signs, and as he patrolled he was constantly finding the upturned signs. When he found them, he rewired them to posts from a roll of baling wire in the back of his truck.

He was twisting the wire tight on a walk-in sign when he heard his cell phone ring in his pickup. He leaned inside the cab and plucked the phone from its holder.

It wasn't Hersig, Ike, or Sheriff Harvey. It was Agent Tony Portenson.

"I tried your office but you weren't there," Portenson said as a greeting. He sounded weary, reluctant. "I'd rather this conversation was on a landline so it was more secure."

"You FBI guys are a little paranoid, aren't you?" Joe asked.

"Listen," Portenson said. "We might have something."

"Go ahead. Thanks for getting involved."

"Fuck that," he said. "I just want to get this thing over with so I can go home. Get transferred, maybe. I hope."

"Anyway . . ." Joe prompted.

"Anyway, the Park County Sheriff's Office asked me to help them track down this Fort Bragg cell phone guy, as you know. It wasn't easy, and it should have been. This is what we're good at, you know."

Joe listened and watched the shadow of a single cumulous cloud move slowly across the sagebrush saddle in front of him.

"I had to call in the big guns in Washington to put pressure on the army down there to break through the wall at Fort Bragg. They just didn't want to talk. But we found out some interesting things. Just a second here . . ."

Joe heard papers being shuffled in the background.

"L. Robert Eckhardt was an army nurse. A real good one, according to his early evaluations. He was a combat guy. He was deployed in Bosnia, Afghanistan, and the Philippines. But he didn't go to Iraq. You want to know why?"

"Yes," Joe answered impatiently.

"This is why the army didn't want to talk to us," Portenson continued. "Eckhardt was suspected of being involved in the 'surgical mutilation' of enemy combatants. That's what it says here, 'surgical mutilation.' Some doctor was accused of it, and Eckhardt was his assistant. The whole incident was kept way under the radar, I guess, like a lot of things are in the war. It was an internal army investigation, and there's no press on it at all. These guys, the doctor and Eckhardt, were pulled out of the Philippines and sent home to Fort Bragg a year and a half ago to face court-martial."

Joe stared the cloud as he considered the information. "Does the report say what the mutilation consisted of?"

"No. Just 'surgical mutilation.' But that's where we might have a connection. Eckhardt and the doctor went AWOL before trial. They've been missing for six months. The army is pissed off about it, and they're still looking for these guys. They don't want to go public with it, and neither do we. But when we told them about Eckhardt's cell phone call reporting the body in the woods they went ape-shit. They're sending a couple of military cops to Wyoming as soon as they can get 'em here.

"Of course, it's possible that somebody has Eckhardt's cell phone, but that seems real unlikely. The army guys asked if the caller had a speech impediment, because Eckhardt has one, but I didn't know what to tell them. Anyway, we're running down other calls made from that number now, and we'll see if we can make any sense of them."

Joe watched the cloud move up the hillside, felt it envelop him as it passed over, sensed the five-degree temperature drop. "The Park County dispatcher had trouble making out what the 911 caller said."

"That's interesting," Portenson said.

Joe's mind was racing ahead.

"Joe, you still there?" Portenson asked.

"I'm here."

"We need to have an emergency task-force meeting. I already told Hersig and he's clearing the decks for seven o'clock tonight."

Joe didn't respond.

"Joe, can you hear me?"

"Yup, I'm thinking." He paused for a moment, then: "Do we have a name on the doctor Eckhardt's involved with?"

"Hold on . . ." Portenson said. Joe could hear him thumbing through the pages again. ". . . Okay, here it is. His name is Eric Logue, Dr. Eric Logue."

"*Logue?* Ah, Jesus . . ." Joe pushed off the sign he had been leaning against, Eric Logue's name ricocheting through his head. In his subconscious a series of formerly random bits of information stopped flying around and began to pause, align, and connect. It was as if the tumblers on a lock were falling into place, finally releasing the hasp.

A doctor.

Surgical mutilations.

Cam said his brother was a surgeon.

L. Robert Eckhardt. *Bob.* The name on the army jacket Sheridan said she saw on the transient who had yelled at her.

Bob. Nurse Bob. A speech impediment. The dispatcher telling Harvey that she had trouble understanding the caller.

Nurse Bob: *Nuss Bomb.*

"Joe, you still there? What's going on?" Portenson said.

"Agent Portenson, let me ask you something," Joe said.

"Go ahead."

"If your parents came to visit you at an inconvenient time and you were telling somebody about it, would you say, 'it's not exactly the best time in the world to have my whole family here for a visit'?"

Portenson sighed. "What in the hell does that have . . ."

"*The whole family,*" Joe said. "Would that be the phrase you would use if your parents were visiting? Wouldn't it make more sense to say *my folks,* or *my parents*?"

"I guess so," Portenson said, sounding perplexed and annoyed.

"Me too," Joe said. "But when Cam Logue was at dinner and the subject came up, he said *the whole family.* Maybe it was just a mistake, but it doesn't sound right. But maybe he really did mean his whole family—including his brother."

"You've fucking lost me," Portenson said. "Who's Cam Logue and why should I care what he said at your little dinner party?"

"Just stay by the telephone for the next few minutes," Joe said. "I've got to make another call."

"What are you . . ."

Joe hung up, then hit 1 on his speed dial. While he waited for Marybeth to pick up, he paced back and forth in front of his pickup.

When she answered, he immediately knew something was wrong by her tone.

"Are you okay?"

She paused. "I've been better."

"Did I do it?" he asked.

"No, Joe. Why do you always think it's you?"

"Because it usually is. Anyway, do you have a second for something urgent?"

"Yes."

"Cam's brother is a doctor, right?"

Marybeth was clearly puzzled by the question. "Yes."

"Where?" Joe asked.

"Do you mean what state? I'm not sure. Marie mentioned a couple of times that he was overseas . . ."

"Was he an army doctor?"

She paused again. "Yes, I'm pretty sure that's what she said."

Joe smacked the hood of his pickup with his free hand. "What's his name?"

"Eric. Dr. Eric Logue," Marybeth said. "Why are you asking? What's happening?"

Joe stopped pacing. "I don't have time to explain right now—and I'm not even sure how this all connects yet. But whatever you do, Marybeth, stay away from Cam. I think either he or his brother are somehow mixed up with the mutilations. If you're at the office, pack up and leave now."

She laughed sadly. "You don't need to worry about that, Joe. I'm at home. But I just got back from the Logues' house and no one answered the door."

"Thank God you're all right," Joe said, feeling a little of the pressure that was building vent out.

"I'm worried about Marie, though," Marybeth said. "I don't know where she is . . ."

Joe called Portenson back: "Does the report give any background information on Eric Logue? Does it say where he grew up?"

"Why does that matter?" Portenson asked, irritated. "I can't find anything here. It may be in the report somewhere but I'll have to look."

"Find out where he grew up," Joe said urgently. "And if they won't give it to you or you can't find it, try to confirm that Dr. Eric Logue was stationed in the same places Eckhardt was."

"I'm not doing jack-shit until you tell me what's going on here," Portenson barked. "You've already screwed my career once, Joe—now, what is so important about where Eric Logue grew up?"

"Cam Logue's a realtor in Saddlestring," Joe said. "He grew up here and just moved back to open up a business. I think our Dr. Eric Logue is Cam Logue's brother. I'm not sure how it all connects but there's something here. Look, I'm out in the field now but we've got to talk to Hersig about this immediately—definitely before tonight's task-force meeting. Then I can explain things better to both of you."

"I'll call Robey right now," Portenson said. "Stop whatever game-warden crap you're doing and head back to town so we can go see Robey. And keep your phone on—I'll call you as soon as I talk to him."

Joe was rolling toward town when his cell phone rang. "Robey's stuck on the phone with the governor," Portenson said without preamble. "The governor called for an update on the task force's progress."

"Do we know how long this is going to take?" Joe said.

"Robey's secretary said she didn't think he'd be off any time soon but she'd 'pencil us in' for five," Portenson said, his voice heavy with sarcasm.

Joe looked at his watch—it was almost three-thirty. "We need to nail down Eric Logue," he said. "The more information we can bring Robey, the better."

"I already talked to the FBI. We should have something any minute."

"Try to get photos of Eckhardt and Eric Logue, and let me know as soon as you've got something. See if you can find out where Cam Logue is right now as well. If Eric is his brother then we'll need to pick Cam up for questioning immediately."

"Who died and appointed you an FBI agent?" Portenson spat. "I know how to do my job. Just make sure you're at Robey's by five—I'll take care of everything else."

———

J oe tossed the phone on to the seat next to him as he drove toward Saddlestring, his anxiety building. He wasn't quite sure what to do to fill the time before the meeting with Hersig. He considered going to Portenson's office to wait for the FBI's information on Eric Logue but Portenson was clearly not in the mood to have Joe hanging over his shoulder. Joe thought about going over to Cam's office but quickly dismissed that idea. After that morning fiasco, he wouldn't be surprised if Cam never spoke to him again.

Joe was almost across the bridge that would take him into Saddlestring, debating whether he had enough time to go home and change out of his work clothes, filthy from fixing the signs, when he remembered Ike's request to pick up Not Ike. He slowed his truck and scanned the river but he could see only one fisherman and he didn't look like Not Ike.

Joe pulled off the bridge and parked his truck. As he jogged down the riverbank, he recognized the fisherman as Jack, the retired schoolteacher and the only man in town who rivaled Not Ike for fishing hours.

"Hey, Jack, have you seen Not Ike?"

Jack was tying on a streamer fly. The glare of the sun on the water behind him made Joe squint.

"He was down under the bridge until about an hour ago," Jack said. "He yelled down to me and said he caught three fish."

Joe smiled.

"He caught a ride somewhere, though," Jack said. "He hasn't come back."

"Do you know who picked him up?"

Jack shook his head. "Didn't recognize him. But he was driving a big-ass truck and pulling a trailer behind it. Big silver trailer, with some kind of writing on it."

Joe froze. "Did it say 'Dr. Cleve Garrett, Iconoclast Society, Reno, Nevada?'"

Looking up from his fly, Jack shrugged. "Could have, I'm not sure. But I've never seen it around here before. I saw the guy driving though, and I swear I've seen *him* before."

Joe took an involuntary step backward. It made no sense—

why was Garrett back in Saddlestring? And why would he stop to give Not Ike a ride somewhere? Then something clicked in his head, a sick pit of worry growing in his stomach.

"You okay, Joe?"

But Joe had turned and was running up the riverbank toward his pickup. As he threw open the pickup door, he called down to Jack, "Which direction were they going?"

Jack pointed to the west, toward the mountains.

Joe jumped into the cab, cranked the wheel, and did a screeching U-turn back onto the bridge, nearly taking out the railing with his bumper.

33

Joe ACCELERATED ON BIGHORN ROAD, grabbing his radio as he drove. "Cleve Garrett has kidnapped a man named George Easter, aka Not Ike Easter," Joe shouted into his radio microphone after switching to the mutual aid channel. "Everyone out there watch for a Suburban towing an Airstream trailer . . ." he described the vehicle, the trailer, and Not Ike as best he could.

It took a few beats before the radio traffic became fevered, with comments, questions, and location reports coming in through the central dispatcher from Saddlestring police, sheriff's deputies, and the highway patrol. Everyone wanted to know what was going on, everyone wanted more details. Deputy McLanahan complained that he was just done with his shift and headed for dinner at the Burg-O-Pardner. He asked how to spell "iconoclast."

Joe's cell phone rang immediately, as he expected it would.

It was Hersig, and he was distraught. "What in the hell is going on, Joe? What are you doing? Everyone's in a damned uproar because of something you just broadcast."

"A man matching the description of Cleve Garrett lured Not Ike out of the river and took him someplace," Joe said. "He was last seen headed toward the mountains."

"Cleve Garrett?" Hersig shouted. "CLEVE GARRETT? What about Eric Logue? I got a message from Portenson about him."

"*I don't know!*" Joe yelled back angrily. "Maybe it was Garrett all along!"

"Jesus Christ," Hersig said. "How do we know Not Ike wasn't just getting a lift to another fishing spot upriver?"

"Because," Joe said, "things are starting to fall into place, and not in a good way. None of us—especially me—took Garrett seriously, because of all his goofy theories. But the fact is that he was in Montana when the first cattle mutilations were reported. When the cattle were mutilated in Saddlestring, he was here too. No one else we know of was around when and where both sets of crimes were committed—except Cleve Garrett. And Garrett pulled up stakes and vanished, so he was obviously trying to get away fast. I couldn't figure out why, before, and assumed it had to do with Deena. Now I'm thinking he must have thought we were closing in on him, that I was closing in on him."

"But if that's all true, why would Garrett come back to Saddlestring and risk getting caught?" Robey said. "Why grab Not Ike, of all people?"

"Not Ike told us how he'd seen somebody, a couple of men, in an alley behind Logue Realty. He called them '*creepylike.*' Remember from the report?"

"Now I do. I didn't put any stock in it."

"Me either, damn it," Joe said. "But I'm thinking that Not Ike was the only living person who may have actually seen the bad guys. Maybe he could identify them."

Hersig paused. "Who would know about what he said besides us?"

"Cam Logue would know," Joe said.

"How in the hell would he know?"

"Because I told him about it in his office."

"Oh no . . ."

"That's right," Joe said. "There must be a connection between Cam and Garrett. I don't know what it is yet but it's the only explanation I can think of.

"Not Ike said he saw two people in the alley by Logue Realty—Garrett was one of them and Cam Logue was probably the other. Cam must have called Garrett after I left his office and told him." Joe mentally kicked himself for being so stupid. If something happened to Not Ike because of him, he'd never forgive himself.

"Calm down, Joe," Robey said. "Just stay focused, all right? We don't even know for sure that Cam's involved. Not Ike could have told the same thing to others and probably did. This morning you told me Logue wasn't part of all this, and now suddenly you're convinced he's in cahoots with Garrett?"

"Forget what I said, Robey," Joe said heatedly. "I may be wrong but if I'm not then Not Ike's life is in danger. You've got to send someone out to pick up Cam right away. He may know where Garrett is heading. Hell, for all we know he could be running now, too."

"Who do you want me to send, Joe? Finding Garrett and Not Ike is everyone's number-one priority," Hersig said. "Barnum and his deputies and basically all other law enforcement within twenty miles of Saddlestring are already out looking for Garrett. I'm not going to call one of them and ask that they turn around to go pick up a respected local businessman who may or may not be involved in this whole thing."

Joe gripped the phone so tightly that he thought it would break. "I don't care who you send—call the goddamn highway patrol if you have to. Someone's got to be around. Cam's involved in this one way or the other and we can't risk losing him like we did Garrett."

"I'll see what I can do," Hersig snapped. "But I'm not making any promises."

"Funnel everything through the dispatcher," Joe said. "I'll keep the radio on and report in if there's anything to report." Hersig clicked off without answering.

Joe tried to tie it all together. Garrett's involvement puzzled him. He had been so focused on Cam Logue that he had paid scant attention to Garrett. Deena had provided Joe with a reason to dig more deeply into Garrett's motivations, but Joe hadn't done it in time to stop what was happening now.

Something else clicked in, regarding Cleve Garrett. Garrett was a publicity hound. He wanted the attention in order to advance his crackpot ideas on aliens and conspiracies. But maybe Garrett was darker, more twisted. Maybe Joe's lack of credulity was the motivation for Garrett to step up his crimes?

And where in the hell did Cam Logue fit into all of this? Joe wondered. He had to be part of this. How else could Garrett have known about Joe's conversation with Cam? Garrett had left *before* Joe confronted Cam. Were they in contact?

Despite the bungling of the rest of the task force, Joe had been the closest to the killer all along and he hadn't seen it. There might still be another explanation—*he hoped so*—but he doubted it. If this played out the way it seemed to be headed, it was his fault for not preventing another murder. He cringed as he drove.

"*Man, oh man, oh man,*" Joe said aloud.

He grabbed his cell phone from the dash, speed-dialed Nate Romanowski's number. For once, Nate answered.

"It's Joe."

Nate was excited. "Joe, I haven't talked to you since we found the bear. Well believe it or not . . ."

"*Nate!* I really need your help!"

"Go ahead."

"How fast can you grab your weapon and meet me on Bighorn Road? I'm heading west toward the mountains."

"Ten minutes."

"I'll pick you up."

As Joe screamed over the hill, he saw Nate climbing out of his Jeep and pulling on his shoulder holster. Joe slowed to a roll, and Nate swung into the cab of the pickup.

Without actually stopping, Joe eased the pickup back onto the Bighorn Road and the motor roared.

"It's Cleve Garrett," Joe said.

"Really?" Nate whistled. "I guess it shouldn't be that much of a surprise."

"No," Joe said sourly. "I guess it shouldn't be. But I think Cam Logue is involved somehow, maybe others as well."

While they drove, Nate pulled his weapon, checked the five-shot cylinder, and shoved it back into his shoulder holster.

"Consider yourself deputized," Joe said, looking over at Nate.

Nate said, "I didn't know game wardens could deputize anyone."

Joe shrugged. "We probably can't. So I'll deputize you in the name of the Murder and Mutilation Task Force."

"Cool," Nate said. "As long as you undeputize me later."

Joe nodded.

"Remember when I told you about what it was like under the calm surface of the river?" Nate asked, his eyes wide, "how there is a whole different world, with noise and chaos?"

"Nate, what does this have to do with . . ."

"Just listen for a minute, Joe," Nate said. "I've come to believe that there are different levels of consciousness and being. There are whole worlds out there with their own different versions of what reality is, and their own sets of natural laws. Sometimes, the laws are broken and things spill over from one level to the next. When that happens, we hope that something from that level is sent to fix the mess or all hell will break loose."

Joe was speechless. "Nate . . ."

"I know," Nate said. "We don't have time for this. But the bear is with me now, at my place. We're communicating."

The radio crackled. It was Wendy, the dispatcher.

"A fisherman just reported seeing a vehicle and trailer matching the description of the suspect's vehicle and trailer at a public-access fishing campground."

Joe and Nate exchanged glances, and Joe snatched the microphone from its cradle.

"This is Joe Pickett, Wendy. There are six public-access campgrounds on the Upper Twelve Sleep River. Can you tell me which one?"

There was a pause, then: "The fisherman says he saw the unit in question at the Pick Pike Bridge campground."

Joe knew which one she was talking about. It was the last public-access fishing location before the start of the national forest. It was small, with four or five spaces, and was located in dense woods. The only facilities there were a pit-toilet outhouse and a fish-cleaning station near the water. Because of the way it was tucked into the heavy timber near the river, it was a good place to hide out. He had ticketed more over-limit fishermen there than any other place on the river, because the fishermen assumed no one would see or catch them.

"I'm fifteen minutes away from there," Joe said to Wendy. "Are there any other units in the vicinity?"

"Sheriff Barnum is rolling now," she said.

"That's right," Barnum barked, breaking into the transmission. "Secure the exits and wait for the cavalry."

Secure the exits? Joe looked at Nate. "Sheriff, there's one road into that campground from the Bighorn Road, but there's at least four old two-tracks that go to it from both sides of the river. That makes five exits."

"Then use your best judgment, goddamit," Portenson broke in from another radio. "I'll take it from here, Sheriff. Follow me."

Joe was relieved that Portenson was taking charge.

They topped a sagebrush covered hill on a two-track road, and the river and campground were laid out below on the valley floor in front of them. Joe slowed the pickup to assess the layout. The Twelve Sleep River, its surface reflecting dusk gold, rebounded in a loopy sidewise U from a cliff-face upriver before it turned and disappeared from view into thick river cottonwoods. The campground was under the canopy of trees where the river bent.

As Joe had described to Barnum, roads that looked like discarded dark threads through the sagebrush came in and out of the bank of trees, offering multiple entrance and exit points.

If Garrett's truck and trailer were down there in the trees, they couldn't be seen from above. To locate them, they would need to be on the valley floor, in the trees or in the campground itself.

Joe had made the decision not to wait for Portenson and Barnum. If Not Ike was being carved up by Cleve Garrett, Joe wanted to stop it as quickly as he possibly could. *I've already screwed this thing up enough,* he thought. *I couldn't live with knowing I was sitting on top of a hill while Not Ike was being tortured.*

Joe asked Nate, "Are you ready?"

Nate said, "Of course."

At home, Marybeth was making spaghetti with meat sauce for dinner when the telephone rang. She was greeted with silence on the other end, although she thought she could hear breathing. "Hello?" she said again.

Nothing. Marybeth put the spoon on a plate and was about to hang up when someone said, "Marybeth?"

It took a moment for Marybeth to recognize the caller.

"Marie? Is that you?"

Marie hesitated, then spoke softly. "I got your note. That was very nice of you. But it was too late, too late." Marybeth knew there was something dreadfully wrong by the soft, vacant quality of Marie's voice.

"Marie, are you okay?"

There was a wracking sob, then a beat while Marie seemed to be collecting herself.

"No, I'm *not* okay," Marie said, her voice breaking. "I'm not okay at all. Cam's gone, and I've done something horrible. They took him."

"Who took Cam? Marie, what are you telling me?" She recalled her conversation with Joe, his admonishment to stay away from Cam.

But Marie couldn't answer because she was crying too hard, and she finally barked out "I'll call you back," between wails, and hung up.

Marybeth found herself staring at the stove but not really seeing anything. She realized that she was suddenly trembling.

Where was Joe? He needed to meet her at the Logues' right away.

34

As they leveled out on the river valley floor and crossed a small stream before entering the trees, Joe punched off his cell phone and squelched the volume of the radio to a whisper. Both windows were open in the pickup, so he and Nate could get a better sense of the surroundings. Joe drove slowly, keeping the sound of the motor at a minimum. He wanted to enter the campground as quietly as he could.

They passed a brown Forest Service sign nearly obliterated by years of sniping and shotgun blasts that read PICK PIKE CAMPGROUND.

Inside the trees, it was dark and it smelled damp, with an edge of forest-floor decay. Pale yellow cottonwood leaves blanketed the soft black earth. Small splats of sun pierced through the wide canopy of trees and formed starbursts on the surface.

Nate gestured toward the two-track in front of them, and mouthed, "Fresh tracks."

Joe nodded. He had seen the tracks as well, noting that they were so new that the peaked impression of the tire treads was still sharp.

Nate had his .454 Casull in his right hand, the muzzle pointed toward the floor. Joe's .40 Beretta was on the seat next to his thigh. Joe's palms were icy with apprehension, his breath was quavery and shallow. He found himself clenching his jaw so tightly that his teeth hurt.

Before turning toward the campsites, the road passed a rusting metal fish-cleaning station near a boat takeout point on the riverbank. They were past it when Joe sniffed the air and eased to a stop. There was a smell that didn't belong, he thought.

He opened his door as quietly as he could, and approached the station. Nate did the same, but walked toward the bank of the river. The fish-cleaning station was old and simple; a flat metal work area perched on angle-iron legs. The cleaning area could be washed clean by a river-water faucet. Usually these things smelled bad, he knew, but the normal odor was of fish guts, fish heads, and entire rotting skeletons if the fisherman filleted the trout and left the rest. The problem with this station was that it didn't smell like that at all, he realized. Instead, there was the pungent odor of ammonia bleach.

Indeed, the metal cleaning counter was scrubbed clean. In the center of the counter was a drain hole. The drain led to an underground pipe that discharged into the river itself.

Either the station had been used by unusually sanitary and obsessive fishermen, he thought, or it had been used for another purpose.

His stomach clenched.

Joe looked up to see Nate gesturing at him furiously to come over to where he stood at the water's edge.

As Joe walked over, he had a sickening premonition of what he might find.

Nate bent down and pointed toward the discharge pipe several inches below the surface of the river. A long white ribbon of some kind had caught on an underwater twig and undulated in the flow. Nate reached into the water and pulled the ribbon free, stretching it across both of his hands so they could look at it.

It was human skin. White human skin. On the bottom of the

ribbon was a dark blue stencil of some kind, a series of three consecutive horizontal lines. Through his horror, Joe realized what they were.

"Oh, my God," he whispered. "That's the top of some lettering, *T-E-E*."

He looked up at Nate. "From the word 'ABDUCTEE.' It's from Deena. She had it tattooed across her abdomen. *The son of a bitch skinned her.*"

Now, Joe was angry. Everything he had been feeling previously—frustration, embarrassment, outright fear as they descended into the trees—channeled into rage.

"Let's find him and take him out," he said over his shoulder to Nate as he strode to the pickup. Tilting the bench seat forward, Joe drew his shotgun from its scabbard. It was still loaded with double-ought buckshot shells.

Nate followed. "Joe, calm down."

"I'm calm," Joe said through clenched teeth. He was thinking of Deena, of Not Ike, of Tuff Montegue and Stuart Tanner, of the circus of humiliation and depravity Cleve Garrett had brought into his valley.

"Let's talk about this for a second," Nate said.

Joe racked the pump.

"We need a strategy," Nate said. "So take a breath."

Cleve Garrett's Airstream Trailer was still attached to his pickup and it was pulled into the fifth and last space in the campground. It looked like a big, slick metallic tube in the dark trees. Behind the trailer, through thick stands of willows, the river flowed wide and shallow.

Joe cranked the wheel of his truck to block the road, and turned off the motor. Garrett could not drive out of his site now, and there were too many thick trees all around for him to use an overland escape route.

The blinds were pulled down tight on all of the trailer windows, and Joe wondered if he had been either seen or heard by the occupants inside. Joe and Nate slid out of the cab. As they had planned, Nate pushed his way into the brush and vanished within it to take a position behind cover near the front of Garrett's pickup. This way, Nate could cover Joe as well as see if anyone inside tried to escape out the back of the trailer.

Joe stood behind his pickup, keeping it between him and the trailer. He had switched his radio to PA and the mike cord stretched across the cab and out the open window.

When he assumed Nate was in position, he keyed the mike.

"Cleve Garrett, come out of that trailer now."

He watched the windows carefully, saw one of them near the front shiver as someone looked out.

"IF YOU HAVE ANY WEAPONS, LEAVE THEM IN-SIDE. OPEN THE DOOR AND COME OUT WITH YOUR HANDS IN THE AIR, PALMS OUT."

The front window blind shot up. Joe crouched down and raised the stock of the shotgun to his cheek. He put the bead on the front sight to the window. A face appeared, pressed against the glass.

"Joseph?" Not Ike mouthed. "Joseph?" His words were silent on the outside.

Not Ike looked confused but okay, Joe thought with a rush of relief. Garrett probably had a gun at Not Ike's head, shoving the big man's face into the glass.

Not Ike was mouthing something through the glass. Joe could read it: *Creepylike guys, Joseph.*

A louvered pane near Not Ike's head was being cranked open. Joe hoped Nate had a better angle on the window from where he was hidden in the brush. Maybe, Joe thought, Nate would be able to see Garrett inside and fire if Garrett lowered his gun or was distracted.

"Joseph, that's you, isn't it?" Joe could now hear Not Ike.

"It's me," Joe said, talking into the mike so that Garrett would be sure to hear him as well. "Plus about twenty officers more on the way. The trailer is surrounded."

There was a beat and Not Ike's face was pulled from the window. Maybe Garrett would speak now, Joe hoped. Maybe Garrett would try to make a deal.

"Nobody needs to get hurt," Joe said, willing confident gentleness into his voice. "No one needs to get hurt at all. Just leave any weapons inside and come out."

There was movement inside the trailer, and it rocked slightly.

With a metallic click, the door burst open. Joe swung the muzzle of his shotgun to it, saw the door slam against the outside of the trailer, saw the doorframe filled with Not Ike. Garrett was behind Not Ike with his forearm around the big man's throat and a pistol pressed into his ear. Because Garrett was much shorter, all Joe could see of him were his eyes over Not Ike's shoulder.

"We're coming out," Garrett shouted.

Not Ike stepped out of the trailer, Garrett pressed tightly behind him. Not Ike took several steps forward, grinning at Joe as if he didn't fully comprehend what was happening. Joe didn't lower his shotgun. For a brief, electrifying moment, Garrett's and Joe's eyes locked.

"Let him go," Joe said, close enough now not to need the microphone. "Lower the gun and drop it into the dirt."

Garrett looked furtively to his side.

"I don't see anybody else," Garrett said. "Where're your troops?"

"They're out there," Joe lied, thinking: *Nate, where are you?*

Garrett pushed Not Ike forward another few steps toward Joe. The pistol was jammed into Not Ike's ear, tilting his head slightly to the side. Joe could see that the hammer was cocked. Not Ike looked strangely serene, Joe thought. Somehow, it made the situation seem worse.

"We're going to walk right up to you," Garrett said, his voice gaining confidence. "And we're going to take your truck out of here. You are going to lower that shotgun and step aside."

Yes, I was, Joe thought. He had no other choice. Unless . . . *Nate?*

Then the door to the trailer filled with someone else, something else, something unspeakably horrible.

It was Cam Logue, with most of his face peeled aside. The

front of his shirt was soaked with blood, and his head slumped forward, his arms limp. He was being held up from behind by a big, dark man with a beard, wearing a bloody camouflage jacket.

"Oh, my God," Joe heard himself whisper. *Why is Cam here and what have they done to him?*

The man behind Cam Logue moved out of the trailer. He appeared to be carrying Cam, keeping him vertical with one arm wrapped tightly around Logue's chest. In the other hand was a scalpel, which was pressed against Logue's throat.

"You din't fo'get about me, did you, Doc?" the man asked Garrett. His speech was garbled and slurred. The man's poor speech and the camo jacket clicked in Joe's mind. It was Nurse Bob, Joe realized.

"Of course not," Garrett said to Nurse Bob, not looking around. To Joe: "It's a messy business, this."

Joe was stunned, unable to process the horrific scene in front of him. Nothing made sense.

BOOM.

The left half of Nurse Bob's head disappeared, blood and pieces of flesh splattering the side of the trailer with a sickening, wet sound, while his body toppled over backward like a felled tree. Cam Logue fell forward, released from the man's grip, landing facedown on the ground.

Instinctively, Joe straightened up and moved to his left behind the truck to get an angle on Garrett. Garrett had wheeled Not Ike around toward the sound of the shot, and Joe could see Garrett clearly now. But Garrett still had the pistol jammed into Not Ike's head.

"*Who did that?*" Garrett screamed, stealing a glance toward Cam's prone body.

"DROP THE WEAPON!" Joe shouted.

But Garrett didn't. Instead, he began backpedaling, pulling Not Ike along with him. Garrett backed up until he was nearly at the trailer again, but veered toward the rear of it. Not Ike was starting to panic now, because he didn't know what was happening.

"*Joseph!*"

Garrett backed into the reedy brush behind the trailer, and before he was gone the last thing Joe saw were Not Ike's arms flailing.

Then he heard a splash.

J oe and Nate followed.

"You didn't tell me there would be two of them," Nate said.

"Nobody told me there would be two of them either," Joe muttered. "Or that Cam would be with them."

Nate said nothing.

They found Not Ike in the river, sputtering but unharmed. Cleve Garrett was gone.

"I've got him," Nate said, leaving Joe and Not Ike in the river and wading toward the opposite bank.

35

For the next three hours, as night came and the campground filled with vehicles and men and the crime scene lights went up, Joe Pickett was in a kind of fog. He was lucid enough to recognize that he was in mild shock. He dully recounted the details of what they had found in the campsite to Portenson, Hersig, and Sheriff Barnum. As activity whirled around him, he stayed out of the way, observing things as if he had no connection to any of it.

Hersig came over to Joe at one point and told Joe that they'd found a duffel bag with some personal items in the trailer that confirmed that the man Nate shot was Robert Eckhardt, the army nurse accused of mutilations who had gone AWOL. The phone number of the cell phone in the man's bag matched the phone number Deputy Cook and Sheriff Harvey had pulled off their Caller ID. Hersig said they were going to run the man's prints through the computer to prove his identification. The extent of his injuries would make a visual ID impossible.

Joe watched as Cam Logue's body was hustled onto a gurney and loaded into an ambulance, followed by Nurse Bob's, and as Barnum put together a team of deputies to cross the river and track down Cleve Garrett.

Remarkably, Deena was still alive. The EMTs brought her out from the back bedroom of the Airstream. She was naked except for the bandages wrapped around her belly and legs and a thin white sheet the EMTs had tucked around her. She was conscious, sleepy-looking, probably drugged, Joe assumed. As they carried her on a stretcher toward ambulance number three, she rolled her head to the side and smiled faintly at Joe.

One of the EMTs, whom Joe recognized from the Tuff Montegue crime scene, told a deputy that Deena had spoken to him when they found her inside.

"She said Garrett was experimenting on her, taking off strips of skin. She said she didn't mind all that much, but she was angry when he screwed up her tattoo. Can you imagine that?"

Deputy Reed came out of the trailer holding a bundle in dark cloth, and someone shined a flashlight on it as the bundle was opened. Steel surgical instruments glinted in the light. Joe recalled Lucy and Sheridan saying something about seeing "silverware" on a cloth in the shack behind the Logues and that the man who chased them away had "Bob" stenciled above the pocket on his jacket. So did the man with half a head who had been zipped up in a body bag an hour before, he thought with a shiver.

"How did this Nurse Bob guy get hooked up with Cleve Garrett?" Hersig was asking Portenson. "Why in the hell did they go after Cam Logue and Not Ike?"

Portenson shrugged and cursed.

"Joe, do you know?" Hersig asked him.

Joe shook his head.

"He's in bad shape," Portenson said, looking at Joe with some sympathy. "I don't think he's ever seen a man's head blown off before."

"Not only that," Hersig said, "but did you see Cam Logue? Jesus, I'm going to have nightmares for years after that."

"You did good," Portenson said to Joe. "You probably saved the lives of two people."

Hersig stood near Joe, shaking his head and staring out into the dark trees. "I'm confused," Hersig said as much to himself as to Joe. "Why was Cam here? How did this Nurse Bob character get involved with Cleve Garrett? Or was he involved with Cam somehow? It wasn't just a coincidence, no way."

Hersig looked at Joe. "So was it Cam all along? Was Cam working with Cleve Garrett? Did he know Nurse Bob through his brother or what? I thought Cam hated his brother?"

Joe barely followed what was being said. He waited for the sound of Nate's gunshot from across the river. The shot never came.

Shortly after, Nate appeared beneath one of the spotlights, looking for Joe, causing the deputies who were milling about to stop and stare. Nate certainly had a presence about him, Joe noted.

"I lost his track in the dark," Nate declared to everyone.

"Shit," Barnum cursed. "Did you see my deputies?"

"They're coming in right behind me," Nate said.

Nate searched the crowd, saw Joe standing by his pickup, and started over. Portenson stepped in front of Nate, cutting him off.

"I understand you were the shooter. There may be charges filed, and we'll need a statement from you."

Nate looked at Portenson coldly. "Charges?"

"I deputized him," Joe interrupted.

Portenson shook his head. "What in the hell does that mean?"

Nate shrugged, and stepped around Portenson.

"We still need a statement, mister."

Nate said, "You'll get one. Right now, I'm going to get Joe home. I'll come in to your office tomorrow."

Portenson approached Joe warily. "The identification came through in the middle of all of this. The doctor who escaped was the same Eric Logue who had grown up here. We should have photos of Nurse Bob and Eric Logue on the computer when we get back. Washington is sending them out. But how in the hell everything connects is beyond me right now."

Joe shrugged. His movements were a beat behind his thoughts.

Joe and Nate left Hersig, Portenson, and Barnum, who were having a discussion about how quickly they could coordinate helicopters and dogs to pursue Cleve Garrett.

"Are you sure you're okay to drive?" Nate asked.

"I'm fine."

"I couldn't get an angle on Garrett, or there would have been two bodies back there."

Joe nodded. The images of Cam Logue and Nurse Bob's exploding head played on a continuous loop just beyond the hood of his truck.

"So Cam Logue is dead?" Nate asked, after minutes of silence.

"Yup."

"So I saved a *dead* guy?"

"You didn't know that. Neither did I at the time. That was a hell of a shot."

Nate repeated, "I saved a dead guy."

Joe looked over. "Nate, are you okay?"

"Okay is the wrong word to use after you kill somebody, Joe. I guess I'm . . . I don't know what. You could say I have some degree of job satisfaction, I guess."

Joe remembered his cell phone and switched it on as they turned onto the blacktop of the highway.

The display read: YOU HAVE 1 MESSAGE.

Marybeth, thought Joe. She's probably worried as hell.

He punched in the numbers to retrieve the message, and held the phone to his ear.

It was Marybeth all right, but her voice was hushed and urgent.

"Joe, where are you? I'm with Marie, at her house. It's a terrible scene, and I'm scared for her. Can you please get here as fast as you can?"

He suddenly floored it, and the engine howled.

"What's going on?" Nate asked.

"I don't know."

36

MARYBETH'S VAN WAS PARKED in front of the Logue home on the circular drive, and Joe's headlights swept across it as he pulled in. The van was empty except for a small, blond head in the backseat. Joe's heart raced, fearing it was Lucy or Sheridan.

He braked, leaving the shotgun in the truck, and slid the van door back. The interior light went on and he looked at Jessica Logue, sitting in the center of the middle seat with her hands on her lap. Her face was stained with dried tears.

"Jessica, what are you doing?"

"Mrs. Pickett asked my mom if I could come out here," Jessica said, looking at her hands. "My mom said I could."

"They're inside?"

Jessica nodded.

Joe reached in and patted her shoulder. "Stay here, then. I won't be long." He started to shut the door.

"Mr. Pickett?"

"Yes?"

She looked up at him. "I hope you can help my mom."

"I'll try, honey."

Nate stood in the dark behind him.

"I think you should stay out here," Joe said. "I don't know what the situation is inside. Maybe you can watch through a window, and if things aren't under control, well . . ."

"I'll be ready," Nate said. "Is the little girl going to be okay?"

"I'm not sure."

J oe knocked on the front door, and tried to see through the opaque curtain beside it. There was dim light inside, from a room on the right of the hallway, but he couldn't see Marybeth. He knocked again, and saw a dark form step into the doorway.

"Joe, is that you?" It was Marybeth.

He tightly closed his eyes for an instant—she was all right—then answered her.

"Are you alone?" she asked.

"Yes," he lied.

"Is it alright if Joe comes in?" Marybeth asked someone inside the room.

His hand was already turning the knob when she said, "It's okay to come inside, Joe."

He stepped in and shut the door behind him. The hallway was dark. Why didn't Marybeth come to him, he wondered. Was someone threatening her inside?

Jesus, he thought. What if it's Garrett?

He quickly reached for his pistol but stopped when Marybeth, almost imperceptibly, shook her head no. Joe paused and pointed outside and mouthed "Nate." She met his eyes and blinked, indicating that she understood.

His boots sounded loud on the hardwood floor, in the still house, as he walked toward Marybeth. As he neared her, she turned her head inside the room and said, "Marie, Joe's coming in now."

"Okay."

Marybeth stepped back and Joe entered. He took in the scene quickly. The room was dark except for two low-wattage desk lamps. Book-lined shelves covered the opposite wall. A television set and stereo occupied an entertainment center, but both were off.

Marie Logue leaned with her back against an upright piano. She had a glass of red wine in one hand and a semiautomatic pistol in the other. Her eyes looked glazed, her expression blank. There were dried tear tracks down her cheeks, like her daughter's.

Across from Marie, in two overstuffed chairs, sat an old couple. They looked shriveled and flinty, and both peered at Joe from behind metal-rimmed glasses. The man wore suspenders over a white T-shirt, and the woman wore an oversized sweatshirt. The woman's hair looked like curled stainless-steel shavings.

"Joe, I don't believe you've met Marie's mother- and father-in-law before," Marybeth said with a kind of exaggerated calmness that signaled to Joe that the situation was tense. "This is Clancy and Helen Logue."

Joe nodded.

"This is Joe, my husband."

Clancy Logue nodded back, but Helen stared at Joe, apparently sizing him up.

"I was just about to kill them," Marie said from across the room, deadpan. "Marybeth is trying her darndest to talk me out of it."

Joe looked at her.

"I bet I can get you to say three words now," Marie said, her mouth twisting into a bitter grin.

Marie, do you mind if I fill Joe in on what we've been discussing?" Marybeth asked, still with remarkable calm.

Marie arched her eyebrows in a "what the hell" look, and took a long drink of her wine. Her eyes shifted from Joe to Clancy and Helen as Marybeth told the story.

"Marie learned last week that Cam has been trying to buy the Overstreet Ranch in secret. That the secret buyer he told us about was Cam himself. Apparently, the only people he told about it were his parents. He told them that he was going to buy back their old ranch but that they weren't welcome on it.

But there was another reason, other than nostalgia, why Cam wanted the ranch. Am I doing okay so far, Marie?"

"Perfect," she said.

"As you know, Joe, the Logue home used to serve as an archive for the old county clerk. Cam liked to go through the old files, to learn about the history of property in the area, he told Marie. But apparently he found the file for the Overstreet Ranch, and discovered that the mineral rights lease signed by their father was for fifty years. That meant that the rights would revert back to the landowner in two more years. The Overstreet sisters didn't know that. They thought the mineral rights were sold forever."

"And Cam would get the royalties on all of that coal-bed methane development," Joe said.

Marie clucked her tongue.

"Were you aware of this scheme?" Joe asked her.

"Well, no. I didn't find out about that part of it until this morning, when he confessed it to me. I was so damned mad at him. You think you know somebody . . . I'm ethical, Joe," she pleaded. "Marybeth knows that. That's why I refused to come to work. I would never take advantage of those two old sisters that way. Cam knew it too, which is why he didn't tell me."

And Stuart Tanner knew it, Joe thought. Tanner found it out when he researched the property. Tanner likely had it in the file he delivered to Cam Logue that day.

Marybeth turned back. "Well, Clancy and Helen decided to come and visit Cam. According to Marie, when his parents found out he was going to try to get the ranch back, they wanted to live there, too. No one except Cam knew about the mineral rights yet. Clancy and Helen thought it would be a good place to retire."

"Damned right," Clancy said defiantly. "The boy does something right for once in his life, and he didn't want to share it."

Joe shot a look at Marie. Her eyes were narrowed on Clancy.

"Please," Marybeth said. "Let me tell the story."

Clancy snorted, but sat back.

"Marie was telling me that Cam has a brother, Eric. He's a doctor with the army and he had some really severe problems a couple of years ago, some kind of breakdown. Eric was accused of deliberately hurting some patients. . . ."

"It wasn't deliberate," Helen broke in.

"Oh, shut up," Marie warned, raising the pistol and looking down it at Helen. Helen clamped her mouth tight, but her eyes smoldered.

"He may have hurt his patients because of his sickness," Marybeth said cautiously, searching for words that wouldn't inflame either party. "Anyway, Eric's friend, a male nurse, came with Clancy and Helen in their truck. You may have seen it parked outside. The camper shell with the locks on the outside of it?"

Joe nodded. *Jesus.*

"That's how they brought Eric's friend here. Under lock and key."

Joe looked at Clancy and Helen now. They didn't look like monsters. They looked like near-indigent retirees.

"Apparently, the nurse got away from Helen and Clancy. He may have been living on the property, in that shack our girls found, but we don't know that for sure yet."

Joe was confused. "Why did you bring him out here?"

Clancy and Helen exchanged glances.

"You might as well talk," Marie told them in a singsong voice. "Or I'll just have to start blasting away."

Helen cleared her throat. "Bob showed up at our house in South Dakota unannounced. He said he was looking for Eric. Our son asked that we bring him here."

"Cam asked that?" Marie said incredulously.

"Not Cam," Helen said. "Eric."

"What?" Marie's face was getting red.

"Marie, please be calm," Marybeth said.

"Eric wanted you to bring that piece of filth to our home?" Marie's voice rose into shrillness. "Where your granddaughter is?"

"Bob's not that bad," Clancy interjected. "Hard to understand him when he talks, though."

"Besides," Helen added, "he stayed out back and never bothered anyone. He just kept to himself."

Maybe you *ought* to shoot them, Joe thought.

"Anyway," Marybeth said, trying to get control of the conversation, "Eric and Bob showed up here today. They took Cam with them."

"Eric was here?" Joe blurted.

Joe knew that something must have shown in his face, because both Marybeth and Marie picked up on it.

"Do you know where Cam is, Joe?" Marie asked.

Joe looked at her.

"Oh, my God, do you know where he is?"

"I'm very sorry," Joe said. "Cam is gone. We were too late to save him. Nurse Bob is dead too. We think he may have participated in killing Cam."

Marie gasped, seemed to hold her breath, then let out a gut-wrenching wail that sent shivers up Joe's forearms. Marybeth stepped back and covered her mouth with her hands, her eyes wide.

In mid-scream, Marie turned and raised the pistol, pointed it at Helen, and before Joe could lunge across the room and grab it, Marie pulled the trigger. The hammer snapped on an empty chamber. Joe grasped the pistol with two hands, and Marie let him take it from her. She ran across the room to Marybeth, who held her.

Letting out a long breath, Joe checked the gun and saw that Marie hadn't racked a shell into the chamber from the magazine. Then he looked at Helen. Her expression hadn't changed from before, when Marie pulled the trigger. Her eyes were dead, black, reptile eyes, masked by the face of an old woman.

"They got Cam?" she asked.

"Yes."

"That's too bad," she said.

"Too bad Marie didn't know how to load a gun," Joe said.

"That's uncalled for," Helen hissed back.

Then Joe froze, and it was as if the room was spinning around him while he stood. On a shelf behind Helen and Clancy were a set of framed photos. The photos were of Cam and Marie's wedding, Jessica, and a couple he assumed was Marie's parents. But there was a single framed picture in the middle that seemed to grow larger and sharper as he stared at it.

The photo was of Helen and Clancy and a much younger Cam. Standing next to Cam, a head taller, was Cleve Garrett.

Joe leaned over Clancy and Helen, snatched the photo from the shelf, and shook it in front of them.

"Why is Cleve Garrett in this picture?" he shouted.

Clancy looked at Joe like Joe was crazy. "I don't know what the hell you're talking about," he said. "That's Eric. Our son Eric. The doctor. *The surgeon.*"

Then Joe recalled Nurse Bob's last words: *"You din't fo'get about me, did you, Doc?"*

37

CLEVE GARRETT WAS DR. ERIC LOGUE. Dr. Eric Logue was Cleve Garrett. And despite the search teams, the helicopters, and the dogs, neither was found. The closest they came to him, three days after the shootout, was the discovery of a crude, abandoned lean-to campsite fourteen miles due west from the river. The camp was in the mountains, in a stand of aspen. They found the remains of a small, sheltered camp- fire and a half-eaten fawn. The investigators determined that the last occupant of the shelter had likely been Garrett/Logue because the fawn's haunches—and face—had been removed. Another trophy.

Following the discovery, the search was intensified. Gover- nor Budd authorized the use of the Wyoming National Guard, and for a week they walked the west face of the Bighorns in concentric circles. No other camp, or track, was found.

Garrett/Logue knew the terrain like someone who had grown up there. Because he had.

The day after Cam Logue's funeral, Marie and Jessica had stopped by the Pickett house on Bighorn Road. According to Ken Siman of Siman's Memorial Chapel, it was the largest funeral in Saddlestring in a decade. Marie was on her way out of town. Marybeth had agreed to let Jessica stay with them until Marie got settled in Denver, which delighted Lucy. Marie told Marybeth they would live in Denver to be near her parents. Cam's life insurance, she said, would take care of her and Jessica for years. Both women embraced and cried, saying their good-byes. Joe and Sheridan stood uncomfortably by, trading glances.

"I think it was finding those files," Marie said, looking to Joe as if he had asked her the question. "They brought it all back to him. I think he was trying to get revenge on his past."

Joe nodded. "Is it possible that Eric was trying to help him? By driving land values down so he could buy the ranch back?"

Marie stared at the floor. "No, I don't think so. I don't think he knew Eric was here until that morning. I really don't."

She looked up. "I don't *want* to think that. So I won't."

As the days passed into weeks, Joe found himself thinking more about Cam Logue and less about Eric. It hurt to think about Cam. He felt more and more sorry for the man, and how things had gone. Cam was the product of cruel, twisted, unloving parents. Parents who had produced two children; one an outright miscreant and the other an emotional orphan. Despite that, Cam had tried to make something better of himself and his own family. He was a hard worker, and as far as Joe knew, Cam was a good husband and father until the end. Much like Joe himself, whose parents specialized in alcoholism, neglect, and lack of direction, Cam had been driving without a road map. Cam needed Marie for structure as Joe needed Marybeth. Under her guidance, Cam had participated in the community, won awards and accolades, received deserved admiration. His doubts, frustrations, and outright fears were kept well hidden. Unfortunately, Cam had likely not shared his fears with Marie, who might have been able to help him. In the end, he didn't so much betray her as allow deeply imbedded inclinations to reemerge.

Cam was guilty of greed, of trying too desperately to provide a better place and a better life for his wife and daughter than he'd had growing up. He was not a criminal by nature, or an unchecked, unprincipled entrepreneur. He had succumbed to his desire to make things right, to try and reclaim and rewrite his past. But his past came roaring back, driving a battered old pickup with South Dakota plates.

Joe thought he had glimpsed the true Cam Logue that day in the real estate office when he confronted him. What he had seen wasn't the cocksure businessman, but someone who was unsure and bitter, someone who was deep into a scheme and situation that he never should have pursued.

Trey Crump had called Joe with startling and disturbing news. "You're not going to believe this," Trey said. "You were right about that bear collar. It was older than hell, and the bear guys said it had been out of inventory for thirty years. We have no idea how it showed up in that sheep wagon."

Joe digested this, his mind swimming. "It showed up there because it came off the bear, Trey."

"The bear guys say no way, Joe. No way a bear wandered around for thirty years without emitting a signal, and then showed up in your district. The only thing they can figure out is that the sheepherder must have found it somewhere along the line."

Joe remembered the trashed trailer, remembered the smell of the bear inside of it.

"Not a chance," Joe said, confused.

Trey cleared his throat. "This is where things start to get really weird, Joe. The thing is, the rogue grizzly bear that came out of Yellowstone was killed by some idiot roughneck over by Meeteetse a month ago. That bear never made it to the Bighorns."

"WHAT?"

"The guy shot him, skinned him out, and crushed the radio collar. We never would have known except that the idiot took the hide to a taxidermist in Cody to get a rug made. The taxi-dermist called me, and the roughneck confessed everything this afternoon. We even found the decomposed body and what was left of the collar."

Joe was stunned.

"There *was* a bear here, Trey. I saw the tracks. I saw what he did to the body of a dead cowboy."

"Must have been another bear, I guess," Trey said unconvincingly.

Joe fought against telling Trey about the bear Nate had been "communicating" with. If he told his supervisor, both Joe and Nate could be faced with federal charges.

The telephone was silent on both ends for two full minutes before they hung up.

Joe stared out his window, confused. A thirty-year-old bear collar? A bear that had vanished off the face of the earth for three decades had suddenly reappeared?

"Nah," Joe said out loud, deliberately shutting off that line of inquiry. God, he needed a beer.

Moments later, as Joe was about to head to the kitchen, Nate called.

Joe said, "You're just the man I want to talk to."

He heard Nate chuckle.

"I just heard some interesting news," Joe said. "They found the missing grizzly. It never got here."

"That *is* interesting," Nate said slyly.

"But we both know there was a bear."

"Yes," Nate said. "I guess we do."

"And I remember there was something you were starting to tell me just before we went out to the campground. We never finished that conversation."

"No, we didn't."

"Maybe we should finish it now," Joe said.

Nate was prone to long silences, and he lapsed into one now. Joe waited him out.

"Hypothetically speaking," Nate said, "if I knew there was

a grizzly still around here and told you about it, you would be duty-bound to report the discovery, correct?"

"Correct," Joe said. "Grizzlies are on the endangered species list and they fall under the authority of the department."

"That's what I thought." Another long silence.

"Nate?"

"I've learned so much. Not all of it is comfortable. But in the end, it gives me hope."

"Why is that?"

"There are bigger things than us out there, on other levels. Luckily, they take care of their own."

"Nate . . ."

"All I can say right now is you need to trust me on this, Joe. It's fascinating, this experience. You'll be the first to know what happens, I promise."

Joe sat back, thinking, recalling things Nate had said.

In my dream, the bear was sent for a reason. He has a mission.

That bear may be more than a bear. That bear is here for a reason.

We happen to be in the right place at the right time where conflicts on different levels are overlapping.

You should open your mind a little.

Using FBI resources, Agent Portenson tracked the path of Eric Logue from his years in the army to his escape in North Carolina to the Riverside RV Park.

Associates in the army confirmed Eric's downward spiral from exceptionally talented surgeon into madness. He was wealthy as well, having invested in technology stocks early and selling just before the bubble burst. Eric first showed signs of paranoia and obsession with paranormal phenomena while in the Philippines. He had been suspected of drug use, along with Nurse Bob. When his patients began emerging from surgery with wounds and grafts not related to the procedure, he was put under a full-time watch. After a suspected Filipino enemy combatant with a minor leg injury died from massive blood loss after being operated on by Dr. Logue, an inquiry was launched that resulted in his court-martial.

While in custody, guards reported that Eric claimed he was in contact with aliens and had regular nighttime visitations with them. Eric said he had been instructed by his contacts to collect samples for them. The guards suspected that Eric's delusions were an attempt to get the charges dismissed due to mental incapacity. Then, while being transferred to another facility, Eric escaped.

He had purchased his name in New Orleans, from a man who specialized in new identities. The pickup and trailer came from a dealer in Birmingham. There was no Iconoclast Society, no wealthy benefactor who financed the research. There was only Eric, so filled with messianic self-confidence that he was practically above suspicion.

Deena had been interviewed by Hersig while she recovered in the Twelve Sleep County hospital. Afterward, he'd called Joe and recounted the conversation.

Deena had met "Cleve" in Helena, and she knew nothing of his past and she really didn't care to hear about it. He had never mentioned having a brother. What she knew was that he had been sent to her at the exact time she needed him most. He knew things that she hoped to learn, and was in contact with other beings on an intimate basis. He was their human conduit. At least that's what he told her, and she saw no reason not to believe him.

If it really was Cleve who did the mutilations, she said, he was simply following orders.

Yes, she had agreed to let him experiment on her. She saw it as no different than getting tattooed or pierced. She was a little pissed off at him, though, when he cut off the top of her ABDUCTEE tattoo.

And yes, she knew Cleve disposed of her skin at the fish-cleaning station. He had told her that.

She had slept through most of the trouble in the trailer the day of the shoot-out, she said. Cleve had given her some medication for her pain, and it knocked her out. The noises from the front of the trailer were awful, in an otherworldly way, but she had thought at the time that she was dreaming.

Despite everything, she said, she still loved Cleve Garrett. And more important, she still believed in him.

Hersig's voice was shaky as he told Joe the story. When he was through, he said, "I think I need to go take a shower."

Sheriff Barnum claimed not to have any idea what Cam had been up to in regard to the CBM rights on the ranch, although he admitted being interested in buying his retirement home there. Joe believed him, but also knew that Barnum had sat by quietly during the course of the investigation, as land values plummeted. He had not revealed his real estate interest to the rest of the task force, and he secretly benefited from the perception that the valley was "spooked." This led Joe and Hersig to speculate that Barnum may have had perverse motivation not to solve the crimes quickly, but they had no solid evidence of that.

Nevertheless, word got out within the community about the land deal that never was, and Barnum's interest in it. There was even talk among the coffee drinkers at the Burg-O-Pardner about launching a recall petition on Sheriff Barnum. As far as Joe knew, the action wasn't followed through. But there was no doubt that Barnum's reputation had taken a beating, and that he would stand little chance in the next election. Not that it mattered much, Barnum declared in the *Roundup,* because he had planned to retire anyway. It had been a good twenty-six years, he said.

For the twentieth time since the shoot-out, Joe sat lost in thought in his office. All but one big-game hunting season had ended, and winter was on the way. Paperwork was piled up in his in-box, and he'd missed three straight weekly reports to

Trey Crump. The mutilations had, of course, stopped. Portenson had gone back to Cheyenne. The Murder and Mutilations Task Force had been disbanded for lack of purpose.

But for Joe, there was unfinished business. The case was still open, and not just because Eric Logue was still at large. There were still too many questions.

Nate Romanowski had all but disappeared. His only communication with Joe was a terse message left on the answering machine: "Joe, I was right. That bear is here for a reason. He's just a vessel, an agent. He'll be here only as long as he has to be."

In the end, as the search for Dr. Eric Logue lost both hope and urgency, the only workable scenario they could give any credence to was this:

Eric had been a boy in the mid-1970s, when the first rash of cattle mutilations in the West was news, so the concept wasn't foreign to him. Perhaps that was when his fascination and obsession with a paranormal answer to the crimes was first implanted.

Eric Logue, in his sickness, had come to believe that his mission was to kill and disfigure living beings and collect trophies. He believed that others were telling him to do it, or he had somehow convinced himself that he was pleasing the owners of these voices through his acts. He used his experience as a surgeon, as well as his tools, to do it. His first disciple in his mission was Nurse Bob, who had problems of his own.

Using his new identity and the cover of the fictitious Iconoclast Society, he returned to the Rocky Mountain West, first to Northern Montana, then to Wyoming. He had a reason to be where the mutilations were discovered, after all. He said he was studying them.

The mutilations in Montana, from Eric's perspective, had gone very well. No one suspected him. What didn't go well, though, was that the officials in charge of the investigation treated him like he was a crank. They didn't take his theories seriously, and didn't welcome his knowledge or advice. There were a few converts, Deena being the primary one, but overall, he was disappointed.

He realized that cattle and wildlife weren't enough. He

needed to up the ante. He needed some help, so he asked Nurse Bob to rejoin him in Saddlestring. No one had recognized him from his youth there.

Eric and Nurse Bob started with animals, as they had in Montana. Then, on the single night in Twelve Sleep County, they had split up, with one of them going after Stuart Tanner and the other Tuff Montegue. Eric took Tanner, Nurse Bob took Tuff. This explained why Tanner's death was similar in style to the cattle mutilations. Nurse Bob, who was not as experienced in technique, had done a crude job on Tuff.

Nate's thought was that while Eric stayed with Tanner's body, his presence discouraged predators from moving in. Meanwhile, Nurse Bob left Tuff's body to the bear while he drove to pick up Eric. Once they were together again, Nurse Bob used his cell phone to report Tanner's body.

This is where the scenario began to fall apart, as far as Joe was concerned. There was still no explanation for why Eric came "home" to Saddlestring, or whether there had been any contact with Cam. If not, why had the murders obviously helped Cam's land deal along? Joe couldn't accept coincidence as an explanation.

They must have been in contact, Joe thought. Either Cam had asked Eric to use the cover of the cattle mutilations to kill Stuart Tanner, or Eric had somehow taken it upon himself to help out his brother. Either way, they must have communicated at some point. Otherwise, how would Eric have known to target Tanner?

The method and aftermath of the mutilations themselves, whether animal or human, still didn't produce a logical explanation. How had Eric actually killed the animals and mutilated them without leaving tracks or evidence? What had he done to the bodies to prevent predation?

What explained the feeling in the air Joe experienced when he first found the dead moose?

What scared Maxine so badly that he was now the proud owner of the world's only all-white Labrador?

The last part of the scenario was just as troublesome. What had driven Eric and Nurse Bob to confront Cam in his home, and to kidnap him? Why did they pick up Not Ike? And why had Eric and Nurse Bob killed and mutilated Cam?

And the biggest question of all: *Where was Eric Logue?*

Joe was still distracted when he and Marybeth cleared the dinner dishes from the table. He had scarcely heard the dinner conversation, with Lucy, Jessica, and Sheridan talking about their day in school.

As he filled the sink with water, Marybeth said, "You're thinking about Eric Logue again, aren't you?"

He looked at her.

"We may just never know, Joe. We've discussed it to death."

"I didn't think it was possible to discuss *anything* to death," he said, taking a jibe at her.

"Very funny."

He washed, she dried.

Lucy and Jessica laughed in the next room at something on television. Joe looked over his shoulder at them. They had changed out of their school clothes. They liked to dress alike, much to Sheridan's consternation. Tonight, they both wore oversized green surgeon's scrubs.

"Why are they wearing those?" Marybeth asked, suddenly alarmed, knowing whom the shirts once came from.

She raised her voice. "Both of you girls go change clothes right now. I thought I told you to get rid of those."

Both girls looked back at Marybeth, obvious guilt on their faces. They had forgotten.

"Sorry, Mom," Lucy said as she skulked to her room.

"Sorry, Mrs. Pickett," Jessica said.

Then it was as if Marybeth's legs went numb, Joe saw, the way she suddenly reached for the door jamb to keep herself steady.

"What?" Joe asked, puzzled.

Marybeth looked at Joe. Her expression was horrifying.
"What?"

"Oh, no," she said, looking pale.

"Marybeth . . ."

She turned to him and whispered, "Joe, Marie didn't throw out those scrubs. She let Jessica keep them and wear them."

"So?"

"Think about it, Joe. A woman wouldn't keep something like those scrubs around her house unless she had a reason. Marie had to know they were there. She washed them for Jessica, and folded them up for her, probably dozens of times."

Joe said, "Go on."

"Why would Marie keep those in her house? Clothes that would remind her husband of the brother he hated? Why would she keep a picture of Eric on her mantel? And now that I think about it, you were more surprised that Eric had come to their house after Cam that day than Marie was."

Joe felt a hammer blow square in the middle of his chest. "Marybeth, do you know what you're saying?"

Instead of answering, Marybeth stepped forward to intercept Jessica as she walked toward the bedroom to change. Marybeth dropped to her knees so she could look at Jessica eye-to-eye. She placed her hands gently on the little girl's shoulders.

"Jessica, how long have you had those shirts?"

Jessica stopped and thought. "A while."

"How long?"

Jessica was surprised at Marybeth's tone. "A couple of years, I guess. I don't remember exactly."

"Who gave them to you?"

"Uncle Eric."

Joe watched Jessica carefully. There was fear growing in her eyes.

Marybeth asked, "Jessica, was your uncle Eric at your house a couple of years ago? Before you moved here?"

Her eyes were huge and she was on the verge of tears. But she nodded.

"Your dad and your uncle Eric didn't get along very well, did they?"

"No."

"Your dad even asked you to get rid of those hospital scrubs when he saw you wearing them, didn't he?"

"Yes."

"But your mom said you could keep them, as long as you never wore them around your dad, right?"

Jessica nodded. "I think they're cool to wear."

"I understand."

Jessica looked over Marybeth's shoulder at Joe. Joe knew that Jessica couldn't determine if she was in trouble or not.

"No one's angry with you, Jessica," he told her. "Just answer Marybeth's questions."

Jessica nodded. "My mom said I could keep them as long as I didn't wear them around my dad, and I never did."

Marybeth asked, "Your mom and uncle Eric were good friends, weren't they? They talked a lot on the telephone when your dad wasn't there, right?"

Joe took a deep breath, feeling a shroud of dark horror engulf him.

When Jessica nodded, Joe didn't even want to see Marybeth's reaction. But Marybeth remained calm, at least outwardly.

"Okay, honey," Marybeth said, standing. "You can go change now."

Jessica didn't move.

Joe and Marybeth stared at each other, neither wanting to say anything in front of Jessica. Jessica watched them both, and her eyes filled with tears.

She looked at Marybeth. "My mom's not coming back, is she?"

38

THREE DAYS LATER, Marie Logue was at the New Orleans International Airport, checking in for a flight to Milan, when she was surrounded by a dozen special agents from the local office of the FBI. The name she was using was Barbara Grossman, and she had a Louisiana driver's license and a four-year-old passport to prove it. Unfortunately for Marie Logue, the FBI had, on videotape, the footage of the transaction taking place between Marie and the same man who had sold Eric Logue his Cleve Garrett identity papers.

Portenson was exuberant and cocky when he called Joe and told him what had happened. He said he had thought it through once Joe tipped him off about the relationship between Marie and Eric Logue, and he figured out that Eric had probably told Marie about the location of the identity thief in New Orleans. Portenson figured that Marie would eventually go there herself, for her new documents. Portenson said his colleagues in New Orleans had arrested the identity thief earlier in the week and had made a deal for leniency with him if he would help them set her up, including the placement of video cameras in his office over a bar on Bourbon Street.

"We want to interview her tomorrow, and we'd like you to be here, since you know her," Portenson said.

"I *thought* I knew her," Joe corrected.

"Whatever. We want you there."

"New Orleans?"

"I'll fax you the address for our field office, and we'll make you a reservation at a hotel nearby. If you take the commuter flight that leaves your little podunk airport in two hours, you can connect in Denver. You can be here tonight."

"I don't think I have the budget to . . ."

"We're covering your expenses, Joe. I already got approval for it."

J oe Pickett landed in New Orleans at midnight, in a rainstorm of biblical dimensions. His Stetson got soaked through in just the time it took him to climb into a taxi at the airport.

Despite the rain, there were throngs of people moving on the sidewalks downtown. Some carried umbrellas, but most just got wet. He checked in at the Bourbon Orleans Hotel in the French Quarter.

As he stood at the front desk, dripping, the flirty blond clerk found his reservation and said, "Are you really from Wyoming?"

"Yup."

"I don't believe I've ever actually met anyone from there before."

"Now you have," he said.

T here was a message on the voice mail in his room from Portenson saying to be at the FBI field office on Leon C. Simon Boulevard by 9 A.M.

"We'll brief you on what we've got so far, and then we'll go in and see her," he said. "So don't party too hard on the Quarter tonight."

Joe called Marybeth to tell her that he had arrived safely, then tried to sleep. He couldn't. The unfamiliarity of it all—Marie Logue, mutilations, New Orleans—kept him awake.

At two in the morning he put on his wet hat and went outside into the rain. The streets were still crowded with people. He walked down Dauphine Street and then Bourbon, and a reveler from a balcony above him called him "Tex" and threw him a beaded necklace.

It was still raining in the morning when he arrived at the FBI field office. The security guard found his name on the computer, gave him a guest badge, and sent him into the back offices.

Portenson was waiting with a bookish woman he introduced as Special Agent Nan Scoon. Scoon had been the leader of the team that arrested Marie at the airport.

Portenson said, "When we brought her in, she had $8,000 in cash on her and records that indicate that she transferred $1.3 million—the rest of the insurance money—to accounts in the Caymans. *That's* what she had spent her time doing after she left your place.

"The calls she made to your wife supposedly to check on her daughter were from all over the country. Not one actually came from Denver, where her parents do live. We interviewed them and she never even showed up there."

Joe whistled. "You did some good work."

"I know," Portenson said, "I'm a fuckin' genius. But the great thing is that we built the case on her while we waited for her to show up here, and last night we dropped it on her like a ton of bricks. First-degree accessory to three murders, child abandonment, conspiracy, racketeering, and fifteen other counts. She was playing it straight at first—she kept insisting she was Barbara Grossman—but we dropped those charges on her like the Mother of All Bombs. And after a little crying jag, she cracked. She gave us a little at first, fishing around for a deal. When she saw she wasn't going to get one, she started yapping. My guys down there said that by the time she was through, it was like she was bragging about it, all full of herself."

"So she's willing to talk?" Joe asked.

"That's why we brought you down here, cowboy."

J oe didn't recognize her at first when they entered the spartan interview room. Marie was now blond, and she wore fashionable, black-framed glasses. She had added a beauty mark to her upper lip. When she saw Joe, her eyes widened behind the lenses.

"Hello, Marie," Joe said, sitting across the table from her. Portenson and Scoon took the other chairs.

Agent Scoon signaled for the tape to roll, and briefed Marie on her rights. As she had done the day before, Marie waived the right to have an attorney present.

"Let's get this over with," she said curtly, looking at Joe.

"So who actually found the file in the basement?" Joe asked.

"*Moi*," she said, and her eyes sparkled. "Cam might have seen it before, but it didn't connect with him the way it connected with me. He was a little slow in that regard. Cam was a fairly weak guy, basically. He looked to me for guidance."

Joe grunted. In retrospect, it didn't surprise him all that much. As he had thought earlier, Cam was driving without a road map. But Marie was the one providing directions.

"Then those mutilations came," she said, "and that's all everyone was talking about. We liked the idea that the land values were sinking, but we worried about whether we could afford the Timberline Ranch anyway. That's when I started pushing Cam so hard to get out there and get more listings. I rode him *hard*, thinking that if even *one* of the ranches sold we would have the down payment on the Timberline."

While she talked, she drew invisible patterns on the tabletop with her index finger.

"That's when poor old Stuart Tanner showed up with his file. We didn't figure that Tanner would research the deed and find the same thing I did. So when Cam told me that we needed to forget about buying the place and move on, I played my hole card."

"You called Eric," Joe said.

"Right. We'd kept in touch for years." She batted her eyes

coquettishly. "He's been *smitten* with me, like *forever*. We'd had a relationship years before that Cam never knew about. I moved on but Eric kept a torch. Even when he started getting sick he never lost his feelings for me. He said he'd do anything for me. Then he'd talk like a nut about his obsession with aliens. I let him go on and on about that. So when I called him and asked him for a favor, he came. Eric and his buddy Bob did Tanner and Montegue. Eric did it to please me, which was kind of sweet when you think about it."

Joe felt his stomach curdle, but tried to stay calm and ask his questions.

"Why did they choose Tuff Montegue?"

She shrugged. "He was just *there,* I suppose. But Eric was clever in a devilish kind of way. He told me that they intentionally messed up the job on Montegue. They did it to draw attention away from Tanner, and as you know, it worked. Your task force would have been working the wrong angle on that one until hell froze over, if it weren't for you, Joe."

Joe said nothing. He was thinking. Most of the pieces had finally fallen into place. But there were still problems.

"So Cam didn't know about his brother being there?" Joe asked.

"I think he assumed he was somewhere close. He told me he thought it was just a matter of time before the family was back together, now that his parents were there. He dreaded the prospect."

"Did he know Nurse Bob was living in a shack on your property?"

"*I* didn't even know that. I thought he was living somewhere out in the woods."

"What about Cam's parents? Did Cam know they were coming? Did you?"

Marie laughed sourly. "That was as big of a surprise for me as it was for Cam when they showed up. I knew about Bob coming, of course, but I had no idea they were bringing him. Old Clancy and Helen really threw a kink into things."

"Did you tell Eric to kill his brother?"

Marie reacted with shock. "Of course not. Of *course* not. I was genuinely shocked when you told me what happened. I just wanted Eric to put a little spine into Cam, because Cam was wavering on me."

"Why was he wavering?"

"You spooked him," Marie said, smiling at Joe. "That meeting you had with him shook him up. When he found out you were checking out the deeds at the county clerk's, he told me we needed to forget the whole damned thing. But I had no intention of giving up."

Joe was chilled by her. She was so matter-of-fact, and actually a little charming. Poor Cam, Joe thought. He'd married a manipulator.

"I never saw it," Joe confessed. "I never even considered you."

"You weren't the only one," she said.

"I kept wondering why they went after Not Ike," Joe said, "but now I know. It's because I told Cam that Not Ike said he had seen somebody in the alley behind the real estate office. When Cam told you the story, you panicked and called Eric."

She leaned forward and fixed Joe with her eyes. "I don't panic," she said.

"Do you know where Eric is?"

"Absolutely not," she said adamantly. "I swear it. I haven't been in contact with him since that morning. I hope you find him, and I hope he hangs or whatever they do to killers in Wyoming. Joe," she said, tilting her head to the side, "he killed my husband, remember? As far as I know, he's still out there."

"You mean in Wyoming?"

"As far as I know," she repeated. Then she looked to Agent Scoon, as if she was exasperated with Joe.

"Don't you think I'd give him up in a heartbeat if I knew where he was? Eric's location is the only thing I'd have to make a deal with. You people have me on so many charges, at least if I knew something I'd be able to, you know, negotiate a little."

It did make sense, Joe conceded to himself. *Damn it.*

"So it was all about money," Joe said sadly. "All about getting the CBM leases."

She turned on him. "*Of course,* Joe. Why would there be any more to it? You've got these rubes all over the state becoming instant millionaires, just because they own mineral rights. It's not like they earned their money by being virtuous, or working hard. Why not Cam and me?

"What did you expect? That we were going to just bump along all of our lives living paycheck to paycheck like you and Marybeth?"

That stung, and he blinked.

"Cam was okay with that kind of existence, but I never was," she said. "When it's raining money, you can either put on your raincoat or get the buckets out. You better think about it too, Joe. You've got your family to think about. Marybeth wants more, Joe. She deserves more. Don't think we haven't talked about it, either."

Joe sat in silence, staring at her.

"Stop staring," she snapped.

"Never once have you asked about your daughter," he said. "Not once have you even mentioned her."

Marie smiled. "That's because I know she's in good hands."

They left Marie in the interview room. Joe and Portenson stood in the hall, shaking their heads at each other.

"Couple of things," Joe said. "If Marie called Eric to come and get Stuart Tanner, then Eric could not have done the cattle mutilations."

Portenson moaned. "Why don't we forget about the dead cows for now."

"Because I can't." Joe didn't bring up the moose.

"Jesus Christ."

"It means that somebody or something else mutilated the animals," Joe said. "It had nothing to do with Eric, or Marie. She used the mutilations for cover to do in Tanner. But she didn't have anything to do with them in the first place."

Portenson sounded almost physically pained. "Joe . . ."

"Don't tell me it was birds, Portenson."

After a long silence, Portenson said, "Okay, I won't. But I don't see where it matters anymore. The mutilations have gone away. We'll never find out who did it, and frankly, since we've got Marie, I really don't care anymore. We'll find Eric. It's just a matter of time."

"One more thing," Joe said. "Jessica Logue."

"Oh, man . . ."

"Are her grandparents okay? The ones in Denver? Can they take her?"

"This isn't my department."

"I know. But you talked to them. Do they seem like normal human beings? Not like Clancy and Helen? Or Marie?"

"They seem normal."

"Are you sure?"

"I didn't give them a psychological test, or anything. Come on, Joe . . ."

"I'm serious." Joe said, raising his voice. "It's important. We've seen too many people screwed up by bad parents. I can't let Jessica go there unless I'm sure she'll be okay. If it's not, we've got to find a normal uncle and aunt. There's got to be somebody."

Portenson sighed, "Okay, okay. I'll make your case. We'll send some people over there, and do some checking. But please understand that this isn't what the FBI does . . ."

Joe thanked him before he could recant.

O n the plane back, Joe sat in his seat and furiously rubbed his face with his hands. He hadn't seen it, hadn't suspected. And even though one part of the investigation was concluded, there was still more. The whole sordid case left a bad taste in his mouth. It always came down to the family, he thought.

M arybeth listened as Joe recounted the interview, watching him. She shook her head sadly.

"It's not your fault," he said. "She fooled everyone."

Marybeth came over and sat on Joe's lap. Her eyes were moist. "We talked about everything, Joe. She told me about her dreams. I told her about mine. Now I find out that her dreams were things she made up for my sake. I feel horribly duped, and angry."

He held her. "Sometimes, darling, we see what we want to see. Remember Wacey Hedeman?"

Wacey had been Joe's closest friend until he betrayed Joe. Four years before, Wacey had shot Marybeth and threatened Sheridan. It still hurt when Joe thought about it. Wacey had twenty more years to go at the Wyoming State Penitentiary in Rawlins.

"Thank you for trying to find the best family for Jessica," Marybeth said softly. "I wish we could keep her, I really do. But after what happened to April, I just can't make the commitment."

Joe nodded. "I knew that. It's okay."

They sat like that for a half an hour, each with their own rumination, holding each other.

Eric Logue is still out there, he thought, *and so is whatever mutilated the cattle.*

She thought, *We're back to where we started.*

39

WINTER STORM CLOUDS were nosing over the top of the Bighorn Mountains and the air was cold and lifeless when Nate Romanowski pulled on his jacket to check his falcons in the mews. Joe Pickett was bringing Sheridan out later that morning, for her first falconry apprenticeship lesson in a while. Nate's special project had concluded, more or less successfully, and it was time to fly his birds again. It had been too long, nearly two months.

On mornings like this, in the quiet of an impending storm, sounds carried farther. It would be a good morning to submerge himself in the river and listen, Nate thought. But the water was getting too cold for that. He needed a winter wet suit.

From inside the mews, he heard his peregrine squeal and flap his wings wildly, and Nate stopped before opening the door. He had put a leather hood on the bird the night before, specifically to keep the falcon calm. Something had alarmed the bird. There was something wrong. . . .

The blow to his head came from above, from the roof of the mews. He hadn't thought to look up.

———

Nate knew what was happening, he knew why it was happening, but there was nothing he could do about it. His limbs wouldn't respond and he couldn't even open his eyes. The heavy blow had temporarily paralyzed him, disconnected his brain from his body. He lay on his back in the dirt near the door of the mews.

Even worse, someone was on top of him, pinning him down.

He felt the deep slice of a blade behind his ear, felt it draw down across his jaw, the sound like a liquid swish, then a jarring scrape of metal on bone that sent a shock throughout his nervous system. It reminded him of how amplified things sounded when he was underwater. He felt the air on exposed tissue as the flesh on his face was pulled aside, and it felt cold.

Eric Logue.

Sheridan had been searching the sky for falcons and lazily eating a banana for breakfast as they drove to Nate Romanowski's stone cabin on the bank of the river, when she lowered her gaze and saw the two forms on the ground near the mews.

"Dad, what's *that*?"

Joe took it in quickly, saw it for what it was, yelled, "Hold on tight!" and jammed the accelerator into the floor.

Through the windshield, Joe saw Eric look up at the sound of the approaching pickup. Eric was wild looking and filthy, with shredded clothing, a scraggly beard, and stiff, tumbleweed hair. He was on top of Nate's prone body with his knees on either side of Nate's head. Joe saw blood and Nate's lifeless, pale hand flung out to the side of him.

As Joe bore down on the mews, Eric stood up, looked quickly at his unfinished business on the ground, then turned and started running toward the river, loping toward it like some kind of heavy-limbed animal.

Sheridan braced herself on the dashboard of the truck, her eyes wide, as Joe drove by Nate and pursued Eric. The distance between Joe, Eric, and the river closed at once, and Joe saw Eric shoot a panicked glance back over his shoulder seconds before Joe hit him.

The collision dented the grille and buckled the hood of the pickup, and sent Eric flying toward the river where he hit the water with an ungainly, flailing splash. Joe slammed on his brakes, and the pickup fishtailed and stopped at the water's edge.

Joe and Sheridan scrambled out, with Maxine bounding behind them.

"Jeez, Dad . . ." Sheridan said, her face white. "I mean . . . *wow.*"

Joe concentrated on the surface of the river. The water was dark and deep, the surface blemished only by ringlets that spread from the center of the violent splash. Eric had sunk like a rock, but Joe wasn't sure he had hit Eric hard enough to kill him outright. He wished Sheridan hadn't been there to see it.

Nate was breathing and his eyes were open when Joe and Sheridan got to him. The cut on the side of his face was deep, and bleeding profusely, and a flap of his skin was folded back and raw. Joe knelt and put it back, seeing that Eric had been interrupted before he could sever any arteries or do fatal damage.

"Ouch," Nate said weakly.

"Stay down," Joe said, still shaky. "Don't sit up. I'm calling the EMTs right now."

Sheridan stripped off her hooded sweatshirt and dropped to her knees to compress the cloth against his wound.

Joe ran back to his truck and keyed the mike.

He completed the call and was told to expect the ambulance within twenty minutes.

"That's a hell of a long time," Joe said angrily.

"They're on their way," Wendy the dispatcher snapped back. "You are quite a ways out of town, you know."

He looked back toward the mews. He could see Nate and Sheridan talking to each other. Nate was going to be okay, Joe thought, although he would have quite a scar on his face.

For the first time since they'd arrived, Joe took a deep breath. He realized that his hands were shaking and his mouth was dry.

He looked at the river, at its deceptive, muscular stillness. On the other side of the river, a high red rock face was dotted with tenacious clumps of sage. Then down river, where the channel began a slow bend away from him, he saw Eric Logue dragging himself out of the water on the other bank.

Eric pulled himself into a clump of willows, got to his hands and knees, and crawled out of sight into a small red rock fissure.

"Stay with him until the EMTs get here," Joe told Sheridan, checking his loads and racking the pump on his shotgun. He had given her his first aid kit so she could use a sterile compress, as her sweatshirt was now heavy with Nate's blood. "You're doing a good job, honey."

Sheridan looked up, concerned. "Where are you going?"

"Down river."

Nate was watching him warily. He started to sit up.

"Nate, stay down," Joe said.

"Joe, you should know something. We've been waiting for Eric Logue to show up. We knew he would."

Joe hesitated.

"They're both vessels," Nate said. "Eric Logue and the bear. It's not even their fight, but you have to let it play out. It has to end here."

Joe looked at him, then at Sheridan.

"The next time you have a dream about bad things coming," Joe said to his daughter, "I'll listen."

She nodded, her eyes wide.

"It's about time," Nate said.

A quarter of a mile beyond where Joe had seen Eric emerge from the river, there was an old footbridge that had been built by a Hungarian hard rock miner named Scottie Balyo in the 1930s. Scottie had used the bridge to work a secret seam of gold somewhere in the foothills. The bridge was no longer safe, due to rotten and missing slats, but Joe labored his way across it by straddling the planks themselves and keeping his boots on the outside rails. The frame sagged and moaned as he went across, but it held. On the other side, he stepped down into soft, wet sand.

He kept to the sand as he crept downriver, walking as quietly as he could. As he neared the willows he had seen Eric crawl into, he turned and scrambled up the loose wall of the bank so he could see the fissure from above.

Never again, Joe thought, would he discount a dream Sheridan had. Like Nate, she was connected to this thing in a way that was real, if incomprehensible. Perhaps it was intuitiveness born of her age, that preteen angst that allowed her to tap into events that were occurring on another level, as Nate had described. Sheridan had seen the evil coming, and tracked it.

With Nate, it was his preternatural animal sense; his interaction with the natural world around him, that drew him to the bear. Joe couldn't explain either circumstance, and didn't want to. But it was there, had been there, and if nothing else he would now open his mind, if only a little, to accept it.

The fissure was narrow where Eric had entered it, but it widened into a brush-choked draw. The floor of the draw was dry now, in the winter, but in the spring it served as a funnel for snowmelt from the mountains into the river. The soft sand was churned up down there—Eric's track. Joe couldn't yet see him, but he couldn't imagine that Eric had gotten very far.

Joe heard him before he saw him; a low, sad moan from farther up the draw.

"Cleve?" Joe called. "Dr. Eric Logue?"

The moaning stopped.

"Joe Pickett," Joe called. "I'm going to arrest you."

"You're going to kill me!"

Joe dropped into the draw. "Maybe so," Joe said.

When he found him, Joe was surprised to see that Eric had managed to stand up, using the help of an emerged root on the side of the draw as a handhold. He was bent forward, obviously in great pain. His head was slightly lowered, but his eyes locked on Joe as he approached. A thread of bloody saliva strung from his lips to the sand.

Joe kept his shotgun pointed at Eric's chest. Joe was a notoriously bad shot, but he figured even he couldn't miss with a shotgun at this distance.

Eric still held the scalpel in his right fist, which rested on his thigh, but he didn't threaten Joe with it. It was almost as if he had forgotten it was there.

"I'm really busted up inside, man," Eric groaned, never taking his eyes off of Joe. "I'm not gonna make it."

"Probably not," Joe said.

Eric coughed, and the cough must have seared through him, because his legs almost buckled. "It hurts so bad," he groaned. He coughed again, then spit a piece of what looked like bright red sponge into the sand between his feet. Lung, Joe knew, having seen the spoor of lung-shot big-game animals many times before. Eric's ribs had probably broken and then speared his lungs when the pickup hit him.

"Think you can walk across that bridge?" Joe asked.

Eric just stared at him. Then: "Why don't you just shoot me? It's okay."

Joe squinted, trying to determine if Eric was playing games with him.

"Pull the trigger, you coward," Eric said.

"Why?"

Eric coughed again, then righted himself. "I'm really sick, man. And they're through with me."

Joe felt his scalp twitch. "Who is through with you?"

Eric tried to gesture skyward, but his arm wouldn't work. "They are. I thought there would be some kind of payoff, but they just used me. No one told me the other side would send something after me."

Behind Eric was a dark wall of Rocky Mountain junipers. Joe thought he saw movement in the lower branches, but decided it must have been the cold wind. The wind did strange things in draws like this.

"Tell me," Joe said. "We know about Stuart Tanner and Tuff Montegue. But why did you kill your brother?"

Eric's face twisted painfully. "It was Bob. Bob did that. I guess Cam tried to get away, and Bob whacked him on the head. Then Bob figured he'd mutilate him to make it look like the others. I wasn't in the room when it happened."

"You were carving on Deena in the other room at the time, I guess," Joe said.

"Who cares about any of this?" Eric said. "You got me. So shoot, you bastard. Give me some peace. Or I'll come over there and start cutting on you."

"What made Tuff Montegue's horse throw him?"

Eric twitched. "Bob said it was just dumb luck. Bob said he must have spooked the horse as he moved from tree to tree."

"Why the animals?" Joe asked, gripping the shotgun tighter. "Why did you mutilate the animals?"

Eric shook his head. "I didn't hurt any animals. Except for that stupid horse on that ranch, and I messed that up."

"*What?*" Joe asked, perplexed.

"I know who did it, though," Eric said, coughing. His eyes shined. He took a clumsy step toward Joe now, and raised the scalpel. "*They* did it."

Again, Joe saw a shiver in the junipers. This time, he knew it wasn't the wind. It was something huge, something big-bodied.

"They're gone now," Eric said, wincing but still lurching forward. "But they'll be back. And if you think *I'm* scary . . ."

The grizzly bear, the one Joe had once been chasing, the one Nate had made his obsession, blasted out of the junipers and hit Eric Logue in the back with such primal force and fury that it left Joe gasping for breath. The bear had waited, and Eric Logue had finally come.

Joe watched as the grizzly dragged Eric's wildly thrashing body into the shadows.

Sheridan still dreamed vividly, and one dream in particular stayed with her, subtly growing in meaning until she would later look back on it as the end of something. In that dream, one of many that took place the night after Eric Logue attacked Nate Romanowski, the roiling black clouds were back. This time, though, the tendrils of smoke or mist leached from the ground and low brush and rose upward, as if being withdrawn. The black horse-head snouts of the thunderheads rolled back, eventually clearing the top of the Bighorn Mountain, leaving big, blue sky.

She believed there had been a battle. The battle took place in plain sight, in front of everyone, but few could see or sense it. She wanted to believe that the battle was between good forces, with the bear as the agent, and evil, embodied by some other kind of beings who had recruited Eric Logue and Nurse Bob. Perhaps the good forces had engaged her dad and Nate as temporary foot soldiers as well. But she would never know that.

It was remarkable to Sheridan how little the incidents—the cattle, wildlife, and human mutilations—were talked about. It was as if everyone in the Twelve Sleep Valley collectively wished that nothing had happened. But they had. Men had died. Maxine would forever be changed from seeing something that had scared her white. A family, the Logues, was destroyed.

Even when the e-mail came to her father from someone named Deena, who had written to him from somewhere in South America where more mutilations had subsequently occurred, her father didn't want to discuss it. Sheridan wouldn't have even known about the e-mail if she hadn't heard Nate try and broach the subject with her dad.

"Too many holes in the earth," Nate had said. "Maybe something was released into the atmosphere that drew in a force like putrid meat draws in flies."

Her dad had said, "Or maybe not," in that dismissive way he had, and changed the subject. When Nate tried to steer him back, her dad told Nate, "I don't want to talk about something we'll never have the knowledge to understand." Then: "Nate, I *hate* woo-woo crap."

Nate said, "I know you do," and smiled, the edges of his new scar twisting his mouth slightly.

She was with her dad later that fall when he slowed his pickup on the bridge to call out to Not Ike Easter, who was fishing in the river. Not Ike hollered back, laughing. Sheridan asked her dad what Not Ike had said.

"He said he's caught three fish." Then he smiled as if he were content, as if things had finally returned to normal.

ACKNOWLEDGMENTS

My sincere thanks to those who provided information, background, inspiration, and expertise in the creation of this novel.

Thanks to Katie Oyan of the *Great Falls Tribune,* for providing her stories, background photos, and information on a new series of cattle mutilations near Conrad, Montana, in December of 2000 and January of 2001.

Special thanks to those who read early drafts of the manuscript and offered expertise and advice: Bill Scribner; Wyoming Game Warden Mark Nelson and Mari; Laurie, Molly, and Becky; RoseMarie London and Lois Chickering; and Ann Rittenberg, who went way beyond the call of duty.

Thanks to Michael Burton for writing "Night Rider's Lament," and Don Hajicek for designing and maintaining the cjbox.net site.

And my gratitude to Joan Montgomery of Murder by the Book in Denver, who two years ago asked, "Have you ever thought of checking out those cattle mutilations?"

As always, special recognition and acknowledgment must go to Martha Bushko, my editor at Putnam, as well as the entire team of professionals at G. P. Putnam's Sons and Berkley.

C. J. Box
Cheyenne, Wyoming

Turn the page for a preview of

OUT OF RANGE

the next Joe Pickett novel by acclaimed author

C. J. BOX

Available in paperback from
The Berkley Publishing Group!

1

BEFORE GOING OUTSIDE to his pickup for his gun, the Wyoming game warden cooked and ate four and a half pounds of meat.

He'd begun his meal with pronghorn antelope steaks, butterflied, floured, and browned in olive oil. Then an elk chop, pan-fried with salt and pepper, adding minced garlic to the cast-iron skillet. His first drink, sipped while he was cooking the antelope, was a glass of Yukon Jack and water on the rocks. By the time he broiled a half-dozen mourning dove breasts, he no longer bothered with the ice or the water. As he sat down late in the evening with an elk tenderloin so rare that blood pooled around it on his plate, he no longer used the glass, but drank straight from the bottle.

He ate no vegetables; unless one counted the sautéed onions he had slathered on a grass-fed Hereford beef T-bone, or the minced garlic. Just meat.

He needed air, and stood up.

His mind swam, the room rotated, his heavy boots clunked across the floor. He paused at the jamb, using it to brace himself upright. He stared at a fly-speck on the wall, tried to will the quadruple images he was seeing down to a more manageable two.

Finally, he opened the door. It was dark except for a blue streetlight on the northern corner of the block. A full moon lit up the crags of the mountains, casting them in dim blue-gray. The chill of the fall was already a guest. He stumbled down the broken sidewalk toward his truck. As he approached, his pickup seemed to swell and deflate, as if it were breathing.

"Something smells good inside," a voice said. It startled the game warden, and he squinted toward it, trying to concentrate, hear it over the mild roar in his ears. A neighbor wearing a tam on his head was walking a poodle down the middle of the street.

"Meat," Will Jensen said abruptly, almost shouting. It was sometimes hard these days to hear his own voice above the roar.

"See you," the neighbor called as he walked down the street, *"Bon appetit!"*

These people here, Will thought. A goddamned poodle and a tam.

His .44 Magum, his bear gun, was on the truck's bench seat where he had left it. Will drew it out of the holster. Holding it loosely in his right hand, he turned back for the house, tripped over his own boots, and fell in the gravel. A red finger of alarm probed into his brain, concern about accidentally discharging the weapon in his fall. Then he snorted a laugh, thinking, *Who cares?*

He didn't know how much later it was when he stirred awake. He was still sitting at the table, but had passed out face forward into his plate. Crisp grouse skin stuck to his cheek, and he pawed at it climsily until it fluttered to the floor.

Angry, he swept the table clear with his arm. Grease smeared across the Formica. The dirty plate cracked in half when it hit the wall.

Where was his .44?

He found it on his bed, where he had tossed it earlier. Along with the weapon, he grabbed a framed photo of his family from the bedside table. He took them both back into the kitchen.

"Forlorn" was a word he had come to like in recent months. It was a word that sounded like what it described. *"Forlorn,"* he had said aloud to himself, *"I feel forlorn. I am a forlorn man."* Something about the word soothed him, because it defined him, made him admit what he was.

What in the hell was wrong with him? Why did he feel this way, after so many years of balancing on the beam?

The roar in his ears was now so faint that it reminded him of a soft breeze in the treetops. His eyes filled with unexpected, stinging tears, and he drank a long pull from the bottle. He cocked the .44, watched the cylinder rotate. He opened his mouth and pressed the muzzle against the top of his palate. There was a burning, acrid taste. When was the last time he cleaned it?

Why did that matter now?

He stared at the photo he'd propped up on the table. It swam. He closed his eyes so tightly that he saw orange fireworks on the inside of his eyelids. He tried to concentrate on the .44 in his fist and the muzzle in his mouth. His stomach was on fire; he tried to fight his urge to get violently sick. He tasted the bitter whiskey a second time.

Concentrate . . .

2

THE WEDDING OF Bud Longbrake and Missy Vankueren took place at noon on a sun-filled Saturday in September on the front lawn of the Longbrake Ranch, twenty miles from town. Everyone was there.

The govenor and his wife, most of the state senate where Bud served as majority leader, the state's lone congressman, and what seemed like half of Saddlestring filled two hundred fifty metal folding chairs and spilled over into the lawn on the sides. Both U.S. senators had sent their regrets. The crisp blue shoulders of the Bighorn Mountains framed the wedding party. The day smelled of just-cut grass and wood smoke from the barbecue pit behind the house, where a prime Longbrake steer and a 4-H pig were roasting. It was a still, windless morning. A single cloud grazed lazily along the peaks. The only sounds were from car doors slamming as more guests arrived, pulling into and the shorn hay meadow that served as a parking lot in the back, and occasional mewls from cattle in a distant holding corral.

Joe Pickett sat in the second row. He wore a jacket and tie, dark slacks, and polished black cowboy boots. He was in his mid-thirties, lean, medium height. His thirteen-year-old daughter Sheridan sat next to him in a new blue dress. She shined brightly, he thought; long blond hair still streaked with summer highlights, a touch of pink lipstick, open, attractive face, eyes that took in everything. She watched intently as her mother Marybeth and eight-year-old sister Lucy took part in the ceremony. Lucy was the flower girl, wearing white taffeta. Marybeth, the matron of honor, stood on a riser next to Dale Longbrake and the rest of the wedding party. The men wore black western-cut tuxedos and black Stetsons.

Joe and his wife exchanged glances, and he could tell from her eyes that she was exasperated. Her mother, Missy Vankueren, was an experienced wedding planner, having been the featured bride in three previous ceremonies. Missy had been designing the event for over a year with the intensity and precision of a general implementing a major ground offensive, Joe thought, and she had enlisted a reluctant Marybeth as her second lieutenant. Endless discussions and phone calls had finally resulted in this day, which Marybeth had come to refer to as "Operation Massive Ranch Wedding."

Joe nodded toward the mountains and whispered to Sheridan, "See that cloud?"

Sheridan looked, "yes."

"I would wager that by Wedding Five, Missy will have figured out how to get rid of it."

"Dad!" she whispered fiercely. But the corners of her mouth tugged with a conspiratorial grin. He winked at her, and she rolled her eyes, turning back to the wedding that was about to begin.

There was a growing murmur as the bride appeared, on cue, beneath an arch of pink and white flowers. Joe and Sheridan rose to their feet with the rest of the crowd.

Applause rippled from the front to the back as Missy appeared glowing, wide-eyed, looking demurely at the throng she had turned out.

"I can't believe that's my grandmother," Sheridan said to Joe, "She looks . . ."

"Stunning," Joe said, finishing the sentence for her. Missy looked thirty, not sixty, he thought. She was a slim brunette, her face and hair perfect, her eyes glistening in a too-large head that always looked great in photos. She held a bouquet of pink and white flowers against her shimmering plum dress.

Joe heard Bud Longbrake say, in a reverent tone of appreciation he usually reserved for great cutting horses or seed bulls: "*There's* my girl."

The reception was held behind the huge log home, under hundred-year-old cottonwoods. A swing band from Billings played on a stage, and couples spun on a hardwood floor that had been moved to the ranch just for the occasion from a vacated mid-forties dance hall in Winchester. The floor was unique in that it was mounted on carriage springs and had been used for Saturday night dances when big bands used to stop over in Wyoming en route to real paying gigs on the east or west coasts.

Joe ushered Sheridan through the reception line, shaking hands. Bud Longbrake slapped him on the shoulder and said "Welcome to the family."

I've got a family, Joe thought.

Missy reached for Joe, and pulled his head down next to hers. He felt the bouquet she still clutched crush into his hair. "Never thought I'd pull this one off, did you?" she whispered.

Surprised, he pulled away. She grinned slyly at him, and despite himself, he grinned back. She was a substantial adversary, he thought. He'd hate to meet her in a dark alley.

"Congratulations," he said. "Bud is a fine man."

"Oh, I think I got the best of the deal," Bud said, wrapping his arm around Missy's slim waist.

"You did," she said, flashing her wide smile.

And her name is already on the ranch deed, Joe thought. *She owns half of everything we see as far as we can see it. She pulled it off, all right.*

Marybeth was next, and had been carefully watching the exchange that took place a moment before.

"You look wonderful," he said.

Thank God it's over, she mouthed. He nodded back, agreeing with her.

"Welcome to the family," Bud was telling Sheridan.

Joe shot him a look.

Joe, are you sure she said *that?*" Marybeth asked later, after appetizers, as they sat at a table under the trees with their plates. Joe had waited for Sheridan and Lucy to find their friends before he told Marybeth about her mother.

"I'm quoting."

Marybeth shook her head, looking hard at Joe to see if he was joking. She obviously determined he wasn't. "She's something else, isn't she?"

"Always has been," Joe said. "What I can't figure out is how you survived."

Marybeth smiled and patted his hand. "Neither do I, at times."

Joe sipped from a bottle of beer that had been offered to him from a stock tank full of ice.

"You two have a very strange relationship," Marybeth said, looking across the lawn at her mother.

"I didn't think we had one at all."

Missy had never made a secret of the fact that she felt Marybeth married beneath herself. Instead of the doctor, real-estate magnate, or U.S. senator Marybeth should have chosen, her most promising daughter wound up with Joe Pickett, a Wyoming game warden with a salary that capped out at $36,000 a year. Marybeth's career as a corporate lawyer or politician's wife, in Missy's view, had been unfulfilled. Rather, Marybeth stayed with Joe as he moved from place to place in their early years together, before Joe was named game warden to the Saddlestring District. Then Sheridan came along, followed by Lucy, and in Missy's eyes it was all but over for her daughter. Because of incidents relating to Joe Pickett and his job, Marybeth had been injured and could have no more children. Then a foster daughter had been lost. It was frustrating for Missy, Joe thought. There she was, providing a living example of how to keep trading up—casting off husbands in exchange for newer, wealthier, and shinier models—and her daughter just didn't get it. Missy literally tried to show Marybeth how it could be done by marrying Bud Longbrake right in front of her, Joe thought.

Marybeth still had fire, intelligence, beauty, and ambition, Joe and Missy both knew. She also had a growing melancholy, which she tried hard to overcome.

"Look at Bud's kids," Marybeth said, nodding toward a table set as far away from the others as possible while still being in the shade, "They just don't look happy. Don't stare at them, though."

Joe shifted in his chair. Bud had a son and a daughter from his previous marriage. The son, Bud Jr., had flown in for the wedding from Missoula, where he was a street musician and professional student at UM. Bud Jr. wore billowy cargo shorts, leather sandals, a T-shirt, and a sour expression. Missy had told Joe and Marybeth that although Bud Jr. had never wanted anything to do with the ranch while growing up, he was content to wait things out, wait for Bud to pass along or sell the ranch. Even after taxes, Bud Jr. stood to gain a huge inheritance. It was the same with Sally, Bud's daughter. Thrice married (like her new step-mother, who had just surpassed her in the race), Sally lived in Portland, Oregon, and was currently between husbands. Sally was attractive in a wounded, Bohemian way, Joe thought. He had heard she was an artist, specializing in wrought iron.

Joe turned back. "No, they don't look happy."

"They don't like it that Bud made Missy cosignatory on all of this," Marybeth said, waving her hand to indicate literally all they could see. "Bud Jr. got hammered at the dress rehearsal last night and shouted some things at his father before he passed out in the bushes. Sally was there last night for about a half an hour before she disappeared with one of Bud's ranch hands."

"Welcome to the family," Joe said to his wife.

The New Twelve Sleep County Sheriff, Kyle McLanahan, stood in front of Joe and Marybeth in the food line. The piquant smell of barbecued pork and beef hung heavy in the light mountain air.

"Kyle," Joe said, nodding.

"Joe. Marybeth. Congratulations are in order, I guess."

"I guess," Joe said.

"Same to you," Marybeth said coolly. "I haven't seen you since the election."

McLanahan nodded, hitched up his pants. Looked toward the mountains. Squinted. "We've got a lot of work to do."

"Yup," Joe said.

Kyle McLanahan had been the long-time chief deputy for local legend O. R. "Bud" Barnum, who had been sheriff for twenty-eight years. Barnum had owned the county in a sense, having a hand in just about every aspect of it. His downfall came over the past five years, as his reputation eroded, then rotted and tumbled in on itself. That Barnum's decline coincided with Joe's arrival in Saddlestring was no coincidence. The Outfitter Murders, mishandled by Barnum, had begun the slide. Barnum's shadowy involvement with the Stockman's Trust continued it. The ex-sheriff's complicity with Melinda Strickland in her raid on the Sovereign compound started the local gossip that Barnum had lost his commitment to the community and was looking out only for himself. The sheriff's deception during the cattle mutilations had turned the weekly *Saddlestring Roundup* against him. Joe had been in the middle of everything, one way or other. Seeing the writing on the wall (and in the newspaper) Barnum withdrew from the running two weeks before the election. Instead, McLanahan had stepped into the race, as had Deputy Mike Reed. In Joe's opinion, Reed was an honest cop and McLanahan was McLanahan—volatile, thickheaded, a throwback to the Barnum style of politics and corruption. McLanahan won 80 percent of the vote.

"Have you been listening to your radio this morning?" Sheriff McLanahan asked Joe. "I saw your truck in the parking lot."

Joe shook his head. "I'm off duty."

Because Marybeth and Lucy were in the wedding, they had left the Pickett's small state-owned home early that morning in Marybeth's van. Joe had brought Sheridan in his green Ford Game & Fish pickup after they had breakfast, but he hadn't turned on his radio during the drive.

"Then you haven't heard that they found a game warden dead over in Jackson," McLanahan said.

Joe felt a shiver run through him, *"What?"*

Sheridan had quickly bored of her sister Lucy and Lucy's friends in the play area that had been put up far enough away from the reception that the children wouldn't bother the adults. The placement had Missy's stamp all over it, Sheridan thought. A swing-set had been erected, as well as smaller-sized tables and chairs complete with plastic tea sets.

She wandered away from the play area and the reception into the makeshift parking lot. It was tough being thirteen. Too old to play, too young to be considered one of the adults. Her parents were fine, she thought. They never treated her with disrespect, although her mother was starting to bug her in ways she couldn't yet say. In a situation like this, with adults all around, she was patronized. She climbed into her dad's pickup truck and looked at herself in the rearview mirror. At least she finally had contact lenses and didn't look so much like a geek, she thought.

Absently, she clicked on the radio. It was set to the channel reserved for game wardens and brand inspectors. She sometimes like to listen to the interplay between the men and the dispatchers, usually women, at the headquarters in Cheyenne. There was a surprising amount of activity on the radio for a Saturday morning in early September.

"The Jackson game warden," McLanahan said, following Joe and Marybeth to their table. "Found him dead this morning in his house."

"Murdered?" Joe asked. He felt Marybeth tense up.

"Naw. Ate his own gun."

Marybeth gasped.

"Forty-four Magnum," McLanahan said. "Not much left of his head, is what I hear."

Joe was out of his chair and three inches from McLanahan's face. He hissed, "That'll be enough with the details right now in front of my wife."

McLanahan feigned hurt and surprise. "Sorry, Joe. I thought you'd want to know."

The new sheriff turned and left, aiming at his table on the other side of the yard.

"Joe, was he talking about Will Jensen?" Marybeth asked.

"No," Joe said, confused. "It couldn't have been. He must have his information about half-right, as usual."

Marybeth shook her head, "I remember when we met Will and Susan. Remember their kids? Sheridan and their son tore around their house while you and Will talked at their kitchen table."

It made no sense to Joe. Jensen was a rock, a larger-than-life man who was considered one of the best there ever was within the department. Will Jensen was what game wardens wanted to be, the kind of man Joe aspired to be.

"I remember thinking," Marybeth continued, looking up at Joe. "I remember thinking how much they were like *us*."

Joe sat back down, shaken. "Let's hold off on this until we find out what the situation really is. Remember, all the information we've got at this point is from Deputy McLanahan."

"*Sheriff* McLanahan," Marybeth corrected gently.

Joe looked up, saw Sheridan running toward them from the cars, her blue dress flapping.

"All I know is that Will Jensen did not commit suicide," Joe said bluntly. "That's not possible."

"Joe . . ."

"Dad!" Sheridan gushed, stopping in front of them, breathing hard from her run. "Guess what I heard on the radio?"